Born into a family of eccentrics, Kate Horsley was raised in a haunted house on the outskirts of London. The daughter of a mad scientist and a crime fiction expert, she developed an early obsession with laboratories and monsters. At the age of 4, she wrote and illustrated her first collection of gothic tales, 'Fenella the Witch Fights the Hairy Sea Lion Giant', but struggled to find a publisher. After some years spent unravelling the mysteries of Medieval manuscripts during her PhD at Harvard, her childhood dreams of being a writer began to haunt her and she abandoned truth for fiction, returning to the UK to take an MA in creative writing at Lancaster. Since then, her poems and short stories have been published in several magazines and anthologies and her work has won awards. Kate now teaches at the University of Chester, where she's a Writing Fellow. She lives in Manchester with her artist partner, a ghost called Ron and a growing museum of curiosities.

D0771780

'That Mary Shelley has a lot to answer for! This is an extraordinary novel, an honourable response (neither venerating nor sneering) to its progenitor, while being startlingly original. Kate Horsley has grounded and voiced her Frankenstein "sequel" in the Orkneys which bring their own mythic load with them and she takes the Gothic to new places, where the darkness of Frankenstein meets the darkness of isolated communities of love and fear and survival. It is brilliantly weird, dark and "horrid" – and it is a tender account of women's friendships and dreams of freedom. It is profoundly touching and weirdly macabre at the same time. I've never read anything quite like it and I think it is wonderful.' – Sara Maitland

'This is a superb debut, an atmospheric and gripping mystery that picks up where the original Frankenstein left off. But to call it a sequel would do it no justice, because this book is fresh and original, and bursting with the most beautiful and lyrical prose. A stunning novel.' - KJ Wignall, author of The Mercian Trilogy

THE

MONSTER'S

WIFE

KATE HORSLEY

Published by Barbican Press in 2014

Copyright © Kate Horsley 2014

First published in Great Britain as a paperback original by
Barbican Press
1 Ashenden Road, London E5 0DP
www.barbicanpress.com

A CIP catalogue for this book is available from the British Library

ISBN: 978-1-909954-05-2

Typeset in Garamond by Mike Gower

Cover Image and Design by Jason Anscomb of Rawshock Design

For my mother, who taught me to tell
stories, and in memory of my father,
the mad scientist.

1

Hoy, Orkney, August 1798

Life changed when he came to the island, the foreign doctor from further away than anyone cared to know. The night he landed, a storm rose and blew boats towards the Northern ice floes, swept Dolphins aground to lie panting on the white scythe of beach. New lambs were stolen and hens found with their throats torn out. Kirk-going women left their cooking and ran wild, reeling home soused to take the distaff to their husbands' heads. All were agreed that this pestilence followed the foreign doctor to the island as Hell follows the pale rider.

'All' was counted as the score and ten who lived in Quoy, the only village on Hoy, though that number varied year on year as a fresh crop of bones fell under the hill and new small islanders were born. Nearest the sea was Old Cormick's tumbledown shack, then Neaquoy, then Norquoy. Beyond the Norquoys lived the Kilpatricks. The turf-roofed crofts of more Norquoys plus a rabble of Moodies, Fletts and Umbesetters dotted the greensward up towards the summit of the mountain with its shawl of grey.

Each croft had its byre and barn and fields of oats or barley and this year, as every year, Oona and May offered their help with the harvest, bending their waists to the oats and binding sheaves. People always gave them a pat of butter, smoked fish or a scoop of ground oats for their labour. Ever since the doctor came, people were saying the year would be thin. No rain, poor seed. The moment he landed, oats and barley soured in the ground and the shoots looked mean.

May was in need of money for her wedding, so she went to work in the big house, scrubbing laundry and keeping the fires lit for its new tenant, Doctor Frankenstein.

Oona had it on good authority that he landed at night, somewhere up the coast from Cormick's beach. Stopping by the Smokehouse, she'd heard Cormick saying you could see the furrow where they'd pulled the boat in, and for once, people believed him. He got a free drink out of Big Dod because of it and was happy and said it was a fine thing the laird had done to leave the big house to rot, because strangers could come, strangers who'd buy his fish.

How the doctor got to the big house from Cormick's beach was anyone's guess. Down by the laundry pool, where the women slapped and pounded their men's breeks, they laughed and leaned closer to May, who was sure to know the gossip. And there was always gossip in Quoy, what with Andrew and Stuart smuggling whisky and Margaret Umbesetter's rowdy boys forever in trouble and what everyone knew was a romance between Hamish Yule, the Minister, and Oona's Granny, Mrs Scollay. For slow news weeks, there were oft-told tales, like the time Cormick had kissed a young girl at the Umbesetters' bridecog and was almost tarred and feathered for it. Or the time Oona's father drifted back from fishing in the North waters frozen into a thing of diamond, his hands still clutching the tiller.

Now was hardly a time of slow news, what with Napoleon's ships gathering in the firth, threatening war. But that talk was worrying and doom-laden. It was far more entertaining to hear Fiona babble about how it was a rickshaw the doctor came on, such as Reverend Yule said Indian princes used.

"No, no, a barouche box surely," said Janet of Flett in her haughtiest voice and looked down her long nose at May, who was rinsing out bed sheets upstream from her. For only May had seen him, and yet it had been a full week now and she'd barely opened her lips on the subject.

"Most likely," began May and paused to savour the spectacle of nine women leaning closer to her, "he stumbled through the mud in the pitch dark and could not find the door key and slept that first night with the pigs in the byre." But she said it wryly, as if it might not be the whole truth, and turned back to her sheets.

The other women turned back with a sigh that came from all their lips at once like a chorus. Oona counted herself above idle talk and was ashamed to be seen wheedling for tidbits like everyone else. She needn't have bothered. On the subject of the doctor, May was resolutely silent. Two weeks after she began her labour as a housemaid, all she would say about it was that she was working her fingers to stubs and far too tired to come over late so that she and Oona could pass a clay pipe between them and talk. Nor did she have time to sit on the beach and eat her piece with Oona, or even walk under the stars to listen to the burn rattling out to sea the way they'd always done.

For the first time in her life Oona smoked her clay pipe on the beach in solitary silence. She swigged rough cider, feeling it was more of a sin to do so alone, but caring little. Her thoughts were wilful and returned unbidden to the doctor. She fancied he was tall, thin and exquisitely dressed, a dandy with a strange accent. Now he stood at the prow of a small vessel, his luggage piled high behind him. Now he dined alone at the head of a polished table upon which candles burned in sticks graven with imps, flickering light upon the frozen snarls of mounted fox and boar and the old, gilt-framed ghosts that lined the walls.

He was always lonely in her imaginings, that brave and chivalrous man, Doctor Frankenstein. So that, before she ever laid eyes on him, Oona dreamt of a life by his side. Keeping him company as he strained his eyes over medical journals, long after midnight rang out on the grand Swiss clocks. Bidding the maid light the tapers. Sitting at the fireside to embroider. Wearing the fine silks and satins befitting a gentleman's wife.

She skimmed stones, seven, ten, thirty of them, one for each humdrum person in Quoy. Not one of *them* worth daydreaming about. Not one of them as dear to her as May was, damn her eyes.

2

Oona fancied that the three long days and nights Jonah spent in the belly of the whale were neither as dark nor as foul as her week had been. No May to divert her and nothing but jobs to do for Granny. Now, when May finally had time to spend with her, she found herself on a beach that stank of carrion and was quite as dark as a sea monster's guts, abroad in a storm, with sideways rain burning her cheeks. As for Jonah's self-sacrifice, it was nothing to hers. For she had put aside her quarrel with May to follow her to the brink of the raging sea on some mysterious errand and a thankless task it was, too.

"See there?" May pointed into the darkness.

"That black shadow in the black night sky?"

"No! That jagged trench, hare-brain." The wind whisked the last word away from them.

Oona strained her eyes. She could just make out the lone candle burning in the window of Cormick's dwelling. It cast enough light to expose a shadowy darkness on the sand in front of the shack. It seemed to be the trench May spoke of. "It's no more than a noust, May, such as the fishermen build for their boats in winter." Even as she spoke the words, though, she thought this one looked rougher than usual.

"That's where the doctor landed according to Old Cormick. He was beside himself."

"Cormick's always beside himself and he's always beside some ale. That's why he tells so many tall tales."

"I believe this tall tale's true." May tugged her sleeve. "Come on."

Oona rolled her eyes, knowing the gesture would be lost in the darkness. "So you led me here at the witching hour to prove that old drunk's story? I thought you knew more about how the doctor arrived here than anyone."

"Ruffled you, did it?" May laughed. "Well, perhaps if you do as I say tonight, you'll discover more."

"Don't care to!" Oona retorted, yet she found herself following May's footsteps across the wet rocks.

The sea spewed freezing water at them. It was hard to stay upright, let alone move forward, so they went slowly, picking a toehold here, bending there to stop from slipping.

Clouds parted and the moon shone. All at once the beach lay before them like a picture in Reverend Yule's storybooks. Perhaps Jonah had felt this way when the whale finally puked him out from the darkness.

Rocks red as skinned things were splayed out in front of them. A white crescent shivered in the tide. Oona thought it was the moon reflected in the water, but when they came nearer to it, she saw a small eye, the dark gouge of a mouth.

It was another dead dolphin. They had been washing up for two weeks now, making a cold pilgrimage ashore. There were five tonight. Oona ached to see their gleaming bodies laid out like a path to the shack. The way they smiled at their deaths was the saddest thing of all.

At the edge of the jagged hole, they stopped and looked down. Bobbing in the tide was a fishing boat loaded with crates. The word Elver was licked round the prow in white. The name and a strange head, half girl half seal, whittled into the prow, told Oona that the old tub was one of Cormick's vessels, heavy with his catch by the smell of it. A rope leading up from it was pinioned to the land above with a slab of rock.

Oona pressed her shawl to her nose. "Foul!"

"Oh quit your carping. You put on airs for no better reason than that your Granny taught you letters. A stranger would think you weren't come from fisherfolk." May jumped down with a splash and clambered in to the boat, beckoning. "Come on. We've crates to sink."

"You've lost your buttons May Edith Norquoy!"

"You promised, Oona. Please?" May beamed up at her.

Oona crossed her arms. "You've cut me this fortnight past and barely spoken five words to me since the doctor arrived. But now you want help, you're all smiles." She wouldn't be gulled this time.

"Suit yourself." May wound up the anchor. "As you see fit." Her face was set, eyes on the water, mouth turned down the way it did when she was displeased.

Oh, suit yourself yourself, sulky minx, thought Oona, glancing wistfully back at the candlelit windows of Quoy, soft constellations of warmth and sleep.

Her feet betrayed her first, falling into the trench, then her hands, lifting her drenched skirts round her waist, and finally her mouth. "You row and I'll push it out." Her head stayed loyal to her heart, though, and firm in its knowledge of May's foolishness.

And yet, when they were through the shallows and Oona had dragged herself aboard, slick as a seal and shivering, and they had an oar each and were slicing the rumpled water, she grew giddy and her belly flailed. She stifled a laugh, imagining Cormick twitching his rags of curtains, seeing his boat gone. How May devised this scheme she could not guess. Perhaps she'd coaxed Cormick into *giving* her the boat. That was the truth about May. She was eternally making people pander to her. *The gift of the gab,* everyone said, an angel's face and the Devil's tongue.

Out at sea, where the earth and sky joined, lightning cracked. Three, five, ten and the thunder rolled. Oona thrilled at the sound, pushing her numb face towards the wind that pinched her cheeks. Then the lightning again and the taste of rain filling the clouds' grey bellies.

She looked at May, whose hands on the other oar were as thin and white as claw bones and she felt them, the invisible wires that had strung them together since they were small.

The wind flung May's voice at her, fine and tight, pushed through the sieve of stormy air. "I'll wager if we row far enough, we'll see tall ships out in the firth—"

"Sailing to France!" Oona finished.

"Or to us *from* France."

Squinting into the blackness, sharp with cold, Oona imagined a convoy of square-rigged frigates slung low, peppery with sulphur, the upper deck gun-laden. French sailors veered larboard and starboard, dancing the tune of the waves. The captain in his blue and gold and black tricorn, stood stern and stiff on the quarterdeck. A lad in the crow's nest used his eyeglass to search out English land, Scottish land, territory. And somewhere in a distant country where they ate raw onions and chopped each others' heads off, Napoleon gave orders - to kill and conquer, to rule the seas. She knew all this from Hamish Yule's confidences to Granny - he always had a broadsheet from the mainland, sour with ill tidings.

"D'you think they'll land here, take us prisoner?" May's arms tensed on the pull back, sinewy and pale in the light of the full moon. "Some nights when I hear cannons, I fancy they'll row onto the beaches, thrash us while we sleep."

Oona pulled a face. "You never have heard them."

"You know, you may be bookish, but it doesn't follow that the rest of us are simpletons." May arched her swan neck, frowning. "The cannons crack loud as thunder some nights."

"That's nothing more than your Da's farts. One of these days a cannon ball will shoot from his bum and amaze us."

May's face split in a grin. "Aye, it reeks some nights, stuffed in that room with the four of 'em when we've had neeps. Don't have brothers, I say, and don't share your kitchen with pigs."

Oona grinned back. "Same thing."

"Two brothers, one sow and her farrow. Comes to nine. The swine makes ten. Can't wait 'til I'm berthed with Stuart, bless his breeks."

Oona's smile faded. Something about May being a married woman, stowed away in the Flett croft, sat uneasily with her. "*He* likely farts too."

May shrugged. "He can snore buckshot and fart cannonballs for all I care. One's still better than nine. And when I'm a wife—"

Oona sighed. "How far are we?"

May's oar stilled. She looked over her shoulder to the endlessness of dark sea. White knives jabbed the sky and vanished on the horizon. Hoy was small now and the yellow nubs of kitchen fires and candles were tiny points, mirroring the shape of slain Orion who sprawled in the sky, his bragging cut short by the scorpion's sting.

The sky blanched. They both cowered, silently counting the thunder's rebuke. They had roamed too far to swim home if things got rough and the boat capsized. The clouds split and spilled their bellies' weight of water. Icy fine points drove into Oona's lips and eyelids. Their vessel seemed to droop, as if it had sailed this far on a last rush of strength and now felt the heft of its cargo of crates. Oona's back ached from rowing now they'd broken off and her gut tightened on sharp things, a growing bellyache, a sense that things were about to turn rotten.

3

May drew her oar in and dropped it, flapping her hands. "It's ill news when you don't feel the chilblains any more." She pulled her blue lips back in a shamming sort of smile, showing her teeth as she never did. She must see it too, that fearful cast to the moon now the storm had hit. And she knew as well as Oona the folly of being out in it.

Another flash, dazzling and eerily silent.

Oona pulled in her oar, dropped it into the murky water that sloshed with the boat's hip-sway. The oars rolled together, like boats themselves on a rough inner tide. "Why are we gallivanting here?"

The thunder again.

"D'ye reckon its cannons?" May slicked her wet hair back from her face. "The Sassanacks brawling with the Frogs?"

Oona's body braced for the next crack. She shook her head. "Cannons don't hum like that. What mischief is this, May?"

With a shaking finger May tapped her nose, turned her eyes to the sea in that skittish way she had. It was maddening, when Oona knew all of her twitches and looks and could read between the lines, could see, now, May's hand skimming the top of the uppermost crate contemplatively. It was closed but not secured with rope or nails.

"Those crates give off a putrid stench. What's in 'em?"

May shrugged. "Bits and oddments from the big house. Rags and old trash I must get rid of."

"Whatever could you need to jetsam at this hour, at sea, in a storm?"

May swayed with the rough clash of waves that pitched the boat to and fro, steadying herself on the stack of crates. "This is rough work. It needs both our strength."

"Here to serve, am I?" She threw the words off lightly, however piqued she was.

May touched her arm. "I wanted to see you. Only I—"

Oona nodded, shrugged, looked away. She saw how it was. Swaying, her hands slippery and stone cold, she lifted the edge of a crate and peered inside. It was heavy and the bottom was slimy. The innards stank. "For God's sake, May, these aren't rags!"

May shrugged. "I don't know what they are. All he said was 'throw 'em in the sea'."

"Who said?"

May cast her a heavy look. "Frankenstein."

In Oona's mind's eye was the man her fancy had painted, his silhouetted figure pacing the gallery of the big house, lamp held high. Settling to a medical book for a while, turning the pages impatiently before throwing it down to stare out of the window. Tall and aquiline of nose, with that slimness of throat and wrists only mysterious foreign aristocrats possess, he seemed to her a dark prince travelling under a curse.

"Is he in hot water?"

May frowned. "Not if we shift these crates."

"Is it the French?"

"God knows, perhaps someone is hounding him." The wind whipped up her hair. The lightning cracked again. "Help me?"

With a weary groan, Oona jammed her hands under the crate. May took the other side and lifted. The boat rocked beneath them, sickeningly hard. They hefted the crate between them and heaved it over the side. It hit the water's rough silk with a crash, spraying their lips and eyes. Oona mopped her face with a sleeve that had grown a stinging pall of ice. The boat pitched. May grabbed her arm and pulled her close.

"Ow." Oona snatched her arm back, chafing the hurt with stupid fingers that hardly felt.

"You almost went overboard. The storm's roughening." May nodded at the next crate, shoved her hands under it. "D'you have it?"

They hauled it up and slung it far as they could, and the next after that. Every one splashed hard and sunk deep, leaving a gob of cuckoo-spit in its wake. With each crate, Oona thought of the pranks they'd played, the hidings they'd had in all their years of friendship. She'd thought it was over, that soon-to-be-married May was too prim and ladylike to come be a tomboy with her. She looked at May over the swing of a fetid crate, the way the glare of the moonlight caught her high, pinched cheekbones. Her eyes, narrowed to slits, seemed utterly black. Her arms worked fast, filled with demon energy. Her brows, drawn into each other, were arched, wicked, wrinkling the flesh of her nose and forehead like a dog's growling snout. When they tossed the last crate, May's lips flew open and the top one snagged on a sharp eye tooth. She was as fierce as ever and twice as wild.

Silver bubbles broke the blackness below them. The moon threw shards of their reflections around the froth. It looked like they'd been smashed, that the crate had hit and broken them and now their fragments bled together in the water, a shimmering whole, as deceitful as any undertow. Wicked girls. The stench of what they'd done still thickened the air. Oona had grown accustomed to it and could now name the component scents: chamber-lye, mingling with putrid offal. A pail of rank slops left in the sun.

Out where the sky hung low, a soundless fist of whiteness struck, bleached it to ash and lime and left a blood tinge to the world. Then the low brrrr of a drum, sea spirits belting heavy barrels towards the clouds. The world blurred. Surely she'd been dreaming this whole night. They sat. Without a word, they turned the boat about and pushed the oars down hard. The rhythm was hypnotic, inevitable, like the push and pull between May and Oona, the flush of nearness – stifling. The ache of running away.

Oona was so cold that the raindrops warmed her. She looked over her shoulder. Hoy was tall, peaked, an old volcano sleeping. Above it, a hole gaped in the storm clouds like shocked lips parting. As they neared the shore, she could see that no rain fell on the island. Dark lashes of grass fringed the ragged cliffs. The crescent beach was licked over with silver. Her neck ached. She turned back. May's mouth moved in silhouette, but the squall was too loud to hear what she said. And besides, Oona was too tired to listen. The water softened, lightened, the sand underneath shining through it. May stood and jumped down. Oona followed and they guided the boat back into its sandy womb.

"Whossere?" The voice above their heads was gritty with hate.

They crouched low. A scarecrow teetered on the brink of the noust, face black against the moonlight.

4

"Traitors!" A loud trickle broke the words, chopped them into mad tees and buzzing esses. Pish streamed down the bank and the hot spray spurted everywhere. The last dribbles were pursued by an earsplitting fart. "Infernal frogs. Stinking cut throats." Cormick lingered for a moment more, weaving side to side in such an extravagant manner, Oona fancied he would tumble into the noust with them. With a hail of soft curses and farting once more, he reeled off into the night.

Oona let out a breath. "Did he spy us?"

"See how soused he was? Grog's not known for making you see in the dark." May scrabbled up the bank, avoiding the furrow made by Cormick's water.

"He saw, I swear it, and he keeps knives in there." Night-blind, Oona felt for the grooves May's hands had left in the sandy mud and sunk her fingers into the melting earth. Grit nudged under her nails and lodged there. Her eyes came level with the laces of May's boots.

"He keeps fish hooks and oyster knives. Don't be so green." May's rough-skinned hands closed round Oona's wrists. The skin burned as May dug her heels into the bank and pulled hard.

"You mind me of an ant with a cobnut on its back," Oona laughed. "Just like you to think you could lift me, when I'm taller by a head."

"Great lump." With a grunt, May let go.

Oona grabbed the earth near May's boots. Her heart was a rusted hinge, creaking. She breathed hard, flailing her numb feet, desperate to drum life into them, calves snared by the wet weight of her skirts. When she flopped onto the sand, she was weak as a new calf and could only lie and suck in air and listen to her heart's dull sound, the snag in its rhythm, that lost fourth beat. She and May had listened to each others' hearts one day after a race across the meadow. That was the first time they knew that Oona's heart skipped out of time.

Now she knew it afresh. Her eyes came into focus and the pale gold oval of May's face swam into view, brow furrowed, eyes fixed on her as if she were another beached dolphin too dead to drag back to sea.

Oona closed her eyes, loathing the pity people seemed to have for her. She hated May for feeling it and herself most of all. She thought of a black hole sucking everything into it, everyone and everywhere she knew, until there was nothing save the purest silence.

Her breath slowed. Her heart hushed. She scrabbled up, keeping her eyes on the black huddle of crofts blocking out square shapes in the starlit sky. The candles in their windows were snuffed out.

"Growing fat without me to keep you busy?" Behind May's banter there was fear.

"Aye, that must be it." Oona laughed uneasily.

Silence unspooled between them, tangling in on itself. Their feet slipped on wet rocks that would be red in daylight but looked black as blood now. Oona heard a noise like the tide's echo in the watery caves that pocked the island. She looked back, her mind on that old crab Cormick, shuffling after them maybe, wheedling and cursing and pleading for a peek under their petticoats. No Cormick. Even the dishwater light in his spiniken of a house had been snuffed.

May climbed fast ahead of her, wedging her boots into slippery toeholds. There was that echo again, the tap tap tap of steps. Oona stopped and squinted at the darkness.

"Someone walk over your grave?" May stood above her.

Oona shrugged. "I fancied Cormick might have spied us."

"Old lecher. Did I tell you he tried to bribe me with that rotgut of his? Wanted a good long look under my skirts."

Oona slipped her hand into a wet groove of rock. "Give him it free did you?"

"Minx!" May's hand skimmed Oona's head in a play slap. "I might have let him take a peek. I do have a kind heart. At the last, I gained the thing I wanted and it was not barley-broo." The lilt in her voice was a taunt - *I'm not telling*. Which was good since Oona didn't want to know.

"Fine sort of charity to give when you want something, May."

They walked up to where the burn pleasured secretly in the darkness and Oona stopped to listen to what the water said. It told her that it cut the island like a long wound, fusing sea with sea, swelling gardens, scraping under the earth for gold and onyx stone. *Thy plants are an orchard of pomegranates.* May took her hand, squeezing her fingers as a child might. She was thinking of how the island would be without Oona on it, how this would be. The burn at night. The moon, suddenly lonely. For all her secrets, her thoughts were easy to guess sometimes.

Still holding Oona's hand, May said, "Let's stay awhile."

They stole past the turn-off to Quoy and without speaking, turned the same way, ended up in *their* place, the wild scruff of dwarf birches that lined the riverbank behind the kirkyard. By summer they kicked their legs in the glutted burn. By winter they huddled under a blanket and smoked and smoked, naming shapes in the trees they'd once been small enough to swing in. Every hatred or infatuation, every secret spilled, each bitter fight had happened here with only the trees to hear it.

In the dark, their stockings and petticoats clinging and the storm rumbling further off, they were silent. It was neither a happy nor a sad kind of silence. It was the same startled hush had fallen upon them the day they went to the fair in Hamnavoe and had ill fortunes read from their palms.

After a while, Oona loosed May's hand, sat up and stretched, head spun and muzzy. She fished the pipe from its hiding place - a wooden box wedged inside a little cupboard of rock - and tamped in tobacco, damp from the storm. It was madness what they had just done, wasn't it? Filching a boat, sinking crates with who-knew-what inside. Like thieves or vagabonds. Although May had said they were helping the doctor, the foreign doctor with his fine eyes and troubled past.

"Pished through?" May sounded like someone speaking in a dream. She stood, shook her hair out, combing the front curls with her fingers. Oona followed her up, steadying herself on the patchwork bark of a birch, half silk sash, half hair shirt.

"Homewards if I don't want a thrashing. And you. Your Granny makes me more afeared than my own dear Da."

"She doesn't whip me nowadays, not since... And everyone knows I'm..." She wouldn't speak it. To speak it made it true. She smiled. "She'll roll her eyes, though, if I wake her."

"The infamous eye-roll! So frightful!" May gave a mock shudder. "I'll be your protector."

"Smokehouse? Dinner-time tomorrow?"

"That's our ritual." May appeared to forget they'd not met there in weeks.

There was no virtue in condemning her. "I meant that we should meet as usual. Farewell!"

They embraced. Oona felt a sharp point dig into her hip, some spiky shape beneath the old oilskin that had belonged to May's Da. Reaching beneath the folds of stiff, stinking cloth that clung to May's dress, she fished out a clutch of nails. Holding their wicked teeth in her palm, she tried to divine their meaning.

May snorted. Her lips puckered, mischievous, "Damn. Ruined it."

"What have you ruined?"

May laughed. "Never you mind."

"Do the nails belong to those crates?"

May shrugged, turned on her heel and walked off, her laughter echoing into the night. Oona went in the other direction, shaking her head about sinking the doctor's crates and Cormick kicking up a row and now some mystery of forgotten nails.

Another of May's secrets.

5

Oona tugged the last peg off the last dishclout and dropped both in the basket. She looked around warily. No Granny and no Toby. She'd been avoiding the pair of them all day, since, in their different ways, they both had a keen sense of smell and the stench of last night's mischief clung to her.

The storm, the crates, Cormick, all seemed like madness now. She slunk to the door of the croft and dropped her basket just inside. Granny was bent over her needles, darning a stocking and Toby snored by the fire, his paws churning the air as he chased dream spiders.

Oona turned from the dull scene and unbound her hair from its kerchief. The road beyond the croft was storm-churned, but the sky was a harebell. Even though the gate was open, she climbed the fence and plunged into the mud barefoot, loving the way it splattered her legs. More May. More adventure. She felt like a creature that slept away the winter and was only now stretching itself awake.

All day long, while she'd ground away at her small jobs of housework, she'd told herself the wild tale of last night: how they'd rowed out to sea in a vicious storm and helped the foreign doctor shake off his pursuers and flown from the dastardly Cormick. By the time she came to take down the laundry, their adventure seemed less like a rogue's last confession and more like the ballad of Rob Roy.

When she'd tired of those fancies, she imagined May labouring in the big house, struggling to keep the grand fires lit and the great floors scrubbed, curtsying to the doctor, her cheeks tight and pink from leaning into the steam of a soup pot, her hair frizzed. She would be bidding him farewell at this very moment, coiled tight round the pleasurable scheme of a smoke and a gossip, lying arm in arm with Oona on the warm rock outside the Smokehouse.

Or a different scene: May whispering in the doctor's ear, intent on their secret. The doctor taking May into his confidence.

This second image prickled her flesh like one of Granny's brushwood hidings. She shook her head, flung the unsettling fancy away.

The Smokehouse sat on a narrow finger of land in the next bay over, surrounded by black rocks and sea. Oona crossed the burn and hiked through two crofts to get to it, squinting against the sun's white point. Lifting her petticoats, she strode through small bogs and over cowpats, down into deep ruts gouged by the plough. When she arrived, there was nobody there. A quiver of temper gripped her, rising hot through her tired flesh. Sweat broke on her brow. May was always late, if she remembered at all.

She threw herself down on the large, flat stone where they often ate their piece and smoked while Stuart drank inside. Above her, the tavern's emblem, Skittery Dick - a mackerel whittled from driftwood - scowled down. Oona scowled back. She held the place in proper disregard.

Once a curing house for the fish, it was now a soaking house for the men. They gripped their beer or whisky in heavy red hermit crab hands while fine threads of daylight filtered down on their faces from the holes in the roof. Whale teeth and shark jaws were nailed to the walls. Women weren't to come in ever. The only reason Oona knew what the inside was like was that she and May had found the door open one night and stolen in and mixed a cog for themselves. They sat there, burning the fish-oil lamp and laughing wantonly and taking turns to drink until they couldn't stand. All the reeling way home, they chewed on clover to hide the smell, but it didn't save either from a thrashing.

"Been jilted?" Though carefree, the voice had an ironical undertone. Stuart. She hadn't heard him walk up. She shrugged, willing May to appear.

"She said she'd be late this morning - we did pass her on the way to the sea."

Reluctantly, she opened her eyes. There he was, May's handsome fellow, weaving a little and a wee bit red in the face, his dark curls stuck to his temples with sweat. He bore an uncanny resemblance to May looked at from some angles. Folk said if they hadn't been betrothed, they could have been brother and sister.

A shadow peeled out from behind him, smirking. Andrew. "Cormick's out of his wits, then," he said, rubbing his hands, "ranting in the alehouse like Ezekiel."

"Out of the Bible, it was."

"Old Testament madness."

Oona sat up. Her neck ached and their cryptic talk was annoying her. Bloody twins, they were. Stuart with his big, lop-sided grin and Andrew lisping alongside him. All the women on the island found them charming except for her. Andrew and Stuart had been inseparable since they were boys. Oona felt certain if Andrew wanted a pish, he'd have to hand Stuart his old fellow first to make sure he was holding it right.

Stuart squeezed in beside her, needlessly cosy. "Who'd have thought it in our modern day, to see the plagues of Egypt washed up onto our shores?" He took out his pipe and stuffed it.

Oona snatched the pipe from his mouth. "What in God's name are the pair of you jabbering about? Ezekiel? Plagues of Egypt? You're soft-headed, both of you, and soused in the middle of the day, and—"

"Tainted! I told you. And my whole catch wrong. Not a single living fish in the stinking lot." Cormick lurched through the Smokehouse door, so deep in his cups he barely looked human any more. He was a small man, dogged as a terrier. Over the years, he'd been salted, pickled and smoked until he looked like the cured cod that hung from a rope over the fire. His deep-set eyes had a dreamy look, but when the whisky hit the back of his throat those eyes dared you to pick a fight.

The meaty fist of Big Dod, May's chunk of a Da, followed him out and gave him a shove. "Drunk as a wheelbarrow. Be off with you!" Dod ran a tight ship at the Smokehouse and stood for no nonsense. The door slammed shut.

Cormick turned to Oona, his flat eyes the colour of whey. He jabbed a finger at her. "The way they spied at you, those horrors, bodies higgledy-pig, poor creeturs."

He was close now and she caught a whiff of his layers of stink, the fishy rankness of his netted vest, the barley-broo on his breath.

"Fish with legs? Frogs with fins?" Stuart roared. "Old rusty gut's lost what little wit he had!"

Andrew chortled, a pale ginger echo of his friend. He always laughed at Stuart's japing. Oona wrapped her arms around herself. She was fearful cold though the sun was warm and everyone else was sweltering.

"Mistress Scollay doesn't like hearing about it." Cormick's face looked chewed, drawn in like the mouth of a bag. "Pishing French I tell you, damnable Frogs in their pannikins, eating their infernal foreign victuals and throwing them in our sea—"

Oona thought about the night before, the crates and their rank contents. She looked at Andrew, anything to keep her tell-tale eyes from meeting Cormick's.

Andrew smiled sweetly at her, as if she'd bestowed a favour on him. "If they'd been eating them," he scratched his gingery beard and held his finger high in the manner of a mildly drunken philosopher, "they'd be gone wouldn't they? Not whole like you say?"

"Whole? Whole? Those freaks, half fish, half frog, half bloody bird, not one thing or t'other! Way you talk," Cormick swilled the spit round his mouth and spat in the muck, "you probably want to swim out and join the blasted Frogs, eat at their table wi'em, suck down their -"

Andrew raised his fist. "Fighting words."

He caught Oona's eye and his brave gesture withered halfway through, fist drooping to his side. She watched the colour rise in his throat and fill his face like wine glugging into a glass. His eyes slipped over her face and away. He'd taken a liking to her when they were children and for her part, she'd formed the opinion that he was a pea-wit. Stuart looked back and forth between them, a smug smile broadening on his face. He whispered something in Andrew's ear that made his colour deepen. Then he ruffled his ginger hair and laughed.

"Don't be a pigeon." Andrew angrily patted his pockets. "You've stolen my pipe, you wretch. Give me my pipe."

Stuart put his hand over his friend's face, pushing him down on the stone. Andrew got him by the neck and they half-wrestled, half-hugged in that way boys do. Except there was something in their manner of doing it that was so soft, Oona felt she had to look away. She watched Cormick's slow progress down the hill from the Smokehouse, heard his prating about the strange haul, the dead things that poured in his nets. No living pollock or cod fighting the net and flapping on the deck, fighting for freedom. Just pale, rotting sea creatures, blanched and bloodless, flopping out belly up and tainting the boat. Disgusting things coming up in waves as if the sea were retching to rid itself of them.

6

Oona let Cormick get a little way ahead before she began to follow him. She flicked a look over her shoulder, but Stuart and Andrew were still prostrate with mirth and did not see her go.

She scrabbled downhill in Cormick's wake. Whatever mischief May was caught up in at the big house, she wasn't skidding down sharp grass on her bare heels, kicking pebbles of sheep shit like hailstones. She was probably setting out the crystal decanter for the doctor's afternoon sherry, blithesomely ignorant of all this. Oona cursed herself for being so eager to help last night, when May scratched a dry twig on the door. She'd been a fool to become embroiled, save that May had been so feverish and her errand so unlike every other humdrum thing that happened here.

She crossed the burn downstream from the copse where the irises thrust their yellow points through the rushes and the birches whispered last night's secrets. Cormick was beyond her, flitting in and out of sight between trees - if such a foul, drunk thing could be said to flit. She scratched her back, surprised at the damp feel of the skin of her back, tallow-greasy and cold against the pads of her fingers.

Cormick stopped to lean on a tree. She feared he would pish again, but he grunted and shuffled onwards. At the far side of the burn, the leaves were a young green against the birches' silver. If she plucked one and rubbed it between her fingers, the scent would be tangy and bitter and new. In the meadow, the poppies burned red in the tall grass that the cows had not yet cropped and the sky was the colour they painted fishing boats. The firth beyond curved around the island, holding it tight, white-burnished spots of it gleaming so she had to shade her eyes. This was Eden as Father Yule told of it in kirk. Every tree and river pleasant to her sight, the sea compassing the land of Hav'ilah, where there is gold and the naked go unashamed.

She'd lost sight of Cormick. He must have slipped off towards his shack. She came to the beach light-blind, wondering whether the whole business was some odd joke between the menfolk, some Bean King prank to scare the women. Or perhaps they'd been in their cups and sun-struck and imagined things, like mariners becalmed too long, tongues swelling from thirst, minds dizzy from the salt caked on their lips and the mad-making seaweed they scraped from the hull to stave off starvation. Men saw the Devil out at sea, Christ too. Their dead bairns and their long-lost fathers spoke to them and they came back touched. Cormick was just such a case.

Hot stone burned the soles of her feet. A strand of dry seaweed was wrapped round her big toe. It was dry and sharp. She bent to pluck it off and straightened. The sea was a too-dazzling mirror. She pressed her hand tight to her forehead and still couldn't see. The stink hit her then, worse than a sheep's carcass. The salt-putrid stench caught in her throat and choked her, the force of it catching her so hard and so suddenly that she doubled up and vomited on the rocks, dribbles of milky spittle beading her lips. She wiped her mouth and straightened, eyes blurred. Someone stood in front of the sun, black against the light. The person bent low, peered at the ground.

"Cormick?"

The figure turned. She still couldn't see the face, only the bulk of his chest and arms. Too big to be Cormick.

"Stuart?"

The man said nothing.

Tears stung her eyes. She scrubbed them and blinked at the light. The man was gone. His going shredded her nerves even more than his silent presence. What had he been staring at, down at the shore's edge? Pinching her nose, she pressed on.

All along the cusp of shore and sea bore whitish scurf. As the sea came, so did the flotsam. She scratched her chest, suddenly itchy beyond bearing. A step further and her bare feet pushed into something softer than wet sand. She waited for her eyes to adjust to the light, wiping tears away. With her hand clamped over her mouth and nose, she looked down. The shoreline was strewn with the bodies of frogs, dead eyes milked over, pale bellies bloated, pushed upwards. This was the plague Cormick had caught in his nets - nothing but frogs!

And strange as it might be if these were what she and May had thrown out in the crates, it wasn't a sin or a crime as far as she knew. Anyway, Cormick seemed to think the French navy was at fault. She let out the breath she'd been holding in, rued it at once and clamped her hand over her mouth.

Things shifted and seethed in the flotsam - dark and gleaming things. She stepped closer. It seemed that young eels hardly bigger than slugs fed on one of the frogs. A crab joined in, its fat, purple hand feeding its little square mouth from which bubbles sprang and popped. The claw reached down and filched another chunk, red and fibrous and nothing like frog guts. She grabbed one of the elvers away. The rest scattered.

The crab stood its ground, waving a claw still clamped around flesh, its little legs keeping precarious grip on a pale hand that bobbed in the Biblical tide.

7

All the way home, she thought about Dead Men's Fingers and how as children, she and May had plucked the yellow fronds of weed and chased each other along the beach, screaming. She clutched the lump in her shirt, begging it not to bloom poppies of blood that would give her away. The fingers were cold against her breastbone - slim fingers, tapered at the ends, the bluish nails ending raggedly. As if the fingers had clawed for all they were worth. Hairless. Dead Girl's Fingers. Nothing seemed real.

At the wicket gate, Toby greeted her, stumpy tail wagging. He stretched in front of the gate and whined, licking his chops.

"Be gone with you." She pushed the gate slowly to stop the hinges from telling on her.

Toby cocked his head to one side, as if he couldn't quite believe she was scolding him. She closed the gate behind her, looking around the croft in confusion. The cottage and the byre and the chicken coop were like buildings sunk beneath the waters of the Firth. Out there where frogs floated and fingers grew. Her stomach roiled. She gulped down a mouthful of stinging bile. Sweat was in her eyes, but she couldn't wipe them, not when her hands held that other hand close. Why had she taken it? The crabs and eels would have eaten it and all this could have been forgotten.

She headed across the yard, too slow for her staccato heart, like swimming through bog water, nightmare slow, her calves pushing through the soft, smelly huddle of chickens pecking for grain and worms. Toby followed close at her heels. He must smell something.

"Go chase a rat," she hissed. She wanted him gone before she took the hand out of her shirt and really gave him something to bark about.

Outside the chicken coop, the cockerel flicked his gold eye up at Oona with something akin to suspicion. She was usually the one whose lap he sought out, whose bed he settled on when it was time to tuck his head under his wing. He puffed his ginger neck feathers and coughed out a salvo of clucks.

"Put your hackles up, will you, Orpheus?" She shoved him out of the way with her foot. "Fair-weather friend."

She pulled out the wooden hatch and grabbed up an egg. "Toby!"

He sat on his hind legs, let out a whine-growl of anticipation. She mock-threw the egg to the far side of the croft. The daft bugger ran for it. In the time it took him to see her trick and circle back, she'd taken the hand from her shirt, wrapped it in her kerchief and stuffed the bundle into the roof of the coop where the hens couldn't get to it, or Granny or Toby either. The little dog ran back just as she was sliding the hatch back in place.

"Don't dilly dally."

She let him take the egg from her open palm and scratched him between the ears as he broke the shell and lapped the sticky yolk with his rough tongue. Orpheus kept an eye on them the while.

Her skin twitched as if elvers nibbled at it. She walked to the croft, her new best friend trotting at her heels. No sign of Granny. She must have gone out on an errand, leaving a stack of dirty dishes by the pail. The basket of laundry still sat by the door, unfolded.

She set to the dishes, glad to find some form of penance. As her hands scrubbed and rinsed and scratched at a soup pot - her pale hands with their rough nails - she realised why she couldn't leave the hand behind. She wouldn't want her own hands or her own body to be left out there for the crabs to scavenge on. She upended the pot to let the water drain from it and picked up a knife. Its blade was stained dark red with beetroot juice. All it took was a swipe of the finger on one side and then the other to make it clean again, to remove the evidence. Wasn't that what she had done?

Instead of telling someone what she'd found, she'd hidden a hand in a chicken coop, the hand of a girl just like her. She no longer felt anything like a heroine. Whatever the doctor had been hiding in those crates, whatever awful thing he might be covering up, she and May were both a part of it now.

8

The kirk bell rang for evening prayer. The sky outside was a deep red, scattered with small clouds, the kind May called Lamb Clouds. Normally, she'd be here and they'd lie and pass the pipe and jug, scanning the curdled sky for cloud faces.

Normally before the doctor came, anyhow. If Oona hadn't grown so used to May's absence over the past few weeks, she would have been worried. Standing at the window, half-heartedly drying spoons, her back ached from holding bad thoughts at bay: crates thrown overboard by moonlight; a girl's hand washed up on shore; the people of Quoy armed with pitchforks and pandybats, swarming onto Granny's land to take Oona away somewhere and punish her.

"There's an awful fug of prattle over Quoy." Granny's voice ripped the fabric of her dark daydream.

"I've barely heard a peep," she said crossly. "You made me jump. I didn't even hear you come in."

"Oona the dreamer. You should go abroad sometimes, see how your neighbours are employed."

Her back turned to Granny, Oona permitted herself a roll of the eyes. "And how are they employed?" She hoped Granny would let the matter drop. She didn't need it rehearsed again, unless it was with May.

"Well, down at the laundry pool, Mad Bridget said the Selkies were up to something, mischievous creatures."

Oona laid down a spoon with a definite click. "There's a story behind her being named 'Mad Bridget'."

"Don't be pert, girl, and look at me when I speak. Your elders and betters deserve your respect."

Oona took a deep breath, turned around, trying not to think of dead frogs, dead fingers. Invisible cords laced her throat. Granny's hair had fluffed up the way it always did when she roused from her nap. Her hooded blue eyes were bright from the fever of loose talk afflicting Hoy.

"We paid no mind to her, and besides, Janice said it must be those Frenchies assaulting us with poisoned frogs to cut off our victuals."

"They're fighting the Sassanacks, not us. Why would they go to such lengths?" Her face was hot. She had no idea why she was scorning Granny's notions, since if any proved popular it might clear her of guilt.

"Stuart called on us. He'd been in the Smokehouse—"

"Now there's a surprise." Oona picked up a dish. Her hand was shaking. She carefully set it down before Granny noticed.

"He observed that who else but the French would possess such a quantity of frogs? It's a sign that they plan to invade us." The puff had gone out of her. "I'm not frighting you, Oona?" Granny's eyes followed Oona's tremulous fingers.

"Not in the least." Oona turned back to the window, hiding her tell-tale hands with her body. "I'm just sick of hearing about it."

"I thought you hadn't heard a peep?"

"Why is the kirk bell still clanging?"

"Evening prayer. It always—"

"It's been ringing continuous."

Granny gasped. "Hamish must have called a meeting."

The kirk's lime-washed walls caught the sun. Moss growing thick on the slate roof made it look like a white pot with a rusted lid. Squashed into the grass around it were herring bone rows of gravestones. Mother's was a tiny pebble in the shade of the far wall.

Oona and Granny hurried past scraggly ewes and grown lambs grazing the moorland, their drift to new grass as slow as white foam in the firth. The big hill loomed above them, its slopes shrugging off the wrath of the wind and the endless crush of the rain, unmoved by each year's fresh crop of bones falling under the hill.

As they neared the kirk's clanging bell and the open door the people of Quoy nodded their hellos to Granny and she nodded back, but not all of them nodded to Oona. The more her fainting fits were spoken of in the valley, the less people liked to meet her eye. Or if they did, they frowned, remembering how Oona's mother had been so fond of a céilidh until she couldn't catch her breath to dance any more. How one fine June evening Granny found her lying by the burn and couldn't wake her.

There was not much use in nodding to Oona, their looks seemed to say, if she'd soon be under the hill. This time there was a darker flavour to their silence, a note of deeper hush running under it. Suspicion perhaps, as if they guessed her secret. Oona shrugged the fear off. She sometimes thought people meant worse towards her than they really did.

The kirk was the same size as Oona's front parlour, small enough that if she stood at the door and spat it would hit the pulpit. Though that would be ungodly. In the darkness, Oona felt the fear of everyone around her like an ache. Stuart's bold young nephews, Jamie and Roy, were huddled against their mother, crying. Big men who usually cursed and swilled ale were pale and shaking. Without really thinking about it, she found herself making an inventory to ensure that none of the women were missing or short a hand.

Only May was absent and that worried her. Part of her wished she could tell the others about the crates and May and the poor girl's hand, come clean right now and ask for advice, for absolution and help. But, sitting in the kirk, it seemed to her that their fear was all her fault. In the midst of those who had cared for her and known her all her life, she had never felt more alone.

Hamish Yule stood at his knotty stump of a lectern, polishing his spectacles, finger pressed into the worn innards of his Bible. He was known for his bloodcurdling sermons and the stern stare he used for rebuking sinners. He had a soft spot for Granny, as everyone often remarked, and Oona often heard a rap on the door and looked up to see his raw, high cheekbones and bushy black brows scowling down at her. When his wife took sick he kept to the manse, nursing her whilst the garden that had been her calling went wild. Since she died, Oona often thought he had an air of having glimpsed another world and lost his taste for this one. Though of course he had Granny to comfort him.

The Minister licked his lips ruminatively and Oona knew that soon he would cut through the babble with the firm knife of his voice and lead them in prayer.

Granny sat down two pews in front of Oona, so she could hear more gossip no doubt. Soon she was nodding sagely at Janice's enervated chatter. Big Dod sat right at the front with May's mother, Effie, and Stuart. When Dod saw Oona come in, he whispered something to Effie. Whatever his words were, they rippled through Effie's thin body. She nodded nervously and turned her eyes back to the Minister. Dod stared back, his eyes on Oona's. His face was sweaty and red as a pig's head left hanging in the byre. When he heaved himself up and lurched towards Oona, she instinctively looked down at her feet, drew back in her seat as if she could stay hidden. Dod had hated her since she was small and always blamed her for anything May did wrong.

It was too late. Dod was on her, towering over her, his sour breath forming a cloud above her.

"Pray mistress Oona, where's my daughter?" He seemed to be trying to whisper, but the hissed words filled the church.

"I'm as ignorant on the subject as you are, Sir."

He leaned into her. "You're her keeper, girl. Saying where she can go, what she can do." Spittle hit her ear. "You must know the answer."

"I'm dumbfounded. What do you mean?" Her voice was harsher than she'd meant. Everyone in the kirk turned to stare.

"I mean, you're lying."

9

Dod's hand gripped her bare arm, his fingers tightening on her freckled skin. Her throat ached around some lump caught in it, as if she were swallowing her tongue.

She looked past him, to where the puzzled faces of everyone she knew watched from the darkness, pale as fingers fished from the sea. Amongst the congregation, Granny's face was no longer flushed with gossiping, just thin and old, sucked in at the lips and eyes. Whatever she might have done wrong, she did not deserve this. And nor did May. Even if she'd known her whereabouts, she wouldn't have given them away.

"Leave me be."

The skin of her arm looked like curds being wrung of their whey, darker where his thick fingers pressed down.

"Release me, Sir." Oona seized Dod's rough timber of a wrist with her free hand, twisted the skin hard. She and May often gave each other burns like this when they play-fought. But Dod wasn't expecting a girl to fight back. His eyes bugged and his grip loosened until it was easy for Oona to slip free of the sweat of his grasp.

She turned tail without looking round again, for fear of seeing a shocked look on the clutch of pale faces. Before the kirk door swung closed behind her, she heard the murmurs begin and Dod's voice growling above them.

First they would voice their concern over her behaviour, wring their hands, momentarily distracted from the plague that had brought them together. Then the people of Quoy would do what they always did when a storm came, or a frost killed the lambs or the sea rose up on the beaches to smite the matchwood of their little boats. They would turn to that great, white eye staring down over Hamish Yule's head, turn to it and stare into it with love as if it was the living Christ. And they would beg and promise their best crop, their firstborn lamb, or their most fertile cow, if He would intercede with His Father for them. As she hiked up her skirts and climbed the stony path towards the coast road, she heard Hamish silence them, his words echoing in the little building, the first solemn notes of song. She clamped her hands down hard over her ears and tramped on.

The big house was just along the cliff tops, tangled in dark heather at the foot of the hill where the skuas made their nests. When his lady died, the laird who'd had it in his family since Hedin battled Hogni left for his daughter's house in Lochailort. He opened it to rich travellers from Europe and America who wanted to play the laird for a summer, drink brandy from crystal glasses and sup on roasted grouse.

It was years since his retreat and visitors were far and few. Each winter draped fresh sheets of snow over the grand estate. The damp tugged stones from the roof and warped the rafters. May had told her that, inside, the plate was tarnished and the tapestries mouldered. Spiders darned fine covers for the four poster beds.

Oona's earliest memories included an imaginary picture of the great rooms of the big house - the sparkling chandeliers and tapestries, the red oriental rugs and gleaming, dark furniture, his great clocks and birds under glass.

All these had been described to her by the succession of maids and butlers and cooks who used to keep the place up back in the old days, when the Laird still graced them with his presence. In their retirement, the old staff delighted in frighting children with stories about the dark cellarage running underneath the ancient pile, an oubliette in the apple cellar that dated to the time of James IV, a damp wall in the upstairs gallery from which a lady in a tall peruke was sometimes seen to wander. And of course, strange smells and screams and things that went bump in the night.

As she sweated her way along the cliff road, Oona thought about how foolish those old ghost stories sounded. The people in them saw terrifying sights and they always acted bravely. She cast an eye on the beach stretching out below her. Gulls had discovered the white-bellied tide and now they gouged and filched and tipped their heads up to swallow, glorying in the carrion.

To them the plague was a cornucopia. They squabbled over it, pecking at each other and flying up to circle the charnel, screeching, before settling to feed again. The stench was so thick, it was hard to think straight as you walked through it. Perhaps that was why, when a real terror came to the island instead of made up ghosts, everyone ran in circles like headless chickens and no-one was brave. Real horror paralysed you. And they didn't even know about the hand.

She groaned inwardly at the thought that there might be more body parts mixed in with the other offal. Those gulls could be feeding on some poor girl. She was surprised at how quickly her guilt about her own role in it all had changed into anger inside the kirk.

Now that anger ran wild in her, driving her toward the big house. It wasn't that Dod didn't know where May was. He knew. But, like all bullies, Dod was a coward at heart and he abhorred the thought of walking to the big house cap in hand and demanding that his daughter halt her cleaning and cooking just because he said so. He was afraid of the doctor and all that had been said about this great off-comer, this man of parts and fortune.

Oona felt no such fear. That being said, when she had passed the gate and the house-cow quietly cropping - square rear-end facing the byre - she slowed her angry march. By the time she had passed the west wing and was nearing the servants' entrance, she was tiptoeing.

Even so, the gravel crunched loudly beneath her bare feet, sharp pebbles jabbing her calloused heels. She had never imagined she would end up creeping over the Laird's domain like a thief, shoulder's hunched, eyes flitting this way and that, poised for some haughty voice to stop her in her tracks.

The kitchen door stood ajar. She stopped and listened. The fire had died down in her and she was half afraid to go in. It wasn't a voice she heard through the door. Instead, it was a sound both delicate and precise. Music playing from a distance, like none she had ever heard.

The notes reminded her of the piano that Annie Yule used to play on Sundays when she and Granny went round for tea after kirk. There had always been sadness in that music quite different to the hymns in church. Even before everyone knew Annie was dying, the notes were melancholy, the melodies stirring and soft like a loon heard through fog.

More curious now than ever, she pushed the door open.

10

On a long table in the middle of the kitchen, a hare lay, half gutted. Next to it was a peeled onion, a large bunch of bay leaves and thyme, a tall jar made of dark green glass, a spill of salt, left untidied, as if May had run off in the middle of cooking.

Oona walked to the table, hearing now how the notes that came from above were tinnier than a piano. She looked up at the high rafters, from which plucked game birds hung, a pig's loin, a mutton haunch coiled round with soft tendrils of smoke from a fire burning in the stone hearth.

She'd always wanted to know what the big house kitchen was like, whether it would have a fire in the middle like a normal kitchen, or blue-patterned dishes on shelves like the Manse. It was twice as big as the Manse kitchen, with scrubbed bare boards and lumpy walls that could use a fresh coat of lime wash and great, cobby rafters running across the high ceiling.

Above the rafters, the song stopped and she heard another sound. Birdsong. Not one bird, but many. A wild chirruping and squawking and trilling like the dawn chorus that came through her window each morning, except that it was evening and this birdsong came from inside. It called to her, luring her past the onion skins and carrot leaves, the green medallions of leek and boiled bones and potato peelings in a pail of cloudy water by the fire into the chill of the dining hall, the pale green walls decorated with gold-painted mouldings of wreaths and horns of plenty.

Crystal doves perched on the heavy chandelier that hung high over a polished table. Despite all she had heard, the stories told through her whole life, she was stunned by the richness of it, here on Hoy where most winters they went hungry, losing teeth and hair in their beds. Losing old folk to the cold in their houses and husbands, brothers, fathers out on the frozen sea.

The Laird never came here now. Until the doctor's arrival, the place had gone years without anyone to grace the table with eight upholstered chairs surrounding it - though only one place was set - or pour their gravy from the gold boat shaped like a galleon that gleamed at the centre.

It was all running to wrack, the mounted stag heads peering from under dust-sheets that were grey and cobwebbed and the mirror at the far end freckled with age. She was surprised it didn't make May angry to see such waste, given how she scrimped. With a cluck of disgust, Oona crossed the Persian rug, headed for the staircase, taking one last look around Gomorrah. Reflected in the spotted looking glass, the red flag of her hair twitched a warning.

The music began again, its metallic twang twisting around the birdsong, high notes rising above their trilling, hitting a perfect scale of notes like tiny hammers beating copper. Whoever was playing was a master, or mistress, of their art, trained to the highest perfection.

She followed the sounds up the spiral staircase, past red walls patterned with gold roses, up to the hallway where a gallery of long-dead ancestors stared down from their eternal prison pinned to the wooden panelling. Here, she stopped, startled by the light streaming through leaded windows, when all before had been gloomy and cool. The music was louder here, the notes more precise, falling evenly spaced. Harder and far more perfect than Mrs Yule's companionable piano playing, jarringly so.

The birdsong drove in the opposite direction - wild, lush, furious. She covered her ears to protect them from the overwhelming noise, blinked and finally saw the hallway clearly. Tucked between paintings, on side-tables, stacked each on each, floor to ceiling, were cages of all shapes and sizes lining the length of the hallway. Some were little more than old snares, their wicker mesh white with bird shit. Others were cubes of metal, ruddy with rust and age, stacked prosaically one on the other like lobster pots, while the cages that hung from wires nailed into the panelled ceiling were gilded and ornate. Inside, beneath, between, poked black beaks, yellow beaks, the fearsome curved maws of black-backed gulls. The birds trilled and sang, croaked and squawked, black eyes staring through the bars of their cells.

There were hundreds of them stuffed into the cages, flapping their wings, forlornly singing mating cries which came to nothing, puffing their chests at each other. As the captives screamed and sang, the precise, metallic notes played on and on and on.

Without thinking about it, she opened a cage door. "Come out, sweetheart."

But the blackbird inside sat unmoving and dumb, head turned to one side.

"Suit yourself then." She went to next cage, flung open the door. A dead bird lay inside. In the next cage, two doves perched heavily, necks drooping, legs ringed. There was no point freeing them. Their wings were obviously clipped. She spun around seeing everything and nothing. Their shit was everywhere, plastering soft feathers to the gilded walls and polished wooden floor. The smell was sharp and foul, making her eyes smart and her tongue click dryly on the roof of her mouth. She tasted bile again. No doubt remained that what she and May had done the night before had caused the plague of frogs. The washed up hand now stuffed in the coop.

Like someone caught in a nightmare, she walked along the corridor of cages, avoiding the fierce stares of gulls, the soft-eyed wonderment of doves. She couldn't meet their gaze because they might see inside her and know that she was an accomplice to all this.

At the end of the hallway, to the left of tall double doors, sat a piano. It was much smaller than Annie Yule's and shaped differently, the bare wood polished to a fine gloss and inlaid with gold. The small wooden teeth moved without the aid of human hands, descending by themselves and rising again. Up and down, up and down in perfect time as if an invisible force hurried the sharp sounds out. It was hypnotic watching the keys jump up and down, and beyond them, through the hinge of the lid, she saw the hammers jump at the keys' command.

"Why in God's name are you here?"

May stood at her side, her lips white, face shaking. Oona was shocked at her sudden presence, even more at the icy tone of her voice.

"Did you open that door?" The question was shrill, almost hysterical, as if May was terrified the blackbird might fly out.

She looked to where May pointed. The blackbird perched exactly as he had before, head turned in the same sad way, eye unblinking as if he were stuffed. "His wings are clipped. He'll always be captive."

"That makes no odds, Oona. How dare you come bursting in here and start touching things?" Their tryst was forgotten. Her voice, her face, were those of a cold little stranger.

Oona bit her lip. The full horror of all that had happened last night returned to her. Worse still, everything she'd risked today. "You're a saucebox, May, to censure me when there's poor birds caged in here that should be free and frogs drifting dead all over the shore and your father kicking up a row. He'll thrash you next time he lays eyes on you."

May's eyes bulged at that last. She frowned and for a moment seemed lost for words. Then she crossed her arms and stood straight, eyes narrowed. "It's beyond me why you think you can burst in here and preach to me. I can't help it if you've been a baby and prattled to everyone. I knew I shouldn't have brought you."

"You pig-headed wretch! Whatever mischief you're tangled in here is wicked." She looked at the doorway behind May's head, wondering what lay beyond it. "Besides, I've told no-one. But now I'm in it too. What I found this morning—"

May pulled her close, held her hard. "Please stop," she whispered.

"What?" Oona couldn't tell whether she knew about the hand. "What I found—"

"Shhh," May pressed a finger to Oona's lips. "We'll speak later on, but not here. He might hear us."

"Who might?"

"*Him.*"

"I'll decide when I speak my mind."

"May. I need you in this moment!" The man's voice, though muffled by the door, was urgent nonetheless. It was accented, but differently than Oona had imagined, not deep and mysterious, but as crisp and definite as the notes on the strange piano. The door swung open.

May slipped from Oona's arms. "Doctor Frankenstein." She looked ashamed.

He peered round the door at them like a startled weasel, raising his eyebrows until they vanished into the blonde hair spilling over his forehead. He wore a stained, white shirt with no cravat, green breeches that were dirty and rumpled. Clothes almost as filthy as Old Cormick's.

He was a slight man, angular and lithe. His nose was large and slightly hooked, dominating the boyish, clean-shaven face and his lips were wide and full. He was entirely unlike the tall, dark and handsome aristocrat of whom she had dreamt.

Appearing to sense her watching him, Frankenstein turned towards Oona. She braced herself for a lecture. Instead, his boyish face creased into a charming smile. His grey eyes, which turned down in a melancholy fashion at the outer edges, squinted shut until they seemed to disappear between thick, blonde lashes. "*This* is your friend? *Bitte schön* bring her into the Music Room. I need both of you."

Oona looked at May searchingly, losing sight of her anger in the moment's turmoil.

May met her eyes. "Don't speak out of turn," she hissed.

11

The music room stank of bird shit mingled with rancid meat and something acrid she couldn't identify. Sharper than lye or rotgut, it stung her eyes. She couldn't see where the smell came from because a curtain split the room so that only a narrow strip of floor was visible, a sort of walkway around the shrouded space in the centre. Cobbled together from dust sheets, the curtain hung from pulleys attached to the white cherubim that flew across the ceiling.

All along the walkway, paintings were turned round to face the oak panelling like naughty children. To their backs were tacked papers covered in angular symbols and numbers. The grandfather clock had stopped. Its pretty face - adorned with a serene moon smiling from painted heavens - hung open. Cogs and the entrails of springs hung out of it. A classical bust in the corner was painted with lurid features and an inky, numbered brain. None of it looked like the stories she'd heard of the Laird's elegant Music Room in which imported string quartets played.

"I have experienced somewhat of a lightning bolt, not to say an epiphany, given the Sisyphean labour of adapting what jetsam we have to hand." In his stocking feet - the yellow silk sadly wrinkled at the ankles - Frankenstein padded over the worn Persian rug, its stars and camels embroidered in golds, reds, oranges. He had a quick way of walking, an air of barely suppressed panic, as if time ran in constant and frightening pursuit of him. "May knows whereof I speak." He smiled broadly, eyes squinting. "My Man Friday, scavenging the wilderness for manna!"

May's lips eased from their white rictus. "Talks in riddles, does the doctor. Never stops working, either," she said under her breath, and smiled confidingly. "He means I've gathered specimens for his experiments."

She'd seen this version of May before, many times: the blushing girl who hung on a boy's arm and laughed at his foolish jokes. Although it grated on her and although she wished fervently for her tactless, foul-mouthed friend to return and drink and smoke with her, she'd learned not to feel too bitter about all the eyelash fluttering, since she knew how much May wanted to be a wife and mother. Sometimes she wondered which May was the true May, though, and which the act. She prayed that this time at least, the simpering was being put on.

"Specimens? Like frogs and birds?" She raised a sardonic eyebrow.

May elbowed her in the ribs. "Oona!"

"Hands?" Although Oona kept her voice low, even she could hear the anger in it.

May looked away, her mouth tightening into a frown.

Frankenstein flicked them a look over his shoulder, as if he had overheard their murmured exchange. "To discover the secrets of life, we must flush nature out of her hiding places, move her into an orderly setting in which she may be observed. Therefore I keep caged birds, not free-flying ones." Walking backwards now, he joined his thumbs and flapped his hands. "I cannot study them when they are flying all around my laboratory, shitting."

The doctor beckoned to May and she hopped over the scattered papers to reach him, hot colour spreading unevenly across her cheeks. Oona looked back at the open doorway. The cage-lined hallway stretched out beyond it. She could still turn back, though it wouldn't erase the fact of coming in the first place, wading deeper and deeper into whatever madness lay here. She thought of the dull eye of the caged blackbird, so used to its prison it didn't even look at the open door that would set it free. She wasn't sure that birds flying around this place and shitting would make much difference to the maelstrom anyway. In front of the dust sheet curtain, smudged papers spilled over the rug and floorboards, notes in handwriting loosely looped and dramatic, as if excitement had overwhelmed the writer; drawings inked so decidedly that the quill had torn through the paper in places.

The drawings, or diagrams, were unlike anything she had seen in the volumes of natural history that lined Hamish Yule's walls. A man who stood with legs and arms spread wide, his belly cut open. A small child curled round on itself in a sack, tied at the belly with a cord. A dog whose wild, round eye gazed down at his own half-peeled face, the tongue lolling through its teeth. That last made Oona think of Toby, the trusting way he padded across the yard behind her when she hid the girl's hand.

The doctor broke away from his whispered conversation with May, running his fingers through his messy hair as he walked to Oona. "The machines here are rudimentary, nothing like those I worked with in Ingolstadt, but I have reconstructed them with what May has been able to procure for me, from this house and the bounty of the island." He smiled at May, nodding.

She pulled a rope that dangled by the side of the dust sheets. They began to part raggedly like the curtains of the puppet theatre in Hamnavoe and Oona had a feeling that their intended purpose was similarly dramatic. For some reason Frankenstein wanted to make his work more mysterious rather than less. A pretty housemaid added nicely to the effect.

"The most abstract inquiries can be made simple through the art of practical discovery, though one must be wary of letting experimental work become an obsession, an addiction. There are always dangers, to a man's own soul, to the flesh itself. I often work here until the stars fuse with the dawn light." He gestured theatrically to the ramshackle stage behind the curtains.

Upon it lay scenery that had clearly been assembled through theft. Oona recognised objects from the rubbish heap on Cormick's beach, the manse and even Stuart's boat: cogs and beams, harpoons and hooks that had been fashioned into great interlocking structures of glass tubes and beakers clutched by metal arms. Springs like those that hung from the broken clock were twisted together with fishing line, great lengths of which ran from the large glass pane in the centre of the ceiling to a great wooden crate in the middle of the room. A circular hatch was cut in the front of the crate, the door that hung open revealing only darkness. Oona looked at May, who stood rapt, staring at Frankenstein. She had never seen her so quietly obedient. She found it hard to imagine chatterbox May working here in the gloom with the mad scientist and his 'machines'.

As if he sensed Oona's unease, Frankenstein came towards her. "I'm sure you must be wondering what all this is in aid of," he smiled roguishly. "Would you like me to explain all of this in layman's terms? I've done as much for your friend."

Oona avoided the grey-eyed gaze that made him seem so sure of himself. She looked at May again, feeling for the threads of lifelong understanding that ran between them.

May glared back a warning at her. She seemed blind to what was obvious to Oona: for all his easy charm, the doctor had brought trouble to the island. Perhaps he was being friendly to them both because he wanted some help up here in the big house. Or perhaps he desired to make them accomplices to whatever dark arts he was in the habit of practising. May had more to live for here and more to lose than the doctor. And Oona? Dead girl walking, she had nothing to lose.

She met the doctor's eyes. She could see he was surprised at her pause and that his smile had faded a little.

"I want to know why our fishermen are hauling in catches of frogs. Can you explain that, Sir?" She didn't look at May because she didn't want to see her mouth fall open or the colour climb up her neck.

For the first time, Frankenstein frowned. Oona's muscles tensed, poised to give as good as she got if he lost his temper with her like Dod had. It seemed to be the only way to deal with men like this and she was in the mood for it. Maybe if he hit her, May would see sense and leave before any of the others realised where they were or what they had done.

He put his hand to his face, stroked his dimpled chin upon which a new growth of golden-brown beard was just visible. "That was a terrible mistake. I brought those specimens with me and they were already ailing when they arrived. I tried to bring them back... to help. But they were decomposing when I began work on them. There was no bringing them back."

"So it seems, Sir, that you asked two girls to dispose of them for you."

He laughed nervously. "You are quite different from your friend... very...direct. I... It's refreshing. I apologise if you think I am exploiting you in some way, if I have done damage. I think the storm played a role, did something I could not predict, brought back... unpleasant remains..."

It was on the tip of her tongue to tell him that more than frog remains had washed up on the beach, but something told her to keep that detail to herself. The girl's hand hidden in the coop could be her secret for now. In any case, she would not find out from whence it came by simply asking.

He smiled. "I am truly sorry if I've caused you trouble, either of you. But really, I'm glad you chanced to visit, because I could usefully employ a woman of your skill. You can read and write, I am told? Even a bit of Latin."

Oona shrugged, surprised that May would have imparted details she so often teased Oona for.

"Most girls are delicate." He looked over at May with a comic grimace. "Not you though, Fräuline Oona, I can see. If I handed you a knife, you'd know what to do with it."

"My Da is gone, Sir, and I've no brothers." She was deadpan, dismissing the skill, even though part of her was secretly pleased to meet with his approval. "The men ask me to gut fish sometimes or butcher a hare, because I'm neat with a knife and nothing bothers me."

"*Mutig!*" he grinned.

She looked past his head, embarrassed at his obvious attempt to win her round, even more at her pleasure in hearing it. She braced herself, mentally repeating, *he just wants something. That's all.* For some reason, it seemed important to resist him.

"I have a small experiment underway today, involving galvanism. Do you know that term from your reading?" He turned to gesture to the long table covered in glass tubes and bottles, festooned with wire slung over it like ivy.

Behind it were two more tables. One was set out with a row of sharp and shining knives. The other was covered with a white sheet that rose and dipped over the landscape of its hidden contents. It was a long, thin table and whatever sat at the nearest end overshadowed the rest. Their tips were scalloped and peaked in the middle. And what lay beyond undulated gently over small, soft hills and valleys towards a shrouded moon from which dark weeds hung. It reminded her of wakes and the awful quietude of things that are dead. *Could that be…? No, surely not.*

Her eyes left the lifeless form superstitiously and looked behind to the windows.

12

Outside, the sky scabbed over and clotted black. Whatever the doctor had planned involved sharp implements and dead animals, perhaps other dead things. Her eyes flicked towards the long table again and away, as if she'd seen a ghost.

She shivered, all at once flooded with the desire to be back at the croft where everything was safe and warm and good. "It's late, Sir and I must beg my leave. My Granny will be wanting me."

"Schon gut," he said gently, "perhaps this is enough for today." He drew a pair of spectacles from his pocket and propped them on the bridge of his nose before turning to his papers.

She felt a light touch on her elbow. May's hand held her gently but firmly, pushing her towards the open door, ushering her from the room and down the cage-lined hall.

At the end of it, she pulled away from May's grasp and they walked through the twisting belly of the house in awkward silence.

On the stairs, May cleared her throat. "He talks and talks infernally, you know. Then all at once he needs to work and he begs you be gone." Her voice was oddly consoling, as if she expected Oona to be disappointed.

Oona said nothing, unsure of where to begin, how best to persuade her headstrong friend. At the kitchen door, she stopped, turned, measuring her words out carefully before spilling them coolly into the night air. "I don't think you should work here, May. I found a hand washed up on the beach. A hand. It seems dangerous to me—"

May rolled her eyes. "And you fancy this 'hand' is something to do with Doctor Frankenstein, I suppose?"

"I do."

"And I suppose you have proof of that."

"My proof is in the chicken coop. I'll fetch it for you tomorrow."

May's mouth went slack and Oona felt a flutter of hope that she'd had an effect. "The chicken coop," May sighed, rubbing her eyes wearily. "Oona, you're losing your wits. This is the real world and in the real world, money is a great necessity. The doctor has money and I need it, so I work for it and he pays me, and at the moment I have cooking to do. So if you don't mind..."

Oona caught her by the wrist. "It's not merely the money, is it?" She looked straight into May's eyes, trying to see past the façade into that busy brain of hers. "It's more than that."

May struggled free and let out a brittle laugh. "You might know your letters and read all sorts of fine books over at Hamish Yule's, Oona, but I am the one the doctor desires by his side. You may not have faith in my judgement, but *he* does, as I have faith in his."

The words pinched Oona and she turned away, mute. Only when she heard the door slam behind her did she let the tears prick to the surface and fall down her burning cheeks, glad that the night wrapped around her like a veil and hid her.

At the burn, she snatched up a fallen stick and beat the bullrushes, making their dark heads snap off and fall in the fast-moving water. Yes, it sounded like a wonderful kind of trusting relationship, slaving as a maid, doing some strange man's dirty work, washing his breeks and cooking his bannocks. No doubt it was a real position of authority. May had made it sound as if she was jealous. What a joke! She threw the stick as hard as she could, satisfied to hear the splash it made in the angry tumult of water.

Halfway back, she stopped on the cliff-top to look at the lights on the mainland. She and May often watched them flickering on and off at night as if someone was sending a message: here is light and life and warmth and possibility.

May was right about one thing. Oona was jealous that her friend got to live her life with all its potential for adventure and discovery, for travelling the world and seeing extraordinary things. Ma had been barely two years older than Oona was now when she died.

She wanted to live, not to be found face down in the burn's cold water, eternally asleep. From where she stood now, the other island looked like a sleeping woman with her hair fanned out under her and her fingers clutching the sea like a sheet and her feet pointing to the heavens.

Feet.

Her heart beat the bony cage of her ribs. She sat down hard. Sweat bubbled from her temples, for she knew with sick certainty what lay under the sheet in the music room.

13

Had it really been a body, or was her mind cozening her? Oona stopped and pressed her hands to her forehead, picturing the long table covered in a sheet and the instruments laid out beside it. That tangled seaweed - *hair*. Those scalloped hills - *feet*. And the soft undulations - *hips, belly, breasts*.

A woman.

In the vampire moonlight that sucked the colour from everything, her imagination took on a dark cast. She saw not just a table and tools, but a winding sheet, butchers' knives.

Squeezing her eyes shut, she winnowed her memories, searching out some bright certainty. The kitchen had been comforting enough, with its familiar smells and food and pots. The gallery full of great ancestors would not have been so sinister without the caged birds and the strange improvements Frankenstein had made to the music room could be seen as no more than a symptom of eccentricity. When she tried to conjure the doctor, however, all she found were fear and fury at the way he'd put May in danger and suspicion of what he had planned.

She watched her pale feet move along the dirt road. Grey grass tickled the curved space between her big toe and its bedfellow. Her feet could walk and run and swing from a tree over the burn or wade in the sea, the salt stinging them. But the ones in Doctor Frankenstein's laboratory were mere meat, cold as the hand washed up on the shore, still as a rock beside the throbbing life of the doctor's menagerie.

She had to know more.

A few paces from the gate of the croft, rain caught her, hard and fierce. The thick drumming on the earth's lid said *dead hand, dead feet, dead girl*. It could be you on that table. Swollen mud suckled at her feet and her clothes tugged her down. She was weak as a beached jellyfish, falling into the cottage and letting the door blow shut behind her. The noise of it flustered the chickens perching on a beam over the hearth. Ruffled and ungainly, they fussed on their night perch, blundering against each other, claws knitting and purling the beam.

The fire had turned to embers under the blackened kettle. The candle guttered on the shelf, lighting the gold-lettered backs of the *Bible*, *Pilgrim's Progress* and *Night Thoughts*. After Oona's parents died,

Granny had made a special effort to teach her letters, dragging her to the Manse often so that she could pore over the beautiful, old books in Hamish Yule's library and ask him her many questions about the world and its history and listen patiently to his long-winded answers. Most folk on the island respected Granny for her wisdom, but others complained that she spoke like she had puffin eggs in her mouth. They thought Oona did too.

The wicker chair was turned towards the fire, its hooped back facing the door and hiding its occupant from Oona. Rain dropped off the freckled tip of her nose and ran in rivulets over her collarbone, down her arms and legs to the floor where it pooled on the flags. She felt like a spirit visitant returning to watch over the living, out of step with the world, little more than an observer. Was this how the dead girl felt, wandering in some limbo?

Orpheus flopped down from his roost to peck at barley husks around Oona's feet. She was glad of his gold eye watching her and his handsome plume bobbing. Vain bird, he was, but he loved her and was waiting for her to strip off her wet things and dry her hair and pull out the drawer that held her bed so he could settle himself in the warm hollow of her belly. Most nights they slept soundly in each others' blood heat as she and May had slept when they were young girls and May begged her parents to let her share Oona's bed.

Wicker scraped stone. Oona's jaw closed uncomfortably tight, the top and bottom teeth chafing each other. The chair turned and Granny's shadow grew long against the fireplace, her stiff limbs poking clumsily forth like a hermit crab opening the shutters of his shell house, revealing his secret hiding place. Toby leapt down from her lap to yawn and stretch. Granny glared at the burned-down fire, still stupid with sleep, then turned her glazed eyes on the spectre in her doorway.

"Where've you been, child?"

Oona shrugged, wiped the drips of rain from her eyelids. "Out." She knew that long explanations would annoy Granny worse than her absence, and lies were no good. Granny had a sixth sense for lies.

The old woman dropped her shawl and marched over to the door. Her hand caught Oona a clip round the ear. Oona reeled back, her hand

grabbing the rough stone behind her to hold herself steady. "What-"
Bells peeled in her ear, cacophonous.

"Leave kirk, will you, in the middle of a meeting? No word to me, no
excuse to the Minister. Is that what I brought you up for, to shame me?"
She raised her hand again, lips white, cheeks quivering. Oona shrank
against the wall. If it had been anyone else she would have hit them
back. But Granny's anger was more terrifying than any and besides, she
could never raise a hand to her.

"Granny I'm sorry." She bit her lip. Needles pricked the backs of
her eyes. She forced the tears back, trying to be braver than she felt with
the whole day, whole week, whole summer rushing in on her in messy
fury. Her legs shuddered. She jabbed her fingers into them.

Granny's eyes followed the movement of her hands. Dull recognition
flitted behind her eyes. *The dying girl.* She shrank into herself with a sigh.
"Oh dear. Come here Toby, come on and give Granny a kiss."

The little dog's ears pricked up and he padded over, stretched and
yawned, following her to her chair. She fell towards it, slow and hunched,
looking her age again now the anger had left her. Toby jumped onto her
lap and she buried her face in his rough fur.

"It was a dark day, wasn't it, eh, Toby?" Granny murmured the
words, speaking, as usual, as if the dog knew what she meant. Her
eyes were turned down, away from where Oona still cowered, fingers
pressed under her eyes to hold the tears at bay. "Bad things happening
in the kirk. Angry words. Everyone so fearful of this plague and nobody
knows what's the matter. Someone's bound to be blamed, eh Toby?
Unless they tell what they know." She opened her arms, sweeping the
dog down as if she was tired of his weight on her lap. "Go on now,
Toby. Don't cling so."

He trotted out the door, ears back with the knowledge of having
been chidden. Oona slunk after him. If she could have put her ears
back, she would have. If she could have told Granny every word of
the truth about May and the doctor and the stinking crates, she might
have done that too. Instead, she must be a supplicant in her own house,
a Prodigal Daughter come to beg forgiveness and lie through her teeth
as she did so.

She knelt in front of Granny and took her hand and kissed its Bible-
paper skin. "I had to go abroad in the world and think my own thoughts
for a while. I went to the beach and skimmed stones."

"Until the witching hour?"

Oona hung her head. "I'm ashamed by my manner of speaking in kirk."

Granny's hand slipped out of hers and coolly folded with the other in her lap. "You'll go to Norquoy tomorrow and make an apology to Dod?"

"Yes, indeed I will." She swallowed the aching lie in her throat, reminding herself that she'd get far worse if Granny knew the whole truth. She rose slowly, feeling suddenly cold, and went to her corner to undress, stepping over the sow that snored thunder on the rag rug. She heard the soft pad and wheezing yawn as Toby jumped up to take comfort on Granny's lap once more.

The sky was the pink of chicks fresh hatched from the egg and promised a good deal less well. Oona rubbed her gritty eyes. All night long, one terrifying dream of death had merged with the next until she felt she couldn't roll over without colliding against chill flesh.

Nerves jangling, she pushed Orpheus from the covers and grabbed up a bucket from the side of the hearth where the pile of peat was dwindling. Granny snored and Toby whimpered by the ashes of the fire, his eyebrows twitching after field mice. If only she dreamt of mice instead of corpses.

In the cool near-night, she crept to the damp byre. She threw down the bucket and unhooked the pitchfork from its place on the wall. Bending low, she let every angry or anxious thought inside her run down into her arms. The tines stabbed the pile of drying peat and every fear or face that had angered her was in the peat she ran through. Again and again, she nicked and jabbed, lifted and sliced until something heavy flew from her, leaving behind nothing but a tense, tingling thrill that she had secrets to keep, or perhaps to reveal.

14

In the birch tree bower, Oona smoked her throat dry, only sorry that it was too early in the day to drink cider. Granny's silences were stubborn and enduring and Oona could no longer tolerate the heavy air of the croft.

The tree she lay in was a lifelong friend and a good place to lie upon while she unpicked the intertwined riddles of May and the dead girl. May did not want help and the dead girl was dead. It was difficult.

She knocked the clay pipe on the branch. Cold ash tumbled onto the ground moss like snow. Poking a straw into the small fire she'd made, she held it to the damp kindling in the bowl, tugged and drew and coughed. The answer came to her framed in blue smoke rings, growing clear all at once as things so often seemed to. She slipped down the worn branch and planted her feet on the ground somewhat shakily.

She had pondered and now she knew that for the dead girl as well as for May, she must go back and she must keep the whole affair her secret. However little she might want to walk through the hallways of the bird prison, the girl deserved her fate to be uncovered. And May, whether she knew it or not, required help.

Oona hadn't considered the whole stratagem, or even decided it. It was simply there, real and firmly planted as the Mustard Seed that is Heaven and grows in the minds of the devout.

As the seed grew, it warmed her and braced her. When she walked into the big house, it would be simple. The doctor had requested her presence and she was obeying him, as girls were supposed to, coming to assist with his experiments; coming to watch him at work, paying only the subtlest attention to what lay beneath sheets, behind curtains, scrawled on papers on the floor.

There was no need to fear getting caught or punished. A person cannot be brought to book for being a helpful housemaid.

To tread the path, though, and hear the crunch of the gravel announcing her arrival, to stand outside a sash window, straightening her skirt, felt quite different to the Mustard Seed. For it was an imaginary Mustard Seed, a madcap plan, bold and unconsidered. As soon as she pushed the kitchen door open and slipped inside, her subterfuge would be real.

She'd be lying to her friend as well as deceiving the doctor, just like some English spy in the stories she'd heard of the Reign of Terror.

Today the kitchen door was locked. There would be no sneaking in and tiptoeing up the haunted staircase. She'd just have to knock. Her fist was halfway to the door when she paused for a heartbeat. A panicky sweat popped up on the back of her neck. She didn't know how to spy on people. She hadn't even considered any of it. Through the door, she heard a key pant in the lock, the rasp of the handle turning. It was too late now. May's pale face appeared, scraped-back hair under her cap making her look strangely childlike. She stood silently frowning for what seemed like a long time. Then she flung her arms round Oona's neck and squeezed hard.

"I'm sorry about what I said." May's words sounded choked.

"Me too." She parted sheepishly from May with a hard laugh, but really she was gladder than she would ever have said. Waves of reassurance washed over her. It was like sitting in the warm shallows on the beach, sun-lavished and worry free. May loved her and she was sure of it. Her darkest thoughts melted in the glow of that.

"He's been asking after you." May rolled her eyes in the direction of the music room.

"Me? Really?" Oona's ribs tightened, bony fingers squeezing. This was worse than a chilly reception, for now she felt guilty at lying to May.

But she was protecting her. She repeated the words like a prayer as she followed May into the kitchen, hearing the now-familiar sounds from the floor above. Melancholy notes, light and crisp and utterly precise as no living thing ever is. On the table lay a brace of pheasants, red masks somehow more vivid in death, throats gleaming.

May walked round to a half-plucked fellow on a board and pushed her hands into the ruddy feathers of its paunch. "Peel some tatties for me? I'll take you up after."

Oona nodded, glad at the temporary reprieve. The idea of going up there again twisted her stomach. She picked up the paring knife May gestured to and dug a spud from the sack at her feet, relishing its cool heft. There was an eye in the side facing her, a green sprout starting in it like a twinkle. She excised it precisely with the tip of the knife, her mind turning inevitably to the sharp implements spread out above them, the prone body of the girl, colder than the bird in May's hands.

"What d'you think he wants me for, the doctor?" Oona felt a lump forming in her throat and gulped it down. "Writing notes?"

"I suppose that's it." May shrugged, her eyes fixed on the pheasant's brindled feathers. "He cuts things up, stitches things together. He's hell-bent on it." Her hand moved to the bird's pink plucked head. "They always look so sad like this. Absurd."

Oona braced, tense as a startled hare, her skin prickling. She must know, must nudge May back on topic. "Hell-bent on what?"

"Discovering the secret of death and so forth."

Cold fingernails clawed Oona's back. *The secret of death.* She looked into May's eyes, wanting to spill the black web of thoughts into her mind and not have to argue against May's inevitable skepticism. "He sounds dangerous, May."

"Oh, not in the least. He's an odd bird though. Half the words out of his mouth are German. He does not sleep for days, picks at his food, paces, tears his hair, then drinks a case of wine, eats like a pig and makes sheep's eyes at me." She laughed, wrinkling her nose. "He puts me in mind of Stuart when he came upon those whisky casks and hid 'em. He turned so ill at ease and sulky, it scarce seemed worth it, being so consumed."

Oona thought of the hand, the body, the doctor, strangling, slicing. "As a person hiding the truth is consumed?"

May frowned. "Perhaps." She struggled a moment with the stubborn tail feathers, pulled them free with a grunt. "Hunted." She grinned, pleased with the insight. "He's like Stuart with his stolen whisky casks, because Stuart was certain people would discover him. And I believe someone is also in search of our friend the doctor."

Oona's mind wouldn't quiet. It churned on through nightmarish scenes. *The doctor running. Screams. People chasing him, desperate for justice.* "The authorities?"

"You have a ready fancy, Oona!" May laughed. "Anyway, how in Jesus' name would I know? When I said we were friends, I was being comical."

"But last night, you said he trusted you. I thought..."

"That I'm his confidante? Don't be daft. I've known him all of a month and anyway, I was just trying to annoy you because you were being very irksome indeed."

"Oh, I see." Oona laughed, relieved that May was not under some spell of Frankenstein's. In fact, she seemed just as prickly and skeptical as ever. May laughed too, shaking her head with mock incredulity. They worked quietly then, smooth as an oiled lock, passing a knife or a dish the other wanted without needing to say a word. It was the best kind of togetherness, that understanding that grafted one onto the other so that their differences vanished under new closeness, like skin knitting over a wound.

Today, Oona grasped at the familiar feeling as a person might scoop up sunlight from a stream and it slipped away before she had a chance to grow used to it. She peeled and gouged and plunged the bald, blank heads of tatties into a bowl of cold water and all the while, unease pulsed under the companionable silence. Even May could see the doctor had some awful secret, had committed a crime perhaps and maybe he would soon be caught. But until then, they were in danger, surely? She must convince May of what she had found and if she could not persuade her to leave, she must at least put her on guard.

She plunged the last potato into the bowl of water and wiped her hands on her skirts. "May, I must tell you—"

A board creaked outside in the hallway, a single footfall. Another. As if someone were listening.

May pressed a finger to her lips and put down her knife, coughing exaggeratedly. The door opened and the doctor walked in. His filthy shirtsleeves were rolled to the elbow, revealing ink-stained arms. Oona and May stopped what they were doing. Along the length of Oona's spine, a wire pulled tight.

15

May curtsied hastily and went back to stuffing minced onion into the pheasant's hole. Wishing she had some fresh task to fall to, Oona clasped her hands together. They were numb and red-knuckled from being plunged into the potato water. Frankenstein closed the door behind him, beaming at the domestic scene he'd come upon like someone pleasantly tipsy or just very happy. His eyes, though, were unknowable slits behind pale lashes.

"Ah, ladies. Hard at work or hardly working?" Eyes on Oona, he chuckled at his little joke.

"Can I do something for you, Sir?" May's question was so informal it sounded insulting. "I've got giblets on my hands, but—"

The doctor held up a hand, chuckling. "No May, do carry on. You have the manner of a person fruitfully occupied. Your friend, though, appears quite idle and must to be set to work. Come Olga, follow me."

May smirked. "I can manage here, Olga." She shook her head very slightly in the direction of the stairs as if to say, *quick, go upstairs.*

Upstairs in the laboratory. Upstairs with the corpse, where she would have to wait until the doctor was distracted. Oona forced a polite smile onto her lips, curtseyed a bit ridiculously and walked to where the doctor stood, jovially patient. He turned, running a hand through his chaotic hair, then halfway out, turned back, smiling charmingly.

"And May, perhaps you could prepare me a little something, a sort of *hors d'oeuvre.*" His voice was a parody of aristocratic speech, playing the Laird. "A scone with small raisins in it, perhaps? I have a terrible craving for sweetness." He winked at Oona.

May sighed. "If I've flour enough." Her tone of weary familiarity struck Oona as odd. She'd said they were strangers. Shouldn't a maid be polite? Oona cast a sly glance at Frankenstein, trying to gauge his response.

He took a step towards the hallway, before answering. "Very well," he said, his smile fading so that his face wore a troubled look. Not just troubled. Lost.

She followed him up the staircase in noon light that had dulled to a sleepy grey. A foot or so behind him, she felt his nervousness like the prickly air before a lightning storm. There was something fascinating in his excitable walk, the agitated tap of his fingers on the bannister.

Each time she looked away from him - at the walls with their red shapes (open mouths, cruel teeth) or the birdcages lining the gallery - her eyes were drawn back to the doctor like coins to a lodestone. She didn't know what she was watching for. Perhaps a layer would peel back and reveal what lay beneath or he would transform into his true self like a charmed beast in a fairy tale. Then she would see the murderer hidden under his smiles.

In the music room, the stench was unbearable. She pressed her hand to her mouth. Something was rotting in the laboratory and each day was making it worse. Without wanting to, she imagined the girl's body distending and blackening as the frogs on the beach had after they began to attract flies.

Gulping back bile, she crossed the camel-patterned rug to where he held the curtain open. Beneath the sweep of his arm, a nebula of candles cast shadow devils onto books and papers piled on a music stand, spilling over on to a lady's escritoire. His body blocked her way. She looked at him, confused.

He looked back, brow creased, grey eyes intent. "This is rather more than a social visit, I hazard. You wish to know what I am doing in the fine house, here on your island."

She tried to smile, but the wire in her spine was too close to snapping. It was sure to show. She'd never been good at hiding things. "You said you were in need of help and for my own part, I desire work, Sir."

He waved her words away, seemingly either bored or disappointed. The thread of connection between them broke. "Of course you will be paid. Although there is more to life than filthy lucre, for wisdom..." He scratched his arm contemplatively. "Wisdom is dangerous. The Faustian pact. The Promethean flame." He leaned close, his voice a whisper. "Is deadly." His fingers clawed harder and left four red lines.

He snatched up a book from the music stand, rifled the pages and turned it towards her. There were words written in a language she did not know. Underneath them was an engraving. A naked man was strapped to a table and connected by wires to a pole with levers on it. A man in a top hat touched his hand to one lever. A coin leapt from the strapped man's hand. Perhaps this was the sort of experiment the doctor performed up here - strapping people to tables, putting them in machines. Perhaps it was why he needed her and May. Her skin buzzed with the remembered terror of a recurrent dream, one where her lungs filled with water and life left her body and she jolted up sweat-drenched.

Instead of turning away from the picture that so repulsed her, she felt compelled to peer closer. The man on the table had a large head, misshapen. His hair stood on end and his face contorted in a freakish grimace. "The look on his face, Sir. It's terrible, like someone hag-ridden."

Frankenstein frowned thoughtfully. "I suppose death is a kind of nightmare, from which most do not wake. This man is fortunate."

Oona gasped. "How can you say that? He looks like a sinner being tortured in Hell."

He shrugged. "He cannot feel it. He's been hung by the neck. His nerves, his brain, are dead, the tissue decaying. Besides which, in life he was the worst sort of murderer."

"He is alive here still!" She jabbed her finger at the book, no longer able to disguise her agitation.

He smiled that boyish smile. It ground against his words like gnashing teeth. "He has been brought back with galvanism."

"Brought back?"

His lips twitched excitedly. "It is a new discovery and has been much debated across Europe. It involves the harnessing of natural forces - the very lightning that splits the sky in a sea storm, Olga - for the purposes of reanimation." As he spoke, his fingers absently flicked the pages of the book.

"I do not follow, Sir," she said dully, unused to feeling stupider than someone. "Why is he throwing the coin? Is it his payment to the doctor?"

Frankenstein laughed. "Pay he should!" he cried, "damned dead wretch! Gold and diamonds for the privilege of being brought back from the grave!" He banged his fist in the book. "And if not diamonds, blood." The last word was sharp and his eyes grew cold, the laughter gone from them. He tossed the book onto the floor as if he despised it.

Oona's head spun dizzily between the conviction that he was a madman and the sensation of falling fast into some deep hole that had opened up underneath everything she was certain of, like the cave roofs when they collapsed and the cliff tops formed blue windows onto the sea's destruction.

16

Oona turned away from the grotesque scene in the book and looked around the room for something real and reassuring. Her eyes lighted on an oak smoking cabinet that stood next to the writing. Behind its glass panels lay neither cigars nor tobacco, but a large jar full of yellowish water and a grey mass of worm-like flesh.

"A cow's brain," Oona murmured under her breath. There was nothing reassuring in that, though it was at least something she recognized.

The doctor seized her wrist, the demonic spark returning to his eyes. "Yes, yes. This is why you can help me, why I have need of you here, for it appears you know a little. Writing. Anatomy. Dissection. Not much but a little. Very soon you will discover more." He pulled her along, his grip surprisingly strong. Too stunned to struggle, she followed him, past the box, getting no more than a glimpse of the sheet-draped table that had been her reason for coming.

He drew her towards a billiard table, abruptly dropping her wrist to reach for what lay in the middle. Whatever it was looked as if it had once been an oil lamp or perhaps a globe, now remolded so that it connected with a large copper wheel supported by a brass stand. He ran his fingers along the spokes connecting the stand to the wheel, checking the thin metal armpits that joined them to blunt-toothed cogs.

"The grandfather clock has been a great patron of mine," he smiled wryly. "The old technology ceding to the new. Can you uncover that please?"

She looked to where he was pointing - the far side of the table, covered by a sheet. If some poor, dead girl lay beneath it, she did not know whether she would be able to keep her composure. Bracing herself, she walked around the table and pulled away the sheet to reveal two glass jugs without handles that were bulbous at the bottom. A shaky breath left her lips and somewhere inside her a wire loosened. *Not yet. It had not happened yet.*

She still had time to turn back.

"Take a closer look, if you like." He gave her a self-assured smile that reminded her of small boys she'd seen on the beach once, competing to see who could pish furthest.

Looking more closely, she saw that one jug was turned upside down atop the other and liquid ran into it from a long tube that fed into the top. Blue-green fluid dripped down into the murky water of the bottom jug. Although the sides of the glass were stained green with the growth of pond slime, a large, spotted bullfrog was visible within, his gold eyes protruding above the water's rim, his broad lips sometimes gaping as he swam to reveal the soft pink skin inside him.

"Hmn. Survived the plague," she murmured.

He looked at her curiously. "What is that you say?"

She stood up straight, inwardly reproaching herself for being such a shoddy spy. "Nothing, Sir."

"Well no matter," he snapped, his fingers twisting at the wires that joined the copper wheel contraption to a length of wire that ran across the ceiling.

Looking up, she saw that it was held to the plaster by metal loops nailed at even intervals. Another length of wire ran down to grasp the tube feeding into the glass aquarium where the frog swam guilelessly round, as if looking for a way out. In between the frog's prison and the wheel was a square of board with something nailed to it. Oona peered closer and saw that it was a long-legged frog, just like the one in the glass house, except this one was held onto the wooden board with lengths of twisted wire looped around its middle. A meat fly that had been buzzing around in the hazy light landed on the frog's head. It walked a staccato circle, stopped, rubbed its front legs one over the other like an old woman chafing her hands. It jabbed its forked tongue once, twice into the milky jelly of the frog's eye.

The doctor waved an impatient hand at the fly. "You see a resemblance?"

With an angry buzz, the fly flew off.

She thought of the severed hand, the hank of dark hair hanging off the pale body, and shuddered. "Resemblance to what, Sir?"

"The picture in the book, of course." His fingers worked feverishly at the wires wrapped round the frog, twisting them together with those that hung from the ceiling.

With a sick lurch, she did see. The frog on the board was the dead man with the nightmare in his eyes. Frankenstein thumped the board down in the centre of the table and gestured to a shapeless object next to Oona, something her height and draped in a sheet.

"Uncover it." He took out a handkerchief and scrubbed at the sweaty band of forehead under his shock of yellow hair.

Oona pulled the sheet away to reveal a great copper spring made of tubing as thick as her arm. The spring coiled around a copper tub that tapered to a cone at its top end. This too was connected to the intricate web of ceiling wires.

"A galvanic coil. It's part of the circuit I've made. And now we are ready to create something so much more mysterious, more astounding than that."

Frankenstein grabbed a handle that jutted from the wheel on the stand and began turning it. Slowly at first, then faster, faster making the cogs spin frantically.

The coil crackled into life, filling the air with a buzz, a storm cloud hum that made her mouth taste of metal and her skin thrill. There was a cut across the frog's belly where the wires probed inside. A spark flew from the place where wire touched flesh, one dizzy star, then another.

Another fountain of blinding sparks shot from the wire armpits that joined the cogs to the stand. The water in the aquarium bubbled and the living frog swam round wildly, panicked. The soft, red strings of the dead frog's innards pulsed against the loops of wire pinning it onto the board. A sticky pool of translucent frog blood ran under the creature's pale, gleaming body. Then its leg twitched once, twice.

With a croak, it bucked against its bindings. Frankenstein stopped the wheel. He bent to the frog, his body obscuring what his hands did. It jumped free of him, slippery and lithe as any pond frog. When it reached the corner pocket of the billiard table, it stopped, the dark ovals of its eyes embedded in liquid gold, gleaming, blinking. *And the dead man came out, his hands and feet bound in graveclothes, his face wrapped in a headcloth. Jesus told them, "Unwrap him and let him go!"*

Oona watched the frog, rapt. A moment before, it had been a dead thing, white-fleshed, belly-up on its wooden board. Now the mottled flesh of its soft-padded fingers shone with new moisture and its cream throat pulsed with each quick breath. Flesh reanimated. What he had said was true. Beside her, Frankenstein stared too, sucking in each moment of new life. His pupils were big and dark, like someone under a spell.

She'd never seen anyone look at something with that sort of mad intensity before. But he didn't seem to share her pleasure in seeing the creature rise from the dead like Lazarus. The corners of his mouth pulled down into a harsh frown and his skin was pallid with sweat. When he turned to face her, she recognised the expression on his face. It was hatred.

17

That night, the storm returned. Huddled in the croft, Oona lay staring at the dark, her mind a busy tongue fretting sores in the mouth. The wind tore angrily at the heavy peats that protected the roof of the cottage. A door banged over and over and a branch clawed the window. Her thoughts spun, endless as the cogs in the doctor's machine, flicking out sparks part memory, part nightmare. *The dead frog waking. The feeding fly rubbing its hands. That glimpse of the sheet and whatever lay beneath.*

After the frog came alive, the doctor's mood had changed. He'd ushered her out before she had a chance to spy any further and slammed the door shut, that hateful look still on his face. She'd walked back home, shaking, the elation she'd felt at seeing the frog come alive bruising into something darker. The Bible would call it necromancy, what he'd done, a practice so abominable it made you unclean even to see it. She sat up in bed, scratching her neck, her cheeks, her legs. She felt achy and sick.

In the darkness, everything shouted and clawed. Necromancers burned their children as offerings. They spoke to the dead. Was that what the doctor had done? Whoever did these things was an abomination to the Lord. M*urderers, sorcerers, their portion was in the lake that burns with fire. Their lot was the second death.*

Unless it was all a parlour trick meant to deceive her, like the man at Hamnavoe Fair who pulled doves from his scarf and rabbits from his hat. Sleight of hand intended to distract her from finding out what he was really engaged in. But she *would* find proof. She would do better than she had and not fall under the spell of his strange magnetism or listen to his lies. Clutching her ears, she threw herself down miserably and pulled the blanket over her head.

She must have fallen asleep, because she woke to hoarse shouts tearing the cloth of her dreams. She sat up and the covers fell from her, the colours of her sleeping life melting so that she couldn't call back the dream's pleasant story, although she knew Ma had been in it somewhere, smiling at her.

The shout rang out again, but it wasn't a person calling. It was Toby, his barks echoing across the yard, though she didn't remember letting him out in the night. With a groan, she swung her legs over the side of the bed and pulled her bedcovers around her. In the cold light, eyes swollen with sleep, she followed the sound of Toby's yelps half blindly.

She crossed the freezing floor, past the long-gone-out fire in the hearth. Granny lay curled in a ball in her wicker chair the way children sleep, with blanket half over her head. She'd taken to spending the night there recently, as if her actual bed was too much bother to sleep on.

Toby started up again. If he kept on he'd wake the whole valley. He sounded frightened, his gruff barking a counterpoint to the squawks of the hens. They shouldn't be outside either, not in a storm. In a moment she saw the reason for the exodus. The door to the cottage hung off its hinges.

Out in the yard, the storm had gouged and torn more than the door. It had taken half the fence with it by the looks of things. She sighed. Sometimes the wind was brutal, hurtling over the flat, bleak land from the sea, smashing branches, tearing off roofs. A crow perched on what was left, hunched low, feathers puffed out, watching her. The wind picked up again and the creature huddled to one side, moving along the wood of the fence post that leaned drunkenly, white in the middle where it had splintered. She took a step closer and the crow jumped up and flew off. Near the fence post, a bucket lay on its side, its water long since spilled. Where the scrubby patch of barley peppered the mud, clods of earth churned up and the green stalks were broken near the root or pulled up whole, scattering chaff and unripe seed.

The wind didn't do that.

With her blanket pulled tighter around her, she hurried across the yard towards Toby's snarls and the still-squawking hens. Her eyes were sharper now, growing used to the gloom even as it lifted and a whey-thin light showed her more - the trail of spilled seed near the byre door, milk trickling near it and pooling round grains.

The hen-house door was latched, clucks echoing within the cramped space. She bent low and unhooked the catch, pulled open the door. A pair of brown hens flung out at her and shot into the mud behind. Then Toby, fur prickling, tongue lolling, reddish dark round the muzzle and mouth.

Holding her breath, she peered into the rank-smelling coop and saw the pale smash of broken eggs, yolks yellow on the scratched earth and the dark, shining stream that reddened as it guttered into the light.

The hens, two, four, seven of them, wings splayed, bloody, necks awry. She'd killed her fair share of chickens, carried them to the block, wielded the axe, plucked them for meat and soup. But that was nothing like this.

There was blood everywhere and the stench of death thickened the air. She stumbled back out, dazed, and fell to her knees. Toby tugged at her skirt, but she couldn't bear to pat him or even look down at the matted blood of his muzzle. He was such a gentle dog. She would never have thought he'd do this.

Her hand pushed into something warm and soft and wet.

She looked down and saw red and black feathers: Orpheus, her bedfellow. Her ribs, breastbone, belly crushed down, squeezing the air from her. For a moment her heart seemed to stop. It lurched into life again, painful, furious so that she almost wished it hadn't. Bending low, she buried her face in the soft feathers.

When she came back yesterday, he'd strutted across the yard to peck at her legs. Then he'd curled up in her lap, his head tucked under his wing. It had been so comforting. She shuffled to her knees. Maybe he was only sleeping. Turning the body round, she peered close. At the end of his neck was a dark hole where the head had been torn off.

She retched, a string of glistening spit joining her to the damp earth.

18

"Toby won't be frighted if he don't expect it." Hamish Yule's brows beetled together when he peered through his spectacles at Toby, a smaller and scrappier version of the sinners he lectured in kirk. Toby, fur damp from splashing in the burn, wagged his tail at the sound of his name. He'd long since licked his muzzle clean. "I'm an old friend of his. I'll take him out into the fields for the deed itself—"

"You'll do no such thing." Granny's voice shook. "I've already lost my cockerel and my silly wee hens." She bent and picked up the little dog as if Hamish might snatch him from her.

They turned to look at Oona, who stood apart from them, peering through wet lashes. She clasped her hands behind her back, not wanting them to see how every part of her shook. She couldn't push away the picture of the dark neck-hole. When she'd looked at it more closely, the wound seemed clean. Not torn as a beast or dog might tear, but severed. She couldn't shake the thought that somebody had come in the night and ripped the front door off its hinges and killed their cockerel with a knife: a good sharp one, such as Doctor Frankenstein kept.

Hamish walked to the front door and ran his hands over the splintered wood. "Yes well, dark things come upon us Mrs Scollay," he sighed. "Even the gentlest beast of the field may run mad at a small provocation. As for your other calamities, the ill winds have brought everyone low."

Granny pressed her lips to Toby's head, kissing him in that fond way she saved for her dogs and her hens. "He's always been a gentle creature and played with the other animals like a friend. Even when they were chicks he didn't bother them."

"Oona was the first to see the thing and found the hen-house shut." Hamish took off his spectacles and gestured with them as he spoke, smiling (as he always did) at the reassuring turn of his logical mind. "Could a fox or a bonxie kill a whole roost and close the door behind itself after?"

Granny countered his self-satisfied gaze with a chill stare. "Could a dog close a door behind itself and shut the latch?" Her voice bristled with the harsh tone she was known for when the time came to stand her ground.

Hamish's brows rose sharply. He looked at Oona. "You never said anything about it being latched." He sounded disappointed.

"Oona?" Granny's voice was sharp.

Truthfully, she'd hardly been listening. Her mind was on the knives in the music room, their blue gleam. Behind her back, her nails dug into her hand. She mumbled her answer, eyes down, hot with that uncomfortable shame she often felt during sermons and never quite understood. "I found it shut tight. And the churn in the byre was on its side, the heavy one. I don't think even I could push it over—"

Granny's eyes widened, as if she had just realised something, "You know, the day before yesterday, Janice said she found her yard in a ruin and thought the goat had done it, or the boys, but later on she noticed meat and grain were missing too—"

"Well, well, I don't listen to gossip." Hamish dusted his hands on his breeches, his whole face puckered in a frown. "You've hard work to do setting the place to rights - I'll help you fix the door and the fence post and then I'll have to make myself scarce. God, in his wisdom, has sent me on many an errand today."

If people passed by the croft that day and heard the hammer thud into the naked wood of the new fence post and saw Hamish Yule - nearly naked himself in his shirtsleeves - they might well have wondered.

Hamish never fixed other people's doors and fence posts and was only seen hatless in kirk. It was often the subject of talk in Quoy - the Minister's near-daily visits to Granny's and hers to him, even when Mrs Yule was bedridden with her last illness. There was nobody who really believed that Bible study had made them constant companions these forty years or more.

Halfway between the burn and the byre, a brimful pail of ice water gripped in her raw-knuckled hands, Oona watched as he rested the hammer in the pouch of mud around the base of the post. Some men looked wrong in shirtsleeves, as plucked birds looked wrong, as a fish, in fact, might look sitting in a tree.

Hamish took out a clean white kerchief and blew his nose, his red, spider-veined cheeks puffing out. He blew twice for good measure and scrubbed the linen square back and forth against the bulbous tip of his long nose. Without folding the kerchief, he wiped the sweat from his head. She wrinkled her nose at the thought that Granny might have kissed that forehead, or other places. It didn't bear thinking about really.

Oona was used to seeing him stand upright as a bannister in the gloom of the kirk, telling her what was good, what was right, how she should be Christlike. She was used to the crackle of his voice, the murmur of prayer, to trying her hand at the virtue he spoke of, pulling it about her, a new vestment of piety, a prickly shirt only the bravest could wear. Even in the yard of the croft, with the smell of soup wafting from Granny's pot, Hamish brought the kirk with him. Toby, the reprimanded sinner, sat arrow straight by the apple tree - as far from the scene of the crime as he could manage - clearly imagining he was invisible. The thud of the hammer on wood along the fence and in the broken byre was the toll of a kirk bell too early of a morning.

The bodies of the hens, neatly ranged side by side, were the melancholy orderliness of the kirkyard, the solemn litany of graves. She looked at the henhouse, its hinges now mended, clean straw covering the bloody earth beneath. It was true what Granny had said. There was no way Toby could have gone in there and latched the door after. Whatever or whoever had killed the chickens had shut him in, as if they wanted the dog to take the blame. Perhaps the doctor had followed her back last night, that dark look still on his face.

How about the hand hidden in the roof? In her panic, she hadn't even thought to check if it was still there. The Minister might find it. She shivered at that thought as if someone had passed over her grave.

Her hands were reaching for the last little corpse when she heard a cough behind her. She turned to face Hamish, her neck twisting at an awkward angle so that something pinched in it and a tiny fire pulsed there. The light was behind him and his face looked even darker and redder than usual, pocked and weighty, graven from sandstone.

He wiped his hands on the handkerchief, brown with farm dirt now. "Your Granny tells me you're a housemaid now at the big house, cooking and cleaning for Doctor Frankenstein."

She nodded, her skin prickly and hot with the guilt of lying to the Minister. "May said there was more work than two hands could do, with so many rooms and fireplaces and things there running to wrack, rusting and half broken, grand as it is."

"And do you clean all of the rooms, the pair of you?" On the face of it, it was a silly question, the kind of domestic detail she had always thought Hamish Yule was blind to, his mind forever following a higher path. It was the tone he said it in, the pause before *pair of of you*, that told her there was something more in it.

"I take care of the cooking and the laundry." The lies pressed through her teeth brazenly. She didn't know where they came from or why they tumbled out so easily. "I might clean the hanging lamps in the big dining hall today. He eats there even though it's only him alone."

"And you've seen nobody else?" He stared at her, eyebrows beetling.

He usually asked for Granny when he came and then they went off on one of their walks, or sat by the fire with a copy of *Pilgrim's Progress* and a bottle of sherry, whispering. Oona wasn't accustomed to him taking such particular interest in the details of her life and her mind couldn't help running back his words of before, *don't listen to gossip*. The Minister wasn't practising what he preached.

Oona had no gossip for him anyway. Not until she found something real and definite. *The girl*. Afraid that this last thought might be read from her face that everyone said was as plain as an open book, she looked down at the cockerel in her hands. The warmth had gone out of him now and he was a cockerel no more. He was nothing now, but a heap of draggled black feathers. His head lay, bright as a poppy, in the mud nearby.

"Well I've mended your fence posts, Oona, and done what I can with the byre. I'm afraid I must hurry back to the manse now. Can you tell your Granny thank you for the offer of soup and sorry I couldn't stay longer." He put on his hat and turned towards the newly mended fence with its naked bird of a new-wood post.

"Goodbye, Reverend Yule." She tried her hardest to smile.

Still bent over Orpheus, still shivering as if with fever, she watched the Minister stride off towards the road. Soon he appeared the shape and size of a walking cane and had nearly reached the kirk, his face whittled birch in the sunlight.

She stumbled up and hurried to the coop, prised out the wooden hatch and reached inside, groping in the darkness for the feel of her kerchief. Her fingers ran frantically over the wooden struts and felt the softness of feathers, the prickle of straw. But nowhere was the heavy bundle she'd stuffed in the roof. She shoved her arm in further until her shoulder burned. Nothing. Whoever had killed the chickens had taken the girl's hand too.

19

The jaunt from Quoy to the big house did nothing to calm her. She marched through the fields, pushing her feet into corn stubble, unmoved by the silvery green of new leaves and the melancholy calls of loons. She even stepped on a worm without feeling the familiar pinch of guilt. Wrapped in a dishcloth, clutched to her chest was Orpheus, his body stiffening. The time for clues and bodies under sheets and hands hidden in coops had passed. She was going to show Frankenstein the fruits of his sin and tell him what she thought.

She flung the kitchen door open and strode past May. All the way upstairs, past the red walls with their macabre faces and the prison corridor of birds, May followed, her voice imploring. Oona didn't hear a word of what she said. Her ears were those of a hound that's sighted a hare. When May tried to block her way into the music room, Oona walked round her.

In the gloom of his curtained laboratory, Frankenstein sat at his desk. Compassed round by candles, his face was strangely lit. When Oona charged in, he didn't look up. His eyes were fixed on a picture of a naked woman in a book lying open on the escritoire. His right hand scratched a quill over the page of his journal.

She walked across the messy rug and set her bundle down in the middle of his papers. "Your crimes have come to light. The dead frogs, the hand of the girl were wicked acts indeed. To add to which, you have wreaked havoc on my Granny's cottage and done this!" She pulled open the cloth.

The doctor looked down bemusedly. Before him lay Orpheus, ruffled belly facing the ceiling, feet splayed, head lolling near his neck, the golden eye already glazed.

"I have done this?"

May bustled up, red-cheeked. "I'm so sorry, Sir. I tried to stop her."

He put down his quill, splattering ink on the papers beneath, on the thighs of the dead woman lying prone and open-eyed in his book. He pinched the bridge of his nose, closing his eyes. "Do not discompose yourself, May. I fancy I understand the reason. The child believes I am responsible for the death of her livestock. I may investigate nature, Oona, but pray don't imagine that I do not value life." He stood and brushed the bird's feathers gently with his fingertips.

"Don't." Oona pushed his hand away from Orpheus.

"Oona," said May, "I can't credit this. Come away now!"

Oona turned, more aware than usual of how she towered over her friend. "Stop your mouth, May. I only wish to shield you, from this... this... necromancer. Dead girls in shrouds. Frogs coming to life. You do not know him for what he is."

May's colour faded to a sick white. "Dead girls. Have you run mad? I wish I had never admitted you here."

"I saw her wrapped in that winding-sheet." Oona pointed to the long table.

But the place where the body had lain was bare now, the dark wood gleaming as if nothing had ever rested upon it.

"She was laid out like a body at a wake, I swear it! I found her hand upon the shore and I put it in the chicken coop and now it's..."

She looked from one to the other with the dizzying sense that they thought she was mad. The room blurred. May was speaking and Oona could see her lips moving, but she couldn't hear what she was saying. The doctor opened his mouth. It was crammed with white knives, gnashing, no sound, just the rush of the burn. His face danced with coloured spots. Their red fire shot out of his mouth and through her chest, up her arm. She couldn't breath because something was crushing her. Dark magic.

Necromancy broke her. She fell under the weight of it. The world above opened and closed - a clamshell, a nostril, a sea snail's shy-breathing door, its black hatch underwater spewing silver bubbles soundlessly.

20

Sun spilled yellow through the windows' fishnet, swam slowly over the pink coverlet. Embroidered with green leaves and white star flowers that mysteriously bloomed alongside pouting fruits, it looked as if it had been a deep red once and the colour had faded. It must have been soaped and slapped on rocks and sun-dried so many times that the once scarlet had bleached to a prudish blush. It was an old lady coverlet, a veteran. A kernel of oatmeal was stuck to the sheet peeking out from underneath. Oona wanted to reach out and chip it away with her thumbnail, but when she tried to move, her arm ached and her chest burned.

"You must please stay still." A calm voice with a foreign lilt.

Her heart bucked. She tried to turn her head but a bolt of pain shot through her neck. "Please." Her voice was a croak.

Frankenstein rested his hand on hers and she was too weak to flinch away. "You have suffered an attack. Your heart, I believe, was the culprit. Your friend says you have had many such episodes. Is this true?"

Unable to speak, Oona nodded.

"This was the worst she has witnessed." His lips were a grave line.

Oona didn't want to look at him. Although it took all the energy she had, she turned her head and stared at the green ovals patterning the wall. The sun shifted over them, painting slanted squares that moved constantly, illuminating one green patch before leaving it in shadow.

"It sounds like a progressive disease, a hereditary one perhaps. Did one of your parents suffer from a similar affliction?"

Instead of answering, she watched the light fall on the polished dresser, the beveled mirror and spotless ewer. How horrible it was to be weak, when she wanted to leap up and run from here as Lazarus leapt up still clad in his grave cloth.

The doctor cleared his throat. "This body you have seen, and the hand you found... They are indeed real things. When I came here, I brought a subject with me, a dead body that came from a morgue in Ireland. Anatomy, dissection - they are medical practices. Not salubrious, perhaps, but not breaking of any laws, either. I did not kill anyone, Oona, and I certainly did not break into your farm."

Coloured spots whirled before her like motes in sunlight. Pink. Blue. Yellow. She squeezed her stinging eyes shut. What he said had the ring of truth, but she did not know whether to believe him. She forced her head to pivot back on her aching neck, facing him, staring into his eyes. He looked back, his gaze plain, a little bloodshot, but unblinking, like a person with nothing to hide.

"May?" she croaked.

He ran his hand through his hair and grinned his easy grin. "May has departed for the day, but on her way home she will assuredly pass by your grandmother's cottage and inform her of your whereabouts, so that your family will not be concerned." He stood and for the first time, she saw how rumpled he looked. His face was grey and lined with worry. "I'm glad you woke. I watched you for a long time." He bent and for a moment his hand touched hers, before he walked to the door. When he reached it, he turned and looked back. "I've given you laudanum to make you relaxed. With any piece of luck you will sleep."

Laudanum. She remembered when Mrs Yule was prescribed it and how she lay in bed for days, not seeing or hearing. Deep down, Oona felt worry kneading her as a cat kneads a familiar human, milk-greedy, claws half velveted. May had gone. She was here alone with someone who cut up bodies and whether he was or was not a murderer, he had, nonetheless, drugged her.

But her fear soon began to sink under layers of softness deeper and deeper, leaving a sense of profound ease she had not felt since a small child. She drifted softly, a leaf on the burn. Was this how Mrs. Yule felt? Was this what it was to die? If so, it was actually pleasant.

Nothing mattered. She had no desire to do anything but watch the sun as it moved round, spots of coloured light shifting over her hands and arms, over the bare skin at her throat and the freckled tops of her breasts. Somebody had stripped her naked and put her in here. All the time the doctor had sat with her, she had been naked. She wanted to turn over and bury her shamed face deep in the pillows, but she was too weak, too tired, too easy. Her eyes were dry, the lids heavy as stones. She closed them just for a moment.

21

When she awoke, the dying sun rouged the bellies of clouds outside the mullioned windows. The room was dark except for a candle someone had placed on the dresser. Frankenstein must have lit it a while before, because the flame flickered low and the wick spat at its own melted fat. She stretched her arms. Her body ached and her lips burned.

She needed water. Slowly, achingly, she rolled over and inched to the edge of the bed. Propping herself on her elbow, she saw that even the dresser was covered in papers. They spilled from a leather-bound book lying open in front of the ewer. She pushed herself up and grasped the cool edge of the porcelain bowl. When she found it to be full, her head grew light. She dipped her hand down and scooped up a palmful of water, drank, scooped again, drank, tasting her own salt.

A drop of water splashed up and hit a sheet of paper. She grabbed up the sheet and mopped the speck with her dry hand, dabbing and rubbing with her finger until the water had almost blended with the paper. Her eyes darted over its contents, a sketch of a delicate woman, her hair swept up in graceful waves. Beneath the drawing, in the doctor's curling script were the words *Meine schöne Elisabeth*. German words. Something something and Elizabeth. The eyes were clear and shining with tenderness. She recognised that expression from looking at May's face sometimes when things were well with Stuart and they were together. Upon seeing it now, a feeling she couldn't describe flooded her heart.

She put the paper back and collapsed on the bed, exhausted by the small exertion. Something flashed against the window, a pale moon pressed close, a bird banging the glass. She struggled up against the pillows, blood roaring in her ears.

The candle painted a flickering image of the room onto the windows. She saw the bed, the dresser, the door, and herself, a loam-white nude, hair spilling like fresh blood over her shoulders, eyes feverish pits. It was impossible to see anything outside, except for the pinky hue of the sunset and something else, pale and indefinite, near to the glass.

Someone was there.

Breath in-held, she rose to her knees and pinched the wick of the candle. The flame bit her fingers. Hot fat coated her skin. Slowly, she looked up.

There was the figure again.

This time she knew it was no fancy or imagining. There was someone outside the window, a face pressed to the glass, staring.

Their gazes met, just long enough for her to make out the blue of his eyes and the thick scar running over the bridge of his nose.

He vanished. The window showed nothing but the mottled red sky and the glow of the yellow moon.

She stumbled out of bed and banged her hip bone, cursed at the pain. The false ease had fled and her drugged flesh prickled. Her hands groped before her, purblind.

She found the door and ran her hands over its seam until she grasped the handle's cold metal. She turned it down, up, again and again, wrenched as hard as she could. Her flesh shook and sweat pooled in the small of her back.

It was no good. The door was locked. Before she had foolishly snuffed the candle, she had taken a careful look around the room. There was no way out save the locked door. No place to hide either. She was stranded here, naked and alone, until someone saw fit to let her out.

Like a child, she ran for the bed, jumped in it and burrowed under the covers. She knew it was foolish. It hadn't been the doctor spying on her, of that she was sure. The man must work in the big house, a servant of Frankenstein's perhaps, though she had never laid eyes on him.

The way he had stared, those blue eyes.

As if he knew her.

22

Oona stayed still as a sepulchre. Night turned and dawn stained the sky orange. Roof beams groaned and ticked as if someone were pacing back and forth, back and forth in the attic above.

She shrank down under the faded coverlet, hiding her face. Coward, she told herself as she hid under the covers, but outside them everything was too loud, too bright, nightmarish. Pushing inside her head, blinding. The boards creaked louder. She slid further down. Her hair clung to her sweating cheek.

In the darkness, she saw eyes.

Blue eyes in a clean-shaven head. A disfigured face, more broken than any she'd seen, the nose pummelled like a boxer's and sliced by a scar that clipped the side of the eye, spliced the brow. A fat, white graveworm crawled up the naked head.

Another scar dragged the mouth down at one corner and crept over the cleft chin. She fancied that if the man spoke, his voice would be thick and his words hard to fathom. His eyes had bespoken shrewdness though, as if he saw inside her and understood.

Pale eyes meeting hers.

Something had stolen between them in that moment, a shiver of recognition. Beads pulled tight on a string, clacking together.

She imagined a great knife slicing the eyes and face, erasing the troubling vision. But each time she pushed the memory from her thoughts and felt peace return, the face pushed under the covers to haunt her. It tangled in the sheets with her, a pestering spirit, an incubus, an unwelcome lover, clutching, suckling.

"No!" She kicked off the bed linens and lay panting in the cold spot her sweat had made.

Her skin shone with fever and there was a pain in her gut like a knife plunged in. She pushed herself off the bed and stumbled to the ewer, retching to rid herself of the disgusting ache. Spittle dripped down. She vomited again but brought up nothing. Pressing her cheek to the porcelain, she shuddered. When she finally pulled away, a necklace of droplets ran between her and the ewer. Beads pulled tight on a string, clacking together.

***

"'Tis the laudanum certainly and it pains me. I ought to have prepared you for its effects: the fever and frightful fancies – *alpträume*, nightmares such as an opium eater might have... All such are normal to the swallower of the suspension!" Frankenstein let out a staccato laugh.

As he spoke, his charcoal stick darted over the page of his journal. He kept it hidden from her, so whether he scribbled or sketched was impossible to say.

She glanced towards the green leaves patterning the walls. At the edge of her vision, the ewer gleamed bone white. She remembered the little pool of vomit in it and, feeling ashamed, shrank down until the coverlet was halfway over her cheeks. She hoped he hadn't seen it. She had no way to wash it out, not with the door being locked. Her eyes flicked back to his face, angrily taking in the smug spread of his full lips, the secretive look of his squinting eyes.

"That is not all of it, Sir. For after you left me here, I saw a man at the window with blue eyes and a scar." She traced her finger down her forehead, slantwise across the bridge of her nose.

He had been scribbling with the charcoal, apparently caught in some daydream. Now he met her eyes, all at once wary.

"You saw this person where?"

"At the window. That window." She pointed to where the grey sky sulked and a bird flew by, black and sharp against the low-slung hips of storm clouds blowing in from the sea. "Win-dow. Or, you know...some German word for it."

"*Die Scheune. Ja natürlich.*" He pulled his chair closer to the bed, the legs screeching harshly against the floorboards. Closing his journal, he rested it on the covers and leaned forward, steepling his hands.

"It may be," he pressed both fingers to his temples, "and I am shameful to admit this. I believe—"

Her shoulders ached. Without meaning to, she'd craned her neck from the pillow, braced her whole body in readiness for his answer as to whose the face was, whose the staring eyes that seemed to know her.

"As I have told you, laudanum is a powerful medicine. I administered it to you for good reasons, for your heart, you see. I feared in your state of collapse that you would over-exert yourself. You needed rest. Ach, so... But I should have warned you. These...nightmares...can seem like lucidity. One such fancy - the man you saw - a terrifying vision assuredly! But no more real than any other dream. And yet...and yet...what we call hallucinations—"

Her neck pulsed and her throat was dry. "He was no nightmare! He was real. I saw him plain as I see you now. I swear it. I saw him there at the window, staring."

As if by speaking of him, she had summoned him, the scarred man was back at the window. His blue eyes fixed on her, his face full of hate.

No! No! she wanted to scream, but couldn't. The words jammed in her throat and choked her. She was unable to look away because her whole body was frozen. There was no choice but to stare back at the pale, blue eyes.

Hands pushed her into the pillows. Metal shivered between her teeth. A spoon pushed into her mouth and scraped over her tongue. It crawled down her throat. A slug. A leech. She tried to spit it out, to retch, to spit. *Get away!*

Colours moved in and out of the air like sounds growing louder and softer. Red *forte*. Blue *piano*. Yellow sweet as birdsong and birdsong a scent. A hundred birds cawed. Some cried. The soaked sheets were cold, *cold*.

May held a damp piece of flannel to Oona's forehead. She spoke calmly, like a mother. "There you are, sweet. All clean now. Clean sheets. Clean you. Be cooler now. Sopping, you were, poor wee hen."

"Have I lost my wits?"

"No, darling."

"What ails me then?"

May frowned and wrung out the flannel in a blue basin, wet it again. "What you saw - that's the laudanum." Smiling, she pressed the poultice against Oona's forehead. "That's what the doctor says." May's sad smile stirred new fear in Oona.

"Am I dying?"

May dropped the cloth in the bowl and dragged her sleeve across her face, sniffing. Her hand fell wearily on Oona's. It was ice cold, but her eyes were eclipsed suns, black circled with red.

"He's a kind man, Oona. A strange gentleman, but one who intends well. A man of medicine, you know. He listened to your—" Her voice broke.

Oona lay rigid. The world was fruit that ripened too fast. Voices ranted inside her, loud and maddening as sticking your head in a hive. *Prick, prick, prick*. The truth stung and numbed with the same poison.

"My life is drawing to a close sooner..." Her mouth smiled the words. She wanted to laugh. "My heart." She'd known it anyway.

May stumbled up and straight away fell to her knees. She pressed her elbows into the bed as if in prayer, half-fell again and buried her head in Oona's lap, sobbing wretchedly. Part of Oona had always wanted to see her cry like that, to know that she was loved and would be missed.

She tangled her fingers in May's curls. She was only a shell on the beach, smooth and hollow. She felt hardly anything, except pity.

The next time she woke, it was night. Too thirsty to sleep and too sleepy to move, she turned her back to the window. She refused to look. Her tongue sought out ridges in her mouth's roof, hard wells in her hind teeth. She tasted coins. Her heart lulled her back, an empty shell swept out to sea.

23

The doctor sat slackly in a red brocade wing chair with his legs sprawled over one arm. Charcoal made soft scratching sounds on the paper that covered his knees. Apart from the ticking of the clock, it was the only noise in the room.

Oona blinked her eyes. They felt dirty. She was so very tired and it was a terrible effort to move or talk, even to think. Sunk deep in the pillows, she heard the thumps and gasps of her heart as if they were waves exploding. He had said she was growing worse. May too.

Closing her eyes, she listened. *Lub-dub, lub, lub-dub, lub.* She knew her heart was different. Today the silence of its hesitation was piercing, as if it faltered in the stillness. Or perhaps she only thought that because of what they had said.

She opened her eyes. The light hurt. Her hair coiled over the pale tops of her breasts. Stretched straight over the coverlet were her bare arms, their whey skin stippled barley brown. On the end of the bed, her clothes lay laundered and pressed and tiresomely out of reach.

The doctor cleared his throat and set down his charcoal. Frowning, he turned the paper this way and that, craning his neck back as if he were too close to see it. He turned the paper towards her.

Through the fog in her head, the lines and shapes began to make sense. The lips were fuller than she thought of hers as being, bee-stung, the corners pulled down pensively. The pale face framed by soft curls seemed fragile, as if the person in the drawing might fade and vanish away. There was no doubt that it was supposed to be her likeness, though. He had been sketching her portrait all this time. Warmth crept up her neck and into her cheeks. It was a not-unpleasant sensation. Was this what coquetry felt like?

Perhaps even a dying girl could feel such things.

"So strange to look upon flesh that seems young and perfect and imagine what lies beneath. The lungs expanding and contracting, the heart pumping blood." He looked into her eyes, trying to read her it seemed.

She stared at the wall, blinking away tears that had welled up as suddenly as her vain blush.

"This drawing took moments and yet it will probably last centuries, after those lungs have seized and that heart has stopped." He stretched out his hand, his fingertips grazing the coverlet near hers.

Crab-like, they scuttled from his.

"Do not you admire my masterpiece?" He ended the question with that nervous laugh and rose to pace before the window.

Oona shrugged. "It's pretty, but it is not my likeness, Sir."

"How marvellous that my serving maid happens to be an art critic."

"I may not be an art critic, Sir, but I know my own face. I am not some fragile flower." Her eyes flicked back to the wounded creature in the drawing. It was difficult not to be lured into its grey strokes, by what he saw: her brokenness, her weakness. Was that what he found worth looking at?

"It would please me... if you would not call me 'Sir', but rather, Victor."

"As you wish."

He bent over the edge of the bed. She thought he would look into her eyes or her mouth or make some medical pronouncement. Instead, he smoothed the coverlet and sat beside her. She wished she could hide under the covers again, either that or push him off onto the floor.

His forefinger soothed the rough lines of the charcoal Oona, blurring the plane of her cheek. "My mother died too young. She had been a wife, a mother, yes. She had known those blessings. But she barely knew life. It seems to me that's why I've always had this passionate need to know what magic curtain divides life and death, to pull it aside and see.

"These last years have taken me deeper than anyone alive. I have seen the darkness, Oona. I have lived it."

He paused. She could feel his skin's heat and smell his cologne. He was too close, too real. The blush climbed her throat again.

He leaned close, whispering to her. "I have never truly beheld... that breath of life that animates our flesh. That force that turns your heart from mere meat to breathing beauty, to this." He pressed his hand to her breastbone.

She held her breath. He pressed his cheek beside his hand, listening intently. Perhaps he could feel it, that wild fourth beat. His hand fell from her and he straightened, murmuring something.

She thought he said, "What a pity."

24

Oona sat alone watching dusk purple the sky and bats replace birds outside the windows. She was bored and hungry, drained and at the same time clear-headed. The boredom reminded her of childhood - that familiar, irritable sensation of growing well again after an illness.

She rose, her legs shaking a little, and dressed, her fingers fumbling the ribbons of her dress. She was recovered from the laudanum's effects. That much was certain. And the rest - her heart, her supposed imminent death - she pushed far down by splashing cold water from the ewer on her face and pulling her untidy hair into a punishing knot.

This time, the door opened easily. Outside it stretched the long gallery of imprisoned birds (no wonder she'd dreamt of them screeching). Candles guttering in brackets along the wall cast shadows. At one end lay the doctor's sanctum, at the other freedom. She stood on the threshold, poised between the two.

To the right lay Granny, a beating and bed without supper. To the left lay another possibility - some way of being sure whether May was right in singing Victor's praises, whether he had told her the truth. Perhaps some proof could be found in there, so that she would know, one way or the other, about the reality of the dead girl and the scarred man.

Before she walked to the music room, Oona made her limbs taut and her back straight. She pulled herself tall. Then she walked down the corridor of cages, eerily quiet now it was night. The birds perched with their heads tucked under their wings, sleeping with the subdued agitation of prisoners. At the end of the gallery she turned the tarnished handle, expecting it to resist her, but it opened easily.

Victor stood directly before her, his arm stretched out in front of him as if he'd been on the point of leaving. He took a step closer until he was nose to nose with her. She tried to manoeuvre past him. Instead of moving away as would have been conventional, he stood scratching beneath his arm and hardly seemed to see her.

She looked past him into the room's chaos, grimacing at the sprawl of papers, half-eaten crusts and sausage rinds, wine-purpled glasses, beakers and stirring rods speckled with unknown substances, crystals of green and blue and brown, compasses and nails and screws and shavings of wood. On the billiard table behind him was a bloody cloth draped over a tall pointed object. Beside it sat a slice of mouldering cake and a parcel of linen. It was utter chaos. How had she thought she could ever find anything useful in here, even if he *had* been gone?

Victor's eyes snapped clear, taking her in for the first time since she'd entered the room. "Hand me that." He gestured vaguely. "Wrapped in the cloth...no, next to the scales. *Ach Gott im Himmel*, must I find *everything* myself?" His hand thumped the wall.

Oona frowned. "Hard to find anything in all this mess, *Victor*," she said drily. He had asked her to call him by his Christian name, after all. It would be interesting to see how long that intimacy lasted.

"Ach, mess mess, what do I care of mess?" Victor pushed his fingers into his hair. "That. I mean *that!*" He pointed to the parcel.

"Open it yourself," she said, not feeling the need to stand on ceremony any longer.

"I need some assistance with it. Truly. *Jedenfalls*, what I am doing, you will like it. It is almost some kind of a gifts for you." He grinned broadly, his eyes narrowing, cat-like.

Moved now by curiosity, Oona crossed to the billiard table and opened the parcel leaf by leaf. She felt a small shock at the contents. The creature inside was curled in on itself, wings folded, yellow legs clenched under the tawny belly, throat blush red as if it had just been bitten. The dark eyes were milk-stained, dead, but the long, fine points of the tail looked as if they might at any moment thrum back to life. Orpheus. His head was no longer severed from his body. He was now a soft effigy of the creature he'd been in life.

Her eyes stung. "What kind of person wraps a dead rooster in a napkin and calls it a gift?"

He lifted Orpheus from the table. "The game's not over for you, fine fellow." He ruffled the rouged throat with his fingertip and moved the fine head up and down in a pale-eyed nod. With deft fingers, he fluffed the small neck feathers and stroked the eyes closed, until Orpheus seemed to sleep.

Watching him work, Oona's head was light. She felt at the same time confused and horribly fascinated. "What do you intend to do with him?"

He did not answer and she did not wish him too. She watched him pick up a pin and poke it into the bird's back, feeling a familiar tingle, remembering the frog on the board, its golden eyes flickering to life. This was what he did: bring things back to life.

He joined the pin to a fine tube, the end of which he poked into the neck of a bottle of green liquid. To the cockerel's throat, he fastened one of the delicate ceiling wires. All the while, pictures flickered through her mind's eye - her own neck, stitched and prone, poked with a pin, the fluid dripping in from a bottle; the dead girl, sunken eyes flicking suddenly open, gold and huge as a frog's.

Her head swam. She'd thought she was lucid, but everything was still laudanum-bright, loud and confusing. Scrubbing her face with her hands, she tried not to hear the crackle of energy filling the room with unspoken anger. Her eyes flew open just as Victor picked up a syringe and poised the needle over the rooster's heart. He plunged the point in hard.

The cock's eyes fluttered open and swivelled in Oona's direction. He puffed up his feathers, raised one wing and blinked his eyes. The actions were discombobulated and oddly mechanical, like the keys that plunged up and down on the little harpsichord outside the music room.

He stretched his legs, flapped and struggled up awkwardly. It was like watching the puppet show at the Hamnavoe Fair, when the wooden limbs became tangled in strings that jerked and twitched uselessly. All at once he righted himself and flapped down to the floor. He strutted, a living cockerel once more.

Her taut limbs loosened and her fizzing anger melted at the sight. She smiled to herself. *And death hath no more dominion.*

"*Zu sehen!*" cried Victor. "I am not so bad as you are thinking."

Oona sat on a wobbly *chaise longue* with a paint-flecked dust sheet flung over it. Orpheus slept on her lap and Victor poured liquids together into bowls with long noses that pointed downwards, stirring them with a long rod. He wrote notes in his journal, held glass rectangles to the light. She watched him work.

She no longer knew whether she wanted to stop him. Nestling close to the warm body Orpheus, she was content to watch him. He was so intent and at the same time abstracted. At times he poked his tongue between his lips in concentration. At times he hummed to himself. Always, whatever he was working on, he left beakers, bottles of chemicals and specimens on the edges of tables so that they seemed certain to topple off and break.

She had never seen anyone like him. His knowledge alone was fascinating. She rested her head on the arm of the *chaise longue* and closed her eyes, wondering whether he had brought the dead girl to pace the cobwebbed attic. Would it be wonderful to wake into such an afterlife after long and dreamless sleep? Would it be like Heaven? She imagined herself rising from the damp of the earth, breaking the grave soil from below, risen as Lazarus to a new beginning.

She woke to the muted cry of a clock chiming nine. Victor was gone. The room was dark except for a single candle stump casting weak light onto the billiard table. Orpheus lay on her lap.

When she lifted him down, the cold rushed in to the damp space where he'd slept. Her left foot was all pins and needles. She stood, clay-footed, stretched and yawned. Papers lousy with inked words and diagrams cloaked the desk and escritoire and floor. Now was her chance. She could pry, spy, neb to her heart's content. Why didn't she want to?

Because Christ has come back from the dead.

She tiptoed to the door, calm spreading through her as if, after long illness, she had woken refreshed, as if this strange house was her real home.

And death hath no more dominion.

She was almost at the door when she saw a dark paw print on the floor, a dry leaf shimmering in the candle's dying light. She bent to look at the small, fallen thing that straddled a gap between floorboards.

It was the frog from a few days before. She knew it at once from the brown mask framing its golden eyes and the ink-splatter patterning the fine bones of its back. Quite dead, it lay in a pool of its own thin blood, its soft tongue bulging. A fly sat on the frog's head, its feet running over its red eyes again and again in a ritual of ablution.

25

Oona hurried into the light of a yellow moon, perfidious as a goat's eye. Her calm mood was shattered so utterly, she couldn't recall it. Waves of fever broke on her skin as unwanted images rushed in: the fly rubbing its hands on the frog's head, black-hearted as a graverobber hunched over a corpse; her own face, sunken and motionless, shadowed by the candles of a wake.

Whatever good Victor meant to do was still subject to rot. She was certain now that he did mean good to come of his work, but to give life back only for it to be snatched away again seemed worse than death itself.

Without thinking, she began to run through the scattering of crofts towards the beach. She was halfway down the path when she saw tendrils of smoke rising up and heard the tinkle of girls' laughter.

She slowed and listened, scuffing her feet on the dirt as she went. Something was happening, something nobody had told her about. Blood knocked at her eardrums, wild with that fear that rushed in on her sometimes – that everyone laughed at her in secret.

She could see the red tongues of a bonfire now and smell roast meat and cider. They hadn't seen her yet, the ghost at the feast. Loud talk drifted towards her, foolish talk that grew from drink.

Two boys fenced with driftwood sticks. "Tis how we'll fight those Frenchies! Death to 'em all!"

A trio of girls with their skirts hitched up round their hips danced over the flat stones fringing the shoreline, bare feet slapping the wetness. At the centre of everything sat Stuart and May, her dark head resting on his shoulder, his sun-brown fingers stroking her calf.

If May had seen Oona, she showed no sign. She drank long and thirsty from the cider jug. "It could be Frenchies," her stage whisper hissed over the stones to lap against Oona's ears, "or it could be some kind of wicked creature, a monstrous thing, disfigured." *A monstrous thing*. Had May seen the scarred man too, even though she'd denied it? The whole world had gone mad and nobody could be trusted!

Stuart's answer fizzed with condescension. "Monstrous? I think you've had your fill." He peeled May's fingers from the jug one by one while she gaped at him in mock horror. "I don't think it's Frenchies or things that go bump in the night. You know what I think and I tell you, I've got a few questions for Doctor Frankenstein if he ever roams from the big house," Stuart's voice was low and terse with suppressed violence. "Things have changed since he got here - the fish in the firth - others may say it's the French, but I have my own ideas."

"He hunts every morning." May's snort. "Well when I say hunts, he lays snares out in the valley along the peat road and he catches up what's been limed there during the night - conies and stoats and great fat rats. He has little cages for 'em..." Her voice sank low.

Oona realised she had been craning her neck and shrank back into herself, snatching glances at the girls dancing in the shallows with their skirts bunched in raw-knuckled fists, their faces shining with sweat. They looked around constantly to see if the men were watching them.

Stuart frowned and drew back from May. What she said had displeased him, it seemed, or at least not had the effect she'd hoped for. "I suppose you know all about his comings and goings, working up there day in day out."

"Well, I mainly stick to the polishing and the pots and pans, but the other day, Oona—"

Stuart cleared his throat. May's face swung in Oona's direction. Her eyes were coals in a shifting fire.

"Speak of the Devil." Stuart smirked and pressed his lips to the jar.

The dancing stopped. All eyes were on Oona. She wanted to turn tail and run to Granny's, even if it meant a thrashing, but May was beckoning her over, smiling sweetly, her sharp-tongued demeanour melting from her. She patted a space in the sand beside her, already hollowed and smooth from the shape of another bum.

"Come sit with us."

Body tensed beyond bearing, Oona obeyed, her eyes turned towards the ground as if she'd never seen grains of sand before, as if the pebbles fascinated her, though really all she saw was Victor alone up there in the big house with creatures not dead nor alive.

Something dark was brewing between the islanders and the doctor. She could taste the anger in the air. He wouldn't be expecting it, not when the island was so new to him and so familiar to them.

Out of the corner of her eye, she saw Stuart bundling May onto his lap, tickling her as if she were a child. He didn't need to try so hard. She knew what he meant. May was his.

Someone sat down opposite her. She saw a pair of pale feet, the ginger hairs on the toes gleaming in the firelight. It was Andrew. If she looked up and met his eyes, he'd stare at her and stutter some clumsy words. She had never been interested in boys that way. What was the point?

She lay back and stretched out her arms on either side, sculpting an angel in the sand. Above her, the sky had shed its red coat and grown a darker one, endless and velvet studded with tiny pearls. Sprites of fiery ash leapt from the crackling flames.

A slender body shuffled into the crook of her arm. Hair tickled her cheek and she heard a confiding whisper she knew well from nights spent squeezed into a too-small bed, sweating in the summer heat.

"Seen your Granny yet?"

"No." Oona was reluctant to think about what would happen when she walked through the door.

"I told her you took ill at the big house and went to bed. She wasn't too huffy, but if you stay here you might catch it, wicked girl."

"Perhaps." Oona shrunk into herself. May was being tiresome.

"I have been wicked too."

"Oh?"

It was the same May as always, well, as some of the time: the dark head on the pillow next to Oona's, invisible except for the gleam of wide eyes; the red lips murmuring secrets, recounting dreams, details Oona hungered for then wished she had not heard.

"I know I should wait until I am wed, but... You won't tell, will you?"

"Not if you don't."

A pause, then, "How do you feel?" Although the words were sympathetic, May's voice was bright and hard, not choked like before in the big house. "You look better, but... Have the effects of the drug worn off?"

"I believe so. I helped Victor after I rose. He brought Orpheus back."

"To life?" May whispered the words, her eyes flicking towards Stuart.

Oona nodded, her mind moving from Orpheus to the dead frog, its second chance spent, not well or knowingly but carelessly frittered away as her life was. The sight of its body had shifted something in her. Now she saw how her life was wasted in small jobs and the avoidance of them. Her days were like berries on a daydreamer's tongue, swallowed unthinkingly. She thought of Victor's mother, his lament for her. *She barely knew life.*

"You have changed your opinion of him." May's voice was oddly accusatory.

Oona swallowed hard, unsure of why she felt guilty. "*You* were the one who cajoled me into working there, May. A fortnight ago, you were baking his cakes and turning down his bed. I don't think you should condemn me for softening towards him."

In the firelight, May's face took on a devilish mien. "Has he told you what he plans to do when he returns to Geneva?"

Oona shrugged, unsure why she was supposed to care and somewhat startled that she did. Across from them, licked orange by the flames, Stuart and Andrew spoke in hushed voices, mouths pursed round clay pipes like old gossips. Stuart swigged cider and swilled it. Andrew's eyes drifted towards Oona's face and slid away.

"How curious he's not confided in you, since you're so close." May arched her back, catlike, and smirked. "You've not been asked to his wedding then?"

Oona stared blankly in front of her. In the background, the mad cackle of dancing girls merged with the bleary cant of the lads.

"So the doctor said nothing about his beautiful bride to be? Oh well." May clapped her on the back and smiled.

Oona's skin prickled, remembering the flush that had risen in her when Victor took her likeness, the pleasure that blossomed in her belly when she watched him work. "Just because I don't think he's a murderer any more, doesn't mean..."

May giggled and rested her head on Oona's shoulder, slurring drunkenly. "If it consoles you, she's no beauty. He showed me a miniature likeness in a locket of his and I thought *what a shrewish face she has, not lovely like my Oona.*" She kissed the bare skin of Oona's shoulder.

Oona barely felt it, her mind on the drawing she'd come upon in Victor's journal - *schöne Elizabeth*. Those fine eyes. Everyone was to be wed except her and they would live a long while and be happy. That was supposed to be a joyous thought. As for her, Heaven awaited. She had often been told she was lucky to reach it so early, but she did not feel lucky. The world jabbed in like broken glass.

She reached for the jug and Stuart passed it, laughing. Tipping it to her mouth, she let the sweet fire warm her throat and drank 'til her tongue was thick and her pain collapsed into an aching stupor. Youth whirred past and the tide butted stupidly on the rocks. She saw and heard none of it.

Like the frog, she would be dead soon. There was so much she did not know. She would die *far too young*, as Victor's mother had and her own mother too. She had not even felt those ordinary things: cradling a baby; kissing and being kissed. Before now, she had never thought of wanting them. For the first time she knew that she must not let her life be swallowed untasted.

26

Time unfolded and folded again in the drunken space of the beach, its pebbles already prickling sea-sweat, its bare feet slapping cool water, glug-glug sipping from the neck of the cider jar. May left her side to go and lie with Stuart in the cool of the shadowed dunes. For a long time Oona drank alone.

When she had finished the jug, she let it slip from her fingers into the sand. Her lips were numb. Her head lolled to the side and she groaned, hoping she wouldn't be sick. There was an arm around her shoulders, propping her up, a face next to hers. May.

No, May had no stubble. She smelled salt and bitumen. Lips grazed her cheek. She squeezed her eyes tight shut and it was Victor stroking her arms. It was his tongue pushing between her lips, his face nuzzling her hair.

She pulled Victor closer, her nails reaching under his shirt to claw his back, amazed that such feelings had lain buried in her, secret desires stirred to life. She bit his ear, urging him on, relishing the hoarse breaths burning her neck, faster and faster.

He stopped moving and collapsed against her, his head in the hollow of her throat. Something warm and wet soaked through the thin fabric of her dress and leaked across her belly. In her mind's eye, she saw blood matted in hair, a limp body rolling from her. Her dream of Victor fell away.

It was Andrew who had kissed and touched her and who now snored contentedly against her neck. She clawed his back, no longer urging him on, but instead trying to shift his weight so that she might get some air. He would not shift and he was so very heavy.

She craned her neck back to stare at the fire that was burning down a bit now. The sea spat salt at it. Embers hissed, making smoke ripple up. Behind the fire, silhouetted, a man watched. Who knew how long he had been there, staring as Andrew pawed her.

She stared back, daring him to hold her gaze unembarrassed. The man's proportions were big. He was tall, much taller than anyone she knew. He turned to the side and the fire lit the sliver of a scar, the gleam of a shaven head, a naked chest. He glanced back once, eyes glowing hate.

Pale blue eyes.

He turned towards the fire and his silhouette parted the flames like red hair before the night's mouth swallowed him.

27

The world was too light and too loud. The stench of rotting fish made Oona want to retch. She hunched by the damp remains of the fire trying not to breathe in too deeply. The silhouettes of tall ships dwindled at the cusp of the firth. Watching them hurt her eyes. She lay back on a pillow of smooth stones.

Fragments of faces painted the insides of her lids. Her head throbbed. The pale eyes of the scarred man watched as Andrew pushed against her, the same man who had peered in through the window of the big house, the man Victor said she'd imagined. But by last night, the effects of the laudanum had faded. What she'd seen had been real, though why the man watched her she could not guess. Whatever the reason, he frightened her.

She sat and cupped her hand at her brow, squinting at tall ships melting into the band of silver light on the horizon. It seemed easy to vanish if you knew how. She wished that she was party to the secret and could escape all this.

From behind came a tumble of stone on rock. She braced herself. It would be Andrew coming back for another roll in the ash. At the memory of his stubble scoring her skin, her stomach rumbled greasily. Perhaps if he saw her like this, he would leave her alone. Footsteps crunched towards her, nimble and light. She smelled lavender. Without turning, she knew it was May. Slender arms slipped round her neck. Dark hair tangled with her hair.

"Still here, pigeon? The céilidh's long gone." May's voice was sweetly admonitory.

Oona leaned and pressed her hot cheek against May's cool one. "I saw him again."

"Who? Andrew?" The last word was spoken with a mocking lilt.

Oona shook her head, the sick feeling rising again. "The scarred man, the one from the big house."

May sighed, exasperated. "You were soused, Oona. How do you know what you saw?" Her tone was almost too certain. She didn't even seem curious.

Oona turned so she could see May's face. "You seem so eager to gainsay me. You know something about that man, don't you?"

"*How much more shall he clothe you, oh ye of little faith!* The man you say you saw is no less a fable than your tale about Victor murdering young girls. Besides," May kissed her ear, "a wee bird told me you got licked by a dog called Andrew."

"I'm serious May. He was right there," Oona pointed to the ashes where the man had stood, "watching us." She shuddered.

May slipped her hands under Oona's arms, making licking sounds and panting in Oona's ear. "Fancy a tumble?"

The kisses tickled and despite herself, Oona began to laugh. "I'll spew if you keep on and I'll do it on you. Besides, I hardly recall it."

"Just as I said, you were in your cups. Don't ken what you saw, but I'm certain of one thing," May's tongue darted out. "He'd never have licked you if you weren't so tasty," she ran her tongue over Oona's cheek. "C'mere lass, let me gobble you up."

They tumbled back into the pebbles, tickling each other and laughing. May licked Oona's cheek and forehead as a dog would. If anyone else had done it, Oona would've boxed their ears, but this was her darling May and she was laughing too hard to do anything other than fall back gasping for air. Her belly ached. All the dark thoughts concealed in her rose to the surface and burst. For their whole lives, May had always been able to turn the worst feelings into raucous laughter as imps weave straw into gold.

The wild sound of their laughter echoed from the cliffs towering behind them, shaking gulls from their roosts. Kittiwakes shot from grooves in the rock and circled the beach, a shrieking carousel of arced wings. Their fierce song wove with the echoing laughter until the bay seemed to fill with a cacophonous symphony of May's making.

They fell from each other, heads touching. Tears streamed from the corners of May's eyes, her mouth a gaping hole of laughter. The fit of mirth died in small stutters, the odd giggle spilling forth as if May was reliving her joke. Oona watched her, thinking, *May is the only real thing.*

The dead girl and the scarred man were far away, her panic the result of laudanum, cider and a too vivid imagination. Everything was well because May made it well. Oona wanted to say that she loved her so much, more than anyone, but in the end she settled for squeezing her hand.

May squeezed back, grinning. "Only three days 'till I'm wed. A bloody week, Oona, and I've nothing prepared. Not even my dress." She sighed and sat and pulled a clay pipe from her skirts.

"Aye." Oona sat too, her sense of ease fading at the thought of May's bridecog.

May tamped tobacco into the pipe and glanced behind them to make sure the coast was clear. "Looking forward to seeing me decked in my finery?"

Oona shrugged. Her thoughts on the subject of married May belonged to the realm of nightmare: losing her friend and fixing a smile to her face so everyone believed her glad... There was little pleasure in that.

"Another céilidh, another tryst with Andy the Dandy."

Oona poked out her tongue. "He sickens me, truly."

"And so you kissed him," laughed May.

"I believed..." that he was Victor, she considered saying. It hardly seemed a good defense, though. "I was dead to the world. I did not know him."

May raised an eyebrow and said nothing. She knelt over the ash pile to strike flints together. She'd always had the knack of building a fire, which was just as well since she loved smoking so much. She lit the pipe and sucked hard, holding the smoke in her lungs before exhaling four shimmering rings. "He fancies you though. We live on an island of thirty - you could do worse."

Oona took the pipe from her. "I've no time for marrying." She did not bother to add I'm too busy dying. May knew that if anyone did.

"Aye well, you could sail off with the doctor, I suppose, see the world. Escape. Seems so tempting at times, even for a *jeune fille à marier.*"

"What's a *jeune fille à marier* when it's at home?" The pipe had gone out. She stooped to light it, but the fire had burned down to winking embers with nothing but tinder to eat. Blowing hard, she roused a flicker of flame.

"A girl that's betrothed, but French words for it. It's the name Victor gave me." There was a wistful note in May's voice, something between nostalgia and regret. Victor, she'd called him, just as he had told Oona to do, and the way she spoke the name sounded intimate.

Oona stifled a pang of envy, inhaled and exhaled, floating a little higher on the earthen taste of the smoke. "Are you looking forward to your bridecog?" She passed the pipe back.

May puffed out smoke rings that drifted out across the sea's dark glass, unknowable. Slick black heads broke the surface, curious seals (or Selkies depending on who you asked). Oona wondered how they occupied themselves under the tide's slick lid, whether they lived wild, sad, intricate lives like some humans do, or dull ones.

The pipe went out.

"Time to launder some linens and sweep some floors." Oona stood, a little dizzy.

May tapped the pipe on a stone. "Help me up?"

Oona grasped May's hands and heaved her upright.

"I need a breath of air before I slave over the stove, Oona. Let's walk a different way today." There was something melancholy in the way May spoke the words.

Despite the swelling heat, Oona shivered, feeling a strange sense of foreboding.

28

Slow and cider-heavy, Oona followed May through the shallows. Rounding the long sandstone nose that divided one beach from the next, they came to the red rocks framing Cormick's beach like bloody hair.

It was a treacherous place when the tide crept in. Twenty steps away, black waves boomed and shattered into silver shards. They roared in Oona's bones as she skidded from one foothold to the next. Over the hunched backs of the boulders she saw that Cormick had dragged the dolphins away from the shore and thrown them upon his stinking midden. By daylight, their bodies looked still more decrepit as well as sad and undignified.

May stopped on a plateau of rock below Oona. She looked up, her eyebrows pinched against light that suddenly spilled from between clouds. "Remember the other night when Cormick took his old feller out and pished on us?"

"Thanks, I was trying to forget."

May smiled, but her eyes were forlorn. She turned and began climbing. Oona followed, wishing she could recapture their merriment on the other beach. She wanted to laugh and laugh until she couldn't breathe. She caught May up, reached for her hand.

"Remember when we played here as wee'uns? We thought there were cities in these sandstone shelves."

May frowned. Her hand slipped from Oona's, moving to hitch her skirt above her ankles. "We shouldn't have come this way." She wouldn't meet Oona's eye.

"Are you well, May? You look so pale."

May said nothing.

There was a plunge in Oona's belly like a skipped stone that won't fly and just sinks down. She chattered on nervously to fill the silence. "I remember we had a whole world made up from rocks and shells and sea," she pointed to a spindly outcrop the tide crashed against. "Over there was the castle Rasteal, built by the King of the Finmen." The light behind it made it look black. It held up the roof of a cave long ago, that the sea had brought down and now this sharp toothy-peg was all there was left. "And that gloup on the cliff where the water glugs we named Younsoun—"

"The dungeon that held Goreen, the Queen of the Trows." May smiled her sad half-smile again. "How odd we were, making tales out of everything instead of playing with the other lasses. I suppose we were always...different."

"Our world was full of finmen and trows and fairy rings. Full of magic."

"I miss it too." May squeezed Oona's hand. Her touch was clammy, as if a fever had come on her. She stopped suddenly.

Oona slipped forward and had to steady herself on the curve of an upturned keel. Their hands fell apart.

They had strayed far from the path to the big house. Oona was afraid to ask why. She thought of May's sharp words about Victor's engagement, the wistfulness in her voice when she mentioned the doctor's pet name for her. *Jeune fille á marier.* Was she having second thoughts?

In front of them Cormick's shack slumped between scuppered boats and a ruddy collar of cliff. The stones had been hewn from the rock and built back into it. Coarse grass swathed the roof and huddled in clumps around the doorway. The midden spreading out in front of the shack was strewn with starfish and the clenched lips of razor clams. A grey cat rootling in the muck dug out a fish head and started licking it.

May peered through the windows, standing on tiptoe to get a better view. She craned her neck, looking too hard, too long for it to be mere curiosity. The cat sidled up and twisted around her ankles, purring. Its yellow eyes gleamed unblinkingly.

"Shoo!" May's leg twitched the cat away, toppling a pail from which mussels spilled. The curtain covering the door opened. She turned to Oona, mouth sprawled open in panic. "Quick. Let's get out of here."

Cormick stood in the doorway of the sagging shack. His eyes were red and there was a mean look on his face. If he was pleased to see them, he hid it well. "Well lookee. Wee Mayflower and her sheepdog barging in nice as you please. After a boat are you?" He shambled towards them, his whisky breath reeking. "Or you just here to wreck my house?"

"Wreck it? This place is a dung heap." She walked up to Cormick.

"Pick that up." Cormick jabbed a trembling finger in the direction of the mussels. "Clear up after yoursen for once, spoiled b—"

"Say it, coward!" May took a step closer. "Say what you think."

"May." Oona tugged at her sleeve, her heart thudding at this sudden squall risen out of nowhere.

May shrugged Oona off. She was trembling.

Cormick stepped back and leaned in the doorframe, smiling. "Seeing as you're here, I'm guessing you wangled some coin from that daft man of yours?"

"Not yet." May stared down at the cat snaking round her feet. "It's coming, though." She ran her fingers through her hair and looked up at Cormick, smiling.

Oona knew the look: charming May getting her own way. It was out of place here. She pulled May's sleeve again. "Come on."

May shot her another look before she turned back to Cormick, twirling a finger in her hair. "I ken where he keeps it. He just needs to go out for a long enough while."

"Aye well. Don't forget, there's a price to pay lassie." He reached in his pocket, hunting for something, a puzzled look on his face.

May nodded, turned, took a step backward. Her smile was fixed but her hands shook harder than ever.

Oona stared at her, trying to make her fogged brain piece the shreds of talk together. It sounded as if money was owed, but who knew for what - something to do with the boat they'd stolen? Oona had been part of that night. She couldn't let May suffer this old sot's extortion alone. "I've got a few pennies—" Her words were directed at Cormick, but he drew into the shack before she'd finished. She turned around.

May was already far ahead of her, scampering over the slippery rocks, her feet as light and sure as the cat's. Oona ran after her, caught up, her hand on May's shoulder. May was clutching her shawl, her nose red and streaming.

"What was that palaver?"

May dragged her nose across her sleeve wretchedly and said nothing.

Oona gently took hold of her shoulders. "Is he after us for the other night?"

May looked up abruptly, her eyes wide and childlike, the dark pupils flitting to the side, as if she was piecing things together in her head. "We came here one day, when we were just...I don't know. I think I was ten and you were eight. The cat had little kittens. You wanted to play with them. Remember?"

Oona shrugged. "Not really." Behind May's head, she saw the curtain of Cormick's shack twitch. "Let's go and scrub a few floors before the doctor gives us our marching orders."

29

In the kitchen of the big house, Oona dropped beef bones into a stockpot. Behind her, May chopped onions, sullen and silent except for the occasional sniff. Onions always made her cry. Oona turned round for her jug of water and saw May blotting her eyes on her sleeve. When she lifted her face, Oona could see that it was red and blotchy. Strings of snot ran between her swollen nose and the rolled fabric buttoned at her elbow.

Oona cradled the jug in her arms. "You might feel better if you told me."

"Oh, Oona, for Heaven's sake." May picked up her knife and brought it down angrily on a pale half-moon of onion. "Learn to keep your neb out, why don't you?"

Oona turned sharply to the stove and poured water into the pot. It sizzled and steamed furiously. "Listen," she said, struggling to keep the anger from her voice, "you've no need to tell me what you're paying him for, but if it's... if he saw us the other night or something. Well, I was part of all that and I've got some money saved—"

May stopped mid-chop. "Chrissakes, Oona, you think because you're book-learned, you know it all, but you don't know anything. Not my problems, not my thoughts and not this. At times I wish you did, but as it happens, it's not your concern." She banged down her knife and ran out of the kitchen door.

Oona turned back and stirred her stock hard. *Secrets, so many stupid secrets.* She threw the spoon down in disgust, splattering the floor with grease. She went to the potato bin in the pantry, shoved her hands in to reach for good, smooth ones. Despite the cool dark, there were hairy spuds growing pale nubs of shoots that would soon sprout waxy, green leaves. She slipped the potatoes into the pockets of her apron. That's when she remembered the feel of the kittens. She'd been drunk on their softness all those years ago, those purring balls of quick-breathing warmth, and the mother cat watching her cautiously, eyes bright in the gloom.

Had it really been there, in that stinking shack?

Walking back into the light, she thought the vision would fade. But instead it grew stronger. She could almost feel her fingers running through the mewing wool. In the vision, May wasn't there. She'd gone somewhere. Oona knew she should be frightened, but the kittens were too soft. Their purring soothed her. She looked up, saw May holding Cormick's hand, like he was leading her somewhere. Then Cormick grabbed the basket up off the floor. He told them to go, shouted at them to go.

On the way home, May stumbled on a rock and fell down. Oona said, *May, it's getting dark,* but May wouldn't get up. She just lay there crying like the kittens. Her shoulders shook the way they shook today when she cried. Oona knelt down and took hold of her hand. She pulled it away. *Don't touch me,* May said. *Just don't touch me.*

Oona was buttering bread to go with the stew when she saw May pulling on her boots. Oona cleared her throat and May stopped and looked up like a child caught mid-mischief. Her anger seemed to have faded. Oona's had too, but the memories that had seeped back made her more troubled about May than ever. Was that awful day with the kittens something to do with all this? She wanted to ask but didn't know where to begin.

After she'd taken Victor his food, they sat on the step, watching the cow crop grass in the pasture opposite. May gnawed the skin around her thumb, biting off hangnails, a nervous habit she had. All the while, Oona tried to think of the words that would pry open the tight-closed clam of May's fears.

"May—"

May tapped her hand and held up the hem of her skirt. A hard circle showed through the fabric.

Oona took it between her finger and thumb and felt the coin's markings. "Is this payment for Cormick?"

May bit her lip. "It's Stuart's. He's torn the croft to bits trying to find it, but he's had no luck. My wages were already spent on food and drink for the wedding..."

"Why did you not give it to Cormick then?"

May smiled wryly. "I don't always fancy doing as folk tell me just because they tell me to. I'm difficult that way. It's probably why you love me."

"Must be the reason." Oona opened her arms, keen to hide the tears that pricked her eyes. They hugged for a long time.

30

Oona woke to a tangle of voices outside the window, hushed voices weaving together with the rustle of leaves in the wind, with the lisp of the burn and the call of loons. Confiding voices, low and intimate.

"'Tis shocking conduct in a young lass. Did you thrash her?"

"Aye, well, not a beating, mind. I couldn't bring myself to that with her ailing and such, but I've kept her to the croft these three days. I worry for her more than anything." Granny's words were weary, but her tone said she was enjoying the chance to jaw.

Today the theme of their talk was Oona, who had returned after three nights' absence to find Granny beside herself. There'd been shouting and, worse than that, late night prayer. Granny decreed that Oona must keep to the croft and not venture out to walk, to work or even wash clothes. Oona must understand the error of her ways, though Granny grieved indeed to mete out such punishment.

"With all these attacks, Ruby, I can't say I blame you. These are dark times." It sounded like Margaret gathering grains of precious gossip to distribute around the island with even-handed charity.

"Indeed. First my hens - and it was Oona found them, poor lass."

"All your hens, God save you Ruby."

"I know," Granny spoke as if she knew she was being listened to. "And now the same thing happening to Jenny's pigs. Throats ripped open, blood everywhere. First we thought it was a fox or stray dog—"

"But a dog would have gnawed at your hens, Ruby—"

"Aye well and the way the cuts looked - *clean*, like a *knife* had done the job."

"Nothing's been right since that doctor came to the island, Ruby. Frogs washed up, fish rotting the nets and now this. It's the work of a monster, not a man of medicine."

Damn them for blaming Victor! She was certain he was not at fault, for she knew more on the subject than they. She had seen, with her own eyes, Orpheus, strutting the big house – a symbol of the doctor's goodness. She had scraped through her feverish illness under his care. For all they knew, the guilt lay with Cormick or the blue-eyed demon she'd spied at the window, or wild beasts. She prayed they would not plot their revenge based on loose talk and dark omens.

"Aye well, today will take everyone's minds off it for a wee while at least. Nothing like a bridecog to cheer people's hearts, and it'll be quite a céilidh this evening by the sound of it. May's been like lightening arranging it all - I've barely clapped eyes on her."

Neither had Oona, and after all that had happened at Cormick's shack, after the sad talk they'd had afterwards, it was torture to stay put and not know how May was. One evening, when Granny was at Hamish Yule's, Oona crept over to Norquoy, only to be greeted by May's small brother Ned with his tousle of black curls telling her his sister was at the big house. She remembered thinking it was late for May to still be working, seeing, from the corner of her eye, the curtain twitch and a dark head slip out of view behind it. Was May hiding from her too?

"Humph, well... If you ask me it should be more a matter of speaking vows before God than an opportunity for merriment, but young folk rarely have much sense."

"Oh well, aye, I cannae disagree with you there, Peg. Now then, Toby, time for such as you and I to drag a brush through our fur and don our Sunday best."

"See you at kirk, Ruby."

"Aye, Peg, aye."

Margaret's's clogs slapped through the muck of the yard. The sound faded under the noise of loons and the door of the cottage creaked open.

Oona shrank under her warm blanket and curled on her side. She could hear Granny chopping something on a wooden board. Toby barked excitedly. There was the soft thud and creak of a basket being dropped, the hiss of water hitting the sadiron and the purr of metal smoothing fabric.

Oona shivered in the sour pocket of air under the blanket until it flew off, borne aloft by Granny's hands. Cold air rushed in.

Oona flailed her arms like an upturned beetle. "Granny! I was sleeping!"

"Oona, the day's half gone. It's time to dress for kirk."

Oona covered her face with her arms. "You bid me stay here in the croft and not go abroad. You said."

Granny folded the blanket into a crisp square and laid it on a shelf out of Oona's reach. "Anything to dodge your responsibilities," she said tartly. "But there's more folk in the world than yourself to think about, Oona. How will things be with May tomorrow and the next day and years after that if you're not at her bridecog?"

"You cooped me up here."

"Well now I'm un-cooping you. Leave that pit of a bed and get to the basin. Your neck is black with dirt. Black." With a poker she broke the ice plugging the top of the water jug.

Oona dragged herself to the ewer. She knew she had no choice but to do as she was told. Granny stood over her while she washed and brushed her hair and listlessly dragged on her best dress, limbs brittle as icicles. The world was moving too fast. It was changing beyond repair. She only felt the pain of it dully, though: her heart had gone into very a deep sleep.

31

Washed and ironed and laced up tight, the solemn pair passed through the wicket gate. The lime-washed east wall of the kirk was a blank page waiting for the day's history. Around the wooden door crowded all the people of Quoy. As she and Granny drew nearer, Oona saw that someone had tied white lace ribbons in pretty bows above the lintel and thrown white petals over the threshold.

Inside the dark kirk, light glared from the kerchief-sized window like God's eye seeing all things. She followed Granny into a middle pew, running her hand along the pocks in the black wood, taking her place on the shallow seat.

In front of her, like bits of flotsam in a storm tide, was everyone she had ever met save for those that were lying in the kirkyard. All in their cleanest, brightest, best Sunday-wear, collected together to be happy for someone else, to make joyful the greatest blessing of her life. Or so they would say if you asked them.

She watched Margaret Umbesetter's lips open and shut like a trout's as she gossiped to Janet of Flett who sat next to her. And there was Fiona Moodie, kerchief white as a daisy, poised at her cheek to catch tears as the bride walked down the aisle. And Stuart. She couldn't help but shiver a little at the chill in her bones when she saw him. He sat straight as an oar in the front pew, braced by his starched collar and stiff new breeks no doubt bought by his mother from Hamnavoe.

Someone shuffled into the pew next to Oona and almost sat down in her lap. He spread his pressed breeks to fill the space between her and possible escape. It made her feel sick to look round, because she already knew it was Andrew and was loathe to meet his eye. He met hers anyhow, his eyes pink - from late night carousing no doubt – and crinkling with mirth at the corners. He elbowed her ribs as if she were a pal of his. Oona slid towards Granny, who cut Andrew dead with a stern stare before turning her eyes to the front.

Hamish Yule stepped into the pulpit and looked over the joyful congregation, his mouth a firm line. His hands rested on his Bible, his fingers caressing a corner edge of the tattered hymnal beneath it as another person might stroke the ear of a cat. She closed her eyes.

An image was there waiting for her, softened from time and frayed at the edges like the hymnal. She lay on her side in Cormick's shack, fishing under the wooden chest, calling, *C'mere gibby.* Underneath was a grey cat. Its eyes shone. May came up behind her and shook her shoulders, *Oona, we have to go.* Now the scene at the big house was before her: May tapping her hand, holding up the hem of her skirt, a hard circle showing through the fabric. She pressed it between her finger and thumb. The markings that told its value were veiled, ambiguous, a cocooned coin, soon to hatch.

She opened her eyes. May was late. Of course she was. It wouldn't be May if she weren't late to her own wedding day, but Oona had a feeling that May wouldn't just be a little bit late today. Something was wrong. The dead men's fingers chilling her belly told her so. Heavy with the kelp-stench of the vengeful sea, they whispered that May wasn't coming at all.

32

If May's wedding had ever taken place, the reading would have told of how Esther married King Ahasuerus, how the great king loved her more than all the women, and she won grace and favour in his sight more than all the virgins, so that he set the royal crown on her head and made her queen instead of Vashti.

May would have thrilled to hear the exotic words warm her bleak island, would have imagined herself an ancient queen wearing silks and commanding the desert. Her dreams of escaping and marrying a real prince and finding wealth, glory, infinite beauty might have ended with Stuart, but through the story, she would see her own wedding painted in the colours of Esther's life.

She never did come to the kirk that day.

Oona heard it foretold in the first cross coughs that echoed from behind her and the third and the tenth. She heard it murmured like a curse when soft whispers began.

"Where's the bride? "

"Fussing over her hair most likely."

"Darning her stocking."

Most there had risen in darkness to break the ice-lid on the ewer's cold bone, to dress in stiff clothes unpacked from chests stuffed with camphor and lavender. They had settled old bones, sick bones, fidgety children on hard pews full of the night's damps. And now the bride was late.

The day brightened outside. Oona could no longer see the moon's daytime ghost through the arched window. Cows lowed in the fields, beckoning the women who were late to milk them. Men tugged at their starched collars, longing to be free. Women turned between shushing their bairns and finding a subtle way to scratch beneath their corsets, itching the places where bone pressed hard into flesh. Granny had long since dropped the kerchief that had been poised to catch tears of joy and now tapped her fingernails on the pew in front.

Andrew snapped the ribands holding his breeches aloft many times, each snap more annoying than the last. Now he shuffled closer. Lye-cured fish and sour cider crept up her nostrils. It had enveloped her the night of the bonfire. Bile rose in her throat. She heard him try to begin a conversation with her, so she turned her attention to

Margaret and Janet, deep in gossip two rows in front. From the tilt of Granny's head, she judged that she wasn't the only one eavesdropping.

"...fine, pale linen with silk ribands in the newest style. Annie's dress was passed down to her of course, but it didn't please her."

"Aye well, lasses like wearing something new. Did she buy shoes at Hamnavoe, too?"

Margaret nodded. "Aye and garters. The something old is her great-grandmother's lace kerchief tucked in her sleeve. Traditional, at least."

"Aye, Peg, tradition is best," Janet nodded, agreeable on every score.

Andrew was murmuring something about how he loved weddings, loved children, loved bonny wee brides, how love was the most important of all things. His fingers crept over her skirts, found her fingers and squeezed.

Oona elbowed him in the ribs. "Hush, for God's sake."

"But Oona, I—"

The angry chatter of the guests swallowed his words. Their hush had been an unspoken promise and now it broke.

"How long must we sit here anyway?"

"Is she pulling a prank?"

"That corset was frightful tight. Perhaps she's fainted, poor thing!"

"Some lasses get quite overwrought, ken. My own Sarah..." Margaret said to the pew behind.

Meanwhile, her boys began a scrap near the tall candles lighting the kirk. Hamish Yule stepped down from the pulpit to part them, his brows burrowing together furiously. Stuart, pink-necked and oily-haired, had sat straight and silent through all. Nobody, it seemed, dared speak to him. When he rose and strode out of the kirk without speaking to or meeting the eyes of anyone, the hush fell again.

Oona's heart reeled. She'd been an observer thus far, pretending not to hear those who wondered out loud whether she might know where May was. After all, it was *just like May,* everyone said, *so like her to be late just to tease us all,* but the joke ended when Stuart walked out.

His face had frightened her. He would search high and low now and he would find May hiding somewhere, in one of her dark moods perhaps, the circle of his coin sewn into her petticoats. Then he would make her suffer for what she'd done today. No-one made Stuart of Flett look a fool.

Oona stood. "Let us go with Stuart and help him search."

Hamish Yule looked aghast. "Oona! Speaking in kirk again? Really—

"Oh, Hamish," Granny tutted. "At last someone has spoken wisely. In my view, we should move outside at once. My poor hands are blocks of ice."

"And mine," Big Dod barked, at the same time gruff and palpably relieved to turn the focus from his own plight to someone else's.

33

There was nothing so ordered as a search party. It was too hard for people wearing their Sunday best to think that clearly, but it was agreed that after their various quests across the island, they would all meet at the Manse where the wedding feast was to have been held. If May were found, then it would be cause for celebration. If not, they might at least compare their findings and plan the next steps.

A few went to Norquoy, a few to Flett. Some searched the cliffs. Launched on their own hunt for May, Granny and Oona caught sight of Margaret and Janet peering fearfully into caves and gloups, afraid, it seemed, that petals of white linen and silk would float up to haunt them forever.

Granny accompanied Oona as far as the big house. Like all who are keenly aware of their status, she was lost for words upon finding herself in grander surroundings than she'd seen before. She fingered the copper pans in the kitchen like holy relics and absolutely refused to set foot in the hallway. Oona left her to peer at the silverware and went upstairs, thinking as she did of blue eyes that had watched her from the window.

Perhaps May had run across the scarred man and was trapped in the cobwebbed attics or mouldering cellarage – hurt and terrified, or worse.

As far as she was able to discover, May had not been there, nor had Victor seen her for days, he said, touching Oona's arm fondly before turning back to his work dissecting a hare's brain.

Granny returned home wringing her hands.

Oona carried on alone to the place she feared going most: Cormick's shack. In her head was an image she couldn't shake, of May aged nine, standing in the doorway to Cormick's bedroom. In her mind's eye, May's face was pale and her eyes were wide, but Oona paid little mind to her friend's fear, distracted as she was by the softness of the kittens Cormick had placed in a basket before her.

At the shack, she found neither May nor Cormick, only a sulky grey cat gnawing bread crusts and fish bones and hissing at her as she searched the stinking pit of a bedroom. When she'd searched every nook, she ran out of the door, her heart suddenly light. Finding May at Cormick's had been her worst fear, worse even than Stuart laying his hand to her. She didn't know why, except for their angry exchange of words the other day, May's tears and the vague memory about kittens.

She ran and ran, not caring about the mud splattering her best petticoats or the sweat staining the crisp lace at her bodice. It was sheer relief to feel the fear fall from her, to feel in her heart that she would arrive at the manse to find May at the centre of everyone gathered in her honour, laughing at her last minute jitters, kissing Stuart and drinking away her nerves.

The manse lay on a high spit of land that meandered into the firth. It was bleak and storm-washed in winter and all-the-year-round precarious. Oona couldn't come on it without wondering what daredevil mason had laid stones on the brink of the sea. It must have been the Minister's grandfather or great-grandfather who'd ordered the chopping of the grey roof slates and the hauling of the small, red bricks from the cliff face. But it was the Minister's wife, people said, who'd made it bonny. Her garden with its trumpet flowers entwining the ornamental arch was the envy of every woman on the island. No-one could understand how she kept the weather from spoiling the heavy heads of the red tearoses. Either she had green fingers or she'd made a pact with the devil.

And then she was gone and the salt air blistered her lilies. Her roses caught black spot. Slugs ate the trumpet vine and began on the wooden arch. Hamish was powerless to prevent these changes or to take care of himself. With much tutting and rolling up of sleeves, the women of the valley took the latter task upon themselves, but even Granny, who'd always been close to him, didn't dare lay a finger to Annie Yule's garden.

Walking up the path, Oona noticed that the wildness that had long since claimed the back of the house was gradually spreading to the front. Honeysuckle clutched the parlour window like bejeweled hands. Mint and rue from Mrs Yule's herb garden waved tall and green on either side of the door. She knocked and stood waiting and for a moment felt that she was in a wilderness such as Adam and Eve had once lived in, roaming innocent until the snake gulled them. The door opened and Hamish appeared, as red-faced and angular as he was in the pulpit and without his usual smile. His hair was wild from running his hands back and forth through it.

"Is she here?" Looking at his face, Oona already knew the answer. He shook his head and turned from her.

There was nothing more to say. Voices in Oona's head jabbered and screamed. She wanted more than anything to sit still. Following Hamish limply through the picture-lined hallway, she saw the eyes of Yule forbears watching her glumly, heard the crackle of the fire, the hushed murmur from the formal parlour. The Yules had each had a parlour to themselves – hers for company, his more of a cubbyhole where he could take cover from company and read. Mrs Yule's, crowded with china figurines and dainty French furniture, was barely used now. Effie and Margaret and Janet and Fiona had come with bunting and ribbons to deck it out for this most lovely of occasions, May's bridecog.

But what Oona walked in on was more like a wake. Effie slumped in a chair, weeping while Janet mopped her brow and gave her sips of the Minister's claret. Big Dod stood by the fire, dark-faced and silent, coughing angrily. Hamish Yule paced, fluffing his hair ever more wildly. Granny plied the search party with bannocks and cheese and they gnawed the food absently, avoiding each others' eyes. Even Margaret had ceased her gossip. The case was too serious now.

There was talk of a bad presence on the island, of slaughtered pigs and chickens, strange things washed ashore. Andrew, sweating drink, proclaimed that if he had womenfolk, he would keep them indoors and guard them with his life at all times. No more roaming free at all hours. His eyes were on Oona when he said this.

She went to the window like one in a trance, her skin hot and tender, and pressed her forehead to the cool glass, staring out in the garden where rain fell on the table laid so beautifully with white linens for the wedding feast. Fat drops splashed on the Minister's best plates, on a silver soup tureen and untouched bread rolls, on Stuart, who sat alone, plucking petals from the pale pink roses of the centrepiece.

34

There were oilskins nailed upon the windows and the woman never knew when the sun rose or set, or if the man had come into the room. Often, she did not hear him enter and cross the bare boards to the bed. She would open her eyes to find him stooped over her.

She had slept and woken, slept and woken in this room for as long as she remembered. She was alone now. Peat embers glowed in the grate. It was hard to draw breath. A hatchet, it seemed, had been thrust through her ribs and shards of it were chewing at her flesh. She wanted to rise and look at the wound on her chest, but if she attempted it, the wires would bite into her wrists.

Fury swelled in her, a storm blistering a cold sea, ripping warmth from the air. Anger clotted her thoughts, pinched her pinioned wrists, her broken body. It made her powerful. She fought the wires and tried to break them, slicing her flesh until fresh blood oozed down her arms and warmed her.

The fog came, though really it was always upon her, making her forget. She knew that the man opened the door, crossed the boards, fed her, made her drink and tended to her wrists. Sometimes she woke to find them wrapped in white strips and her hair smelled clean. But each time she slept, the fog rubbed out her memory. She knew neither her name nor where she was from, nor if she had ever been loved.

She didn't feel love. At times she howled. The space in her chest grew empty then, until it filled with the one thing she was certain of: her need to hurt the one who had put her here. Sometimes she fought the fog back so she would have a chance, but sleep always took her too soon. And so she had nothing to do but sing to her anger and swell it each time she woke.

The fear she always felt was high and fierce like the sharp scream of a gull before it dives, sharper than the blood-flecked bill, tighter than the agile, angry wings that spread wide, swooped for the kill.

Her teeth rattled in her head the same way the wind rattled the stones around her. She screeched and clawed her own skin, a hare biting off its foot to free itself of the snare.

She wanted to remember people, places, her own name and the days before this one, but all she knew was that she had been free once. She knew it like the sound of blood beating in her ears. She had been free, had run and laughed and held someone she loved. She had loved them so fiercely!

She didn't know their name, though, or their face. In the blackness, all she could see was a red sheet of spreading blood and her own cut skin, red cherries smashed in milk, spilled curds, a tub of blood pudding sucking her down and swallowing her and a pale face, the mouth frowning.

She'd angered it. Her teeth had sunk in. Then she'd been thrown in here and damned to Hell, to here, crushed down and smothered. Now the wires bit her and there was no room to breathe. Her bones were piled in on her like bones in a charnel house, layers of dead fighting for space in the kirkyard, her own bones, crushed and bloody, falling under the hill.

There was nothing but her own sharp stink and the pulse of her blood in the darkness, the thirsty darkness, the furious darkness.

The darkness that went on forever.

35

It was more than a week since the wedding, long days of drudgery keeping the fires lit and sweeping and listlessly watching while Victor laboured over his works of alchemy.

He was always kind. Alone of her acquaintance, he seemed to understand her sadness and do what he could to help her. Together, they had searched every hallway and staircase, the cobwebbed attics of the big house and the byre, even the famous oubliette (seen by lamplight, it was little more than a blackened trough for emptying chamber pots).

May was nowhere.

The men of Quoy formed a kind of hunting party from which women were barred in case a body was found. Led by Stuart and Dod, they combed every cave and pool and crossed the valley to the far coast only to return silently each night and drink themselves senseless in the Smokehouse.

Oona never slept any more. Instead, she kept a vigil by the window. It drove Granny mad to see her hunched over her candle. Like a dead soul caught in some limbo, she drifted down to the burn to pound laundry or up to the doctor's study to scrub the muck from his floor. She haunted the kirk Sunday morning only so she could hear May's name whispered between hymns and feel a hair's breadth closer to her.

Oona closed the door of the servant's entrance and dragged her tired body to the beach where they'd laughed like fools that last time. The sea – it was the last place left to look for May and the only place that could not be searched, though sometimes the tide brought sailors back... She pushed the bitter thought from her mind.

Night was drawing in. In the dying light, she stood on the cusp of the sea watching the waves carry a boat to shore. It was in calling distance and she thought she saw the shadow of a man at the tiller. He was neither reeling up lobsters nor moving to bring them in. He was just staring.

She thought of the man with the blue eyes. She was surer than ever now that he was real and that he had watched her through the window, through the fire, had killed hens, pigs, ripped out their throats. People on the island spoke of him in hushed tones, not as a *him*, just a presence, an evil, lurking. Only Oona seemed to have seen him, really seen him, the look of hate in his eyes. If he'd done something to May, if he was on that boat now, drifting ashore, would she take him on?

She bit her lip. Yes, she would do it.

And she would lose - weak Oona, too feeble to help her friend when she needed it most. Her vision blurred and she dragged her sleeve angrily over her eyes. The boat was so close to the shoreline now that she could see the wicker creel she'd taken for a man. The boat had a red line painted around it. Elver was licked over it in white and a strange selkie-girl was carved into the prow. It was Cormick's boat, the one they'd stolen that night to sink Victor's stinking crates.

The crunch of feet behind her made her turn. Andrew had come up softly. He set down his baskets. Rolling up his sleeves, he showed arms peppered with small cuts from gutting fish.

He pointed at the Elver. "Must have slipped someone's grasp."

"Maybe." She turned away. He was the last person she wanted to clap eyes on and yet she seemed to see him all too often these days.

"We should go out to her."

"I'll do it." She started to run through the icy breakers, anything to put distance between them, to do *something*, instead of merely waiting for May's body to drift in like flotsam as the dead girl's hand had.

"Oona! Come back. Don't run."

He'd heard she was delicate. Everyone had. He probably thought he could save her by marrying her and keeping her like some costly piece of crockery. Looking over her shoulder, she saw him grow small enough to crush between her thumb and forefinger. She squashed him like a fly with her mind's eye, smiled to herself and flung her face back into the gritty wind.

He began to run and soon caught up to her, panting, "Why don't you do what you're told?"

"In charge of me, are you?" she said wryly. "The thing is, I don't need any help with anything." The wind whirled her words around her. He must have seen her lips move, though, because he shook his head dumbly and pointed to his ears.

When she reached the boat, she stopped and clutched her chest. Her shoulders ached. She couldn't catch her breath. She gripped the rim of the boat, gasping. Behind her, Andrew's feet pounded in the water, churning over the sound of her heart in her ears.

"Told you not to run." He laid his hand on her back.

The touch brought back that drunken night by the bonfire, him moving against her, the pale eyes watching them. She flinched it away. "I -"

"Rest. You'll be right in a moment."

His hand stayed stubbornly upon her and she was too tired to shrug him off. She doubled up over the side of the Elver like an old man, gasping for air. It was too hard to fight off her illness and Andrew all at once. She was stuck with them both, it seemed.

What if she died here and he was the last person to speak to her?

But at least she'd go to a better place, to May. As she thought the thought, the pain across her shoulders began to fade, though her heart still drummed. She leaned low, listening to her wheezing breaths, then blinked away her dizziness and looked at the boat.

The hull had some water in it, but not enough to cause trouble. The oars floated on the water, rolling with the tide. The creel behind the tiller was soggy and salt-bleached as if a storm had caught the boat. A morsel of dark cloth was snagged on the catch. Her breaths came easier now, but a sick feeling was growing in her.

"May." Her voice was a whisper.

"Hush, now." He stroked her hair.

She reached for the cloth, but her arm wouldn't go far enough. "I need to-"

He leaned over her and caught up the cloth. It was knitted from blue wool and despite being weathered the skill of the needle was plain. Threaded through the collar was a wisp of scarlet - a colour that would suit black hair and eyes. "Why do you want this damp rag?" Andrew wrinkled his nose.

With shaking hands, she took it from him. "Because it's May's."

All the way down to the croft, Andrew stayed by her side and she didn't think to shake him off. Her mind circled round furiously. That night the pair of them had taken the Elver out, May had been wearing Dod's old oilskin, not the cloak. It was hard to see this scrap as anything other than a sign: that May had been in that boat since they'd rowed out in it together and had worn her cloak; that she was alive somewhere not on the island.

Oona didn't see the grass or the heather or the other crofts go by because her mind was on the hard circle of metal trapped in May's petticoats. Perhaps it had been her fare to freedom and that's what her business with Cormick had been. How happy a thought it would be to be certain that May had escaped, was alive, was free.

As she went passed Norquoy, she looked at the scrap in her hands, knowing she should run in and tell Dod and Effie the news. But her eyes were caught on a frayed end of wool that had run away from the cloth's weft. It was just a twist of blue that had fled its loop, but soon a hole would grow. When she ran her thumb across it, she could feel the absence swelling. She held it to her face and smelled May's scent of lime and ash and lavender. If she had gone, Oona would never see her, never hold her.

Andrew stopped, took Oona's arm. "Why would bits of May's cloak be in that wreck?"

The golden picture of May's freedom hadn't faded yet from Oona's mind. "Maybe she went to stay with her cousins in Kirkwall." The dreamer in her believed it. But there was another, darker part of her that thought of the boat and the crates, of Cormick's anger and all the mess that May could have dropped herself in.

Andrew's jaw tightened. "And abandoned Stuart at the altar." The thought seemed impossible to him. But then, of course, he worshipped Stuart as some sort of deity.

Oona could not meet his eyes. Her optimism depended on May having left Stuart behind: it was the only way of believing she was alive. "You've missed my point, Andrew. We never found a mote of her until this... Now...this. This is a sign, I believe, that we must search harder, that we... What if she went in the sea..." She couldn't bear to finish the thought.

Andrew shrugged, seemingly untroubled by the thought. "And if she did, how should we look for her - hold our breaths and paddle round the bay? I can't even credit that scrap is hers."

She broke away from him and walked to the door. "Granny knitted it for her. I know it like the path to the big house."

"Then you know it well." Sighing, he followed her into the croft. "Still think you're fussing at nothing."

At the door, she turned to face him. "I must rise with the lark tomorrow."

"As must I." Andrew cast a wistful look at the soup pot on the stove. "Go on and tell your Granny you had another turn."

"Who made you my keeper all of a sudden?" Oona turned to make certain that Granny was napping in front of the fire.

Andrew's jaw became tight as a fist. He said nothing else, but walked to the door, stooping to fit his head under the low sedge thatch. Outside, he turned to her and his face softened. "Don't run around hunting for May."

She rolled her eyes. "What am I supposed to do, walk slowly everywhere I go?"

"Chrissakes, woman, you're maddening."

"Why don't you stay far away from me then, save your sanity?"

She said it sweetly, knowing that was worse than if she'd snarled and slammed the door. A few scraps of her anger crumbled away at doing this small unkindness.

Her words weren't lost on Andrew. His lips flinched and he nodded, dazed, and slouched away down the sheep path, past the byre, towards the surge of the sea. The darkness made ghosts of the rushes that were washed by the rattling burn. Andrew faded into it and only stars pricking out patterns round the cliffs gave any light.

Out in the firth, the fish slept open-eyed and dreamt of nets. The Elver lay on the empty beach and kept May's whereabouts a secret.

36

The thought of paying Cormick another visit gave Oona about as much pleasure as the thought of clearing cow dung from the byre, but she'd skimped on her morning duties at the big house to give herself time to find what he knew about May.

She rounded the hill, her boots pushing softly into thick, black heather. Behind her cows lowed for the milk pail. She looked over her shoulder towards their call and saw the westerly wind take a twist of smoke from the chimney at Norquoy and spin a fine ply towards the clouds.

Beyond Quoy the cliffs stretched like a penance. Every day she walked them alone, looked out over the firth alone, watching ships sail out into the world, and every day the likelihood of seeing May drifted further away from her. She slipped her hand into her pocket, running her fingers over the scrap of wool from the Elver. Maybe there was a chance still. She strode over the cliffs, tense with hope.

Over rocks bearded with slimy green weed, she made her way silently, eyes on the kirkyard of festering boats Cormick kept. A shriek broke the quiet. She looked up to see a buzzard, dark and rumpled as a shawl flung from the cliff top, another hunter in a world full of hunters, sharp-billed, keen to draw blood.

The tide crept up the beach shyly. Foamy water sucked at her ankle bones. She half expected to see a hand float towards her, or some mockery of nature, an undead freak from the big house. Had this all begun that night with the storm and the crates? Perhaps it was their punishment for colluding with the doctor in making a Hell out of Eden.

Her feet crunched the husks of seahorses, smashed lugworm cases. She pinched her nose against the stench of Cormick's midden, nodding to the cat that slunk out to stare at her with witchy eyes. Its owner reeled out behind it, the look on his face a good deal less friendly.

"One thing I can't abide is folk charging in here."

"I must ask you something about May."

"May? I've not seen her," Cormick's jaw toiled a short time between each word, "not for a very long while." He turned away.

She recoiled at his obvious lie, wishing it were possible to intimidate him as Stuart or Big Dod would, to challenge him to a fight. Even if she never knew the truth, it would provide some small release for the grief and anger that had built in her since May disappeared.

"You saw us only the other day. I discovered that vessel of yours, the Elver, with a piece of her shawl in it."

Cormick turned and drew inside the shack. Oona pulled back the curtain-door, blinking at the darkness. Though the drapes were ragged, they did a good job of keeping out the light. The cat pushed between her legs, purring, and stalked over to the fire where it curled up and began to lap at its hind leg. She followed it inside. The shack stank of whisky and fish oil and was nearly as foul as the midden.

Cormick delved his hands under the half-mended net that shrouded the table. "Always coming here carping. Always borrowing things without a by your leave, and women the worst of it." He lifted his stained jersey to hunt in his pockets. The bone handle of a fish knife gleamed over the top of his breeks. He pulled a clay pipe from his pocket and gave it a good whack on the table. A clot of dark dottle went flying. "Women the worst of it. Grasping hands. Devilish fluttering hands." He jammed the pipe between his gums.

It was hard to keep her own hands from fluttering to his throat, the way he was talking. "This is babble and gibberish. I know you had some covenant with May, for I know she had coin to pay you from Stuart. Was it her fare?"

He lit his pipe from the fire. "Pay me no mind, lass. I like to talk. I like to sing." He broke into a grin.

It was maddening to see him, miles from the real world now when she needed an answer. She had half a mind to snatch the pipe out of his hands but she knew that it would do more harm than good.

She took a step closer, towering over him now. She was brittle as a wafer inside her tall frame, but he didn't need to know that. "She'd purchased passage to the mainland. I'm certain of it. Where did you leave her?" She made her voice low and cold as she'd heard the men talk in the Smokehouse when they'd a bone to pick.

His grin faded. He scratched at his black stocking hat. "I don't ken a May. I ken you. Take a pew. Take a pew."

He gestured round the room grandly, as if pointing out a chair, but there was none, except in the bedroom. Anything a guest might sit on was clarted with old nets, creels and pieces of boats. On the table, a herring lay open with a knife inside it. When his gesturing fingers brushed the handle, she wasn't slow to notice. Dark spots were visible on the blade.

"There's blood on your knife," she said, quietly. Her throat was dry. "Was May short on her payment?" She stood her ground, measuring the distance between Cormick and the sill and the door. "Things have befallen us... Bad things. We are tangled in something... May might have wished to escape it. I would understand. I could understand if she—" It was the first time she had said this or even thought it: that May might have wanted to leave and had more than good reason to, and that she understood.

"I last clapped eyes on you two years ago, lass, for you came here to look at my kittens. Boots recollects it." He looked down at the cat that groomed between its splayed legs. "Do you not, Boots?"

She looked away from him, squinting at light that framed the curtain. Ten years. Boots could be the same cat she'd found on the rocks that day, the one May had warned her not to pick up. She remembered cradling the grey thistledown to her chest, May uncurling her fingers and the cat jumping free. She remembered following the kitten towards the tumbledown shack that was forbidden them. Stroking the kittens while May stayed in the bedroom for the longest time.

"You did May a mischief when we were bairns. I know that now." The words fell dully from her, as much a confession as an accusation.

"You're pale and wan, lass. Fancy a drop – warm your heart?"

It was painful to continue, but she must. "Did you hurt her again?"

He grinned. "Hard to get warm here. Had a nice, healthy lass in the old days and then I was warm as pish." He dug around under the table and surfaced clutching a jug.

She stepped closer, near enough now to smell the stench of whisky and reel from it. "She asked to be freed from her troubles, so you gave her passage in the Elver but she skimped on the fare. Did you demand that she pay a different way? Did she anger you when she said no?"

May, small May, had spent her life looking at men as if she might do what they wanted if they only gave her what she desired. This would not be the first time she'd fallen foul of it. The vision Oona had conjured was fearful and all too believable. She closed her eyes, trying to will it away.

"Prating on, I don't ken what..." Cormick turned the jug upside down and shook it. "Naught but cobwebs... so long I've forgot the taste." He licked his lips.

Oona's temples throbbed. She wanted to pick up the knife and press it to his throat. "May showed me the coin she'd put by for you!"

"Had no coin for a very long time and tasted not one goddamn drop." Cormick scratched his chest. "It gets ugsome. Sometimes if I can't find a sup, I lay my head down. Warm as guts in my bed, so it is."

Telling him he was a liar seemed pointless. Perhaps if she appealed to whatever small spark of fellow feeling was left in him. "Imagine her out there alone, Master Cormick. We must find her and go to her aid."

Cormick reached in his pocket and brought out a twist of paper. He undid it and took out a pinch of tobacco and tamped it in his pipe.

Oona's head spun from the rotgut smell, but she kept on, her voice imitating the shaming tones she heard so often from Granny. "You meant well, I'm certain. I'll wager you rowed her halfway before it grew dark."

His face turned the colour of liver and his eyes narrowed. "Her and her and her and her and her and her and her and fecking her."

She felt a surge of pleasure at having hit the mark, whatever that mark might be. Pressing her advantage, she bent her face near his, whispering. "You took a liking to her when she was still a wee lass, her manner of walking, her lips and her hair, her way of looking into your eyes as if she might make you a gift of the world. Her soft skin. And you so lonely."

Cormick pushed her away. She fell against the table. He lurched at her, grabbing her arms, shaking his head from side to side, slapping his lips.

His voice was shrill. "Perhaps she tired of you fancying yourself so canny. She wished to be left. It's good to bring home what the sea gives and cook your meat and eat it and take a sup now and then, but when you do, they say you sup too much and if you like someone, they say you like them too much and you touch them too much. Is it any wonder?"

His face was red. He pressed it into hers. The fish knife pushed into her belly, a short jab, just enough to hurt without cutting.

She ripped herself free from him, spun around and ran from the shack, past the midden where the gulls lunged at herring guts and the green crabs shuffled by like drunks.

Clambering onto the boulders, she breathed hard. It began to rain, slicking the places where her hands gripped. On top of the last rock she bent double. It felt like she was being stabbed in the back. She slid down and landed on her tailbone, fell forward palm down, face pressed into the earth.

37

Oona lay listening to her heart and tasting the sweetness of crushed clover. She pushed her face into the small white buds and closed her eyes. Her heart was a poppy and the wind was tearing at its petals. She counted the beats – one, two, three, and the fourth, the dull string on a fiddle, the squeaking wheel on a cart.

Hands could fix carts and fiddles, but there were no hands clever enough to mend the fourth beat of a heart and hers was weakening by the day. Ever since May went, it was growing worse. She could almost feel the long sleep coming on, her tired bones falling under the hill and bleaching. She must find May before that day came.

She rose to her knees and dragged herself home, light-headed and heavy-boned, a cruel thought grating away inside: she'd paid too little mind to May. How else could she have let her come and go to Cormick's when the man was spitting mad?

She pressed her hand to the place where the knife had dug in, hearing his vile words and feeling his hate. He'd had plenty of time to use his knife that way on May and worse. Oona had been too busy hunting shadows at the big house and flirting with the doctor to watch her. She had let her keep secrets and now she might never know what they were.

Inside the croft, twists of firelight licked the threadbare linens on the dresser and nuzzled the flagstone floor. Granny was frowning at the task of untangling the wool from the bird's nest it had got into inside her knitting basket. Rugs and quilts covered her knees. Toby, who cocked an ear when Oona came in, then yawned and lay back down. One of Granny's hands stroked the worn velvet of Toby's ear and the other traced the edge of a pale square of quilt.

"Where did you get to, lass?" She said the words without turning, but her voice was sharp with worry as it had been all week.

"The beach." The lies slipped from her tongue with ease these days.

Granny picked at a stubborn bird's nest of wool. "Stuart came visiting, asking after you. Something to do with Andrew, he told me."

"Oh?" She yawned, wishing to sound bored, but the thought of Stuart pinched her guts still harder than the knife had. She'd kept her distance since his wedding day, knowing full well he would blame her for May's disappearance, or worse, catch some gleam of truth from behind her eyes and know that she knew a deal more than she was telling.

She shut the door, went to the fire and knelt in front of the chair, laying her head in the space between the blue quilt patch and Toby's belly. It was something she'd used to do as a child when her need to be mothered overcame her fear of Granny.

Granny's hand stilled. Oona could feel her knees tense under the sudden heaviness of Oona's head, but she didn't care. It was warm and she was so very tired.

"You've not had one of your fits?"

"No."

For a brief moment, Granny's hand rested on Oona's hair. "Your Ma's was just like this, as red as this."

"Is that why Da fell in love with her?" Oona closed her eyes.

"Who's to say? They were chalk and cheese, screaming and fighting."

Oona had no wish to hear about how they'd hated each other. It seemed sad to come from that. She knew Granny blamed her mother for her father leaving, for him dying too. "Tell me the one about the Finman."

"That's a tale for bairns, not for big girls."

"It's my favourite."

"Well, it was the summer your Ma turned eighteen," Granny scooped up a length of hair and wound it round her wrist, "and she was as bonny a lass as any on Hoy, with a bairn on her hip and that was you..."

Her voice carried on, crackly and soothing, but Oona didn't hear the tale of the Finman who caught sight of Ma from his boat and took too much of a fancy. She heard the hoarse sound of a jackdaw and saw men carrying a wooden box. There were black diamonds sewn on the elbows of their jackets. At the kirkyard, the women whispered Ma's name. May came to hold her hand through the Minister's stern words. After the prayers were done she kissed the top of Oona's head. "You're my kin now. We're sisters."

Granny's hand stopped moving on Oona's hair. "Why, I'm prating on and I don't believe you're even listening."

Oona sat up. "I had a strange dream. I fancied that May was trapped somewhere with no-one to free her."

"Trapped?" Granny's face closed tight as a prayer book. She frowned. "May left no hint of her whereabouts, so all that remains is to look, which is what we have done. Making up tales to torture ourselves is senseless."

"Sometimes dreams show the truth of things." Oona stared into the embers. They were round and bright as coins, the ashes in between them dark as bruises. "She may indeed be trapped, or hurt and day after day passes by. She may lose hope..." Her voice caught on the last word.

Granny looked at her sharply. "Are you keeping something from me, Oona?"

"No."

Granny frowned deeply and patted her lap. Toby climbed into it yawning and she petted his ears. "Oh Toby, the clouts never bring themselves in. Fetch them for me - there's a good lad."

38

Drooping between the wind-crushed sycamores were blouses and stockings, aprons and skirts. Toby followed Oona down the length of it, settling on his haunches to watch as she smoothed and folded, trotting behind her when she moved from one peg to the next.

She wished there had been some way to press Cormick harder. She was surer than ever that he knew something, had done something wrong. Guilt was written all over his face. She shivered, her hands working thoughtlessly on unpegging a worn woollen blanket. Toby barked and ran around her ankles. The blanket fell into her hands and revealed a pair of staring eyes.

She dropped the blanket. "You frighted me." Toby ran between her legs and barked at Andrew.

"Why does he whine so?" Andrew stepped closer. His skin had a beer-sheen and his voice was tight.

"He's a dog. That is their language."

"I've hunted for you everywhere."

"And now you have found me." A dot of rain landed on Oona's cheek. "I must fetch these inside." She picked up the basket.

As she turned, he took hold of her wrist. "Have you visited Cormick?"

Toby's ears flicked back and he trotted inside with his tail down. Oona turned towards Andrew but kept her eyes on the ground. "I went there to ask about May. He said he never saw her, but—"

"Did he confide in you, Oona?" He pulled her towards him. He smelled of beer and sweat.

The basket fell onto the ground and the clothes spilled out of it. "Stop!"

His eyes came into focus and he let go of her. "If you have discovered something, you must tell Stuart."

"I have told you all I know - last night, I did. You paid no heed to it then."

Andrew nodded, his hand moving to his eyes and scrubbing at them like a child.

"Save that, I know nothing more than you." She picked up the basket, brushing at the dirty folds of blanket. "I would say if I did."

He caught hold of her fingers, gently this time. "Please come and we'll call on Stuart. He has need of a friend."

She snatched her hand away. "I was never his friend, or yours."

"But we could become friends." He smiled in a manner that seemed intended to please her. "I could begin our friendship by carrying this laundry for you as a gentleman does for a lady."

She sighed, too tired to resist him today. She let him take the laundry from her and carry it in. Granny smiled at excuses from Andrew that would have made her scold if Oona had spoken them and gave her blessing to their taking a walk. She probably had some foolish notion about wanting to see them married and living in Neaquoy surrounded by bairns. It made Oona sick to think of it.

The old Flett croft had gone to rack since Stuart's father died. When he and May were betrothed he'd built a room onto the end of the byre for his ma, laughing that his women would fight like cats if they were kept together. The cottage was slate-roofed and built from red stone that Stuart's folk had risked their necks to bring down from the cliffs. But Stuart didn't like risking his neck too much, so the wind whistled through gaps in winter and the house sagged at one side where the stones sunk into the peat bog. Old churns and broken ploughs cluttered the field nearest the house.

Stuart sat on a pile of stones with a bucket of tar between his legs and an upended boat in front of him, painting. When Oona and Andrew approached him, he looked up, scowling.

"Any closer to the bride-cog?"

"Small chance of that," Oona grimaced. She'd felt certain that people were talking this nonsense.

Andrew laughed. "Oona's a wild beast, but at least I've managed to herd her here."

"Well, don't linger, will you. I've a great task before me with this wreck." Stuart picked up his brush.

As they came closer, Oona got a better look at the boat Stuart was mending. A red stripe ran across its prow like a wound. The Elver. She leaned over to look at a jagged hole in the hull, clumsily patched with an old plank.

"Why are you tarring Cormick's boat? Short on barley-broo?" She tried to make the words sound light, but Stuart looked at her sharply.

Andrew laughed nervously. "She does love a joke."

Stuart let the brush drop into the bucket and moved between Oona and the boat. "Long time since you last called here, Oona. You were in the habit of visiting with May when you both were close."

The words cut her, as they were meant to. "We are close still."

"Then tell me where she is." His lips stretched in that unctuous line that made the other women swoon. "For you do know. I'm sure of it. You and that damned foreign devil, your employer. I think he's done a mischief to my May and you're protecting him. We all think that, everyone on Quoy, all of us running about searching like fools while you laugh over your great secret."

She gulped back the lump in her throat. "I don't know anything and Doctor Frankenstein certainly does not. How dare you."

"Oona..." Andrew's voice wavered.

She flicked her eyes towards him, as if to say *is this the reason you brought me here, to accuse me?* "You keep more secrets than I do, Stuart, such as patching a hole in the same scuppered boat that had May's cloak in it."

Andrew turned pale as a sheet, the brave beer sheen gone. He stared at his boots. Stuart hovered closer. Oona closed her eyes, bracing for a slap.

Nothing.

When she opened her eyes she saw Stuart wiping tears away.

"We had our bad times as everyone does, but I can't credit her running off as folk say... She always swore that she loved me."

The look on his face as he sniffed and sobbed and let the snot drip down seemed to demand some sort of forgiveness, and though it was on the tip of her tongue to tell him it wasn't a case of happy so much as May being ten times too good for him, it would have felt too much like kicking a dog when it was down.

"Maybe she'll come back." Oona looked away, wishing more than anything that it were true. Then her eyes found the boat with the jagged hole gaping in it like a maw. Something hid under its carapace, there in the darkness, something worse than any secret May had ever kept.

39

The morning was heavy with wet bed linens and foggy with the steam of the sadiron. Oona drifted listlessly from room to room with the keys that May had once managed, folding quilts into chests and pushing pillows into cases.

Working alone, she had more time to notice the curiosities built into the big house: old chutes that began in kitchen cubbyholes and ended in some cabinet upstairs, bookshelves that she delicately dusted until she found the books were wooden and painted, a dark thing in the cellar that May had said was for punishment. If you looked down deep inside it, there were supposed to be old bones. Most of the upstairs doors required a spell spent trying each key in the lock until it finally clicked and let her in.

She was in the east wing, her arms aching with a burden of sheets and her fingers stiff from jiggling at the lock when she found that she was a key short. Some had been lost over the years and May used a knife in place of them. Oona laid the bedding on the floor and knelt to peer through the bothersome hole. It was dark inside. Something sat on a table and bubbled like a pot of soup. A copper barrel gleamed in firelight. She couldn't see a bed and lacked May's skill with a knife.

With a sigh, she picked up the sheets. The keyring slipped down to her elbow, clinking and clanking, making her sound like some old ghost wound in chains as she trudged down the hallway, down the stairs, to make the doctor's breakfast and try not to think of how May had done it, or the song she'd be singing under her breath if she were there.

She trudged from the burn with pails of water slung on a pole across her shoulders. On the long trip up the brae, she remembered May's arms around her that last time they hugged. Surely nobody here was wicked enough to harm such a fragile creature. She remembered Stuart's hard words and Cormick's knife stuck in her belly. They were a rotten pair and had malice enough, but the thought of them hurting May and working together to cover their crime made no sense. Why would they?

And now Stuart was blaming her and Victor. She must warn the doctor as soon as she could.

In the dining hall, the air was ice and the windows were fogged with dripping mist, because she hadn't remembered to light the big fire yet, only the one in the kitchen. She set her pails down, spilling water onto the rug.

"Lovely."

Despite the cold, an angry heat flashed through her, at having all this to do alone, at Stuart's horrible words, at her own foolish weakness. At May, damn her eyes! Damn her secrets!

She pulled out the brush and threw it hard. It collided with the table leg, knocking a chip from it. Half-sobbing, her hands as raw with chilblains as her head was hot, she sank onto her stiff knees and scrubbed the floorboards with all she had left. May had always left them spotless. She must do as well. She must. She looked up and surveyed the one patch she'd left slick and gleaming, then saw the rest stretching out endlessly. There was so much more to do. She scrubbed and scrubbed, pressing her anger, her sadness into the brush, letting the noise lull her, suck the feelings from her, until she was numb.

She had just lit the upstairs fires and was on her hands and knees sweeping ash from the kitchen hearth when she thought she heard Victor calling her. She stopped, head tilted, watching water ripple in one of the pails. The chandelier shook. He was moving something heavy upstairs and, she felt certain, calling her. The noise seemed to come from the Master bedroom. There it was again – a blurred word she couldn't make out. She set down the brush and got up, dusting her hands on her apron.

She ran up the narrow staircase, her knees cracking like an old woman's. On the landing, she turned into the hallway that ran in the opposite direction to the gallery of caged birds. In this (less peculiar) corridor, a dusty tapestry showing men and dogs cornering a wounded stag ran the length of the wall. At the end of it, a door stood ajar. Victor's silver breakfast tray lay just outside, the napkin genteely folded over a plate, a kipper's glazed eye peering out from underneath.

A board creaked. She slowed her step, her fingers ghosting the balcony rail ornately carved in oak. She felt the intricate shapes of cool, wooden petals brush past her thumb. When she reached the door, she listened again but heard nothing. She had never been into Victor's private chambers when he was within them. In the mornings, at his request, she always left his breakfast outside. She was about to turn back when she heard the sound again, although this time she couldn't make out a particular word or name or whether it came from this room or the one beside it.

There was only one way to know. She put her hand to the door and pushed gently, fearing the squeal of hinges. But the door was well-oiled and moved silently open, revealing a big bed with tapering wooden pillars rising from each corner. The red comforter was rumpled and flung back as if someone had just risen from it. Papers spilled from the carved chest at the bed's foot and were dotted across the rug like fallen blossom. Force of habit made her stoop to pick up the first. She tidied her way towards the bed, feeling a bit foolish at the thought that the doctor had probably been calling her to make his bed and take his tray. As she worked she followed the blooms and swirls of the rug. Some of the pale curls in the pattern looked like faces.

By the time she reached the chest, her arms were full of papers covered in inky scrawl she couldn't make out. The last piece of paper was half in, half out of the chest. It was larger and whiter than the others and when she picked it up, she felt the heaviness of the paper, its rough grain.

Turning it over, she saw that this time the dark lines were arranged in sweeping curves instead of letters. She carefully slid the other papers into the chest and held the sketch out in front of her to get a better look. It showed a woman lying on a table. She was naked except for a sheet thrown over her mid-section. Her arms stretched above her head, the wrists pressed into each other. There was something wrong with them, as if they were cut or bound in some fashion. She peered closer.

"Do you like it?"

Oona dropped the paper. She saw a bare-chested Victor wearing the black silk breeks she'd ironed yesterday and the beautiful shoes she'd polished into mirrors. "I was not spying, only squaring your papers away." She stared at the floor.

"Don't you appreciate my drawings?" The words sounded half offended, but he ended them with a laugh.

"They're beautiful."

"Ah, do you think so? Well you have marvellous taste." He sat down on the bed and patted the space beside him. "Come and I'll show you something much better."

She took in the sinewy strength of his chest, the smooth hairlessness of it, then looked away quickly, ashamed to feel her cheeks grow hot.

"Come," he smiled. "I won't bite."

On the bed, she hid her swollen knuckles and ragged fingernails in her skirts. Victor smelled of cologne. From his open valise, he drew a small book and opened it to a page marked with red ribbon. She saw a delicate drawing of what looked like a smooth grey stone. Four thick stalks rose from it, curved, twisted and neatly cut short. Leaves and roots undulated down from the stalks, some thick and branched, some fine as hairs.

"Can you tell me what this is?"

"It's a mossy stone, at the base of a tree I think."

He laughed, shook his head. "It is a human heart, the body's most vital organ. As long as this beats, blood courses through the veins and arteries, bringing necessary elements to the organs and nervous system, pumping life upwards to the seat of human identity - the brain - and downwards." He turned the page to a drawing of a sweet pea flower, its round fruit curving up from it on long tendrils. "Down to the organs of generation, the seat of the feminine. Eve's curse...or blessing, as the Minister in your church might deem it to be." He closed the book and laid it on her lap, let his hand rest there.

She searched his face. There was a new aspect to it, a tremble of the lips, a feverish gleam to his silver eyes. She let herself float for a moment, existing in nothing other than his steady gaze and feeling more than ever that she might confide in him.

"I visited Stuart yesterday, and Old Cormick - they know something of May's whereabouts, I feel it. They did something to her." She spoke the words quietly, measuring each out carefully because they were all so heavy.

"Did something?" His eyebrows flew up and she thought how expressive his face was. You could read each tiny change of sentiment upon it. She almost felt that she could read his thoughts.

"I've told you many times now... I feel certain that something bad has befallen her and that she is hurt, or worse." A drop of water fell on the book's cover, ran into the finely tooled lettering of the Latin words on the front, *De humani corporis fabrica*.

His hand slipped over hers, the fingers closing on her palm. "You fear for her."

"She's my dearest friend." Her voice broke.

"She is near to your heart." He pulled her towards him. "And what a kind heart it is."

Her head was on his shoulder, her face fitting the hollow of his neck as if the space was made for her to hide in. "She is my better half," she murmured, letting the tears run now.

His hand was on her hair and he was whispering words she could not understand, but they sounded more tender than any she knew. She felt his fingers under her chin, lifting her face to him. For what seemed like a long time, he just looked at her, then his mouth was on hers, soft and hot. His hands pressed into her back, pulling her closer, kissing her harder.

Suddenly, he broke away. "Sorry. I should not have... You're distraught and I—"

She touched his hand. "I took no offence."

"It is merely that..." he stood, walked to the window, running his hand over his flushed face, through his damp hair. He stared out at the fields' patchwork, the mountain's veiled green. "At home I am to be married." His voice sounded far away.

She stood unsteadily. Air rushed into her ears and made a harsh whining noise. "They are certain it is you, you know."

He spun around. "*What* is me?" He looked angry and at the same time inscrutable. Whatever foolishness had made her think she could read his mind had vanished. "And *who* is certain?"

"Everyone on this island believes that you killed May and that I am your accomplice. They think we are murderers, both."

40

It was one of those golden days where the sea was blue as blue and you could see the whole world from the shore. Yesterday's clouds had cleared. The mist round the mountain was gone. Loons sang from sand banks stranded in the ebbing tide, sounding half-human, half like ghosts.

It might have been beautiful to some, but to Oona it felt like what she imagined Hell must be. When she rose, she'd splashed her face with ice water, but she could still taste Victor. Worse, she could still see the anger in his eyes. Whatever hope she'd had of asking his help had shrivelled.

The sun brought flies - fat, thirsty ones. She swatted them away and tapped her foot on the dirt, counting out the moments it took for Granny to make water before they went to kirk. Usually she felt sleepy at the thought of the Minister's sermons. Sleepiness sometimes became dreaminess when her eyes turned to the bright day outside and her mind turned to the thought of dangling her legs in the burn. Once in a while the angry words read from the Good Book stirred her and she resolved to be more Christlike. Today an eel bit at her guts. It was the twelfth day without May and for all Oona's turning of stones, she'd found nothing.

Granny walked up, already out of breath. They left the croft and Oona shut the gate behind them to keep Toby from following them to the kirk.

"Och, Toby, we don't fancy jawing wi' her now do we?" The little dog sat watching Granny from the other side of the fence as if he knew just what she was saying.

Oona glanced up at the grass track leading from their front door to the kirkyard and saw what Granny meant. Mad Bridget stood in the middle of the path holding counsel with a russet cow. Bridget was the same age as Granny, a fair-haired scarecrow who'd blow away if the wind hit her hard enough. She was never seen without a bundle of grey rags she cooed to like a baby. Those that were mean-minded enjoyed asking her how her bairn was getting on, to which she replied, "My Wully loves a nip of whisky and a suck of the tit just as much as his Da does." Her tormentors would reel off laughing while Bridget smiled. If there'd been a Da in her life once upon a time, he wasn't there to lead her home any more.

"Good day Mrs Scollay. Good day young lassie. Mrs Umbesetter has been telling me your news."

"Good day to you Bridget," Granny pulled her shawl tighter round her shoulders, as if it might keep the madness at bay. "What news from Mrs Umbesetter?"

Bridget turned back to the cow and patted its dewy nose. "I heard tell all about the lassie's bride-cog. She said everyone will sup their fill at the wedding, even the likes of me, didn't you Joan?"

Oona looked from Bridget to the cow. "I fancy the likelihood of my being wed is far smaller now than ever it was."

Granny gave her a look.

"Can Wully come too?" Bridget cradled the rags tenderly.

"He can come to my funeral, both of you can, and have a sup there for me!" Oona smiled brightly and chucked the rag baby under his grimy chin.

"Heavens, Oona." Granny gripped her arm hard. "Come, we are already late."

"Farewell Bridget!" Oona waved, undeterred by Granny's disapproval.

"And a very good morning, a very good, good morning to you. Now, Joan, on the subject of my husband—"

When they were through the kirk gates, Granny dropped Oona's arm and turned to face her. "Why must you say such foolish things?"

Oona's eyes followed the stately shapes of Quoy women moving inside the kirk. "They all know I will soon die. It may be a matter of weeks."

Granny's voice shrank to a whisper. "Whatever they prate about is their business, but for God's sake don't give them—"

"The truth? If I speak my mind will I be cast out like poor Bridget?"

"Oona, you do not know what it is to die like that, with everyone talking and shaking their heads as your coffin sinks under the earth."

"Nor do you."

Oona's head was light with anger. She saw spots of white and colour spill from the sun behind Granny's head when she said, loud as she pleased, "In any case why should I not? It is our family tradition. Everyone talked ill of Ma the day she was buried, how she was with the men, how Da'd rather freeze in his boat than stay by her side, how you hated each other. Everyone says you could have helped her that day by the burn and you damn well left her to—"

Granny raised her hand, staring Oona down through narrowed eyes. "Shut your bone box girl, before I slap you quiet."

She turned and placed a trembling hand on the fence and straightened her back until her head was high, then marched towards the clanging bell and the open door, where the people of Quoy nodded their hellos and she nodded back, superior as she had been her entire life.

"Die," said Oona, to the flies and the loons and the sunlight, "everyone knows you left her to die."

She followed Granny, smiling and nodding, laughing a bit inside at her poor imitation of a lady. Even fewer people than usual returned her greeting. They were wary of her since May's wedding day.

She sat on the Scollay pew, far enough from Granny that she would not provoke her. She'd never spoken such harsh words before. She'd never dared. She still trembled from it, a chill sweat slicked over her, and yet, as the rest of the village filed in and squeezed themselves onto the hard, narrow seats, preparing for worship, for obedience, she felt a certain triumph at using her prerogative. For the dying may speak their minds.

Hamish Yule stepped into the pulpit. "Take out your Bibles and turn to Genesis 4 verses 1-16."

There was a thump of heavy books, a chirr of dry pages.

"When Cain killed his brother Abel, God spoke to him and said, *Where is your brother Abel? What have you done?* For he had killed his brother and the blood cried out for vengeance! When a man does evil, God speaks to him through his soul and convicts him of his sin. *What have you done?* he asks. He judges us more harshly than fire or storm when we do bad, yet he is gentler than the summer rain when we do good. A man must do what is good even if it grieves him."

A shout made Oona sit up straight. It sounded like the blood of Abel crying out. But it was Stuart, not Abel, who stood up unsteadily. "I must do right by May."

Everyone stared at him.

"May's been gone more than a week." Stuart's white-knuckled fingers clutched the pew like the legs of a crab. "And still we've done nothing to find her."

Big Dod stood. "Minister, may I speak?" He turned to face the congregation. "Stuart, lad, we've searched for her everywhere - the caves, the cliffs, the valley. We've done what we can to find her, torn ourselves to bits doing it..."

Hunched beside him, Effie sobbed wretchedly.

Dod's big face grew dark. His jowls trembled. "It may be time to leave the matter in God's hands. We may have to let her—" His voice broke.

Effie reached up and grabbed his hand. "No!" She cried, "No! My girl..." She clung to him.

Oona stared at her lap, clutching at some last shred of hope, some golden speck that kept her from the abyss.

Stuart's voice began again, sly as a snake's. "I catch your meaning, Dod, and I respect you for all that you say, but I do not think you are apprised of everything. The truth is, this woman here," he jabbed his finger in Oona's direction, "knows more than she will tell us. She knows that the doctor up at the big house has sinned—"

"Liar!" Oona stood.

Granny grabbed her wrist and pulled her down again, hissing, "Be silent."

"You've been playing the Devil up at that house, bringing the wrath of God upon us, the Plagues of Egypt, killing our chickens and pigs while we sleep. Witchcraft, I call it. Evil." Stuart started towards her, but found himself fenced into the pew by a row of knees.

The Minister dashed off his spectacles. "Master Flett. This is the Lord's house and you will—"

Stuart thumped the pew with his Bible, "Cormick saw you, the pair of you, rowing out in his boat like Devils in the dark, and now May's gone and the very same boat drifted back with a hole in the hull. Did you put it there, Oona?"

"Did *you*?" Oona wrenched herself from Granny's grip and stood, her whole body trembling at the words. She felt Granny's hand on her wrist. This time she paid it no mind. "Did you do her an injury, Stuart, out of jealousy? Is that why you're mending the Elver's hull, to hide what you've done?"

All eyes turned to her. The Minister's spectacles hung midway between his face and his book. Oona met his gaze, hoping he knew she was sorry. He'd been a father to her since her own ran off.

Stuart's face darkened. "Make her leave."

The Minister put his spectacles back on. His hands shook on the Bible, but his voice was calm. "What, and cast her out, and everyone? There are but thirty of us in Quoy, Master Flett. If we cast out all the sinners, I'll be preaching to the sheep. Now sit."

Stuart stayed and spoke his piece, albeit in a quieter voice and with just a tinge of contempt. "Our island went to hell when that man came here. This place was an Eden. The serpent crept in and everything rotted and died: my fish, my livestock, my wedding day. I say we've been idle too long and let evil flourish under our eyes. The time has come to put that Devil down."

41

Oona followed Stuart and Andrew down the hill watching Stuart's arms swing briskly back and forth. A white cloud in front of him made it look as if steam was coming from his ears. Anyone watching probably thought she looked that way too.

After his impromptu sermon, he'd bolted from the kirk, though at least he didn't have half the village following him with torches to burn down the big house. Not yet anyway. They'd sat stunned at his words and the kirk had been silent except for Effie's loud sobs.

It wouldn't be long until they listened to him, though. Whether he really believed his own story or was acting this way to conceal his misdeeds was impossible to know. She must stop him regardless.

She followed the pair over to the next bay, down along the finger of land on which the Smokehouse sat. Perhaps they were headed there to blow the cobwebs away. Anything was better than going to the big house.

She crossed the burn, scowling at the bright sun and the swallows skimming buttercups in the long grass. She'd lived here her whole life and now she felt like an outsider. She would die as Granny said with people talking and shaking their heads, relieved to see her go, while men like Stuart and Andrew would live out their three score and ten surrounded by fat grandchildren.

She followed them through small bogs and over cowpats, down into deep ruts gouged by the plough, cursing her life and everything in it. By the time she reached the Smokehouse, it seemed the pair were inside and a buzz of low voices flowed from the half open door. She couldn't see through it, but she imagined Andrew would be sitting close by Stuart, topping up his beer and listening. She picked a clover flower from the damp grass between her feet and plucked the petals off.

Footsteps scuffed the dirt behind her. She turned to see Stuart climbing the road from the beach. His fists were clenched. He came towards her fast, walked by without seeming to see her, and knocked the Smokehouse door open with his elbow. It slammed behind him.

From inside, she heard a thump like a fist on wood, more voices, louder this time. She still could not hear what they said. She stood and went to the door, her skin tingling. As quietly as she could, she pressed her ear to the door, heard scraps.

"D'you reckon it's true?"

"When I get hold of him –"

"Don't be daft. Wait!"

Chairs scraped. Another thump. A crack. Her hand moved to the door. She shouldn't go in. A cry. It sounded like Andrew. She threw the door open and stepped inside. The place was dark and stank of ale and smoke. There were beer jugs stained with dottle. A half-gutted halibut drooled fish blood down the table leg. Behind that, two men reeled around the small space. Drunks dancing. They knocked into Dougie Flett who spilled ale down his shirt.

"Christ, watch yourself!" He raised his fist.

They paid no mind. It was only when they reeled into daylight that she saw it was Andrew and Stuart. Dougie banged down his pint. "Calm yourselves. No need to scrap."

Oona bumped past the table. "Stop!"

"Keep that petticoat away." Stuart grabbed Andrew by the nose, fingers jammed in his nostrils.

Andrew yelped and punched him. "I'm saving you from yourself."

Oona thrust her arms between them. "Leave each other be."

Stuart's elbow caught her chin. She fell against the table. The corner caught her in the ribs and she slid to the floor, watching the room sway. The men broke apart.

Andrew skidded to her side. "Are you hurt?" He touched her face.

"It's a bump, no more." Stuart scowled, his body still braced for a fight. "You're forbidden this place. Did you not hear me in kirk? You're not welcome anywhere in Quoy."

"Stop your mouth, Stuart. It does nothing but lie." She gripped the table edge and dragged herself up.

Andrew rested his arm on her shoulders. "Go home to your Granny, eh?"

She brushed him off. "I must know why you were fighting."

They stood stupidly, breathing hard. A fly buzzed through the open door. Dougie took a moment to stare at the scene between slurps of beer as if he wasn't quite sure it was happening. The peat fire in the middle of the room gave up the ghost.

After a while, Stuart smiled with one side of his mouth, as if he had just conceived some new mischief. "Very well. I went to Cormick's shack to ask him a question or two. He was out, but I found this." He opened his fist and slapped something hard on the table. A coin glinted. He dragged his sleeve over the thin stream of blood that trickled from his nose, smearing it onto his cheek. "I have searched for this high and low."

Her head felt feathery, her eyes seeing the round shape of a coin sewn into a hem. "How do you know it's your coin?"

"I marked it so no-one could steal it from me." He held it up. Light fell through a hole in the middle.

The fly buzzed round her, looking for a place to rest.

"I'll wager anything May took it for her fare to Hamnavoe." Andrew clenched and unclenched his fists.

Stuart squinted at him. "That's only part of it."

"What's the rest?"

He pulled something from his pocket. "This."

It was a long length of fabric, dark red with darker patches splattered on it.

"May's stocking, stuffed in a rusted old creel. Bloodied."

Oona's legs grew weak beneath her. She fell on the floor with a thump. "How-"

"I thrashed him half to death to make him talk." Stuart smashed his fist on the table. The jugs jumped. One fell to the floor and smashed. "His eyes rolled up in his head before he'd tell me-" He paused and took a long look at his audience.

Andrew clenched his fists. "The wretch! How'd he do it? We'll hang him up high."

Stuart shook his head. "I'd have sworn by God's blood it was Cormick, but the story that rusty guts told me rang true. He was rooting in the midden at the big house and found it with blood crusted on it. Now the time's come to discover the reason and it's as good a moment as any, because by all accounts the good doctor spends his Sundays hunting in the valley."

Oona wrenched herself up from the floor and stumbled outside. Even though she stood still, the world rushed past her, grass and trees and sky spinning so fast they bled together.

May's red stocking, knitted for her by Effie. There was no doubting it was hers. She'd had the pair as a gift upon her engagement. She must have hurt herself working, fallen and torn the stocking and thrown it out there. It was the only explanation.

Andrew came out behind her. "Go home to Granny." He kept his voice low. "What we're about is nothing you should see."

Stuart grabbed Andrew by the shoulder and dragged him away. "I would go home and hide if I were you Oona. Don't fear – we'll deal with you anon." He started up the path to the valley.

She stood by the door of the Smokehouse, fists clenched, watching their figures shrink and darken as they went from her. Their angry talk blew back, twisted by the wind.

When they faded from earshot she started after them.

42

The woman forced her gritty eyes open. Squares of peat glowed in the grate. Inside, the pain burned as it always did. She pushed her wrists against the wires binding her and felt them sink into her wounds like an old friend.

The man would come soon and give her small sips of beer and sit silently next to her, turned so that she could not see his face. Usually he was kind, though perhaps he was only biding his time until the moment came to take whatever it was he wanted from her.

The smell of the peat, of the room, was different today. She didn't know why, but the scent of the air brought a feeling like her mind becoming clear water. Old feelings swam to the surface of it and she fancied she saw a high place she'd been to with a burn and hills on either side, where she'd dug down in the heather, nicked and cut the wet peat, stacked it in the open to dry. She remembered so many fragments but not who she was or where she came from, or even what her own face looked like. She strained at her bindings. The wires broke the swollen skin of her wrists and ankles, opened old wounds, scored new ones. Biting her lip to stop herself crying out, she sank back onto the pallet.

The door opened. What stood behind it was dark and she saw neither what lay beyond the room nor the face of the man, only his shadow leaning to shut and lock the door.

He crossed to the hearth and knelt to blow on the peat. Flames spat and crackled into life. She closed her eyes and feigned the low, deep breaths of a sleeper. She did not want him to know she was watching.

There was a long pause and she began to think he'd left the room. She had never heard him speak. He was always silent. Pins jabbed her hands and feet. They were numb and painful at the same time and she wanted to move them but didn't dare. A chair scraped on the flagstones and its suddenness jolted her. But she kept breathing slowly and deeply. Even when she felt his hand stroke her hair, she was stone.

She squeezed her eyes tighter, shutting him out of her head. Fragments of some lost scene flickered across her vision - the grey sky, heavy with rainclouds, the dark sea growing rougher and the edge of a boat with a woman's hand on it. The scenes made her feel things.

How open the sky was, how huge the sea and the horizon stretching out forever. Being rocked too hard, the taste of bile. Being free.

His hand left her head and air pressed coolly on the damp patch his sweat had made. Stone screeched on stone and liquid glugged into a cup. Her tongue clucked dryly on the roof of her mouth.

She opened her eyes and saw his hand hovering. He lifted her head and tipped the cup to her lips. She drank the warm beer, some of it hitting her tongue and running down her throat and the rest dribbling down her cheeks and pooling under her. As she drank, she watched his chin, the dark holes of his nostrils, his shadow cast on the roof beams bloated like an ogre's. He held her head gently but still she was bound hand and foot.

When she'd finished drinking, she turned her face so that he'd take the cup away. He rested her head back on the pallet and put the cup down somewhere behind him. In a moment, he'd leave and she'd be alone again for an aching stretch of night. Or day. It was hard to tell. This was her chance.

"What is your name?" Her voice sounded broken.

The man stood listening, his face turned from her, his arm paused mid-stretch. He said nothing. Her heart kicked into a gallop. The wound in her chest burned. She coughed, trying to clear her throat.

"What is my name?"

He turned towards her. Flame shadows licked the planes of his cheeks. He rubbed his hand over his eyes and coughed into his hand as if he, too, was unused to speaking.

"Your name is Eve," he said, as if she should have known already. "I must move you to another place. You are not safe here any more."

43

The mountain was a dark beast sleeping – one hip raised to nudge the sky, the other slung low in the soft-breathing, secretive valley. Heather grew thick on the high ground, drunk from the burn that scored a groove across the island. The sky was hot and clear and lichens marked the boulders with their patterned blood. From the fields, the higher reaches of the island were nothing but white cloud.

Oona stopped to let her heart slow and saw in her mind's eye the red fabric that had lain against May's skin. To think of it lying tangled in an old creel made her legs weak. Maybe it was Cormick who had taken it and put it there. Maybe Stuart.

He and Andrew were far ahead of her now, crossing the shallow part of the burn. She could make out their outlines and could see but not hear Stuart whipping the stocking at bullrushes as he climbed the boggy meadow that led up to the Scollay croft.

She dug her nails into her palms, hoping fervently that Victor was holed up in the music room dissecting something, miles away from the valley and ignorant of this whole affair. Later, when things had calmed, she would ask him what he knew about the stocking and the blood. Stuart had seemed very quick to call it that given that it was dried and black, as if he knew more than he was telling them.

She followed the pair of them over the burn and fallow fields. It grew rimy, rain filling the buttercups and trembling the frail leaves of poppies, and the wind howled through high ravines, startling the gulls and stirring them into a chorus of shrieks. A crow ghosted her steps, resting on a tumble of stones to stare her down until the wind took it by the wings and tossed it back.

They were closer to the mountain now and the air tasted different. She could see silver ravines and the green scars of burns gouging a path through rock. The Scollay place hunched its shoulders against the mountain. A squat pile of red stones, it might have been her home in another version of life. Instead, wind whispered through gaps in the stones and the only known inhabitant was a nanny goat that had once belonged to the Umbesetters. Renowned for her sharp horns and sharper teeth, she ruled the abandoned croft with ireful grit.

The shower eased, leaving a shroud of rain on everything. When he came level with the rotting byre Stuart turned, sniffed the air. He said something to Andrew. She didn't hear what. Chest puffed out like a cockerel, he started towards the byre, then swerved past it and walked to the cottage. At the door, he paused, bristled, walked inside.

Oona crouched low behind a lichen-crusted ledge of rock. Wild garlic glowed white from the dark places under the thorn trees. Breathing hard, she watched Andrew follow Stuart and disappear. A few feet away from her, a stoat peaked out from under a pile of rocks, flicked her a look of black-eyed scorn and darted down a hole. Above, a great skua circled, staring down at the place the stoat had been a moment ago. Inside the cottage, a man's voice cried out brokenly.

She ran without thinking or really feeling her legs, ran towards the cry, for it was a voice she knew. Over the clutter of old cart wheels and rusted hay knives that grew around the byre, to the narrow window that sagged under the roof of the cottage. Grass sprouting from the slates tickled her forehead as she squinted through it. Nothing but darkness. After a moment she realised that someone had boarded it over. She knew Victor went hunting near here, searching out hares and birds, gathering the fruit of his snares. Maybe he'd gone inside the cottage to escape the rain.

The rear of the building had collapsed into a tumble of broken stones, muck and thorn bushes. She groped over the rubble, scratching her feet with each step. There was another small window. She squatted next to it and peered inside. It was boarded up like the other, but there was a small crack between the pieces of wood. Through it she saw the blackness of an empty grate, a pile of broken furniture against the far wall and a jumble of straw and wool shaped into a rough palette.

The palette was covered in crumpled clothes and sheets and a blanket lay in a heap at the foot of it. They looked clean. Strange when the place had been abandoned all these years, as if someone had been hiding out in the ruins. The crumpled clothes moved. A face emerged from them.

It was Victor.

44

Stretched on his back, Victor's arms and legs sagged off the sides of the palette. It grieved Oona to see him prone like that. Stuart came into view. He hunched over Victor, gripping his collar.

"Tell me the answer, monster, before I beat it from your lips."

"I don't. I wouldn't —" Victor turned his face to the side.

Andrew stood by the door, biting his nails.

Stuart straightened and opened his hand. Balled inside it was May's stocking. "We found this outside your door." He let the length of it fall, dangling it so that the sock foot brushed Victor's cheek. "What else is there, her petticoats? When those are discovered at the big house, what will you say then?"

"Please." Victor squeezed his eyes shut and Oona realised that for all his boldness, he was smaller than Stuart and weak in comparison. If Stuart wished, he could kill him easily.

"Stop hurting him!" Oona blurted the words before she could stop herself. Three pairs of eyes turned to her.

Stuart dropped Victor and came to the window. "I told you to stop following us, damn bitch." He reached out, his fingers grabbing at her.

She shrank from him, tumbling back into the muck. Something sharp jabbed her in the ribs. Her heart raced and it was hard to breathe. Now would be the time to run, but she couldn't leave Victor. However tangled and strange their friendship was, she knew she cared for him in ways she did not yet understand and it hurt her more than she would have thought possible to see him lying there. She must protect him.

She pushed herself up and hurried around to the doorway. Andrew stood before her, blocking her way.

"Go home, Oona." His eyes were flat.

"I cannot." She pushed past him.

A pile of snares blocked her way, some with small birds chirruping and squawking inside them. She climbed over them the same way she had the rocks and the thorns, anger driving her forward. From inside, the room looked even sadder. It had collapsed in on itself until it was a fraction of the original grandiose plan her father had made for his family seat.

The main room was a tip crowded with mouldering furniture and heaped peat. Stuart nearly filled what space was left. He dangled

Victor over the bed with one hand. The other gripped a distaff. Oona thought he would shout at her when he saw her, but instead he smiled and caught Victor a jab to the ribs.

"Where is May?"

Victor shook his head from side to side, his slim body hunched round Stuart's fist.

Another blow. "What did you do?"

Victor's yowl was high and strange. Oona flung out her arms as if it would make the beating stop. Stuart let him go with a grunt. Victor fell into the snarl of covers and curled over on his side, his head tucked between his sinewy arms. Stuart reached into his pocket and pulled out a fishing knife. He flashed a tight grin at Oona.

Stuart twisted the knife between his fingers, his eyes never leaving Oona's. "Come now, you clever devil. I ken what you're like, drawing dead girls, cutting their naked bodies. How would you like to be cut?"

Victor mumbled into his folded arms, but Oona could not hear what he was saying. She leaned in.

"I would never hurt a living girl," he muttered the words over and over like a half-forgotten prayer.

She took a step forward, wrapping her arms around herself, a mirror of Victor. If only she could get between them, but in this mood, Stuart might snap her neck.

He leered up at her. "You cold, girl, when the sun's high? We won't be long, then Andy and I will take you home, make you a nice warm fire." He smiled. His eyes were wet. He picked up the distaff and smashed it into Victor's face. "You poisoned the water so that all the fish died and the beach filled with flies and frogs. You stole my livelihood and took the only other thing I had."

"I..." Blood bubbled from Victor's nose.

Stuart raised the distaff above his head.

"Stop!" Oona stepped forward and put her hands in the space between Stuart and Victor. "You'll kill him if you continue."

Stuart gaped at her. "You're coming to his aid now, after all your cant about helping May?"

"He has nothing to do with it. Can you not see he is ignorant?"

"Ignorant?" He took a step towards her and brushed her cheek with his fingers.

His touch was the sting of a jellyfish. She pushed his hand away. "I thought he was wisdom itself, a genius May said."

She stared him down. "Just as you are a genius with your hands. Why not tell us about the Elver that you were fixing? It's you should confess."

"Useless damn woman." He spun away from her. "Aren't they all? Now tell us, doctor, what did do you do? Cut her up for one of your experiments?"

Victor raised his head, the slight curl of his lips a shadow of his usual wry smile. "It does not work like that, my friend. If you knew anything…"

Stuart smashed the distaff into Victor's gut.

Victor screamed.

Something snapped inside Oona. She no longer cared if he hurt her. She must act. She flung herself between them and tried to seize the distaff from him. He just held it higher over his head.

"You must stop this." She tried to wrestle it from him.

"Andrew, come and take this daft woman of yours." Grunting, Stuart pulled the distaff from her grip.

Oona stumbled back, steadying herself on the doorframe. Andrew walked in, his mouth tight.

Framed by the crook of Stuart's arm, Victor's face was a mask of blood. His right eye was swollen shut. He breathed raggedly.

"If you keep on, he will certainly die and then everyone will know you are a murderer." She made the last words as cold and measured as she could. If pleas had no effect, maybe the threat of the valley's disapproval would.

Stuart and Andrew stood at the foot of the bed looking down at Victor. Stuart's face twisted in disgust. Andrew turned pale. He reached out to Stuart. "Hand me that distaff." As he said the words, his eyes met Oona's.

"The pleasure is mine." Stuart gave it to him, spat and wiped his mouth with his sleeve. He turned away from the bed. "I've had my fill for now, anyway." With that, he walked out.

45

Oona ran to the bed, her eyes blurred with tears. Victor's left eye looked at her vaguely, the pupil large and dark, the white bloodshot. His face was grey, the veins at the temples hard ridges. It was heartbreaking to see him lying there like the husk of a dead crab, fighting to stay awake.

She turned to Andrew. "I must prop him against the pillow, or he'll choke."

Andrew nodded. Together, they lifted Victor's until his head rested upon the pillow. She dabbed the blood from him with the edge of the blanket, hearing his breaths grow slower and calmer.

Andrew wiped his hands nervously on his trousers. "I'm going to... I need to find Stuart... stop him running mad."

She nodded. "Thank you for putting an end to this. It was the right thing to do."

Victor coughed hard, bright blood staining the blanket and his lips. "Thirsty," he gasped.

There was a flask by the bed. Whoever had been sleeping out here had brought a few home comforts at least. Oona tilted Victor's head back and gave him a sup of whatever was inside it.

He drank, then pushed the flask away, coughing. "*Mein gott, feuerwasser.*"

She sniffed the leather mouth of the flask. Whisky. "It might help with the pain." She put it to his lips again. Some ran down his chin and cheeks, mingling with blood.

"It stings!" He winced, his hands flailing.

"Sorry." She put down the flask. She'd never seen someone as weakened as this. He hardly seemed aware of her.

At the foot of the bed was a rumple of blankets. She pulled them over him as gently as she could and tucked them around his body.

"I wish I knew how to stop the bleeding." She turned away, looking around the room for something she might use as bandages.

He caught her by the wrist. "Don't leave me here."

"Of course not." She laid her hand over his. "You will be well again, I promise."

"I'm so sorry." He coughed hard.

"For what?"

Victor kept coughing, his hands pressed to his face. "Bringing him here."

"Who?"

"Death."

She braced herself, wondering if he did know something after all. Then she looked in his eyes and saw that he was far away somewhere, mumbling nonsense like a child who's woken from a nightmare.

She gently touched his face. "You're talking nonsense. A good blow to the head will do that to you." She tried to laugh, but one glance at the wreck that was Victor killed the sound in her throat. She bent and kissed the top of his head, her lips grazing his matted hair. Pride no longer mattered. He needed her.

His hands were as bloody and bruised as the rest of him. He lay them very gingerly on hers. "The man you saw at your window, the scarred man..."

Her throat tightened. "The one you said I dreamed because of the laudanum?"

He squeezed his eyes shut. "It was wicked of me to lie to you. That man is real, a monster, he followed me to this island. He is shrewd, cunning and..." He broke into a fit of coughing. She tipped the flask to his lips.

He swallowed painfully and cleared his throat. "This beast knows the land and the sea, how to survive, to remain invisible from ordinary men who might shun him. Even if your friends were to track him down, he would destroy them before they could..." He looked at her with his one good eye. "He is a murderer, Oona, cold-blooded. Evil. May saw it too. She knew."

"Do you think...he...that May..."

His hands slipped from hers. He looked at the wall.

She rose and ran from the shack, out into the sunshine where the flies droned and the blackbirds taunted. She flung herself against the wall of the byre, choking down sobs. The kirk bells in her head were loud and the angry pulse of her heart drove her to claw her hands on the wall and beat her head against the cold stone until it stung and blood ran into her eyes.

Second to May, she'd trusted Victor most of all and he'd lied to her, told her she was imagining things when really she'd seen the person - the monster - who could have taken May.

She pressed her hands to her face, rubbing grains of dirt into her skin and feeling the salt sting her lip where Stuart's hand had caught it. Her breath came in ragged gasps. She scrubbed at her face, making the earth grind into her, tasting its rawness.

For the first time, she had begun to believe that May was dead.

46

A fall of pebbles.

The sound of it echoed from the valley's looming rocks.

Oona looked up, expecting to see a scarred man with staring, blue eyes. Instead, a potbellied goat stood before her, chewing on a turnip top, gold eyes unblinking. The nanny goat of legend brayed sourly and lowered her horns. Oona dragged her hand across her nose, jolted out of her dark reflection by the oddity of the sudden appearance.

"Don't point those things at me."

As she spoke the words, a shrill cry rang out, echoing off the slack stones of Scollay's outbuildings.

"Who's there?"

No-one answered. She pulled her shawl around her, cold and conscious of the valley's bleak lull. The air was so still it took her breath away.

She struggled up from the heap she'd slumped into, staring past the goat at the wreck of her family farm. She'd been a baby when her father went fishing for the last time. Granny said it had been a calm day, no storm except for the one in the Scollay house, the constant shouting and hurling of objects that by all accounts only paused when her parents slept. Maybe her father had left to get away from it. That was what Granny always said.

Whatever the reason he went, he wasn't back that evening or the next. Some people whispered that he'd angered the sea spirits and they'd taken him, others that he'd been greedy, casting his nets in the far North waters where icebergs groan. Oona's Ma left her with Granny and waited on the beach for her husband night after night, week after week, growing thinner, paler. Until one day something inside her cracked like ice falling in a cave and she came back from the beach for good. It was only a short while afterwards that Granny found her lying face down in the burn.

It was night. The fire she'd made warmed the room, but wind still whistled under the pile of old chairs and cupboards she'd used to block up the door. On the bed, Victor shivered. His face was slick with sweat and he kept kicking off his sheet, pulling at the torn strips she'd used to wrap his wounds and moaning. Half of it was a babble of

German she didn't understand, but sometimes his eyes flew open and he cried out in English about the creature being in the room with them.

Sometimes he cried for Oona and she went to him, soothing his head with water from a pail she'd found outside. As she tended to him, she thought about how he had lied to her and kept terrible secrets. May too. Strange how you never really saw what was inside someone. Perhaps the more you cared for them, the less you knew. More than anything, she wished May were here again, so they could talk. She was far too tired to blame her or even Victor for all they had kept from her.

Bone tired, and yet she could not sleep in the ruined croft where the ghosts of her parents rattled the windows and whispered from the walls. Or perhaps it was the monster who whispered and knocked and made that steady sound, like footfalls circling the cottage.

Oona paced the room, sometimes pausing to peer through the crack between the window boards. Nothing but darkness and a sliver of yellow moon slipping free of the clouds. Wind howled down the chimney. She hurried from the window, pulling her shawl around her. It was growing colder. She went to the stack of peat, so dry and neatly kept (and recent, surely) and grabbed up new sods for the fire, laying them carefully down. Tucked under the shelf beside it where her mother would have set bread to rise, was a stack of bed linens. No cobwebs on these. They were fresh. She took them out, stood and let the cloth tumble free of its folds.

She drew a sharp breath when she saw the shape that lay against her body, a little too short to fit her perfectly. No bed linens, but a crisp white nightgown, bloodied at the cuffs. A few faint drops were spattered over the breast of the gown. Someone had worked hard to scrub them out and hadn't quite succeeded. She held the gown to her nose. It smelled cleanly of lye and lavender, of May.

Her hands shook. She dropped the gown and circled the room, peering in one dark corner, then the next, under an upturned table, up on a shelf, all the time scratching her elbows and neck that suddenly itched enough to drive her mad.

She stopped, forcing herself to be calm and see what she hadn't yet managed to see. She had turned over everything, looked beneath each piece of rubble, all save a wicker chair that lay in the corner, its round back unravelling. She ran to it, heaved it up. Underneath was a black leather bag, worn but clean and softly shining. She undid the clasp and pulled it open.

Knives. A neat row of them. They gleamed silver in the firelight. Scissors and scalpels like the ones Victor used to cut things apart.

Her head whirred, skin filmed with sweat, cold though the room was hot. Her hands dropped from the bag. She fell against the wall, reaching behind herself to clutch the rough stone and feel something, anything real.

47

Victor was deep in some fever dream, his eyes beetling under the thin-skinned lids. Oona picked up the jug and threw the remainder of the water over him. His head jerked up, the good eye blinking furiously. She held the bag where he could see it.

"You have been staying here." She couldn't keep the fury from her voice.

"What?" His gaze moved blankly between the bag and the scalpel she held in her other hand.

"Do not lie to me, Victor. I know you have been here. Who else would keep knives like these in such a bag? Did you bring May here? Did you hurt her?" She waved the scalpel wildly. She was losing control, eyes blurring, voice cracking.

Fumblingly, he caught her wrist, his fingers slipping from it almost at once. "Oona I would never..." His hand moved to her face. "Oona, please, listen."

She wiped her eyes angrily and put down the bag, but not the knife.

"Please...sit." He smoothed a space on the palette beside him.

She shook her head, crouching on the floor, her hand clutching the scalpel so hard that the join between blade and handle cut into her. "Is this story about a monster...is it even real?" Her voice was high at the end and sounded mad even to her. She was losing any sense of what was the truth and what was lies.

Victor reached for her again. His hand found her arm, the fingers pressing her skin. Despite herself, she found the touch reassuring. She looked into his eyes. They were clearer now. If only she could see inside his head and know the truth.

When he began talking, his voice sounded far away. "I grew up in Geneva with people I love with all my heart. Mother, Father, my cousin Elizabeth and my young brother William, a beautiful boy... When I reached manhood, I followed my passion for natural philosophy and went to study in Ingolstadt. There, I undertook research into the secret of life. It was dark work. I dissected not only animals, but humans..."

He paused, his eyes flicking anxiously over Oona's face. "My work required illicit connections. During the course of it, I became entangled with a most unpleasant man. Barely a man - no I would not grace him with such a name - a *monster* - a vile fellow, ugly as sin, scarred and hairless and wicked. The man you saw."

He pulled his hand from her and pressed it to his face. For a long time, there was no sound but the rattle of the window timbers, the howl of the gale down the chimney.

When Victor spoke again, his voice was barely a whisper. "This creature murdered my brother William. A young girl - a maid like yourself, who worked in our house - was hung for the crime. Later, he stalked me into the mountains and even in the icy wastes where I had gone to grieve, he found me.

"There, he admitted the crime and struck a Devil's bargain. He ordered me to continue my research into the secrets of life, work he would use for his own dark purposes. In return for this, he would refrain from killing the remainder of my loved ones." He held her gaze, eyes wide and intent so that she couldn't look away.

She pressed her hands to her temples and closed her eyes so she didn't have to see him. Instead she saw the dead girl's hand washed up to shore and May, so slight and so reckless, so easy to hurt.

She took a deep breath, drawing her fear and anger inwards, letting it swell before she spoke. "So you came here and he followed you. That is what you meant when you said you brought Death to our island."

He turned his face towards the fire, frowning. "Indeed, the beast is here, bound on ruining me once more."

Oona stepped back, squeezing her body into a small nook by the door. Her sympathy had contorted into something else. A vision of the chicken coop flickered before her eyes: torn necks, congealed blood, Toby's whimper of shame and the look of blank shock in Granny's eyes.

"Everyone I love lives here, or did. You are so compelled by the sorrow of your own story, you've neglected to think of the cost to everyone else."

He looked at her vaguely as if the words only made partial sense, then he waved his hand. "No, no, the monster's vendetta is with me. He will only harm those dear to me. You and the others, you will all be quite safe."

Oona swallowed hard, stung and at the same time ashamed that she felt so. She went on, her voice a notch more waspish than before. "And what about May? Has he harmed her?"

"Oh Oona, I hope not."

She leaned over, turning his face towards her. "So this is not your hiding place?"

He shook his head.

"Then whose is it? Who would be keeping a bloody nightgown and a bag full of knives in my parents' house?"

He covered his face again. "*Gott im Himmel.* It is him."

She watched all night by the dying light of the fire, the knife clutched in her fist, her back pressed to Victor's sleeping form. For all her anger, she was glad of the warmth that bled from his body to hers. It gave her some comfort at least.

Grey light spilled through the cracks in the shutters and around the makeshift door and still her bones stayed clenched. She must see the monster first if he came to the window and be ready for whatever he planned. Even if those footsteps circling the shack were his and his voice sounded somewhere out there, she saw no sign of him.

When the light was strong, she turned to look at Victor's sleeping face, wondering whether she should simply abandon him here. He had brought so much pain to the island. His face was softened by sleep, the fair hair falling back against the bedding, the full lips parted and innocent as a boy's. For all his cleverness, he did not know right from wrong. In some ways, he knew less than her. He was at his weakest now. She couldn't leave him alone.

By noon he was able to walk without shaking too much. Oona broke apart her makeshift barricade and they struck out, her arm around his waist, her eyes scouring the rocks and grass around them for any sign of Stuart and Andrew. Or the monster. When they reached the big house, her arm dropped from him and she took out her key. The kitchen door opened and they staggered in and sat down wearily.

"Thank you," he smiled weakly. "You may have saved my life."

She nodded, shrugged, with an exhausted sense that whatever she had hoped for from him, he could not give it to her. He could neither love her nor help her find May.

She stood, her knees and back creaking. She wanted to crawl somewhere and sleep for a hundred years, sleep and wake up and have all be well again. When she went to the door, he came to her and put his arms around her and held her tight. He pressed his lips to hers. They were dry and hot.

She flinched away. "You still do not see."

Still holding her tight, he stroked her face, brushed his lips against hers again. "See what?" His pupils were dark, his voice soft, seductive, as if he'd forgotten the terror of their night together already.

She held herself rigid. "When you said you brought Death here, I believe you spoke the truth. What you've done, what you're doing, is wrong."

He let her go, nodding. His face was sad and he turned from her. "Ah well, you are right, but you will only be able to see when you are truly put to the test what mad things you are willing to do to protect those you love."

She opened the door and went out.

48

The woman named Eve did not stir when the man walked in. She kept her eyes closed when he sat down next to her and stroked the tangles from her hair. Something in his voice when he said her name was familiar. It made her afraid. He was murmuring now, gentle words, *the sea is blue*. She saw the sea from the cliff tops, the way it changed colours with the light and sometimes when the clouds swelled overhead, the colour drained away.

He grazed the back of his hand across her cheek. Sometimes in the sea, there were monsters – seals that split down their spine and sloughed their skins like plums. In one story, the Finman rowed from the underwater realm in seven strokes of the oar to catch a human girl. In his sea cave, the girl became a selkie wife. But how did the story end?

Beyond the new room he'd carried her to, it rained. A storm was gathering. She could hear it creeping under the roof, rattling the windows. The fire spat and sizzled where raindrops hit the peat. The man got up and walked over to the smoking fire. She opened her eyes, watching the way he moved, careful, precise. Her arms ached and she felt as if the wound in her chest was venomous and that the venom was seeping through her body and killing her. The man knelt by the fire and stoked it. He picked up bricks of peat and piled them onto the embers and stoked again, then he straightened and turned back towards her.

"What do you want of me?"

He said nothing, staring. His eyes were burnt moons in his blurred face.

"Please let me go."

"You wish to go?" He picked something up and walked across the room. When he came close, she saw the curved blade of a knife. Eve flattened herself against the pallet. She couldn't cower any further from him. The lower half of his face split in a smile. She cried out. The sound was no more than a whimper clawing its way from her charred throat.

The knife came closer, the tip taunting her. She squeezed her eyes closed, felt a cool flick against one wrist, then the next, then her ankles. Her skin screamed with new pain. She kept her eyes tight shut, waiting for the next swipe of the blade. When she opened them, the man was gone, although she hadn't heard him leave. She turned her head to look at her left wrist, although she couldn't see much of anything in the darkness. She turned it to make sure that he hadn't cut it off. Her arm flopped off the pallet. Her wrist was loose.

She was free, every morsel of her. She had asked to go and he had cut her bonds. She must run. Her hands and feet were still numb, so she shifted herself down the pallet on her back until she reached the end. She tumbled down in a broken heap, the cold floor hard on her knees and palms. She lay for a while, just breathing, feeling pain in each bruised part. Her limbs were floppy. She had to creep across the floor, bit by bit to the door.

It was locked.

It was a long night in the cold room. She could almost hear his hollow laughter at her for thinking she was free. Each time she tried to get up, her legs shook and crumpled beneath her. So she lay on the cold floor by the fire listening to the rain crashing down on the ground outside, rubbing the numbness from her wrists, feeling the swollen flesh sting with new pain. The storm came straight over the room and the wind howled fit to break the house. She wished it would. But it just rattled until it was spent and the wind died down. Threads of light spooled through cracks in the heavy shutters. Eve slept.

When she woke, the rain had stopped and the light was cloudy. She looked around and saw her pallet, the dark shapes of shelves, the glitter of bottles propped against the walls. She looked down at her lap and saw her white smock smeared with dried blood, the bracelets of scabs on her wrists. There were bandages wound around her chest.

Had the man done this to her or had she always been this way? A tear seeped down her cheek. More fell and her ribs ached with the release of inheld coughs and sobs. She thought of the story, of how the Finman rowed from the underwater realm in seven strokes of the oar to catch a human girl. *In his sea cave, the girl becomes a selkie wife, skin roughening to fins and scales. She can never return to the human world, for her kind don't know her again.*

49

Between the big house and Granny's croft was the kirkyard. Every stone in it, be it the wall or the graves or the tiny kirk itself, had been blown sideways by winter storms.

Oona wandered between them, letting her hands skim the lichen-stained tops, thinking of the restless bones lying under her feet. They said if you laid your ear to the ground, you could hear their voices complaining about the living, always messing things up, quarrelling amongst themselves. The Minister said good folk make a quiet kirkyard, but who was truly good down to the bone? The far wall was the emptiest. It was there under the trees that the smallest stone read *Stella Scollay, devoted Mother and Wife, 1784*. She knelt down beside it.

"Everything's broken, Ma." She lay down and closed her eyes, her fingers tousling a clump of green moss. "Just as it was for you."

For a long time, she'd had a memory of Ma rocking her when she was a baby and singing *tura lura lura sheer the sheep*. Ma's face hung like a bright moon over her and she tangled her fingers in the soft, red fronds of her hair. She used to remember the song every night and it would send her to sleep. But when she asked Granny about it, Granny said her Ma had never once sung to her and didn't like to sing. It bothered her for years, thinking maybe the memory came from someone's story or hearing of someone else's mother. Her fingers stroked the green moss, stroked and stroked it like hair and she lay there for a long time thinking of the song. Whoever's memory it was, she had it now.

There was a rustling in the trees by the burn. At first she thought it was the wind kicking up, but then it sounded too loud. She opened her eyes. The light was pale gold now and thick with meadowsweet. She squinted at the darkling copse, expecting to see a crow fidgeting. A shadow moved, making twigs crack under it. No crow or cat, but broad and heavy as the man on the cliffs had been that day, hidden by the trees and watching.

It was the man with the scarred face and the hateful blue eyes, the one who was stalking Victor, the one who might have hurt May.

Oona could feel his stare from the shadows. She walked slowly along the path to show she felt no fear, tucking her hands under her folded arms to keep them from trembling. Birds sang and the sea lapped, but she heard no footsteps behind her. She couldn't look, couldn't turn back and see that hooded face. Her chest was so tight, she feared the bones of it might fuse.

At the croft, stockings and dresses and sheets hung in a droopy congregation. She stooped under them, feeling the safety of the house beckoning. If she could only get inside and into the nook bed, then nothing could hurt her. She would pull the door closed and bury her face in the blankets and sleep and sleep until a sunny morning came and the dark clouds melted away. She ducked under a clammy grey stocking.

Stuart leant in the doorway, his legs crossed casually at the ankles. "You're late, Mistress Oona. Your Granny's afeared for you."

50

Stuart looked still bigger than Oona remembered. There was only a small gap between his arm and hip that allowed her see where Granny sat staring blankly into the fire. Had *he* been the one watching her?

"I needed to wash Doctor Frankenstein's linens." She swallowed and stared at the floor, knowing he'd know she was lying and not wanting to be found out in front of Granny.

"But that's not the whole truth, is it?" Stuart smiled, though his eyes were as cold as ever. "The pair of you are...intimate...now. Is that the word for the sort of folly that befalls a maid and her Master, a dying girl and a soon-to-be-married man?"

Her heart seemed to stop for a moment and the world stopped too. She could hear herself just breathing, clinging onto life though everything she heard and thought was mad. Granny stood behind Stuart now, her eyes wide.

Stuart hooked his finger under Oona's chin and tilted her head to face him. "Have you not heard about your killer lover's other wife? Perhaps you were otherwise engaged at the Scollay place and found no time for talk?"

"What is his meaning, Oona?" Granny rubbed her hands anxiously. They sounded like dry leaves rustling.

Oona could not answer her, or Stuart. Her thoughts were too tangled. Before Victor told her about the monster, she'd been certain of Stuart's guilt, but now she did not know who she really suspected.

She took a step back and Stuart's finger fell from her chin. "I was in the kirkyard, visiting my mother."

"I am sorry." He bowed. "Since your lover has left you alone for now, why not ask me inside for a spell? We can talk like gentlefolk."

"Can we?"

He smiled wide. "It doesn't much matter what you say to me. Your Granny already made me welcome."

"I cannot prevent that, but if you don't mind, I'd like to go in, too."

"So charming, you Scollays, I've always said so." He went in ahead of her and looked around at the dresser and nook bed and half-full peat bin like a hawk coasting over a henhouse.

Oona marched after him, racking her brain for a job she must see to right away, a reason to tell him to leave. "I must get supper ready."

Granny frowned and turned to the fire as if to check that her food was still a certain fact, however the rest of life tipped and tilted. When she saw the old black iron pot the Scollays had cooked in for centuries, she nodded, seemingly reassured. "It's already done, Oona."

"Oh."

"And what will you eat today, girls?" Stuart lifted the lid of the pot and peered in.

Granny looked at him, affronted. "Cockaleekie. You're welcome to a dish if you've not eaten, Stuart."

Oona took the lid from him and put it firmly back on the pot. She stood between the two of them, hands on hips. "We mustn't spoil Stuart's supper, Granny. I'm sure Ma Flett has been cooking all day."

Stuart nodded. He went to the table by the window and sat down turning his neck from side to side as if he had a cramp. He smiled that oily smile of his and beckoned Oona over with his head. She went to the table and sat down, keeping her trembling hands folded in her lap. Between them lay a lump of cheese and a blunt-ended knife, home comforts that looked out of place with him here.

"It's a sad case, how Ma must cook for me still. The plan was that May would be doing it."

Oona shrugged, unable to keep the bitter irony from her voice. "Well that's likely the worst thing about her not being here."

His face turned from charming to cruel in an instant. "Be clever all you like, Oona. You'll be punished for it, you and your doctor friend. I'll see to that."

"Why should we be, when we've done nothing?"

"Do you have any proof of that?"

"Do you?" she snapped back. But as soon as she did, she saw how hopeless things were if it became her word against his. He was trusted and loved by everyone on the island and who was she really, to anyone here? The misfit, the dying girl. Worse now that her greatest ally was Victor.

She stared down at her lap and picked at her thumbnail. Ever since she was a child, Stuart had always seemed invincible to Oona. He was the big boy who climbed along the crags and stole puffin eggs and shot snow hares with a sling. If he lit a fire it always caught and when he told a joke everyone laughed. They all wanted him to like them, even grownups. The scrawny orphan everyone pitied, Oona had envied Stuart his swagger and ease.

Then one day she and May were playing hide and seek out at the Flett place and they heard shouting and thumping loud enough to shake the snow from the mountain and send the birds squawking into the sky. They peeked in through a window and saw Old Man Flett beating Stuart with a battledore, saw his thin back covered with thick, purple knots of scars. His Ma cowered in the corner crying and his Father just kept on hitting and hitting him until they couldn't watch any more. After that day, May took a shine to Stuart, the seed of pity sprouting into love. For her own part, Oona was wary of him. She'd seen dogs that had been beaten all their lives, knew how when they sunk their teeth in it was sudden and fierce and they were loathe to let go. The only way with a dog like that was to let it know you were giving the orders.

Oona stared Stuart in the eye. "I've searched everywhere for May. I don't know any more than you do." She spoke the words with a guilty sense that she *did* know more: the scarred man, the monster. Had he rowed May out in the Elver to further revenge himself on Victor, tipped her over the side somewhere? How could she tell Stuart she thought that? The first thing he'd do was lead a mob to the big house to finish what he'd begun at Scollay.

"I can't credit that, Oona. I believe you were jealous. May was your boon companion all those years and after all that, she was about to marry to me. I think you couldn't stand it."

Her throat pulsed, choked with anger. She thought of May's sad eyes the last time she saw her, the coin hidden in her skirts. Whatever had happened, she hadn't seemed so keen on marrying Stuart in the end. "I think she couldn't stand you. She was saving, maybe to run..."

The warmth died out of his throat and face until he was pale as whey. "That's not the reason she's gone."

Oona kept staring, forcing herself not to blink. "Then what is?"

Stuart's eyes began to water. He looked as if he might cry again, then he reached under the table and took her hand. If Victor had done that, it would have been romantic, holding onto her where Granny couldn't see. But with Stuart it was like a slug oozing over her skin.

Granny's wicker chair creaked. She turned round, crumpled, as if she'd been dozing. "Want some soup now, Stuart?"

"No, thank you Mrs Scollay. I'll be off home, soon."

"Oona? Set the table for me?"

"Yes." The bones in her hand crackled like twigs. She tried to pull herself away, but he wouldn't let go.

"You know, May was always your shadow, doing your bidding." He took her hand between his and stroked it gently. "How do you know it's not you she's gone from? Maybe she wished to be free of you."

"Or perhaps you thought she had another lover, so you killed her—"

Stuart pushed his chair back from the table. He took a step towards the door as if he was going to leave. Instead, he turned to her, hand poised and trembling level with his face. She was cornered, back flat to the wall. He grabbed up the cheese knife and stroked his thumb along the edge of the blade, his eyes on her throat.

"There's something wrong with you, you ken?" He waved the knife. Cheese crumbs fell onto the floor. "Maybe you don't have a mother or a father. Maybe you can't get a man. But you shouldn't be running round this island making trouble. Doing that's a sure way to end up in the kirkyard with your Ma. Be better for it, maybe."

"What is all this, Oona?" Granny's voice was sharp with fear.

Oona pressed her shoulders into the wall. "Nothing." The word was no more than a whisper.

Stuart leaned in closer, his spit spraying her nose and cheeks. "Now that I look at you near-to, you're blue around the lips. It's a wonder, really, that you're still dragging those bones around and causing a fuss. May told me you've had a few bad turns. I bet it wouldn't take more than a strong wind to knock you flat."

The chair by the fire scraped back slowly over the floorboards. Oona heard it, knew that Granny was getting up to come check on her and prayed for her to stay where she was. Her heart stomped and it was hard to catch her breath. "I want you...out of here."

"What did you say?" Grinning, he leaned in close.

"What's happening there?" Granny came into view behind Stuart.

Stuart held up his hand. "Nothing to fear, Mrs Scollay. I only want to hear what Oona is saying."

All she could do was sit still and listen to her own wheezing breath, feel the burning it made in her chest.

Inside, something cracked into pieces.

Stuart's face was so close, she could see the roots of his eyelashes. She wanted to push him away, but didn't have the strength. She squeezed her eyes shut, remembered peering through that window at Flett, seeing the Old Man beat Stuart's purple-scarred back, the screams and boy-tears egging the beating on. She was glad no tears came for Stuart to see and laugh at. "I think...you were the jealous one...I think...you hurt her."

"Shame you've got so much blather in you and barely a breath to say it with." Stuart ran the knife between his fingers, seeming to relish the metal's smoothness, before dropping it back on the cheese dish. "You act so prim, but you knew she was making a fool of me if anyone did. One of you so much as farted and the other knew." He cracked his knuckles. "About to be my wife and she was dancing attendance on that doctor, making eyes at him behind my back, both of you after him and me in the dark. You were just laughing about it, weren't you?"

Oona shook her head. It wouldn't do any good to try speaking, not when the veins in his temples swelled and his fists were bunched. She closed her eyes, panting for air.

"Stuart, I think you should go home now." Granny's voice had changed to its scolding tone.

"I'll be but a moment, Mrs Scollay." He sounded like his charming old self.

"Aye well, I know what you boys get like when you've had a sup."

"I've not touched a drop today."

Oona opened her eyes. Something inside her pushed her to keep fighting him if it was the last thing she did. "Could you blame her if she preferred him to you? Victor's a man of the world. And you're what? Some fisherman living on an island. Nothing. Nobody. You blame him because you're jealous of what he is. He's done nothing except save lives. He's a good man, more than you'll ever be."

"You can talk about being nobody!" Stuart reeled forward and grabbed Oona's hair by the roots. He yanked her head to the side and smashed it into the table.

Stars of pain burst out in her cheek and lip. She tasted blood.

His fingers wound tighter in her hair. He jerked her head back until she thought her neck would snap and twisted it so she was facing him. She gasped for air. He watched her the way a stoat watches a chick, black pebble eyes sliding all over. His other hand closed round her throat, fingers probing for the place to squeeze. He pulled her up close, hand pressing hard, then he flung her into the wall.

Granny's hand covered her mouth. Her eyes were rimed with tears. She took a step towards Stuart. Her paper-skinned fingers closed around his arm. "Don't you hit her again."

"Lucky I don't hit you in her stead."

"You leave us alone." Granny gripped his arm. "All I need to do is shout loud and the Minister will come running."

"Oh the Minister." Stuart laughed. "That old loon will see to me, sure as eggs."

Granny knelt at Oona's side and clutched her hand. She smoothed the hair from Oona's forehead. "You'll be right as rain in a moment."

Stuart kicked a chair and it cracked over onto its back. "You're a fool if you say so. She won't be right. She's another year at best, less if she keeps on with the doctor. His number is surely up. We'll all see to that, every one of us on this island."

"Get out." Tears streamed down Granny's cheeks.

"Look at her. She can hardly breathe."

"She's got more spirit than you'll ever ken."

Stuart made a sucking noise deep in his throat, swilled his mouth a round and spat on the floor next to Oona's head.

"I'll pay my respects at the wake."

51

It was hard to sit up straight and hot, even though the rain drove down outside. Eve slumped in the chair and let the man wrap the linen strips and pull them tight. She rested her head on her shoulder to watch him take a pin from his mouth and fasten a pale edge of bandage with it. Her skin didn't feel as much pain as it had last night.

The man laid her arm in her lap and went back to his chair and picked up one of the things he'd been fixing. She was so tired. She let her head loll down, staring at her two bandaged arms. They didn't seem like hers. The door was on the cusp of vision, almost invisible from where she sat. It was closed and locked. He made sure of that each time he slipped in and snicked the latch behind him.

When he found her crumpled by the fire, he wasn't angry. He picked her up as if he had found one of his things tumbled onto the floor, turning the broken pieces over in his hands; then the salve and linen strips and pins and him dressing the cut wrists and ankles. Sometimes he said a few words she didn't quite catch, murmuring to himself until she began to feel she wasn't there anymore. She asked him who he was, more so that she could hear her voice speaking than anything. As usual, he said nothing.

He worked by the light of a lamp on the table beside him and his back hid whatever his hands were doing. The oil in the lamp smelled strange. She saw her own hands pouring fish fat into a lamp and felt the creeping embers singe her fingertips. A man's voice spoke to her. Not this man. A different man who had been close to her. He wanted his breakfast. She could hear the familiar way he spoke to her, the tone of it, but not the words, not his voice speaking her name. Trying to remember her other name or the place she'd been in when she lit the lamp was like grabbing a trout - getting hold of its slimy skin only to feel it slip away.

With a sharp snap, the man set something down on the table. He said something weary in words she didn't understand. Then he folded his arms behind his head and leaned back in his chair, yawned and stretched.

It was night and he was usually gone by this time, sleeping somewhere while she lay awake on the mattress. For some reason, he was still in the room tonight. He sat up, ran his fingers over his eyes, turned back towards the light, squinting down at the thing on the table. When he picked it up, she could see the shadow of it turning and turning between his hands. The flickering light showed interlocking circles and long thin wires. He pinched his fingers along a wire and smoothed out a bump, pulling it tight.

Beneath the wires was a coiled circle with something like teeth. In the lamplight it glinted yellow. When the man put his finger inside it and turned it, it clicked. The man picked up a key and twisted it in the circle and set the thing down. "How is your chest?" He spoke the words without turning to look at her. His words sounded strained, as if he had to think of each one before he said it.

"Good." In truth, the skin burned there, as if someone had tried to cut her in two.

"And your wrists and ankles?"

"What's that you're making?"

He let out a small sigh that was half a laugh. "Not making. Fixing." He picked the thing up again and held it at arm's length, squinting, brought it to his face to look at up close. "Just as I fixed you. Are you strong enough to come over here and sit beside me?"

"I cannot say." She pressed her swaddled hands into the arms of the chair, trembling with the effort of pushing herself up.

She began walking slowly, swaying from side to side. The man turned to watch her clumsy movements. It was like trying to move wooden blocks fixed to her legs. With each step, she sped up until she was out of control. The table loomed close. She was going to crash. Planting her hands on the wooden edge, she came to a clumsy halt. He pulled out a chair and she tumbled into it, panting. He turned back to the table and picked up a thin metal tool.

"What is truly remarkable about living things is that they work at all." His hand was on the wire thing, but his eyes were watching her. There was a smooth, metal flap in the middle of it. He untwisted the pins that held it shut and stared inside at the metal circles, at their teeth, knitted tightly together.

"Now, let's see..."

He sat hunched over the thing for a long time. As he worked he told her strange words. *Engine. Coil. Screwdriver.* Sometimes he took her hand in his and curled it around a part and she felt the shape through her wrappings. He oiled her fingertips and ran them along cogs and wires, over teeth and sharp edges. When the light guttered and choked in the lamp, he rose and stretched and told her to rest. Crossing the room, he slipped his key in the door. She glimpsed a sliver of the world outside - a hint of red wall, a gleam of polished floor. The panel of dark wood closed behind the man and the lock clicked. His footsteps faded.

She got up and went to the door and crouched down. Her knees creaked. She winced at the ache in them. Peering through the lock she saw the red wall outside the door. There were gold flowers and birds painted on it and they shone. She sat back on her heels, thinking about the key he kept in his breast pocket. It was the secret of how to get out.

52

Granny helped Oona into the chair by the fire, the round-backed one that Grandpa had carved from a big piece of driftwood before Oona knew *driftwood* or *a chair*. Granny tucked a rug around Oona's knees and handed her a cup of ale.

"Drink that. It'll bring you round."

Oona nodded, breathing hoarsely, half in a daze. She'd never thought Stuart would do that to her. Her fingers moved to the back of her head where an egg-shaped lump felt tender to the touch. Looking down, she saw the necklace of plum bruises that adorned her throat. If he'd choked her any longer, she'd be dead.

She sipped the lukewarm ale. It stung her throat.

She only closed her eyes for a moment, but she must have fallen asleep for a long while, because she woke to find the dawn light coming through the windows. She watched Granny hobble around the room, stoking the fire and murmuring to Toby, casting the odd glance at Oona and the chair. She was never long out of it and was probably missing it.

Victor, meanwhile, would be injured and alone, quite unaware of Stuart whipping up hatred in the Smokehouse, gathering a rabble of islanders with fishhooks and torches...

She stood, wincing at the ache in her back. "I must go, Granny. I must warn the doctor."

"I'm sure Doctor Frankenstein can look after himself, all the trouble he's brought. And what about you, poorly as you are? You might run into Stuart again and then what will happen?"

"I don't think he's lying in wait for me, but in any case, I can't skulk here hiding." Oona picked up her shawl. It was still hard to breathe. "Then he'd have won."

"You're a stubborn lassie." Granny frowned. "Just like me." The last word caught in her throat. "Your shawl's tangled. Here." She straightened the worn cloth around Oona's shoulders and her hands were as frail as blossom petals. "Take care at the doctor's. You haven't known him long. Can you trust him to be a good man, as you said?"

"Aye Granny, I can." Oona opened the door and felt the morning air knock into her like a pail of ice water, purifying her.

The burn was one of two places on the island where a gathering of trees could be found. Crouched in the swaying boughs of willows were small birds hidden in bowers of green leaves. They trilled as Oona trudged down the hill with Victor's sheets and shirts in a basket on her hip. It had been a relief to go to the big house and find him in the music room just woken, bruised but otherwise unscathed, with Orpheus sitting in his lap clucking contentedly. She made sure to lock the doors and windows before she left.

Under the willows, women scrubbed their linen and sang. They were as small and grey as willie wagtails from where Oona was and she felt a rush of affection, not for any one woman, more for the thought of working beside them. Every so often a song arose as it did at harvest time when the women took their sickles to the fields. It was best to pound laundry with a song in your head. Then the burn's rattle and the rhythm of cloth on stone were more than empty noises. They were fiddle and drum for the song on your lips that drowned the sound of your life slipping off down-stream.

Oona saw an empty spot on the bank in between Joan Umbesetter and Janice of Flett. It would be good to kneel between women, safe somehow, as if Stuart and the hooded man couldn't hurt her there. She knelt and placed her basket down beside her.

Chatter tailed off. A woman's song died mid-note. Oona nodded a hello at Janice of Flett. Instead of nodding back, Janice dragged the dead weight of wet clothes into her basket, lumped them onto her hip and walked off. Frowning, Oona pulled out a sheet and plunged it into the burn's dark water.

Shivering beneath her, the water told her the reason Janice left - that black smudge round her eye. Janice probably knew her brother had done it. Edith too. Oona wished she had friends enough that they would come to her and offer comfort, sisterhood, as May would have done and as all these women would have done for May. Under the burn, the knobs of her wrists turned to hailstones.

When the sheet was sodden through, she hefted it up onto a flat stone and reached for the next. Down the bank from her, Joan rose clumsily to her knees. Oona caught her eye and smiled. Joan turned her head sharply away. From that moment until she was upright with her hamper on her hip, she kept her eyes averted. Oona stared at the slack, white twist of her neck with a sinking feeling. Janice's guilt couldn't have made Joan avoid her eyes. Some other stone had been hurled into the burn, making Janice leave, then Joan, then all of the women. One by one, they got up and flapped the water from a sheet or wrung out a shirt, folded up things for their baskets and left with their lips pursed and their necks turned. Though the birds in the branches stayed where they were and chattered on.

In the end, only Bridget was left washing the rags for her bundle, quite unaffected by whatever was in the air. They knelt and scrubbed and pounded in silence, each woman keeping her own reflection company. Oona drowned another sheet in the icy current and her lopsided self with its black eye and swollen lip faded from view. The world was nothing but a billowing stretch of cloth and the floating red berries of her knuckles, then up and out and today, a certain pleasure felt from pounding cloth on rock. Squinting her eyes, she could see Stuart's face thumping onto the flat stone, his look of surprise.

She was reaching for the last sheet in the basket when she felt breath on her cheek and saw knobbledy feet being dangled into the burn.

"I've washed all the clouts for my wee'un."

Oona smiled. "Now he'll be neat as a new pin."

"Aye." Bridget cradled the air against her breast, a soppy look in her eyes. "I ken. I ken."

"What do you ken?"

"That all the folks say he's not real."

Oona felt a twinge of guilt. She'd said the same things about Bridget as everyone else. For the first time, she wished she hadn't. She pulled a scrunched shirt from the basket and plunged it into the burn.

"I ken. I ken. I ken he's not real."

Oona looked more closely at Bridget's face than usual, saw the spider veins on her cheeks and the down of fair hair that fringed her forehead. Bridget stopped smiling and her eyes grew clear. When she leaned close to Oona, there was a tender look in them. Her hand hovered near Oona's bruised throat, but when Oona blinked, it fluttered away.

"You can't see what will be."

Oona blinked hard. "No one can."

"No. No, you're right. It's better being honest than being loved."

Bridget got up, her movements as agile as a hare's. Her hand rested on Oona's neck and then it was gone and she was away into the valley, singing out of tune. Oona rubbed her throat, not knowing why Bridget's words had made her heart ache. She looked back down at the shirt, blooming in the water like an ungainly flower - and there in the centre, a ragged red mark. Held to the light, it looked like blood.

53

Oona stood in the big house kitchen with her back to the stove, her fingers tingling from the heat flowing too quickly into them. Unless she took care, she'd grow chilblains again.

The still-damp shirt lay plastered to the back of a chair, stain-down. Outside the window, linens hung on the line threw flickering shapes that reminded her of puppet figures made from hands and a candle to entertain children. In their shadows flickered an image of May's face that last time. The dark eyes gazed at Oona sadly before bleeding into Victor's drawing of the woman tied by her wrists. A sheet flapped in the wind and the picture smashed. It was now a black vision of Stuart's hands choking her while the scarred man at the window watched, bent on revenge.

Maybe this was how Bridget felt, flooded by pictures that wouldn't come clear.

A board creaked upstairs. Oona straightened. She grabbed up the shirt and swung into the dark hallway with its mothball scent and ticking clock, then took the stairs two at a time.

Victor stood at the top of the stairs, elegantly coiffed and crisply dressed, poised to descend.

She held the shirt up to him, unfolding it to reveal the rust red mark. "I was washing your clothes and I found this."

He took the shirt from her and leant on the bannister, peering down through his silver eyes as he turned the damp cloth in his hands. Then he handed back the shirt and took out a handkerchief. She remembered his lips on hers and wished she hadn't shown him the stain.

Victor blew his nose, folded the handkerchief and put it back in his pocket. "You wanted to ask me about this…*blood?*" His eyebrow flew up at the last word.

"I want to know how it happened." She listened to her own voice, so suspicious and bitter these days.

His eyes moving from her cheek to her swollen lip, her necklace of bruises. "Were you not with me the other day when I was beaten bloody?" He laughed his boyish laugh.

"Yes, but you weren't wearing this shirt."

"I changed into it after I dressed my wounds and burned the other that was ruined." He smiled wryly. "That is an old one given to me by my cousin Eliz..." His eyes blurred. He looked out of the window, cleared his throat. "Burn it also if you wish, but don't kill yourself trying to clean it."

She nodded and turned away, feeling the heat prickle along the nape of her neck. He'd been kind, considering.

"Wait, I have something to show you."

She stopped, the prickle turning to a shiver.

"Do you not wish to view my little invention?"

In the music room, the noon sun painted gold squares over the white walls. It was tidy for once and even the floor around the billiard table was free of scrawled papers. Orpheus strutted across the floor, chasing the sunlight, a dazed look in his red eyes. He barely seemed to notice her. Victor crossed the Persian rug, beckoning to her to follow.

Long limbed and angular, a doe-hare lay on a board on the writing desk. As Oona came near to it, she saw that the doe's dark-lashed eyes were half open. Her body was stretched apart, slit along the belly. Though Oona was as used to dressing game as the next girl, the sight of the doe's guts pinned out across the board made her wince. There were wires tangled with the veins of the small heart, cogs and a circular piece of metal serrated inside, with what looked like teeth gripping the spine. In the centre of the metal contraption was a smooth, metal flap. Victor untwisted the pins that held it shut and stared inside at the metal circles, at their teeth, knitted tightly together in the centre of the doe's entrails.

"I have struggled with some means to begin things...to find the spark that animates flesh! It is in nature, in lightning. It's what has made this place so fruitful, all the storms from the sea, all that electricity filling the air. But even here there are calm days when there is nothing... Well, I have tinkered and pondered and stumbled upon a way of making bodies become their own source of energy, their own source of power. I have harnessed the lightning within the body, Oona."

Oona looked at Victor's face so that she didn't have to see the pitiful thing anymore, undignified now as any creature could be. He seemed so pleased with himself, as if all his tortured tale of the monster stalking him was no more than some act he believed was expected of him, as if he had no conscience at all. "And why do you need all this? So that you can keep killing animals and turning them into toys?"

He laughed and it chilled her now. "I need it...to keep a promise. That is all. Anyway, enough. Observing the living tells as much as any study of the dead ever does. Sometimes the living can be so instructive." He was staring at her chest, unashamedly. "May I?"

"What?" She looked down, expecting to see that some moth had landed on her bodice for him to pin.

He reached out and pressed his hand over her heart. "Do you ever wonder how long it will keep working for?"

She stood still, letting him touch her. She wanted to move, but could not. "Yes." Her voice sounded defeated.

"It must trouble you, the uncertainty... your heart, May vanishing, not knowing..."

She stared into his eyes, the silver of knife blades. Was he toying with her? He was so composed and impenetrable, it was impossible to tell.

"I'm sure you've searched, Oona, but have you asked the right questions? Who was the last person to see her, that you know of?"

She stared sideways at his smooth face that might have been handsome had the lines of thought not etched themselves into it. "I think it must be Old Cormick, the ferryman who lives in that shack by the sea."

Victor's hand dropped. He drew his chair back from the desk and sat down, as if drawn there by magic, as if he couldn't stay away from his ghoulish work. "And did he tell you all you needed to know?"

She shrugged. "He's always drunk and full of nonsense."

Victor looked over his shoulder at her, his hands busy with a copper twist of wire that coiled between the hare's neck and the lever-like knob on the flap. "Doesn't it seem suspicious," hands twisting, smoothing as he spoke, "that he had a stocking so conveniently tucked away to accuse me?"

The doe's ears twitched and her paw grabbed the air. Oona stepped back, her heart knocking into her aching ribs. "She's alive." She didn't know why she was surprised. It was the way of things here. Dead. Alive. Alive. Dead. It was just that she hadn't seen something spring to life with its entrails hanging out before.

Victor flicked the lever on the rusted box and something left the air, like a song ending. The hare stopped moving. "She's not, as it happens, but a touch more and she might cross back over the line."

"The line to where?"

He smiled back at her, his hand hovering over the box. "The land of the living."

54

The man slipped his arm through Eve's and they began to walk. In the flickering dark, the objects in the room were ghostly versions of their daylight selves. He was talking to her about birds and the sky and things outside the room but she was hardly listening, thinking instead of the names of things – quill and manuscript, pliers and screws, the door, the keyhole, the key. She murmured the words under her breath.

"Eve – stop – you move... too fast." He let go of her arm, pressing his hand to his ribs the way she had when he first made her walk.

"I am sorry." She almost meant it, but all the time, her heart, her mind, were racing. She must move again.

"You are far stronger than an ordinary woman. You have the heart of a wolf. It will endure long past the time I've turned to dust." He caught her wrist. "You're...perfect..."

Her bandaged fingers moved to her face, rough threads of gauze tickling her cheeks and eyelids. "What do I look like?"

"Soon you may look in the glass and see for yourself." He straightened and smiled his mysterious smile.

When the clock chimed midnight, he left her to bend to his work. She felt the creak of the door, the panting breaths of the key in the lock. She hated him then, for locking her in once more. She wanted to pound the door, to smash her fist through it and step straight onto the other side, to stride down the unknown hallway and be free.

But she could not picture either what lay beyond the room or what she would live on if she left it. Each day, he brought her soup and bread and beer to drink. He carried in peat and kept the fire burning. He unwrapped the pale tongues of her bindings and checked underneath to see that she was well. If she left, there would be nobody to do these things for her.

For a long time, she stared at red haloes of burning peat. The smoke curling up from it changed into the foam of a burn, the lick of a wave on the sea, the violet flowers of hill heather. There were other pictures, too: blurred faces and eyes intent with feeling, lips moving, although she couldn't hear the words. She got up, paced the room. There were people out there who belonged to her. She didn't know who they were or where they lived, but they might be looking for her at this very moment. She went from one table to the next, trailing her muffled hands over the contraption of wires and teeth.

On the table beside it was a dead mouse, soft muzzle slightly agape around the twin prongs of yellowed teeth. Its furry hide was split down the belly and pinned to the board beneath it. The tangled grey string inside it was hardening, although she couldn't smell it, only the sour whisky stench of the liquid the man painted over it. Cradled in the basket of its ribs was a small pink pearl that he had said was the mouse's heart.

She felt her chest ache and looked down to see her clumsy hand pressed to a painful place in the middle of her breastbone. It drummed her fingers, wild and fast, full of desire to love, to know. Her hand moved downwards like a thing with a will of its own, fumbling across the gleaming tools that surrounded the mouse. Pins. Clippers. A slender knife that slid easily between the layers of white gauze and pressed coolly into her skin.

Eve went to the door and knelt down before it as if she wanted to pray. She pushed the knife into the lock, jiggling it back and forth, listening for some tell-tale click within the door. She had some memory, blurred as a dream, of a girl's hands doing just this, of a door opening onto the secrets of a hidden room. If only she'd looked more closely, remembered more clearly, then she would know the deft twist that would set her free. But her fingers were clumsy and the knife slipped about between layers of gauze and her sweat-greased skin.

She was just about to give up on the thing when she heard the rasp of metal grinding metal. She tried the handle. The door didn't open. She attempted to turn it in the other direction, unable to remember which way it went. This time the handle seemed to push back at her. It wouldn't move. She pressed her ear to the door and, on the other side, heard breathing.

55

With a decanter of whisky tucked inside her shawl, Oona stole past the kirk, looking to one side then the other like a ne'er-do-well. She couldn't hear anyone, but she had the feeling that the herringbone rows of dead folk tucked into the ground judged what she did. Thieving from the big house, creeping out while Granny slept had made her feel she had become her own mistress at last. She was bad and bold. May would be proud. Her parents, though, must watch from under their mossy stones and count themselves blessed they'd never lived to see such a daughter grow tall.

Drawing her shawl tighter, she skidded over the tumble of fat stones that led to the red rock beach. Cormick's shack crouched in the middle distance, no smoke or light in it. He'd be mad as a beaten dog and curse when he saw her, supposing he was even there. She caught herself hoping he would be in his boat or passed out somewhere, so that she wouldn't have to be brave, but then she glimpsed a slight, dark girl sitting on a boulder, chewing her hair and humming. May. Her sad eyes said *find me*.

Through the bone-yard of boats, the thought of that girl kept her upright and moving forward. However insane he might be underneath his charm, Victor was right about one thing: Cormick had done wrong or at the very least seen wrong done. Perhaps he'd seen enough to help her find what had happened to May. The one thing she knew about him was that he loved whisky, so she'd stolen a crystal decanter from the sideboard in the music room, right from under Victor's nose.

The waves beat the beach in time with her off-kilter heart. It was as if her feelings were driving saltwater needles into the rocks' grazed knees. Their fury buffeted her along the sliver of red, through the midden's crunch of shells to the shack door. She stood facing the grey curtain, shivering at the thought of what lay beyond before riving the sodden door aside and walking into the darkness.

Cormick sat at his small table by the remains of a fire. His lap was draped with a tangle of net. He looked up nervously when Oona came in, then his eyes flitted back to the hemp in his hands.

"I'm busy." It sounded as if a chunk of herring was caught in his throat.

The roomed smelled sourer than before, felt colder, as if Death had come calling of late.

"I brought something for you." Oona took the decanter from under her shawl. "To say sorry for the other day." She went to the table and placed it there. A splash of whisky spilled past the crystal lip and dribbled over her fingers.

His haunted eyes were on her hand now. He never looked at her, just sat there, licking his lips. She could see the fish knife glinting in his lap, the cords of tension in his sinewy hands as he gripped the broken net. She took a step back, wiping her hand on her shawl. The scent of whisky drenched the room, replacing sour air with heady sweetness. Cormick's hand closed round the decanter. He dragged it towards him like a fisherman reeling in a pike. When it was near enough, he grabbed its throat and pressed the crystal mouth against his mouth, not swallowing, just letting the drink drip down.

Oona felt for the windowsill behind her. She rested on it, poised to run if he came too close with the knife again. "That day I came here, you said May had run off, but Stuart found her stocking hidden in your creel."

Not seeming to hear her, he kept the bottle pressed to his lips, Adam's apple bobbing as he drank.

Anger jabbed Oona forward. "Cormick, you were the last to see her, weren't you?"

He banged the decanter down on the table and dragged his sleeve over his mouth. His eyes were wet, his cheeks flushed. "I'll sing you a merry tune," he thumped the table, "about a wee lass in a boat."

"I don't want a song. I just want—"

"May!" Cormick lurched up and reeled across the room to her until they were nose to nose and she could see nothing but his cheek veins, smell nothing but his whisky reek. "Everyone wants May, don't them? Rotten-gut husband, aw-e-aw doctor, poor, wee, meddling you!" He grabbed her shoulders. "I'm sick of folk coming here spying." He shook her. "Sick, d'you hear?"

She wanted to go somewhere quiet and clean and lie down. She pulled herself away from him and slumped back onto the windowsill. "I only want to find her and no-one…" Her heart tapped out of time against her ribs. She pressed her hand to it. It was growing bigger and soon it would fill the whole space inside and choke her.

She closed her eyes and gulped down a mouthful of bile. It would be bad to fall down here.

"You look pale, girl. Are you sickly?" His voice was different when he said it, almost kind.

She kept her eyes closed. "I'm dying."

It was strange to hear the words out loud. She almost laughed because they sounded so stupid. To be alive one moment, and then... Cormick said nothing. For a while she was alone in the darkness of her own head, listening to the waves crash down, feeling her heart slow. She'd been so afraid of everything and now she knew there was no reason to be. It would all be over soon. She heard him cross the room and pick up the bottle again. She was probably the only one in his list who had sunk so low as to bribe him. A thought struck her and her eyes flew open.

"Do you mean the doctor from the big house? Was *he* here?"

Cormick swallowed a mouthful and nodded. "I'll tell you something." He picked up his knife and held it between his hands, pressing the point into his finger. "Because you said that you're dying." Their eyes met. "I am too. Come sit before you fall over."

Oona slowly got up and moved across the room to him, her eyes on the knife in his hands, and yet not caring somehow. She sat, thinking of May with her lost face and the coin sewn in her skirt hem.

"Did you give her passage to Hamnavoe?"

He shook his head and took another drink. "She gave me coin for her fare, said she needed to go quick. Sun was sinking, mind. We had to wait for him first, though, that was coming with her."

Wait for him. The charcoal sketch of the naked woman on the table flickered in front of Oona's eyes. The doctor might be betrothed, but it hadn't stopped him from kissing Oona. Maybe Stuart was right about May's betrayal.

"She was waiting for Victor."

Cormick shrugged. "She never would say. We stood and the clouds drew down some and I said, *it's a foul night lass.* But she...she wanted to wait and wait and wait and wait. I came in here so thirsty and when I got back to the beach she was laid there..."

Oona pressed her hands to her eyes. "No."

"Blood all over and *him* stood over her."

"Oh God. May." She rubbed her fingers over the raw, bruised flesh of her face. "No."

"Said I could keep the coin, buy myself a whole crate of whisky, long as I didn't tell what I saw him do to his wee wifey. Told me to put her in the boat, row row row her out into the bay. Broke the hull. Folk'd think she drowned. Left me to it. I couldn't. Just sat there. Held her bonny head. Watched her breathe. There was blood in her hair and I couldn't—"

"Watched her breathe?" The words were like Victor's machine, its small sparks bringing life. Oona dropped her hands and looked into Cormick's face, afraid to ask for more.

He took a long drink. "That doctor came down."

The spark flashed into lightning. "May *was* waiting for him."

Cormick stared at his hands as if he could still see blood on them. "Remember when you came to look at the kittens? Boots remembers it."

She took hold of his arm. "What did the doctor do?"

"Gave me coins, so many coins. Shinier than Stuart's. Said take the Elver out into the bay and scupper it, just like Stuart said. Lifted May up, said he'd help her. I did what he said. I took my boat out and I broke her." He put his face in his hands and his shoulders shook. "She was so bonny."

Cogs whirred, filling her flesh with new life. "Did the doctor take her to the big house?" This was why Victor had pushed her towards Cormick, so she would find out the good he had done.

"She loved those kittens and I loved her." His eyes were soft.

For the first time Oona was certain what had happened that day with the kittens, how Cormick had ruined May. He knew it, too, that what he'd done had come to this. She pressed her hand to her mouth and ran out.

On the beach, the crabs came, their stiff bodies inching sidelong over rocks like bloody hair. Their mouths frothed bubbles. Small crab shrieks she couldn't hear. She ran through the midden, crunching shells underfoot and for once, not caring if she stepped on living things. Somewhere along this stretch of bleak rock, May had lain, only just alive. The gulls had circled over her, crying hungrily at the scent of her hurt. Oona couldn't look or think about where it had been, or how Stuart had done it. Or why Victor hadn't told her directly what he had done, why she felt certain she shouldn't ask.

She reeled into the boulders blindly, hands and feet slipping on slimy strands. Her back ached and she felt the salt chill of night drawing in. On the last boulder, she stopped and looked up at the cliff top where the big house crouched, hiding everything she loved most in life, taking her world for itself.

56

Oona crept through the kitchen door, cocking her head and listening. In the hallway she was glad of the clock's ticking, stepping in time with its metal teeth so that she might go stealthily up the stairs. Around her wrist hung the bracelet of keys. She clutched them in her sweaty palm to stop their tongues. If she and Victor could not speak honestly to each other, she must to find the truth another way.

On the upstairs landing, she stopped and looked along the hallway. It went in two directions – the gallery of birds and the master bedroom. Glancing towards the music room, she saw no sign of Victor and heard none either. His door was closed. He would be twisting wires together in there, stitching flesh. The guest wing might have been her first guess as to where May was hidden away, or the oubliette or the attic, but she'd cleaned them all top to bottom and there was no nook, however small, she hadn't peeked inside. That left the room next to the master suite. As soon as she took a step towards its door, she remembered hearing a noise coming from it the other day, the way she couldn't open it. It was the room he'd said didn't need cleaning. There must be a reason for that.

Oona tiptoed up to the door and pressed her ear to it, listening with every grain of her being. All she heard was the tide ebbing inside her. The pot bubbled no more. She squeezed her eyes shut, thinking of May in her bloody dress, May waking, trapped and afraid, the woman in Victor's drawings, the hand on the shore, the hare pinned to the board.

There had to be a key. May always kept spares lying around. And Victor would have one too. Now was the moment to go to his room and look. If he was in there, she would say she'd come for his sheets. Crossing the hallway, she clenched her fists and willed herself to be as stone.

Victor's door creaked open beneath her trembling hand. The room was empty and tidier than usual. The bed looked as though it hadn't been slept in. She could search for the key. Her heart kicked up a gallop at the thought. The desk was clear of papers now, holding only an inkwell and quill, a few stray shreds of parchment.

She opened the long, curved drawer in the middle first. It was lined with a rough cut of flowered wallpaper and there was a letter opener and a scrawled note in a foreign language. She lifted the paper lining and peeked under it. Nothing but a dead woodlouse, legs in the air. She did the same with the other drawers – all empty. Next, the valise.

He that passeth by, and meddleth with strife belonging not to him, is like one that taketh a dog by the ears. That was what they would say in the kirk if they knew what she was about, but this was for May.

Victor's clothes were stuffed willy-nilly into the valise, stained with all sorts of things she didn't wish to think about. She almost cut her hand on a knife that was wrapped in a shirt, its edge hair-fine. She dumped the rest out on the bed, scrabbling through rolls of paper and notebooks, soap, brush and straight razor. There was no key, so she stuffed everything back in as near as she could to the jumble she'd found them in. She ran her hands over the lintels of the doors, looked under the bed and rug and finally sat down on the bed, closed the valise with a snap and admitted defeat.

The moon outside the window lit the kitchen. Should she leave now and admit defeat after all this? Maybe tomorrow... She stared at the cod she'd left on the chopping board for the morning. It seemed to watch her, mocking her with its gold-black eye. *You're just so weak and miserable.*

She picked up the cleaver and chopped the cod's head off, then ran her thumb along the blade, gathering shreds of raw white flesh and a dribble of watery fish-blood. The anger drained out of her and she felt tired and thirsty and drained. She put down the knife and walked into the pantry for the jug of beer she kept there.

In the dark, she rooted around, hands fumbling over big bags of flour and oats, a tub of lard. Her fingertip caught on something sharp. She winced and sucked on it, looking between two boxes to see some rusty nails driven into the wood at the back of the shelf. A ball of string hung from one, a loop of washing line from the next and from the third a bracelet of keys, bigger than the others.

She wanted to kiss May for hiding them so carefully, as if she had known Oona would find them here. She slipped them over her wrist and scurried upstairs, not bothering to take her apron off, her mind fixed on that door, a lump in her throat like a round pebble from the beach. She got up to the library and knelt down, glancing down the hallway to see if he'd sneaked back in without her noticing, but wherever he was he must be taking his time for she did not see him.

She pressed her ear to the door and listened, heard nothing, tried the first key. It didn't fit. Another slid in but got half stuck, so that she panicked and twisted it about and thought it would be jammed in there for good. When she finally jiggled that one out, there were some too small and others too big, until she was down to two keys. One had a big, square tongue with a cross cut out of it and the other was slender with a bare smidge of a gap-tooth.

"One of you had better work," she told the gap-toothed key as she tried it.

It went in smoothly, turning neatly to the side. She heard the lock's belly click and release the door and her heart sang. Her hand trembled on the handle, thinking of May holding her hand through gold wheat fields like the Red Sea parting before them, May braiding daisies into her hair and saying they were jewels. The door creaked open like a door that's not been used much. The room was small and dark and smelled like scrubbed floors and old whisky. Dust motes danced in the light that spilled between the curtains. When Oona got close to them, she realised they were flies.

She held her hand over her nose and mouth. There were dark patches on the floor, dribbles and spots and pools of spilled something leading up to a curtain that hid one half of the room. On the table next to it was a cup of water, a thread and needle, a long knife. Next to the bed sat a glass cylinder with coils of paper inside. The coils went up and down and when they did, they made a wheezing sound like noisy breathing. Tubes ran from the glass case and between the folds of the curtain.

She drew the curtain back. Behind it was a bed covered with rumpled white sheets, as if someone had hastily made it. The tube disappeared under the sheets. Oona ran her fingers along it.

A fly landed on her cheek and she brushed it away. There was a gasp from under the sheet. Oona stumbled back, tangled in the curtain. Something jerked under the sheet and there was another gasp. The noise was strange, inhuman. Hardly able to breathe, she reached for the top of the sheet and slowly drew it back.

What she saw made her fall to her knees.

For a moment she just crouched there, listening to the wheeze of the machine, praying that the thing on the bed would stay where it was. She turned around on her hands and knees like a child. Each part of her shook too hard to move forward. She was a block of ice, heavy and cold. Her fingertips were red. She crawled forward numbly, holding her breath. When she reached the door, she got hold of the handle and pulled herself up on shaking legs. In the hallway, a face turned and stared. Her eyes came into focus and she saw Victor.

Then she was running down the hallway, past Victor who shouted something angry-sounding, flying downstairs on legs she couldn't feel, out of the house, to the sea.

Footsteps thudded behind her on the grass, heavy ones. Her head was light as air and it was hard to force it to turn. She thought she would see Victor, but instead it was a tall figure wearing a hooded sealskin. She could not see his features, only his blue eyes staring at her, the yellowish tint of his skin and the long, white scar. He was like a Finman with his strange-coloured skin, running in long, heavy strides. She looked ahead of her and saw the beach stretched in a silver line like the haft of a key. The sea bit at it. She could run down there and run and run until she fell down, but there was nowhere to hide from the man.

57

The red rock beach was in sight. As she slipped and slid over the boulders, Oona glimpsed Cormick tipping out a pail of brown water. He saw her and stared, his hand shading his eyes, then he shrank back into his shack. The world knew she was in trouble and was deserting her.

Behind her, it had fallen quiet. She looked over her shoulder and saw nothing but kittiwakes brooding their eggs in clefts in the cliff. Out in the firth, the dawn was breaking. A gull circled and landed on the water, its blood-tipped beak locked round a squirming fish. The way it writhed echoed the body in the big house. When Oona looked under the sheet, something had looked back at her. It had May's hair and skin, but the eyes were dead, as if May had been in there once and had gone. No. It wasn't May at all.

Boots crunched on the loose stones at the top of the cliff. The man was gaining on her. Sucking in air, she ran faster, heart punching ribs and always that fourth beat awry. Someone had thrust a fire iron between her shoulder-blades. It was hard to breathe. She stumbled between the last two rocks, where the King of the Finmen had once sat on the gold throne of Rasteal, pitched forward, hands gripping the side of a small, blue boat with an oar bobbing in it, as if God had put it there.

His heavy feet slapped the wet rocks, slipping around. Fear turned to strength and she dragged the boat over the sand where heat rose in mazy ripples, warping the tangle of weed-crusted fishing nets Cormick left lying around. The prow hit the water with a slap, slipped in, floated, smooth as an oiled lock. She staggered with it for a few steps and tumbled in. Grey water soaked her skirts. The old tub needed bailing out. No time.

Picking up the oar, she saw May sitting spread-legged on the seat and her perched on the other side, their hands guiding each stroke of the oars in unison, laughing. Rowing out into the dark firth, free.

The man stood on the cusp of the beach. A gust blew his hood back, showing a head smooth as an egg. He went from boat to boat, peering down at the hulls, hunting for an oar. She plunged hers into the water, surprised at its weight. Surely oars weren't always so heavy. She was pushing and pulling, but rowing alone she was only a few boat-lengths from the beach and now the man was heaving at the prow of a red boat, dragging it over the sand like a dandelion seed.

Cormick ran out, his mouth open, words lost in the wind. The man didn't look at him. His dark hollows of eyes were fixed on Oona, his mouth set in a deep frown. With his spray-wet sealskin, he was just like the Finman in the stories, the one that rowed from under the sea in seven strokes of the oar and caught a human girl.

Oona's hands were numb. The pain in her back had gone. Above her, clouds parted. The sun had half risen. The sea changed from black to deep blue. It was going to be fair, the kind of day when young folk would loll on the cliffs looking out at the silver scythe of bay that held the green hills close. The women would go slowly, singing, to pound clouts in the burn and would take their time pegging out shirts. The men would drag their fish-full boats carelessly inland and stroll to the Smokehouse for ale. They'd be carefree because they didn't know that in one dark room of the big house May lay on a bed and wasn't May any more.

They were a long way from the shore when the scarred man pulled his oars in and sat still. Oona rowed a few fast strokes in wonderment, her arms loose, like husk peeling off from a seed. The man had given up. *It's a short way now to Hamnavoe. She's free! On the mainland she'll find a bailiff. She'll sit in the sun and dry out her sodden dress.* Her dress was so wet, even the bodice and sleeves. The wet made it tighter, squeezing the air from her. An ice shard plunged into her back. Her fingers were numb. The oar fell from her.

She leaned after it. The boat dipped low. The oar rolled against her fingertips, slid further away. A wave slapped her face. Wood groaned underneath. She fell into the water, kicked against the boat, paddling the way Toby did when they were out on the beach. But she couldn't move well for the band round her chest. It was happening. Her heart's cogs stopping. Her life's sand running down. She scrabbled. Her breath hurt. The boat slipped away. Her head went down. She was going to die. She bobbed up, mouth full, eyes burning. The man stepped out of the boat.

She went under. The water was so blue. Sunshine, silver-white, above her. The kind of day when women take their time. The sun soft as a kiss. Her chest on ice. Swallowing salt. Granny said *don't wade past your knees – a finman will catch you!* May held her hand, screaming at the waves.

She was dying.

Her chest sings. The sea is sapphires and silver. A selkie swims up to her with green weed snarled in her dark hair. Under the sea, girls become selkie wives, soft skin roughening to fins and scales. They can never return to the human world, for their kind don't know them again. When the selkie comes close, she smiles and Oona knows everything will be alright, because it's May and her arms are open wide.

58

Something sank inside Eve, a beast giving into a riptide. The door opened slowly. The grey-eyed man stood, hands in pockets. His face was cut into squares with knives of moon. Eve clenched her hand, pushing the penknife back inside her gauze windings. The tip bit into her and she prayed that it wouldn't bleed much. She must distract him before the bright red blooming on the bandage gave her secret away.

"Do you have something hidden in your pockets?" She moved her face in what she hoped was a coy smile.

He stepped forward, forcing her back. "I was nearly ready to lay my head down when I had an idea." He laughed, closed the door behind him and turned the key.

"You mean the mouse?"

Shaking his head, he walked over to the machine and drew from his pocket a pointed piece of metal. With great delicacy, he fitted it into a screw in the middle of the spine. He turned the tool round a few times. There was a crack like breaking bones. He took hold of the device and pulled sharply. The two halves came apart, a single copper wire the only thing that held it together. He picked up his pincers and with a small snip the thing was broken.

"In order to make something work properly... sometimes you have to take it apart." He was still hunched over the thing, squinting, the tool poised as if the cogs might whir into motion without him willing it. But it was just scrap. He turned to her. "Now, off with your gown."

She looked at the tools still clenched in his hands, then past him at the tangle of wires. His eyes followed hers and he laid down the pincers, smiling. "I'm only going to examine you, Eve. It won't hurt."

She thought of how strong she was, how he couldn't keep pace with her now, of the way her heart galloped. She thought of the knife sticking in her fingertips, how easily it sliced. She looked at the shuttered window and wished she could see outside. But she couldn't imagine it and she was afraid of the world outside.

Gulping back the sour taste in her throat, she lifted the hem of the loose white gown and pulled it up. Here and there, it caught on her bandaged body and when she got it around her head, the rough cloth jammed on her elbows. Her clumsy hands tugged and twisted, palms sweaty. She was a fish in a net until the man's hands untangled the knot and soothed her.

When he'd laid the gown aside, he knelt in front of her and took her foot onto his lap. He unpicked a pin from the gauze around her toes and stuck it between his lips. The furthest edge of her cocoon unfurled in his hand. Gathering more pins in his mouth, he slowly unwrapped her, moving along her foot and upwards, revealing her ankle and calf. Every inch of the pale skin was new to her and she watched him with an excited flutter.

When his hands climbed to her thigh, she knew why she'd been afraid – there the skin puckered like lips bound in silence. It was coarsely stitched. She closed her eyes. She was afraid to breathe as his hands freed her hips and waist, paused at her breasts. He was standing now and she could feel the warmth of his steady breaths when he unpinned her wrist and unravelled the last of the gauze. She opened her eyes. He was so close to her, his eyes strangely blurred as if he'd just woken. He wetted his lips.

"I must check the rest. Keep still."

His hand skidded up her thigh. His touch was rough between her legs. His eyes met hers, the gaze intent and the curve of his lips cruel. He jabbed his fingers inside her. It burned. She felt something break, heard something snap, like the back of the metal beast. For a long time, his hand moved against her, breath quick, brow slick with sweat. After a while, his hand dropped from her. He stood and drew out a handkerchief and wiped the blood from his fingers.

59

Between her legs, the thing he'd done to her felt raw. Gingerly, she parted her thighs and peered down at the coil of coppery hair between them. Her eyes were drawn to black stitches running between fair, freckled skin and a darker area. The grain of her skin changed at the seam, downy hairs becoming long, fine ones that gleamed gold. She was a stocking darned with the wrong wool. Dark blood mottled the patchwork. She brushed her fingers over it, feeling their tenderness now they were free from the gauze. The blood had dried. Four bruises ripened on the top of each thigh. She fitted her hands over them, felt the rest – the puckered flesh between her breasts, the lurid skin puffed up between black stitches. A scream was building inside her, but she hardly dared breathe.

In a moment he'd return. Meantime, the door was locked again and she was a prisoner still. With a sigh, she rose and went to the table to look at the roll of red cloth he had left on the table for her. In the light of the taper that burned from the wall, Eve spread out the softly shining cloth and found the slippers nestled inside the dress. Something else fell out - a string of dark gems like drops of blood.

She emptied the shoes and jewels onto the table, ruched up the sides of the dress and slipped it over her head, relishing the fabric's cool slither. Smoothing the gown against her breasts and hips and turning in the candlelight, she saw how it shaped itself to her body. But the slippers pinched. Her feet were rough and broad and she had to squeeze them and pat them as if she was shoeing a horse.

When she'd dressed, she looked at the other thing the man had left - a square thing that gleamed. It made her think of the sea at night when the moon is on it, a pool of silver light. It drew her to it as the moon draws the tides, her heavy limbs inching towards the light.

In her mind's eye she saw moths fluttering at candles, spinning around in dizzy circles, their bumbling wings an ungainly echo of flame's golden dance. She was face to face with the light, with a girl who had pale, freckled skin and wild, red hair. Her eyes were large, the whites yellow in colour. Behind her ear, the ghostly skin puckered around black stitches. It looked like a bad cut. Eve stepped back. The girl's face shrank. Eve hugged herself and took a wary step forwards.

The girl's face grew, the skin between her eyes knitting together, the lips tight and frowning. The skin under her eyes was bruised, but there was something in their look that was familiar, in the whole face. It was like looking at the backs of her hands. She glanced down at the raw knuckles, the freckles, the bloodstained fingertips. She reached for the square of light until her fingers touched other, cool fingers.

Now there was a dark hand in front of the face, reaching out to touch her in turn. She flattened her own hand against it. The two fitted. She leaned in close to kiss the face. The girl's lips were cold and smooth. Eve fell back, her head fuzzy with that old fury, the gathering storm. She raised her fist, drew it back, forced it towards the light. A dark hand blotted out the face. The square smashed. The face burst into pieces. Her hand burned and bled.

The lock clicked and the door creaked open. The man held out his hand, "Come."

She faltered, remembering the sting of his fingers. She glared at the broken square, stained red. "I killed that girl…"

The man smiled. "Shame. She was rather lovely, I thought."

Eve shrugged. "She looked sick so I ended her pain."

He took a step towards her, "Do you not recognize that girl in the mirror? That's you, Eve." He rested his hand on the scar between her breasts. "Your heart is special. Did you know that?" He rested his face on her chest, pressed his ear to her skin. "Listen. It beats beneath your breastbone like a wolf's heart. It was so broken, I never believed it would work." His lips slid over her skin, caressing the fused flesh. She rubbed her bloody hand over his fair hair, down the slender nape of his neck.

It looked so fragile.

They left the room and Eve's eyes darted around at new things, ticking, flickering things, red and pale, furred and smooth. With her newly bandaged hand, she gripped the man's arm until he muttered something and peeled her fingers away. They came to a big room with a long table. Plates and glasses and knives and forks and spoons were set on it. As they walked along the length of it, Eve had a dreamy memory of rubbing beeswax into the top of a table like this and teetering on top of it to dust the glass pendants of the light. At the end of the table, they stopped and he drew back a chair, gestured for Eve to sit.

She obeyed, shivering. "Why are we here?"

"I want you to meet someone. It's a sad day, but also a happy one, so let us toast." He lifted the stopper from a decanter and poured two glasses. He handed her one.

She looked down, unsure. She was thirsty, but the red liquid smelled sour.

He clinked his glass against hers and sipped. "You're promised to an acquaintance of mine."

She choked on a mouthful of sour stuff. It ran down her chin. She stared at him, hoping he'd smile and say it was a joke.

"Oh, Eve, don't behave like a child." He took a handkerchief from his pocket and handed it to her. When she turned it over in her hands, she saw it was the one with her blood on it. She dabbed at her mouth with a clean edge, watching the man's hands close over a white box that sat in the centre of the table. He picked it up and opened it, handing her the thing inside - a small red bag.

"Look inside. Go on. Do not be afraid."

She undid the small gold clasp. Inside was a small mirror and a pot of something red, a bottle, a knife. When she saw the last one, she snapped it shut and handed it back. "No." Her eyes itched and blurred and she gulped back the stone in her throat.

He shook his head. "The hour has almost come, Eve. You'll have need of these. The bottle holds a sleeping draft. When your new husband has taken his fill of you, I want you to slip the contents of the bottle into a drink and give it to him. When you're certain he is slumbering, use the knife."

Tears ran down her cheeks and the side of her nose. She couldn't see. "I don't want a husband."

He knelt in front of her, clutching her hands until they ached. "The man you're to marry is a murderer. If you do not kill him, he will most certainly kill you." He let her go, stood up, paced.

She closed her eyes and let her tears run down, hearing the man's angry coughs.

60

The man paced and drank. When his glass emptied, he poured himself more. Each time he passed by Eve, a floorboard creaked. Her teeth clenched and her hair bristled when he came too near. It was too dark outside to make out land or sea or croft, but she could hear the storm blowing. In the hall outside, the big clock ticked away the hours. Her skin pimpled with cold and her shoulders sagged towards the table, gathering in like petals. The jug ran down to its lees.

"Our visitor is late." His fingers shook on the cork of the second bottle.

Red liquid splashed on the starched tablecloth. He pushed a full glass towards her and she pretended to sip at it, dribbling wine into the handkerchief when he turned away. He sighed, stretched, leaned on the mantelpiece, watching dots of rain spatter the window and run down jaggedly. She thought of the man who was coming. Maybe it was some new test she had to pass. The things in the bag – the knife, the sleeping draft – were things from a fairy tale. She should open the small bottle, slip the contents into the decanter, then she could go.

The storm howled down the chimney and shivered the bricks of the house. The man paced the room. His footsteps were heavier now and his eyes were smudged underneath. He sat down in the chair by the empty grate and steepled his jittery hands. He looked sad, as if the passion he'd felt for this new game or plan or whatever it was had faded from him. Eve watched him slip down in the chair, lids drooping, mouth growing slack. Eventually light snores puffed between his teeth.

Outside, an owl called through the gale, or maybe it was a dog that howled, or a man coming to marry her whistling. She had to get away, just a bit further away, to breathe. Edging up from the chair, she winced at the stiffness of her back. She was almost standing when the man moved and muttered to himself. His head lolled onto his shoulder, spit flowering damply on his white shirt, hand trailing the floor. He began to snore deeply. She let out a heavy breath. It would be such a simple thing to put her hands around that fragile neck and snap it. She knew she had the strength to and part of her wanted to for the things he'd done, the way he'd hurt her.

Another part cried *no*! After all, he was the only person she knew, or remembered anyway.

Sidestepping the loose board, she slid over the smooth floor on slippered feet. The door was ajar. It led down the corridor, down to somewhere else. She remembered her arms full of laundry, a bucket, heavy and sloshing, the smell of fish frying, potatoes roasting. Was there a kitchen through there? She felt sure she'd cooked there, cleaned and sung there, that once she'd worked here. And there'd been another with dark hair and sweet, sad eyes. It was so real, the thread of that memory tugged from some sampler upon which her past life was stitched, a half-known name on the tip of her tongue.

Softly, she crossed the room. She was almost to the door when a board creaked. She stopped mid-step and looked back to the chair. The man didn't stir. He lay there snoring as she crept through the door and tiptoed along the dark hallway. Light flared. A dark rumble followed, thrilling her skin. She spun around. A sheet of light whitened the window. A man stood behind it.

Eve shrank into the wall. Darkness. Another burst of lightning.

The man was gone.

She'd only seen him for a moment, but she was sure he'd been there. Thunder snarled. Maybe the man had woken from his stupor and was looking for her, or maybe her husband had come.

It was hard to breathe. She clasped her throat. Something was wrong. She shouldn't be here. She peeled away from the wall. It hurt between her legs and in her chest. She knocked into something that stuck out, hard and cold. A doorknob.

She turned it, stole into a room where the lightning showed a stove and hanging pots. Rain spattered a small window. She knew this smell of fish and potatoes. This was the place in which she'd scrubbed and cooked and sung. She opened a door and found a small room full of sacks and hanging meat. A board creaked above. She stopped to listen to another creak and the banging of boots. Heavy steps moved overhead.

61

Eve knew there was another door. She went to the stove and turned around to one side, bumping against one wall, the other. More footsteps thumped and her heart's clock ticked.

Her hands groped in front of her, felt plaster, a panel, a handle, a door. And she knew – *knew!* – that this one did not lock with a key, but with a heavy bar that always jammed, except that when she lifted it, it slipped out easily and the door swung open and out and she lurched through it, feet touching soft, wet stuff, the moonlight making her skin glow white as pearls. There was a round thing, dark shapes, a byre, a path.

She looked behind: nobody there. She began to run, the things she knew pouring into her like rainwater flooding a burn. If she turned round and ran past this house, she would be close to the sea.

Running was like walking, but faster. She put one foot in front of the other, the other foot in front of the other, breathing harder. She could see it now, like the square of light but so huge.

The ground punched her in the face. Her chin throbbed and her mouth tasted bitter. She spat and let out the hiccup of a sob. Pushing herself up on all fours, she crawled through damp grass that soaked her slippers.

Then up on her knees, her feet again, and running until the grass thinned out and turned to rough stubble that scratched her calves. And behind her still nothing, nobody following. She ran through the field, across stones flung over a burn, ran until her chest burned and her feet sank into something soft and white. Sharp stones poked the soles. Others were large, flat, slippery. Then she was there in it, swallowed by it, lapped by it. The sea kissed her and stung her. She loved to walk in it, smell it, look at it. It was a place to hide if you crouched down as she was now. It lapped and nibbled her legs, running back in a smooth little suck.

She swam in up to her shoulders. It bit her, but it soothed her too. She splashed her neck and breasts and face, kicked off her slippers and pushed her toes deep into the sucking sand beneath that welcomed her like a friend. A big wave pushed her over, knocking the breath from her, filling her mouth with salt. Her nose and eyes smarted. Spluttering, she crawled back to the shore and lay with her legs in the shallows, letting the sea nibble her pale legs stretched in the moonlight like a sea creature.

The sky was fading, the darkness ebbing from it. The stars were becoming less clear, the moon sinking down at the end of the sea. Closing her eyes, she saw green grass stretching out, and birds, a house, a woman with white hair and pegs in her mouth and a dog who ran in circles round her legs. She could feel its hot tongue lick her palm.

If she could find the place, she'd be safe there. Opening her eyes, she struggled up. Her shoulders and buttocks and the backs of her legs prickled with grains of …sand, it was called, sometimes soft and sometimes hard and sharp. She swiped it off and climbed up the bank, over the wet grass to a place she knew would be trodden down and easier to walk on. She followed along that to a long stretch of smooth, waxy earth. The sky lightened and birds began. Looking over her shoulder, she saw nothing but the fields and the sea stretching out endlessly.

On the crest of the hill, she stopped to stare down into a dip of land where a cottage sat, surrounded by bare dirt. Beyond it stretched other land and other buildings. She knew them all. Inside the cottage, the woman with white hair and a girl with red hair slept in a big bed and the dog slept there too. The fire would be burned down to ash by now, so that you had to keep all of your toes and fingers under the coverlet, or they swelled up with cold.

Stretching from the house was a line hung with sheets and shirts and skirts. Usually, that was only there in the daytime. She walked down the hill, her feet treading the smooth dirt at the bottom as if they'd trodden it many times. Her body felt good to be here, the ache inside her ebbing, although her wet dress clung awkwardly. She went to where the clothes hung. There was a white shirt that looked familiar. She pushed her face into it and though it was damp and cold, it smelled nice.

A woollen scarf hung next to it. It was a bonny red colour and it smelled nice too. She plucked the pegs off and clutched it to her, sniffing and sniffing. This smell was her, the old her and the white-haired woman and the dog. It was home. She went to the window and peeked inside, but all she saw was darkness. There was a loud noise from inside the house - a ruffing, angry noise, an animal whining. Then a small white face appeared, baring sharp teeth. It snarled and snapped as if it wanted to tear her up. Eve took a few steps back. Something wet caught her and clung to her. She turned round in a panic, came face to face with white cloth. There was a shuffling, a click, a creak. The door opened.

A woman with white hair came out. "Hello? Who's there?"

Eve untangled herself from the sheet and stood where the woman could see her. She felt her mouth stretch in a smile, because she was so happy to see the woman, who was kind and loved her. She took a step closer, arms spread wide. Still the dog barked and the woman said harshly, *Toby, down!*

The woman stood blinking at the half-light, rubbing her tired eyes, her shawl huddled round her. Eve inched towards her, wanting to be held by her and comforted, to sit and grow warm by the fire. She tried to remember the right name, to think of the words to say. But instead of a word, a low moan escaped her lips. The woman with the white hair shrieked, fist pressed to her mouth, eyes wide.

"Granny." The word came out twisted. She reached out to Granny, wanting to hold her, to bury her head in her skirts. If she could only do that once, then all would be well.

Granny stopped screaming and stared as Eve came closer, was just a step away, almost near enough to touch. And then there was a loud bang and Granny was gone and the door was shut.

Eve tried the handle, leaned on it, pressed her face on the wood. But it wouldn't open. She heard a keening sound and thought it was Granny, then knew it was her. She banged her head on the door again and again and again.

"Oona." The muffled voice was Granny through the door.

"Please?" The keening again.

"What are you?" Granny's voice was so close, it was almost inside Eve's head. "A demon returned to torment me?"

A demon. Eve hugged her arms around herself. She felt very cold. She cuddled the clothes to her chest and stared down at her muddy feet and then she ran out of the yard, up, up, into the light that was sluggishly white as a dead sea-thing. The birds shrieked too loud. She ran up to the brow of the hill where the fields had been shorn short. There were tents of gold straws there, propped against each other and bound at the top, stooks of wheat. The bundles leaned together and in the middle was a warm space. She crouched down onto the stubble and crawled into the dark place and lay down.

62

Birds filled the world with noise. Eve lay in her straw cave, shivering, smelling the damp of rotting wheat stalks. This would be fodder for the cows in winter. The men would come and heft it up and carry it to the hayloft. *A demon come back to torment me. Oona. Oona with red hair.*

She sat up, hearing the chords of a hymn from long ago. The words were still there, buried under layers, pushing pale and waxy horns of raw growth towards the light. Eve was Oona and Oona was Eve. She remembered that, but not the part where she'd gone from being the other her to being *this*.

For a long time, she watched the field birds drop down like seed scattering and wondered how long she had lived that life with that man. Victor was his name, those eyes like knives. Was it weeks, months, or years that she'd lain in the dark with just a few bright threads of memory to keep her company? Then Victor caring for her, loving her, though the things he'd done always seemed to hurt.

Last night's wine and talk of murder seemed like a nightmare now, but the thunderheads she'd heard then still hung low over the fields, their dark bellies splitting and merging. The fine rain that had streaked the windows dripped steadily from the thatch above her and beaded the corn stubble.

It blew through the opening and coated her face, gathering in the curve of her lip as if she'd been crying. Her feet that had been satin-clad wore slippers of cloud. The mansion with its gold and glass, the neat kitchen and the ticking clock were gone as in some dream. All around her, the wet earth sent up a sweet-sour smell, the scent of turned milk, and a breeze played its comb harp in the grass. She'd left the warm place for a wilderness. Who would look after her now?

She lifted her hands to her cheeks and smoothed away tears of rain. When she'd gone into the yard, everything had smelled and looked and felt like home and she'd known how it was to have Granny hold her and Toby lick her face, but Toby had snarled as if he'd seen a fox and Granny had talked to her the way you'd talk to a beast. It hurt to remember the words.

She should have grabbed that dog and squeezed his soft neck until the last weak cry, then Granny would be sorry. Tears ran and soaked the neck of her dress. She cried until there was no water left.

There was a laugh, the ring of boots hitting the hardening earth, the sounds of men's voices talking low and easy. They'd be coming to the fields to shift hay and mend stooks after the storm. They were coming nearer, their voices growing louder. They came so close she thought they were sure to smell her, but then their footsteps passed by, fading as they plodded down the hill towards the crofts.

Before long, Granny would tell other people about the demon. The men would come back to the field armed with sticks and knives. She crawled out of the stook, staying down on her knees, out of sight. A brown mouse scampered out with her and turned, stood on its hind legs its currant eyes gleaming then ran away with a squeak, like the dog, like Granny.

As she rose to a crouch, a red thing fell to her feet. The scarf. She folded it and wrapped it around her head, tying a clumsy knot at the nape of her neck, remembering that weeks or months or years ago, she'd used this to keep the sun off when she worked in the fields.

She took one last long look at home, the place where smoke twisted from the chimney and chickens scratched in the dirt. The two men were almost there. She began to walk, feeling the looseness of her dress, as if she'd shrunk in the night the way fruit does.

She walked for a long time, watching her bare feet moving between stalks or over grass, not following any particular direction. Crows called to her from the stumps of trees, their hoarse voices mocking, their grey hoods warped by the wind. She followed the path the burn cut through pastureland down to the beach. Where the grass thinned, runnels of brown water cut grooves in the sand. The rains had glutted the burn and all its channels, toppling pale towers into the flood. She heard the splash of them falling, the burn gurgling, her feet padding steadily on.

At the stepping-stones, she stopped and looked down. Her face was a distant moon lost in a halo of red hair and wool. The water flowed through it, making it look as if her lips and nose had been worn down. She held her body still, trying to see the demon inside.

Sighing, she pressed on, clambering through tussocks of spiky grass onto a stretch of beach where a lone boat rested on a bank of black seaweed. The sun was high. Most of the fishermen would have been out for hours, casting nets, hauling up creels. Soon it would be time for their meat and they'd lie across the boat with their brown feet hung over the side, drinking beer. She kicked at the sand as she went, until she stubbed her toe and sat down like a child to cradle it.

That was when she heard their voices. At first she couldn't work out where they were hiding, but then she saw the coils of white smoke drifting up above the lip of the boat. Some fishermen must be leaning on the far side, passing a pipe between them. A picture of them doing just that filled her head, real as life. She even saw their faces, sucking on the blackened clay.

In front of her was a big piece of driftwood, sun-bleached as a bone and smooth from the sea's caress. She crouched down behind it, her head resting on the salt-smelling surface. There were round grooves that had been worn into the wood by people sitting on it to watch the sea. Maybe she'd sat on it once, too. From her hiding place she watched the smoke and listened.

"He said she stole the boat and that was why God struck her down, but this one's Uncle's. It won't be stealing at all." The voice tangled in her head with a picture of a dark-haired boy flailing a stick.

The other blew out smoke and spat. "Aye, it is, Roy. You know we're banned from it. I don't want the belt again, thanks." He picked up a stone and skimmed it into the shallows. Jamie. Jamie and Roy. They were something dear – not to her, but to someone she cared for.

"He beats us for everything since Aunt May left. Might as well be hung for a sheep. I say we row out now. We'll be back for our meat. No-one will ken."

"And what if a ghost comes and finds us and drowns us?"

"Oona's or May's?"

"They both drowned, isn't it? They'll both be ghosts."

Drowned. They were talking as if she was dead.

Roy laughed. "Great big lassie you are. I've no fear of of finmen, don't believe in 'em."

"Well then, what of the demon Cormick saw chasing after Oona? He might come after us."

"You'll believe anything, you. Cormick's only an old drunky, making up tales."

"Then why did she have that face on her when they buried her, as if she was frightened to death?"

"Well…I s'pose it's no céilidh to drown."

Oona needed to talk to them. She got up, and with trembling hands brushed the sand off her dress and smoothed the scarf over her hair. She took one step closer, then another. When she was almost in reach of the boat Roy appeared by the prow. His mouth fell open.

"What have you seen, Roy?" Jamie stumbled after him.

They both stared.

"Don't it have a look of…?"

"They laid her in a wood box six feet down…" Roy picked up a stone. Jamie did the same.

Oona held out her hand. "Jamie." It was her voice, as always, except she heard the sound of the wind moaning under it, the same sound that seemed to come with all her words.

Roy held his stone over his head. "Away with you!" The hatred burning in his eyes told her he meant what he said. They'd hurt her if she stayed.

She turned around and walked back over the sand, her chest a furious fist. There was a horrible picture of white sheets and black hair before her eyes. That was something she'd seen and forgotten, someone she had loved. When the first stone hit her back, it felt like God punishing her, almost a relief from what was inside.

The boys were following a few steps behind, talking low to each other. The next stone stung her haunch. She broke into a run. Granny. Toby. Jamie and Roy. They all wanted to hurt her. Slate skimmed her shoulder. She heard a triumphant laugh. They were enjoying it. She ran through the dune grass and over the burn. Just past a stand of dwarfed trees was a white building circled by stones. Its roof had orange spots like rust. The door was open. She ran inside and thrust it shut and leaned on it.

63

Inside the white building, the room with benches was hardly bigger than the stook Oona had huddled in. A tall wooden box stood near the end of the room. With her back to the door, she stood stunned, chafing her arms and listening for the sound of stones striking the wood behind her. None came. Maybe the boys had gone.

Above the wooden box, a square of light dazzled her. In the light, she saw Victor working, his skilled hands creating and destroying, heard his voice telling her to kill. She closed her eyes. She saw people crowding in here week after week, grovelling on their knees on the floor. She'd done that, fallen on the hard ground, her lips moving silently.

She wove between the dark wood benches that were empty now. She'd walked down here once before, to see a woman in a white dress carrying a posy of pink flowers. She never came though everyone waited. Instead, she became a woman wrapped in white sheets with dark hair tangled over the pillow like seaweed. She seemed so peaceful and then the sudden lurch of the body under the sheets and the empty eyes staring.

Jesus died for our sins.

He died with his hands nailed and Mary Magdalene washing his beautiful feet with her tangle of dark hair. Blood everywhere and dark hair growing out of it, a hand hanging down - she'd held it, kissed it. She should have ripped it off.

She reached the wooden box and fell down on her knees. She pounded at her heart, forcing the images out. She clawed her face, trying to tear off the skin that made everyone scream, get back what once was. Her cries echoed through the church like some wild hymn and her tears pooled on the floor beneath the box. She tore at her hair, tugging out wispy curls, then pressed her hands together, lacing the fingers tightly, pressing them to her wet lashes.

"Please." When she moved her hands from her face, they were covered in blood.

"Are you in need of help?"

She turned around. An old man was walking across the room to her, his knotted hand leaning on the backs of benches as he passed them. His skin was sun-reddened and his thick black brows made him look fierce, but she felt in her heart that he was like a father to her and loved her. She opened her arms. His mouth twisted and he stepped back, fumbling in his black coat. She crawled closer to him.

"Father."

Biting his lip, the man pulled out a metal cross and held it up the same way Roy had held the stone before he threw it. "Depart from me, you cursed, into the eternal fire prepared for the devil and his angels!"

Oona stopped crawling and sat back on her haunches. His voice was weak and white foam flecked his mouth. His hands shook on the cross and he kept on whispering, "They shall be stoned with stones. Their blood shall be upon them. This is the second death. This is the lake of fire." His eyes were blank, like the body under the sheets.

She scrambled to her feet and edged past him, her back pressed to the benches. "Father, it is Oona."

He followed her movements with watery eyes narrowed under wild brows. "I buried Oona Scollay with my own hands. She was stone cold. I sent her soul to heaven."

"I am warm. Feel." She held out her hand.

He shrank from her. "You must be lost here. You need to find the light again and rest. You do not belong here with the living, not in the kirk, not anywhere in this world. Go!"

She stumbled towards the door, wrenched it open and ran out into the light. It slammed shut behind her. She stood in the green place with its half-buried stones, blinking. The boys were gone and the clouds were grey and furrowed as the man's brows. Through the doors, she heard him. "Jesus lived among the tombs and no one could bind him anymore, not even with a chain. Night and day among the tombs and on the mountains he cried out and cut himself with stones."

She could listen no more. She drifted between graves looking for a place to sit. Each had a name, half hidden under its moss wrapper. She glimpsed letters and dates as she passed by. The grass became a strip of earth, freshly dug over and bordered with stones. She sat down on the edge of it and raked her fingers through the soil. At the far end sat a wooden board with a name carved into it.

Oona Scollay.

Her chest grew heavy and she was very tired. Deep underground was a box. She should be inside it, lying with her arms crossed and her eyes closed. She had been down there and now she was here again, walking around. The man in the white building had seen her dead body.

He'd laid her to rest here and sent her to Heaven, a peaceful place. She'd been resting and everyone here had bid her farewell. And then for some reason she'd clawed her way up, climbed into this white light, this Hell.

64

The sky turned from white to yellow, yellow to crimson to dark. Oona stayed by the grave watching the heavens bruise. The old man was still inside. He must be hiding, murmuring his prayers.

Dusk thickened and swifts skimmed low over the mossy stones, snapping up midges with their open beaks. She thought of picking up the wooden board that bore her name and breaking it over the old man's head. Victor had said she was stronger than anyone. It would be so easy. But the image of the board breaking, of blood and pain, felt like Victor's tools boring into her head. She clutched her face and rocked until her mind was blank again.

Night came. Stars shone and the waning moon looked down on her, one side whittled away. They'd called her *cursed, a ghost, a demon.* Victor had fixed her with tools. She was broken, but she was alive and strong too. She had a second chance. The thoughts padded through her head like night things, yowling. They gave her no peace and none seemed to be the answer. Owls whooped oaths and the burn babbled curses at the sleeping sky. The night was half gone by the time she knew what to do and stood.

She untied the scarf from her head and picked up four of the stones that marked her grave, laying them gently inside the cloth as if they were food. The sling dangled by her thigh as she wove between graves. She swung it in time to the gurgling burn as strode down the brae. When she got to the beach, the firth stretched out darkling and strange. The tall white torches that men put on the small islands flung their silver over the sea. Under the water's rough weft was a selkie who'd once been a human girl. The Finman took her down there with seven strokes of his oar and when she came back, her kind didn't know her again.

Oona tied the scarf round her waist so that the round stones were cradled in the small of her back, the ends knotted tightly over her hip. Waves licked her feet, inviting her to take another step closer, one more step. She began to run through the shallows, remembering another time when she'd run like this and turned round to see a young man watching her from the shore.

The cold water climbed her calves and thighs, planting salty kisses on her breasts. The sea was a lover warming his cold hands on her, tickling up goosebumps along her bare arms, holding her so tightly it was hard to breathe. She closed her eyes and felt the world below open for her.

Her feet tiptoed along the soft mush of drowned sand. Salt seeped between her lips. She opened her mouth, letting it trickle down her throat, burning and cooling, filling her. Underneath, seed pearls spilled from her, surged to the surface and burst. She smiled. She was going home.

Hands grabbed her hard around the waist and dragged her back. They gripped her from behind, knocking the last breath from her. She broke the surface, spluttering scalding salt, face smacking the frozen air, chest on fire. The scarf was ripped off and plunged away. Silt scorched her heels, then her calves and thighs. She gulped in air, hearing the hoarse notes her body made as if they came from somewhere else. She flung her arm back. It collided with hard flesh. She kicked back and clawed, gasps turning into shrieks. But whatever had her kept on hauling her back through the sea until they were on dry land and it set her down.

She lay in the sand, her eyes blurred and stinging, rough coughs ripping from her lungs. Through a haze of saltwater, she saw a tawny face half hidden by a dark hood. A man knelt over her, smelling of peat ash and sealskin. He put his hand under her neck, gently tilting her head to the side so that the water trickled from her mouth. Her hand flailed out and struck him a blow to the head. He caught her wrist and smiled with one side of his mouth.

"Be still."

She tried to shout No, but the word was no more than a splutter of water. He let go of her and she heaved herself onto her side and retched. She must run, but she was still too weak. She closed her eyes and saw a hooded man staring from his sealskin covering, watching her from a boat as she rowed. Had he been following her?

She hauled herself onto her haunches, saw the sand and red cloth stuck to her scarred thighs swarming with pale dots and flecks of gold. She sat back down and retched more salt water. His hand was on her shoulder. She looked up. A scar ran down between his nose and his top lip. Another began on his sun-brown cheek and vanished from view beneath the hood. His blue eyes had yellowed whites, like hers when she stared in the mirror.

He gripped her shoulders. "Why did you do it?"

She tried to twist free, but he was too strong. "Leave me be!" She eyed the distance from the sand to the grass, from the grass to the field and the stooks.

"I promise not to hurt you." His hand moved to her neck, a thin layer of grit dividing skin from skin. He turned her face from one side to the other, staring.

She seized his wrist, pressing down hard, crushing the bones. "I make no such promise."

"You seem better at hurting yourself." He peeled her fingers from his wrist as if she were a child.

Her hands and feet scrabbled the sand at the same time. She balled her fist and smashed his face as she had smashed the glass. He reeled back, bleeding. Then, with a kick of pebbles, she was up and out of his reach, halfway down the beach with his feet crashing behind her.

She glanced back, tripped over a branch and landed flat on her palms. He picked her up by the waist and she kicked him hard. He turned her round in his arms and she bit his hand, drew more blood. It pleased her to see it run between his knuckles.

"Stop fighting me. I want to help you."

"No," she kicked his shin, "no!"

"I know it hurts when you wake up," his arms clamping hers. "People scream. You want to break everyone and at the same time, you want to die. I know it. And if you stay in plain sight, they will kill you. To them, you're a monster, a killer."

"No." She clawed his back. He held on, unyielding as the grave, his strength matching hers. She smelled the blood drying on his arm, the faint scent of blight that hung over them both.

"You are like me." His breath was hot on her neck. "We are the same."

65

The owls hushed in the fields, their deep voices growing sleepy. They had stayed on the beach a long time, locked into that strange embrace, half death, half life.

When the stars began to fade and the first cord of pink light rose over the brim of the sea, the man's arms loosened and Oona was free. She had thought that when he loosed her she would run and keep running until she left him far behind. She could not say why she stood looking into his face, except that it was a kind of glass in which she saw her own life and her own pain flicker back towards her. Damp air settled on her arms and the small of her back where his skin had warmed hers.

"What…" she began.

"What will you do now?" It was as if he read her mind.

She nodded.

"You have made yourself known. As soon as it grows light, they'll come."

She hugged her arms around herself.

He looked over her shoulder, along the beach. "There are boats a small way down from here. Take one. Row until you find a place to hide."

A place. It looked blank in her mind's eye. She knew nothing of the world beyond. She must have lived in this place her whole life and never ventured out. In the shadows that had begun to fall around them, she saw the ghostly forms of men with torches, hunting for them.

"What will you do?"

He was silent. She followed his gaze to the gold light clasping the bellies of the clouds. Beneath the soft grey haze, red and yellow smudges melted into each other. The rocks and a shack and a row of boats were all black silhouettes, a world of dim shapes.

His eyes were on her face – a familiar look, as if they'd known each other once, though she couldn't remember it. He rubbed his eyes and when he was done, he seemed older than before. "I'll come with you until you find somewhere safe to stay and then I'll leave this place."

Aside from death, there was no other choice.

As they walked over the wet sand the life that had slept all night began again. Fish leapt and the dark heads of seals nodded from a wave or behind a rock before dipping from view. The white birds babbled from the rocks and the gulls began to circle, idly curious about the creatures beneath them.

They came to a big boat settled in a noust. Rimy air drew out the pitch stench of the half-tarred hull. It was a big old tub and too wrecked to go out in. Mute and furtive, they hurried on past bristling sea-grass and clear runnels of burn to where two smaller boats lay in a tidemark of dried kelp. The furthest had a black cross on it and a strange face carved on the front.

He ran his hand along the edge, peering in. "This one is sound."

"Aye."

They took hold of the sides and ran with it into the shallows. It was easier than she thought it would be. They were both strong. When the boat was in the shallows, he told her to climb in, and kept running until he was waist height, leaping in, wet breeks showering her. He took something from his shirt and laid it in her lap - an oilskin, bundled together. It smelled of bread and cheese.

"Wrap that around your shoulders, or you'll freeze on the crossing."

She picked up an oar. "No."

"Suit yourself." He raised the other oar, turned around and plunged it into the water.

They kept to the line of the coast, sometimes hitting a rhythm and other times off-tempo – he yelled back at her then. It was hard to keep up, the way he wielded the oar, neat and quick, nicking and cutting the dark sea like peat.

The sun grew burly. It dappled the man's back with pale light. As she kept time with him, she watched his shoulder-blades rise and fall, the pale hairs gleaming on his nape. He rowed faster than anyone she'd seen, just like the Finman in the stories, taking the human girl down to the undersea.

They'd been on the water a while when he stopped rowing. She must have been half asleep, aimlessly sculling, when she felt the boat slow. Her feet were wet and numb. Dark water rose to her ankles. The man sat still, head cocked, listening for something.

In front of them, the rock went straight up, climbing in vast red and black steps. Giant steps. Rime shrouded the cliff-tops, twisting into veils of golden light where the rising sun caught drops of sea spray.

The man's back and face were black and seemed carved from the dark wood or the hearts of burnt peat. The boat lurched forward on the crest of a wave and the sun unfurled a flaming mist around the man, like an angel's wings. *His body was like beryl, his eyes like flaming torches.* She knew the words from long ago.

He put down his oar and turned to her. "Hand me the oilskin."

She took the skin from her lap and passed it to him. He unrolled it and drew out a small red box and opened it. The lid flipped back. It was brass inside, the lid graven with the sharp prongs of a sun and with letters. Cradled in the golden circles of the lower part was a glass eye with a dancing arrow inside it.

"This is a compass," he said. "I use it to guide the boat after the stars have disappeared, when it is day or when I am lost. The needle points to all the directions, North, South, East and West. We're headed round the coast to the South bay. If anyone follows us…" He snapped the compass shut and slipped it in his pocket. "Do you understand?"

Oona nodded and she was only half lying. They picked up the oars again and rowed towards the cliffs. The surf crashed on the side of the boat and washed inside. It was up to their knees. They rowed hard. When they were a few feet from the shore, they laid down the oars and jumped out.

Together they hauled the boat through waves that spit salt and foam at their faces. Without the sun shining on him, the man lost his wings and no longer seemed like an angel. He held out his arm and Oona stopped. They stood hip-deep in the freezing sea listening to the men's voices.

66

There was a snatch of rough talk, a dragging noise, the words *haddock* and *noust*. Perhaps the men were hauling fish onto the beach. She looked down at the water, where the sun had melted to butter spooned between waves. She saw her own pale hand floating under the sea with long fingers wound around it. For a moment, she thought it was seaweed entangling her. But it was the man's hand gripping hers. She could have bitten it again, but the pressure of his fingers gave her comfort somehow. After all, they were the same. Dead things. Monsters. Hunted.

Whether it was that a wind blew up or that the men were wading into the sea, their voices grew louder in Oona's ears. Her wolf's heart beat faster. She looked up at the man. His grip tightened.

Boots crunched on sand. A prow sliced through water. They were pulling their boat back out to sea. There was a cry of "Whossere?" the splash of wading thighs. The man's hand moved to her wrist, dragging her away from the voices. Her legs moved too slow, caught in treacle. The men were almost on them. There were more words, chopped up by the booming sounds of waves hitting rocks. *Killed that lass o' mine. We'll string him up.*

She knew the gruff voice that spoke the words and cudgelled her brain to remember who it was. Nothing came. Her feet had no feeling in them and she was glad of the man's hand keeping her steady. *Murderer.* The word, spoken in a familiar voice clutched her heart like a frozen hand. The word caught in some sea cave and shuddered up an echo. *Murderer. Derer. Rer.*

A pair of kittiwakes startled from a sea stack and whirred up screeching. Oars hit the water. *Can you see anything?* A different voice and yet she knew it too. It made her think of being held, being kissed. Those were meant to be good things, but she'd never been more afraid. She knew the men were looking for someone, a killer who deserved punishment. The thought split inside her. The men were looking for them.

A big wave pushed her forward. She plunged down and hit the bottom. The water rattled as it sucked sand out from under their feet. Salt stung her eyes and throat and chest. The sea was a frozen fist gripping her. Hands closed around her waist and hauled her out. The man lifted her up and waded through rough swells, clutching her to him. She spluttered brine, forcing herself not to make a sound that might give them away.

The man's voice was low in her ear. "Hold on. There are rocks on the left."

She squeezed her eyes shut, face pressed into him, smelling salt and seal hide. In the darkness, she felt the tide drawing them towards the rocks. Then there was a glimmer of sunlight and the sound of surf growing shallower, dragging them ashore. He laid her on the sand and fell down beside her.

"They took the boat. It's lost to us, but we can hide here."

She listened for the men, but could hear them no longer.

They were in a small cove. The beach was shallow and pale and unmarked. The rocks rose sheer and tall out of the powdery sand. Set into the rust-red cliff face was a dark mouth that echoed their breathing.

"A cave."

He nodded and scrambled up. Shivering, she followed him across the sand to the mouth of the cave. Inside, the ceiling dripped rhythmically and something in the depths made scratching sounds. The clouds behind them parted. Light silvered the wall in front of them. The whole surface was covered with crosses gouged into the rock, carved in deep with some sharp implement. Some were circled with whorls of hectic scratches as if whoever marked them was angry. She looked at the man. He was squinting at the crosses, his blue eyes curious.

"A man lived here, but not any more, not for a long time."

"I can smell him."

"Me too." He walked on.

A few steps more and they reached the back wall of the first chamber. It was about the same size as the white building where the old man lived. Near their feet, a smaller mouth led off somewhere. Water gurgled inside it.

The man turned and faced the beach again. "We can build a fire."

She followed him from the cave, blinking at the sun that hung over the sea, new-minted. For a while, she stood watching the man stoop and straighten, stoop and straighten, as if he was picking flowers from the sand. Then he turned and she saw the small sticks of firewood in his arms, the scowl on his brow as he scanned for more. It would be a mean crop on a small beach like this. A memory shimmered up from some past time, turning her towards the cliff face where she saw dry grasses sprouting from the ledges of sandstone and felt joy at knowing they'd be there.

She went up to the cliff and started to rive the brush. At first she came away with handfuls of dried straw. She stuffed them in the lap of her dress and tugged harder. Sharp twigs bit into her hands. She wrenched at the roots of dried-out bushes and whole plants came away from the cliff, the knotty wood spraying her with sand. She fell backward with a small cry of surprise that was half a laugh. The man was there, looking down at her.

"What are you doing?"

"I've found kindling."

He looked at her curiously, then put down his bundle of driftwood and scanned the rock face.

"Good."

After that, they worked side by side, reaping grass and twigs from clefts in the sandstone. The man clambered higher and snapped off dried branches from ledges. When they had as much as they could hold, they carried it back to the cave. Oona found dry, flat stones and gathered them into her skirt. She brought them in and set them down, laying out a rough circle.

When she'd finished the makeshift hearth, the man laid out the larger pieces of driftwood, setting aside the damp bits, nestling the kindling inside it. He took two pieces of flint and struck them together until a spark hit the kindling. It started to smoke. Oona blew soft breaths, willing the embers to grow. A stick of driftwood caught and the yellow flames licked up, casting shadows around the cave, making strange shapes from their bodies as they knelt to warm their hands.

Oona looked at the man's profile in the firelight. His lips were finely shaped and half hidden by his beard. His hood had fallen back and she could see the scars that ran jaggedly over his shaven head. His wide blue eyes were fixed on the fire. She touched his arm.

"What is your name?"

"Adam." He said the word without looking at her.

"There's a man in the Bible called Adam."

Her cheeks grew hot, remembering the name Victor had called her by. Eve. She looked away from Adam at the walls speckled with crosses. A person had put them here, some lonely hermit chalking the walls, muttering prayers to himself; or a madwoman, grinding the Xs with her blunt knife and shouting loud to keep the Devil at bay. Prayers and cries had echoed through the tunnels of this cave once. And they would have to sleep here side by side.

"Are you the man that was coming for me?" She couldn't say 'my husband'. It sounded too strange.

He didn't seem to hear her, but kept on staring into the fire. She remembered the purse with the knife and poison, Victor's words: *he's a murderer.*

"What happened there?" His voice was sharp.

She looked down to where he was pointing and saw the cluster of bruises spreading over her thighs. They'd darkened into sooty fingerprints. "Victor did that."

"He hurt you."

She said nothing.

He took her chin in his hand. "Look at me. Did the doctor do that?"

"Why should I confide in you when you won't in me?" The tears ran down her face and splashed his hand.

He closed his fingers on them and she watched the salty water catch in the creases of his palm, then stood up so abruptly that she cringed back, thinking he might hit her.

Instead, he turned and ran at the wall of the cave, smacking his head against the cold stone, punching the hundred mad crosses carved there again and again, a low cry croaking up from his chest. His blood stained the wall. Oona hid her head, hands pressed to her ears. All she could hear were Victor's words: *if you do not kill him, he will kill you.*

67

On the floor of the cave there was a large rock. Oona saw herself pick it up. She would feel the heft of it in her hands, the crevices inside it salty and damp. Her arms would strain as she lifted it above her head. When she brought it down on his soft nape, she would be released and when he slumped to the floor, she would have done as Victor wished.

The rock sat on the cave floor, waiting for her. Adam stood facing the wall, blood running from where he'd cut himself. Pale hairs gleamed against the golden skin on his neck.

She took a step closer. She should be bending, picking up the rock. The hair at his nape silvery white, like a child's hair. Why weren't her hands on the stone? He turned around and their eyes met. How blue his were. The blue of the sea roughened with winter ice. He brushed her fingers with his own before walking back to the fire.

She followed him and sat down, her hands clutching her knees, the hard rock digging into her haunches. She stared into the fire, feeling its heat like a reprimand for what she'd almost done. When Adam crouched low to pick up scraps of kindling that had blown loose, she saw the rock, the blood and imagined him dead. She shivered, thinking of the body growing cold, being alone in the cave.

Victor's words echoed in her head – *he will kill you*. If it was true, why was he waiting? She watched him throw the dry grass onto the fire, tug his shirt off and wipe his cut forehead. His chest was covered with lines that ran from his neck and arms, meeting in the middle of his chest like knots of fishing net. Some were faint and white, some puckered and crimson. She scratched the place between her breasts where the stitches of her own scar prickled.

"Don't scratch." His tone was harsh. Maybe he knew what she'd been thinking of doing to him. Her hand dropped into her lap.

He looked down at his chest, scowling at the blackthorn branches of wounded skin. "Do these frighten you?"

She hugged her arms around herself.

"You have them too." He reached for the neck of her dress.

She grabbed his hand hard. "Don't touch me." She squeezed his bones, crushing down, so easy to break.

He wrapped his fingers around hers. For a moment they arm-wrestled. She felt the sweat blushing to the surface of her skin, a film of it forming between them. Then he gained the advantage and pulled her to him, placing her fingers on the plum furrow where his arm joined his chest. He forced her fingertip along the scar so that she could feel how smooth it was. She tried to wrench her hand back, but he held it hard.

"See how the skin on my arm is darker?" He moved her hand to the left. "And the scar over my heart? I do not know where I came from, not as you do, though I have searched long and hard for a mother, a father, a home."

As he traced her finger over the scar she saw the lighter shade of it, the tightness of the pink flesh like the skin on boiled milk.

"At night I tell myself stories, that my skin came from a nobleman, my heart from a general in the war, my brain from a philosopher in Ingolstadt. For that is where I was born, in a graveyard, under the shadow of a hanging tree. That is where he made me."

"Victor?"

"Yes," he spat the words, "*Victor*. Herr Doktor Frankenstein." He dropped her hand and stared down at her lap where the dirty dress had ridden up, not far enough that the bruises were visible, but enough so that they could both see the seam along her thigh, how the skin of the thigh was milky smooth though the calf was freckled.

He pulled open the neck of her dress and peered down at her left breast. It was smooth and creamy white, the nipple dark and large, the stitching round it forming a ragged circle. Her other breast was smaller, paler, its nipple pink and hard. She twisted away from him and shuffled back against the wall of crosses, clasping her dress tightly over her breasts.

Adam sat back and began to fold his shirt. "He needed a new heart for you. Yours did not work any more."

"No." The coldness of his words froze her bones, shrivelled her up inside. She hid her face in her dress.

"Your friend... He used her heart. Her skin."

"May." The word was muffled.

She saw it more fully this time - the lurch of the body under the sheet, the hand reaching out to her, imploring. Dark hair matted with blood and the eyes staring blankly. She had turned on her heel and run and left her friend, her May. All the memories were there at once - May's trembling hands, her sad eyes the last time they held each other, whispering goodbye.

68

For a long time she sat with her head buried and her back pressed into the wall. She had let him touch her, care for her - Victor, with his calming words, so wise and easy to believe. *He* was the killer and yet she'd loved him because he was all she knew. He had dug her up and pried inside her, forced her to steal her friend's heart – the friend she'd left behind.

Knowing that was worse than any other pain. She should find a sharp flint and cut the heart from her chest, but each time she tried to rise, to go out on the beach and look for a weapon, the rhythm of her new heart's beats played in tune with the lapping of the sea outside. Inside her chest, beneath her ribs, lay everything she'd loved, all that was thriving in the world. It wasn't hers to destroy.

She sat up, head sore, throat dry. Adam was gone. After a while, she heard the shuck and scud of stones thrown in the sea. The fire was just glinting embers by the time she curled on her side and fell asleep.

Some time in the night, Adam must have come in and lain down with her, because she woke to the warmth of his body behind her and the gentle sound of his breath in her ear. He murmured something, a foreign word spoken in sleep. *German.* That was the name of his language. His hand rested lightly on her hip and she thought of moving it, was surprised to find that she didn't want to. Instead, her body nestled against his and she liked the warm smell of it, calming her until she drifted off again.

She woke to grey light spilling gloomily in, changing the carved crosses into a spectral graveyard. A fine spray of seawater hit the mouth of the cave. Her back was cold. The space behind her was empty. She sat up and took in the dead fire, the empty cave. Adam was gone. May's heart struck hard against the tender flesh of the scar as if it blamed her. She bit her lip and fought back a sob of despair. What would she do? Where would she go? Her skin stung.

She looked down to see her fingernails scratching wretchedly at the scar on her thigh - May's thigh. They dug under the dark jewels of dried blood, scratching until fresh blood bloomed on the milky skin and trickled onto the cave floor. She kept on, scoring angry, pink lines until a voice stilled her hand.

It came from the beach and was soon joined by another man's. They spoke in the bitter tones that had sounded so familiar the night before. Crablike, she scuttled to the wall and pressed her back to the sharp crevices of it, breathing shallowly as the voices came steadily closer.

69

"I heard someone banging about in here."

"Ach, you're dreaming, man!" A dark-haired man walked inside the cave and kicked a stone. From her corner, Oona saw his stout boots and heavy fisherman's coat. She shrunk back, pressing herself between upright shelves of rock.

His fair-headed friend was smaller, thinner, his voice high and nervous. "If they left the boat, they'd have ended up on this stretch of coast." It was that last word - *coast* - that made her remember. They'd lain on the beach, his mouth pressed hot on hers.

"It could've been anyone last night, dark as it was. We don't even know if the doctor was telling the truth. You were soused then and you still are." The dark-haired man punched his friend's shoulder, cocky and cruel. Oona remembered him using his fists on Victor, over and over. That must be when Victor told him the truth about things. His name was Stuart and the other was Andrew. He squatted down, searching the floor for something.

"Can't credit the doctor lying. Why should he? May lost her life to those monsters and her bones won't rest until the pair of them are brought to justice." He straightened and walked over to the ashes. "Look here, a fire." He kicked the ashes. He was so close, one step more and he'd see her.

"Bones won't rest, eh? You babbling about the sea ghost your nephews chased after?" The fair man ran his hand through his hair and laughed. "The ghost with slime hanging from her locks? Now I know you're drunk. Come on man." He pulled Stuart's arm. "Let us take the boat out now, before the sky turns black."

Stuart took one last look at the cave. For a moment his eyes seemed to rest on Oona. Some hidden part of her willed him to see her, the real her, to come and tell her she wasn't any kind of fiend, but his lost love. It was her heart that wanted it, May's heart that had loved Stuart. She felt it still with the sense of how good it would feel to be kissed and held close and taken home.

Stuart shook his head and turned around. He followed Andrew outside. Wind caught their talk and threw it booming at the rocks. Then they were gone. Oona let out a ragged breath. Her eyes stung.

She sank down. It wasn't too late to go after them. But if she did and they shouted and threw stones like the others had, she would lose the will to go on.

For a long while after the voices faded, she huddled by the wall of crosses, her forehead pressed against her knees. *Can't credit the doctor lying.* What had Adam said last night? *Victor. Herr Doktor Frankenstein.* The doctor was the one who'd told them to come here. She saw him sitting by candlelight, his deft fingers mending things. A different time, when she was another person, those fingers had touched her breastbone, felt the fault in her heart. He'd sighed and she thought she'd heard him murmur, "What a pity."

He'd known what was wrong with her. Perhaps he'd even hoped she would die, so he could take her apart and piece her back together. Now he'd told May's old lover - and her old lover - to come out here and find 'the monsters', *his monsters.* He'd allied himself with the same men who'd beaten him senseless. The other Oona would have wept at knowing that and the tears would have made her feel better. But this Oona was numb, a cold creature lulled by the strange heart beating inside it.

Her back was stiff, her motley skin goose-pimpled by the time she slowly stood and walked outside. The small beach looked bleak in the daytime, the grey sea stretching out cheerlessly until it melted into a slab of slate sky. She picked up a stone and flung it at the waves with a scream, another stone and another, each with a furious cry. A hand clamped over her mouth.

"Hush."

Oona bit down, thrust her elbow back. A groan. The hand fell from her mouth. She spun around. Adam stood, clutching his gut. His face twisted with rage. He growled and raised his hand. She braced for the blow. His hand dropped and he turned from her.

"Why did you leave me?"

He kept his back to her. "I needed to find more firewood and something for us to eat. I found a good place for us on the far side of those rocks, but the waves are too strong to fish in."

"Why did you not wake me? Men came. They nearly found me."

"I thought you would be safe."

"Victor sent them after us. He told them we were killers."

Adam turned to face her slowly. His mouth was a narrow line. The scar on his head gleamed like a slowworm in the dull light.

"We must leave this place."

70

They waded through a roost to find the next cove. Oona's body was taut and as charged as one of the wires Victor used to bring dead things to life. Each rock they scrambled over seemed like some trick. Seals came up to watch them, eyes dark and curiously human. From the corner of her eye, they looked like men lurking with nets, with knives. Rounding a spill of red stones, they came in view of a curve of white beach.

At the far end of it, two immense black sea stacks rose from the spray. Oona followed Adam across the last of the rocks and onto the beach. The sand that sunk under her toes stretched in a long, silver crescent that ended in the sea stacks. Red cliffs towered behind them, cloaked in mist, and green hills thick with heather rose from the beach. She felt like an ant that had wandered into Eden.

There'd be a snake somewhere. There must be. The whole place was far too open to give them shelter from the men, but Adam seemed not to care. He told her he was going to find wood for a fire and walked away over the sand. She watched his shrinking form clamber over the round stones on the cusp of beach and hill. Then he vanished into the heather.

If he wanted a meal, it was all around them, clinging to the rocks. She turned back to a red rock-pool where mussels and seaweed grew. Swags of sinewy shells came away easily in her new, strong hands. She held up her skirts and dropped them into her dress-lap. The clouds broke as she picked whelks from rock-pools. The sun shone and the sky bloomed cornflower blue. She found a large crab and killed it with a rock between the eyes.

Adam returned with dried ferns, driftwood and a few berries. He squinted at her catch with disgust and piled stones for the fire. She wrapped the shellfish in layers of green weed and baked them on hot stones under the burning sticks. Adam waded into the shallows with a sour look, but when she unwrapped the bundle and he caught the scent of it, he came back and sat down. She handed him a stick and showed him how to poke the meat from the shells, how to crack claws with stones. In the end, he even ate the seaweed. A pair of skuas circled above them, squawking.

Adam stood and stretched. "We must find shelter for the night."

He took her hand and dragged her towards the ferns, where the dried bed of an old burn made a path. When they got higher up, he let go of her so that she could climb, grabbing onto clumps of bracken, grit driving under her nails. It was slow going and he disappeared over the brow of a brae while she was still struggling. She'd almost reached the top, when she lost her footing. She seized the trunk of a gorse bush, knowing how its roots were strong and went down deep into rock. Her other hand flailed.

His hand caught her wrist and lifted her easily. He held her by the shoulders, steadying her. Their eyes met. Last night, she'd been planning to kill him. As she stared into his broken face, she imagined how he would have snapped her neck if she'd tried. *He will kill you.* His hand brushed hers, took hold of it. Their faces were so close she almost tasted him. The skua flew over them, casually vicious. When a skua did that, it meant a death was coming they said. *White sheets stretched in her mind. A hand reached out.* She dropped Adam's hand and walked on, feeling that if they stood there staring at each other any longer, what was left of their world would go bad.

71

Oona walked close to the brow of the hill, too close, so that she could feel the valley's undertow. Adam fell in step with her and tugged at her sleeve.

"What is it?"

She stopped. "Look at that." She pointed to where a hawk hovered in the wind, fierce and alone, waiting to plunge. "It feels nothing when it kills, save hunger." She looked into his face.

He ran his finger over his lips. She wanted him to tell her, without her even having to ask, that it was all lies what Victor had said. That he'd never so much as stepped on a worm. But she already knew that wasn't so. If they were really the same, he had fury running through him, like her. And he thought about killing, like her.

In the end, he said nothing.

They walked on. There were strands of bramble here and there, snaking up from the cliff edge, pish-the-beds and sorrel hidden in the grass. She knew they'd soon be hungry again and began to pick the fruit and flowers, dropping them in her skirt lap, murmuring under her breath, *because the vine bloomed crookedly, the heavenly gardener could not spare his son.* She wouldn't think of blood or sheets, or Victor, or the men. She would cast them from her mind.

"You move slower with each step." He stopped to let her catch up, but didn't reach for her this time.

"I found these." She showed him the tangle of plants in her skirt. "We could make a soup from this sorrel if there's a pot."

"Sorrel soup?" He grimaced. "There is something like a barn over there, piles of stones but no roof."

She followed his gaze. "Not a barn. There are old tombs here. Cairns, they call them. No-one goes in those." The clearness of the memory made her smile.

"Good place for us, then." He struck out towards them.

"Wait," she caught his arm. "They stay away from those places because people buried their dead there."

"You fear that the dead will rise from their graves?" He smiled wryly. "And what do you think we are?" He turned back towards the tombs.

"We are the dead," she whispered.

The sun shining overhead looked bleak and her thoughts of making soup seemed foolish now. She let the leaves fall from her dress. Near her feet, a slow worm slithered between blades of grass, its nightshade eyes gleaming. *And I will put enmity between thee and the woman, and between thy seed and her seed; it shall bruise thy head, and thou shalt bruise his heel.* Above her, the sky darkened. The first fleck of rain hit her cheek.

It was damp in the old cairn and the air smelled of mouldering leaves. When she crawled inside, she remembered the tales of bitter ghosts who sucked breath from the living. She crouched low, cradling her knees in her arms. He curled on his side as an animal would, turned away from her.

In the night she woke and found his arms wrapped around her again. When she pulled him closer, he woke and murmured half in English, half in German. The parts she understood seemed to be about living beneath a pile of wood and digging turnips. She closed her eyes and imagined him alone, as she had been. Outside an owl hooted. His lips brushed her neck. She fell asleep clutching his hand, her fingernails digging a little way into his skin in case he thought of running off.

72

Oona knelt on the grass outside the cairn breathing shallowly. She picked up a flint and began to rub it on a dry patch of stone. Adam had made it look easy before, striking the flint, hitting up sparks so that they touched fire to the curling hairs of tinder snugly tucked between pebbles. She'd known how to do it once, but her memory was fogged. Angry now, she pounded until her arms ached and the flint bit into the soft flesh of her palm.

As the sun came up over the next hill and stretched yellow fingers between dark lashes of fern, the flint struck sparks in its furrow and the tinder caught, tentatively at first, then bolder. Red light ate along the tawny threads and she laid lengths of dry grass across it, blowing gently, building a thatch, until she had the beginnings of a fire. She threw the drier twigs over it, coaxing, her back tense with the fear that she would smother it. She rocked back on her heels. It was good. It was alive.

She picked up the roots she'd dug from the hillside, weighing their cool heft in her palm, brushing off clods of that good kind of muck. When the fire had burned a while, she pushed them into the ashes. She stood and stretched and smiled. She'd woken with a warm feeling inside her, like when she reached in the hen's nest at home and felt a chick's wings unfolding. She turned so that the sun would stroke her face, closing her eyes, remembering Adam's teeth on her neck, gently biting her in his sleep.

A hand on her shoulder startled her. She turned to see Adam's face tattooed from sleeping on the seam of his shirtsleeve. "Burning things? In the middle of the night?" His voice was throaty.

"I rose hours ago. I'm cooking." She brushed a spider's web from his shoulder.

He crouched by the fragile fire. "What are those?"

"Roots," she smiled. "I've eaten them many a time."

He stared at her and for a moment she thought he would hit her. But instead, he pulled her hard into his chest and kissed the top of her head.

"What was that for?" Her laugh was muffled against his skin.

"I don't know." He held her at arm's length, looking at her intently.

She wondered at the strange, stung look on his face. He bent and kissed her, just a press of the lips at first. Then she felt the soft warmth of his mouth, mingling with hers, tasted salt and seaweed and heat. She put her arms around his neck and held him closer.

His hand moved to the curve of her back, his mouth pressing harder. His fingers fumbled for the hem of her dress, catching the flimsy cloth, pushing it up her thigh, feeling for her, touching her roughly so that she gasped, her back arching. He took her hand, slipping her fingers inside his breeks. She felt the rough tickle of the hair there, the tautness of him, caressing with her thumb until he groaned into her neck, a dewdrop of wetness slicking the flesh she held in her hand. He hoisted her up and laid her on the ground, pushing her dress up to her hips, untying the rope at his waist, poised between her legs, just watching her, flushed and trembling.

Stones rattled somewhere below them. There was another noise, maybe a muttered curse. Adam's eyes widened. He rose to his knees, retying the rope. "Someone is there."

Oona scrabbled up, pulling her dress down. She felt ashamed, as if someone had seen. Adam tiptoed to the brow of the hill, gesturing to her to keep back, but she followed him anyway. From where they stood, she could see a pile of fallen rocks, churned-up reddish earth and turf from the bank below, but no sign of a person. She reached for his hand. He slapped her away, his fingernails scratching her skin. She crouched back, frowning, sucking on the scored flesh, tinny with new blood. He turned to her, his face dark. "Stay here."

As he walked to the fallen rocks, fists clenched, the words forced their way into her head again. *He's a murderer, cold-blooded. A monster.* She pressed her hands to her ears to block out the echo she suddenly seemed to hear around the valley, squeezed her eyes shut, feeling the white blankness of those first awful days enter her head. Her knees weakened. Before she could steady herself, she sank to the floor.

"What is the matter with you?" Adam stood over her. His face was still dark and instead of putting out his hands to help her, he made fists of them.

"My head feels hot." Tears stung the rims of her eyes.

He knelt down by her, brow furrowed, his face looking heavier, older. He held his hands out. Cupped in one of them was a metal object. "I found this in that heap of earth. Someone was climbing there and fell down the scree and ran off, left this."

She squinted at the letters graven into the handle. She turned away, her hands over her face.

"It is his, isn't it? Victor's." His voice shook. "Did you tell those men to bring him here?"

She said nothing, feeling hot tears slip between her fingers. He trusted her even less than she trusted him, despite what they'd been about to do. Her throat was dry, her head filled with rough noise. She felt Adam grab her hand and press the cold shape of the knife into her palm. He forced her fingers closed until the carved initials pressed into her like a brand. She yelped and dropped the knife. He stood. She could smell burning. It was roots. They'd be turning black in the fire, the white flesh inside growing hard and yellow-brown. It didn't matter now. She stayed hunched over the knife. It glimmered wickedly between her trembling knees. He paced the hilltop like a trapped dog, growling.

At last she opened her mouth. "What will we do?"

"Be quiet."

Her nails dug into the soft flesh of her thighs. She couldn't stay where she was. She knelt by the fire, pulling out burnt roots like the black shapes of sinners, burning her hands. It was penance. It felt bad and good. She whined softly to herself at the hurt and sucked her scorched fingers.

Adam's face appeared next to her. "Stop that."

"Stop giving orders." She poked at a burnt root.

"He is out here still. He'll see us." He wrenched her by the wrist like a naughty child, dragging her towards the cairn, half pulling her arm from the socket.

She pulled herself away, rubbing her burning shoulder. "You're not my master."

"I am as long as you behave like a child." He dropped her hand, scowling. "You'd be helpless out there on your own."

"Who fed us yesterday and today?"

He crouched down, eye to eye with her. "And who led that monster to our door?" He held her by the chin. "Was this a trap set for me?"

"No!"

He squeezed her face, his fingers a vice. "Liar!"

Her jaw ached as if her teeth would pop out, or her eyes. His grip was iron.

Her fist shot out, her sharp knuckles splitting his lip. Blood spurted from his mouth. He stared at her, startled.

She rubbed her cheek. "He told me to kill you before you killed me. He said you were the worst kind of fiend." She looked into his eyes, hoping that he would deny it. He did not.

Instead, he licked his lips, smearing blood around the edges of his mouth. "Why did you not break my skull as I slept?"

She shrugged. "I might still."

Grimacing, he dragged his sleeve across his face. "Did you speak with those men in the cave? They work for him now."

She closed her eyes. "I hid from them."

"You have not done as he commanded you. He knows that now. Those men are the new instruments of his wrath. He has followed them here to make certain they finish me as you did not."

She opened her eyes and saw the fear engraved on his face, but the hatred for her was gone. He picked up the knife, tossed it in the air and caught it. "He's not careless. He is precise as clocks are precise, with neither sensibility nor conscience. This knife is his sign. He's hunting us."

She reached for his hand and this time he didn't smack hers away. She drew strength from the warmth of his skin, feeling the anger slip from him. A welt was growing in the corner of his mouth, the lip puffing up, the blood drying. Her fist had done that. They were alike, after all.

73

By the time they left the cairn, the morning's brazen blueness had sunk into a plain grey. They went carefully, looking from side to side, sniffing the air like beasts. It seemed fitting that the sun was hidden in the clouds, that a skua shrieked and that the water rattled through a nearby burn too loudly.

As they trudged down the sodden braes and up again, scouting for hill caves or hollows, Adam would catch Oona by the sleeve and stop and take a long look behind them, sniffing the air as foxes do, though he never said a word. Sometimes, Oona thought she glimpsed a shadow flitting out of sight, one that always hung way behind, making the odd twig crack, the occasional stone fall.

No place seemed secret enough to keep them safe. The rimy air clung, tasting of tar when it caught in the throat. It began to rain, just a spray of chilly pinpricks at first, then cold drops that ran between Oona's shoulders and made her dress stick to her body. They forded the shallow burn and came into a field someone had ploughed and sowed, though she'd never heard of anyone living this side, up in the high, lonely crags. A few shaggy ewes with shy, black faces and curling horns straggled over a hillock. Adam walked between them and they scattered, bleating, leaving snagged wool and smooth pills of dung that stuck to the soles of Oona's feet.

At the crest of the hill, Adam stopped, his body tensed, staring at something below. She came abreast with him and followed his gaze to an old heap of byre tucked between field and burn. Adam pointed, unwilling, it seemed, to break their pact of silence and risk the echo of his voice across the valley. As they tramped through sheep dung to the barn, a jack hare shot out from behind it, racing away from them, the air around bristling with his fear. Oona watched the leanness of the taut loins, the long legs crossing each other mid-stride, the blur of black eyes and the back-flying, ink-dipped ears. It was strong like them and wary and alone. There'd been one on a board, spread out, gutted. It was at Victor's house. He'd caught the doe hare and rived off every bit of it, put a machine in the heart. Maybe she had one inside her too, a lightning spark, a cold clock ticking. She could still see the dull veil over the hare's liquid eyes, the scant white hairs left from its winter coat - dead as she'd been, for a while.

They huddled under the part of the thatch that was still sound, watching the rain thicken. The place was abandoned, but other people had passed through not long before. The grey remains of a fire lay near them and the peat was only half burned.

Oona pointed at blackened bones left round the cusp of the fire like an ogre's necklace. "Will they return?"

"I cannot say." He pressed his face bluntly against hers, as a child might. "My mind keeps returning to his creation of me, and you, for the fault is mine."

"Why do you say that?"

"Your suffering weighs heavy on me. That's all."

She took his head in her lap and stroked the hairs bristling from his chin, surprised at their sharpness. His shoulders shook. She kissed his neck and wiped the tears from his face. When they lay together it was different than before. They took off their clothes and made a bed of them, touching each other gently. His body warmed hers, his mouth hot against her mouth, her breasts. He planted a row of kisses between them, his tongue lapping between her legs. She liked the way he felt inside her, the deep sigh and shudder at the end, the sense of calm. The rain slowed outside. She heard the nagging cry of a lamb, the murmur of water trickling from the corners of the byre.

Afterwards, she began to feel the cold again and struggled into her damp dress. The blackened roots were knotted in the lap of it. She untied them, half-laughing and laid one on Adam, an offering. He lay with his brown arms folded under his neck, his pale chest gleaming around the wintry blackthorn shape of his scars, frowning down at the root with puzzlement.

"For myself, I hunt hares and rabbits and seize the occasional chicken from a coop. Red meat is what I require."

"The occasional chicken?" A picture flashed in her mind: bloody feathers; severed necks. Then it was gone.

She nodded and began to peel the black flesh away, forcing her fingernails under it, scraping the charred skin off until she got to the bruised brown meat. She broke it in half revealing soft, white flesh and handed a piece to Adam. He bit into it and grimaced.

"I feared for you before, but now I believe you'll survive long after I'm gone."

She bit into her half, her throat thick before she even swallowed, her heart heavy with what he had said, the sense that soon it would all be over.

74

Peat was stacked in one corner of the byre. As night drew in on them, they gathered up the dried sods along with tangles of spilled hay and piled them on the circle of ash. Oona watched Adam strike stones until they sparked, his large hands cupping the flame to the tinder and making the peat start to smoke. When the first flame licked up, she went to him and took his hand. She did not know whether they would sleep, but more than sleep, she wanted to feel him warm and naked against her again, to take comfort in him.

She slipped her hands under his shirt, running her fingers over the puckered scars. She looked up at his face. His eyes were moist. She pulled him close and kissed the tears away, hearing a sob catch in his throat. He held her tight and kissed her, his tongue meeting hers, their breath growing faster, their strange hearts keeping time with each other.

A twig snapped. They fell from each other. He pressed his finger to his lips and tiptoed to the byre door. She peered round him and saw the silhouettes of a dozen or people or so in the twilit field. Perhaps they had been there for a long time, watching. Or they had spent the day following the small signs she and Adam had left in their wake without knowing it. Whichever way, they were there now, their breath riming the air, each step drawing the net tighter.

"Stay."

She shook her head. But before she could stop him, Adam was off and out, a pale outline in the dusk. The shadows chased him up the hill. She heard him cry foreign words into the night. Like the jack hare, his shape whittled down and vanished from view.

She peered into the empty field, alone with the vicious beating of May's heart. Her legs tensed, ready to run after him. *Stay*, he'd said. She heard her own voice murmuring as if it was someone else speaking. *Our Father, Who art in heaven, Hallowed be Thy Name. Thy Kingdom come. Thy Will be done, on earth as it is in Heaven. Give us this day our daily bread.* Adam was tall and strong. He could snap a man's neck like a wishbone. But there were a lot of them and Victor was wily and knew things before other people dreamt they might happen. She turned and stared into the fire. Between the flames, there were sharp tongues whispering death. *And forgive us our trespasses, as we forgive those who trespass against us.*

And lead us not into temptation, but deliver us from evil. She turned round and ran through the door.

Her feet flew out from under her. Someone grunted. A knee pressed into her back. She smelled bitter chemicals and wine and cologne. Victor. He knelt into her spine, pressing the breath from her, crushing her into the ground. Her fingers scrabbled weakly in grass and dung. Her vision blurred. Something was in front of her, a pale thing, cupped in a palm. A smooth stone from the beach, the kind you might use to beat sheets and shirts in the burn.

"The most ancient tool of all." His breath was on her neck. "Cavemen used them, Eve…and you dropped a rock like this one on the beach when you…when you were engaged in that terrible act of *Selbstmord*, of self-annihilation, trying to wash away your original sins, your Biblical sins in the sea, the great sea that forgives all, cleanses all things. An elemental force, like lightning, something to dowse the spark I put in you. All my ingenuity in making you and my genius so near to being wasted."

Spots of pale light danced on the stone. Her chest burned. *For thine is the kingdom…*

"A prayer?" He spoke softly. "Dear Eve, have you learnt nothing from your work with me? Do prayers seem to you to be as useful as science, as the great experiments we did? This is a brave new world we have created, you and I. And in it, Oona, God is dead! There is nothing up there except for the stars…those blazing stars that are millions of miles away and down here there is only us." His lips pressed the back of her neck.

She flailed behind her, nails catching his breeks and scoring them. He grabbed her wrist and pressed down hard on her bones.

"Please don't struggle so. It breaks my heart to see you waste your greatness on that…*creature*."

Whimpering, she tried to pull her hand away. "If he's a creature, so am I."

"True," his voice had an edge to it now. "To the primitives on this island, you are abominations. They have Adam, tied hand and foot. They are nought but savages and they will hang him up and burn him for their amusement while the moon is high, as in some ancient ritual. You are worth more than that, even if you do not know it. You are the only thing, perhaps, the only thing I have ever done right. Which is why I must…please understand…you must be out of their way when they kill him. You must…" She thought she heard him whisper *Amen*.

The cool force of the beach stone struck like a storm wave falling. Her thoughts swam down the current of the burn and out to sea.

75

Song woke her, the strident trills of birds singing out of tune. She needed to make water and now she'd have to inch out of the covers and cross the freezing floor without waking Granny, who sometimes slept late on a Sunday. She'd lay fresh peat sods on the fire to boil the water for their meat because the bannocks in the cupboard were stale. The light pinched her eyes. It was cloudy-bright, as if Granny had forgotten to pull the curtains closed, and the birds were too loud, singing inside the croft.

Deafening. The pain in her head was bright and hard. It had been thick night inside her, but now the light pulled her back to a world of shrieks heard under water. There were moans all around her and the ground beneath smelled of dung.

She moved her mouth to speak but could not find spit enough to swallow. Her neck throbbed and her head buzzed. Her eyes opened. She saw scant grass. Running up alongside it, a blue strip. The hooves of dirty white ewes made sucking sounds in the mud. Fat lambs butted bellies for a teat. Their bleats were shrill bells tolling. Oona sat. Patches of bald earth shone. Turds lay coiled on them, black and dry. Adam was gone. She was alone. She struggled to her feet, her head fit to burst.

When she stumbled towards the brae, some of the ewes thundered off on hooves too small to carry their fleece-burden easily. Others turned their yellow devil-eyes on her while the lambs squinted out from under curls of their mothers' muddy wool. The yellow eyes watched her climb. At the top of it, she saw a black cloud over the cliffs. Shading her eyes, she looked into the direction of the rising sun. Motes of white drifted down in her sight like fiery bees and her bones rasped each time she looked a different way. The cloud was so big it could have been the start of a storm, except that a twist of black tailed down from it into the unseen ground. Up on the high ground, where the cliffs met the clouds, someone had a fire going, a bigger one than she'd seen before. She could smell it now, taste the salt tang of the charring wood. *They will hang him up and burn him.* That was what Victor had said before he smashed the stone down. She began to run.

A few times she stopped and bent double, her hands pressed to her thighs, trying to breathe. Her head pounded and her chest ached, but even when she closed her eyes she still saw smoke and thought of Adam up there with Victor or maybe all the angry people on the island, out for blood. She ran on. Brambles that webbed the track scratched her calves and snagged on her dress. Fiddleheads crushed underfoot were bitter as lies. Gulls scavenging in the dried bed of the burn found nothing and flew off shrieking hunger. The sun hit Oona's raw face and dried her dress and a cold sweat settled on her.

A stone gulley led to the cliff top and it climbed straight up. She scrabbled above her for finger-holds, toeholds. She couldn't see the smoke anymore, but it smelled stronger. Small dried grass sprouted between stones, tempting her to cling to it, but she knew better than that. Perched on a ledge, her hands wiggled the loose teeth stones and avoided them, found firm stones that wouldn't give. Pebbles the size of shelled peas rolled loose and blinded her. Sharp edges cut her feet. A heavy stone above seemed sure. She gripped the flat top. The stone slithered out and plunged past her. Far below, it shattered on rocks. She thrust her fist into the cool cleft of soil where the stone had been and clung on, just breathing.

Looking up, she saw the smoke again. Beneath it, black heather starred with the tiniest pink flowers. The gulley widened into a crisscross of ledges, each broad enough to sit on. She heaved her body up onto the first and found a straw nest with two speckled eggs in it. The shells were broken, the yolks dried sticky over feather and lime and a pink nub of wing. A skua must have found it. She reached for the next ledge, feet firmly planted now. Looking down, it seemed that she was wearing red slippers again. Blood stained her toes and the sides of her feet. Beneath them, the sea shook the rocks and broke into furious, white beads. Her head whirled. Sickness gripped her gut. Her fingers loosened. She would fall down there, into the roiling white. *Don't look down,* that's what they said. *Never look down.*

Hands clasped her wrists and hefted her up. Surely only Adam was strong enough to lift her so easily up and over the edge of the cliff. She never saw his face, just tumbled on top of him, his arms firmly holding her. Fear flooded out of her. She lay on his chest sucking in ragged breaths, her body floppy with relief.

"I thought you were dead."

"Aye, well…"

She looked up and saw blonde hair, a red beard.

Andrew smiled and ran his hand over her hair, over her cheek. "We fancied you were dead and all."

She squirmed from his arms and got to her knees. A group of people stood behind Andrew, their faces and bodies darkened by the flames that leapt up behind them, roaring from a towering stack of driftwood and boat beams and straw.

One man stepped forward and his face came clear from the rest. "Look what the sea swept in. Our own Oona, back from the dead." Stuart grinned. He looked happy to see her.

Andrew got up. "Come here, lass."

She remembered his kisses, his hands running over her on the beach by the bonfire while Adam watched. Her head was a jumble of their memories. She took a step nearer, feeling sure somehow he would never hurt her. His arms closed around her and she smelled salt and tar. He'd wanted to marry her, loved her maybe. She'd known that once. But still the smoke burned behind them. She broke away.

"Where's Adam?"

He took her by the shoulders and held her at arm's length, still smiling. "The doctor delivered him to us, told us he was a monster and that we must deal with him. As it happens, he threw us a half-truth, for there's two monsters need dealing with."

His arms dropped to his side. The fire twirled in front of her and her skull shrieked. She lurched forward. Stuart laughed and pushed her lightly back. The fire turned black. The sky bled.

She staggered through burnt heather and fell down. Another face. Big Dod, May's Da. His heavy jowls glowed red. His face came near hers, hand reeling back. It plunged down.

She felt the sting of each knuckle. Stuart's fists joined Dod's. She kicked their legs. Stuart stepped out of the way. He was the devil who'd crushed the life from May on Cormick's beach. Her fist flung out at Stuart, hit air.

Dougie Flett's boot caught her in the ribs while Stuart's aimed at her knees, between her legs. She was slack as wet cloth pounded over and over in the burn, the part that was Oona running off downstream, guttering out while the people she'd known all her life kicked her and laughed.

76

Their boots fell still, as if they'd lost interest. It was dark inside Oona and in the darkness, everything screamed. The men spoke in low voices but the words were chopped into sharp pieces so they didn't make sense. She tasted nails, felt her cheeks swell inward and smother her tongue. Pain ground her down. It pulsed and gouged. She smelled burning peat, sharp and salt. Light beat her swollen lids. The sharp bits of sound merged together.

"She looks dead to me."

"Dead for the second time."

"You'd think she'd have learned from the first."

Her lashes lifted a hair's breadth.

"Drag her over with the other beast. Let them be man and wife."

Hands grabbed her. Her arms flew over her head. She went wrist-first over the ground, the heather scoring her back. Her wrists seemed to loosen. The fire roared next to her ear. Her cheek burned. Cooled again. The hands dropped her. She peeked through her lashes.

Andrew's fair hair was limp and yellow as wet straw. He dragged his sleeve over his brow. He didn't smile this time, just looked down as if he was searching for something in the midden's muck. He smoothed his hair back and wiped his eyes, then vanished behind the fire with the rest.

Her head rolled away from the fire, bones grating in her neck as it moved. She opened her eyes. A body lay in the black heather next to her, not moving but not burnt either. It wore Adam's shirt. She stretched her arm towards it, felt the warm skin, the shallow rise and fall of breathing.

"Adam." Blood and spit sprayed from her lips in a haze like pink steam. The name sounded broken. "Up."

He didn't move. She sat up and the pain throbbed between her legs, in her knees and ribs and head. He was wrapped in fishing nets, his hands joined with a hook, as if in prayer.

She shuffled next to him and pushed at the metal spike gouging the back of his hand. Blood ran from the hole and slicked her fingers. The hook sunk down low enough for her to slip her fingers between his skin and the curved haft. It stopped, stuck. She pulled harder and heard a sucking sound. The hook came free. She straddled him and began to tug at the nets. They wouldn't budge. With a groan, Adam woke and looked up at her. His glazed eyes fixed on a point behind her head.

She turned around slowly, hiding the hook in her sleeve. Stuart stood over her. He bent down and stroked Oona's cheek. "What are you thinking of wee'un?"

"Killing you."

He laughed. "Much as you sicken me, I ken you've got guts."

He yanked Oona's head up by the hair and pulled her up from Adam. He dragged her a few steps further, pushed her down and drove her face into the heather. His fingers twisted harder in her hair. He jerked her head back until her neck burned and slammed it forward. She cried out, rolled over. He stood and she heard him spit, felt the warm wetness of it on her face.

She staggered to her feet. Stuart grabbed her by the waist. She stumbled forward, clawing at the flesh of the arm that choked her, the world a blur. Wood fell in the fire, raining sparks on them. Stuart's arm lost its grip. They slid apart in a slither of sweat. She slipped the hook from her sleeve and swung round fiercely. Stuart hit the earth hard and fell face down. She jabbed the hook into him. He cried out. His blood wet her hand. He staggered up, clutching his back. She faced him, the hook between her fingers like a claw.

Smoke whirled above them like ghosts, gold embers dancing. Over Stuart's shoulder, she saw the others scatter, their forms shrunk and darkened against the green of the hills. Another man appeared, face dyed red by the flames. Adam walked towards them, blood-shod, smiling.

He wiped his face, slicking it black with the mark of his kill, licking his lips, a monster, a killer, like her.

Stuart didn't see Adam. He cocked his head and charged. Oona swung the sharp point. It sunk in to Stuart's gut. His blood sprayed over her, soaking her clothes, blinding her. She let go and he sank to his knees.

"For May," she muttered to the red world in general.

Adam reached for her hand. She took it and their skin touched, blood-joined, kin. Then her feet were moving under her and they were running, flying, over the heather, away from the fire, running hard and fast until they reached a huge hole in the rock by the cliff edge.

Oona knelt down and peered at the turquoise water rippling below, glugging and sucking against the black rock. "We call them gloups, caves with broken roofs. The water flows fast in them, straight out to sea."

Adam knelt beside her. "See where that ledge angles down. We can climb to the bottom."

He sat on the ledge, lifting his body's weight onto his hands, lowering himself until he almost lay on the puckered rock. She let him go before her, watching him work his way over clefts in the rock. Sometimes drunk men fell into gloups and the tide pulled them out so fast, they woke up half frozen in the Northern floes. Sometimes their heads were dashed on the rocks and they had to be pulled up with ropes, their broken bodies hefted along the coast road to crofts where their stoic wives sat by candlelight, stitching their shrouds. She started after him, swinging herself onto the ledge, the rock digging into her back. Her arms ached. Her fingers slipped from a shallow hold and she grabbed the side of the ledge, almost fell, skinning her palms and scraping the skin from her wrists. Salt sweat pooled cruelly in her cuts. She bit her lip, waving her foot out, groping for the next ledge, forcing her mind not to see the broken shapes of those men.

When she had almost reached the bottom, his hands closed around her waist and he hoisted her down. Wordlessly, they waded through the glugging tide that was paler and dirtier than it had seemed from above. He took her hand. She trusted him, strangely, more than anyone she knew. She would follow him anywhere, she thought, as they wound through black, craggy rocks where purple anemones crouched like glistening pimples.

They turned a corner and their splashing footsteps caught an echo. They were in the darkness of a sea cave where small waves lapped against the rock's cool throat. It was so black she couldn't see the wall of the cave or his face beside hers. A crash from the shore echoed through the honeycomb of caves. Water rushed in freezing, flooding, knocking her back, filling her mouth, tearing his hand from hers.

77

In the darkness, she called to him, hearing nothing but the slap of water on rock and her own voice echoing, seeing nothing until her mind made shapes in the blackness. The sea roiled, treacherous. Perhaps it had knocked him down and pulled him out of the cave already. Perhaps he had hit his head.

She groped in front of her hopelessly searching, calling his name. The dark played tricks on her. She saw Stuart's face looming before her, bloody and beaten, then May's, the eyes dark and sad, then Victor's, his smile like a boy's, his hands held out in front of him. Her fingers clutching the cold rock, she tried to picture Adam, but all she could see were fragments – the curve of his ear, the scar snaking over his head.

The water splashed near her. Footsteps boomed on the cave roof. A hand clasped hers and she squeezed it.

"Adam! I thought I had lost you."

The fingers gripped harder. "You love him, don't you?" Victor leaned close. "You would offer your own life in place of his."

Her hand burned in his. He was crushing it. She tried to pull herself away. "Please." She smelled his cologne.

He caught hold of her wrists and pinned them behind her, pressing her into the wall. "Why, Eve, when I made you, healed you, brought you to life? When I taught you everything and tried to save you? How could you fall in love with your murderer...like some...some common ballad!"

Her flesh was numb.

"I prepared you. You ignored my advice, my teachings. Eve, it is worse than you imagine! That monster watched you drown, destroyed your life so that he would not be alone."

Like a dream it came back to her, slivers of light pinning the nightmare to the darkness - the hooded man she'd seen before rowing so fast, the water taking her, sucking her down, him stepping out of the boat. "No."

"Yes...yes...it is true! *Gott im Himmel*, I would not lie to you. How could I? But Adam...he waited, to be sure he did, waited patiently for you to sicken, to die, for the sea to do the rest, waited for your funeral to pass. Then he dug you up and brought you to me and I... *Gott hilft mir*...devil that I am, I did the rest and will be damned for it! Please understand that he held me to ransom with threats against my family. I had no choice. He would have…he may still… that monster forced me to replace your heart with your friend's. The dear soul – I believe she loved me in her way. Poor doomed thing, I found her too late and she wasn't…fit…couldn't be fixed…not like you, Eve. You were strong."

"No." She thought of May lying under the sheet, her hand lurching up, her empty eyes. "No!" The word flung against the rock and splintered.

"He was lonely, he told me… there in the ice caves when we spoke for such a long time. He begged me for a wife to keep him company in his damnation. That wretch! He blackmailed me in the cruelest way. And yet you would give your life for his." His hand found her face and rested there. "It is truly a loving heart I placed within you, but how could I predict *who* it would choose to love?"

Bile rose in her throat. She saw Adam looking at her and felt him touching her, tasting her. He'd taken her life and yet he had saved it too.

"He loves me as I love him."

"Then I pity you dear Eve… for I cannot save you. It seems I have brought you back from Hell only to damn you in a new way. I'm so… I am sorry. The creature brings only death and no-one will stop him now." Victor pressed his face to hers. His lips brushed hers for a moment before he slipped back and dropped her wrists. She slid down the wall of the cave until she was waist-deep in the icy water.

The suck and splash of Victor's footsteps faded. Through the maze of rock, she heard the waves beating the shore, the gulls shrieking and the gurgle of trapped currents in the caves. She was shut off from the world, *damned,* he'd said. It was just a dream now. She'd trusted Adam and he'd betrayed her. When the splash of feet swelled in her ears again, she didn't know who she feared finding more. Adam, Victor, Stuart.

"Oona! A wave knocked me under the water and dragged me from the cave. It's rougher than Hell out there, but I discovered where they hid the boat. I swam past it. Where are you? Are you hurt?"

"I'm here."

He came to her and knelt down, took her hands in his. "I'm sorry we were separated. Do you forgive me?" His hand touched her cheek.

She swung her fist in the direction of his voice. It slammed into his chest. He growled in surprise. There was a loud splash as he stumbled back and fell over. Echoes thundered around the cave.

"Victor told me you did this to me."

She knelt on top of him, heard the bubbles fly out of his mouth, felt the wild beating of his heart under the lapping waves. She pushed his head into the sand.

"I should let you drown in vengeance for what you did to me. But we are different." She pulled him up by his shirt and stood.

He coughed hard and struggled up. "You were already…by the time I got there…your heart…"

"You drove me towards that fate. You wished me dead so you would have a friend in the world."

"You were dying already." His voice sounded broken. "I loved you. I wanted you to live."

"Don't lie!"

He caught hold of her hand. "Oona please. We must go. The boat's not tied. It's merely floating in the cave. Please come."

"If I do, it's only because I want to live." She pulled her hand away.

She followed his footsteps through the caves, half of her wanting to hit him again, half wanting to climb into the boat and row out into the light. He stopped still. She bumped into him, reeled back, heard the clucking noise of a hull tapping the rock. She squinted, her eyes finding dull light through a cave mouth somewhere ahead of them. A boat's curve gleamed in the blackness.

She waded towards it, her skirts bobbing round her hips, translucent as tissue in the cave's dark well.

They each took a side and ran the boat through to the mouth of the cave where the rock gaped wide and the day poured in, blinding. He took her by the waist and hoisted her into the boat. A wave picked the boat up and hurled it forward.

She leaned over the side. "Climb in!"

His fingers touched hers. "Head south."

78

In four beats of the heart, he was out of sight – back there in the darkness where the echoes of their last words circled. The sky turned dark. It was a black shroud poised for a storm. A thunderhead hung heavy on the horizon. The wind froze tears on her cheeks, words in her throat. A wave rolled under the boat and bumped her high. She clung to the edge to stop herself from flying out and fell back, hitting her head on the oars.

She struggled up, pushing back the folds of her sodden dress. The shafts of the oars pressed into the backs of her knees, but when she tried to reach for them, her hands were too frozen to move.

She closed her eyes, feeling the cold creep through layers of her flesh. Icy spray pricked her breasts and throat, the places where Adam's warm hands had touched her and the salt air stung her mouth with harsh kisses.

It wouldn't take long to die out here. It happened at least once a winter to some foolish soul trying to poach a night catch with a sup of whisky for company. They said it was a quiet death and came upon you slowly, though the men who drifted back to their wives carved from ice never spoke a word.

Oona saw herself from the outside, a still thing hardening to a white glaze. She would be pure, every scrap of impiety gone, no longer a monster but a girl made from glass, a prism catching the scant rays of the evening sun. The boat rocked and spray hit the deck. Above her, a swart-back called out, hoarse and plaintive. When the tide turned, she'd drift back to shore just like the fishermen. Adam would find an ice princess, an ornament, his mouth open in wonder at the wife he'd forced Victor to create.

She opened her eyes and shook her arms clumsily, the fingers clumped up like an old man's. She beat them together, knocking the blood back into them, forcing it to flow. Needles of pain brought her back. Opening her mouth, she cried out, hoarse as the gull, shuddering with the return to life. She fell onto her knees and scrabbled up the oars, fingers slipping over the smooth wood like a seal's flippers at first, then gripping, holding, lifting.

Though her mind was lost in the frozen sleep she'd almost succumbed to, her body still worked. The oars slid into place on each side. They churned the water. It resisted, pushing the blades back up. Her arms worked harder, growing stronger with each stroke. May's heart beat loud and livid, forcing her on as they had gone on that night, laughing together in the dark. Her hands began to remember the rhythm. One oar sliced the sea, then the other, then both at once. The boat moved where she willed it, back and back and the island shrank into its icy mist like a woman stepping into the firth, wrapping her shoulders with a pale wool shawl.

Adam would be out of the cave by now. Maybe he'd already have found Victor. In spite of what he'd done to her, her skin ached with his absence. The oars' cadence was a prayer pulsing from her. Back. Forth. Back. Forth. *Our Father who art in heaven.* What if Victor killed him? She paused and let the oars drag on the water. It was hard to breathe. She gasped for air. A breaker tossed the boat forward. She heaved the oars back, forcing a beat. He'd said to head South. She looked over her shoulder, saw nothing but the blank sea.

No choice but to keep sculling. Staying still let the waves get the better of her. She saw herself from a distance again. This time, she was rowing into the firth, her heart clotted with fear and Adam rowing after her. The boat had filled with water. Her heart had given out. He'd said she was gone by the time he got to her. The sea had beaten her then. She looked down between her tensed knees at the green water, expecting it to rise and fill the wooden shell. And then she would sink down again, the cold brine setting her on fire.

The boat pitched and threw her to the side. Clutching the oars, she prayed they'd anchor her. She landed with a thud and dragged the oars into the boat, letting them fall on her lap. Her hands were raw and covered in blisters. She ran her finger over one, feeling the tight pillow of water underneath. There were no landmarks now, only a rimy veil and leaden sea tapering into it. Propping herself on one elbow, she peered behind the boat and saw the mirror image of what lay in front. She fell back. It was hopeless. She was lost.

It was easier to drift and let the sea carry the boat whichever way it would. In fact, it made her feel calm. There were no sounds except the lapping tongues on the hull, not birds or wind or the bells of other boats. Water swathed her back and sides, pulling her to it. Something floated on it: the small bundle he'd pressed into her hands.

It bobbed on the boat's inner tide.

She reached out and snagged it with her finger, laying the damp weight on her breast. Her numb fingers worked on the knot, loosing it, folding back leaves of brittle sealskin. The thing inside gleamed golden. The bundle was open and the round face with its flickering pin lay in her palm.

When she turned it one way, the needle bobbed around to the left; the other way round and it chased itself back. It always pointed the same way, halfway between the curlicued *N* and *W*. *Head South*. Right now, she was going North-west. That was what the little machine told her. That was what it was for. She sat up and laid the compass in her lap and picked up the oars, feeling sparks of new vigour in her arms. Pinioning the oars, she began to turn the boat about. It was hard, but with many jabs and twists of the oars, she made the stern face north. Her body and the boat's smooth lines aligned themselves with the hopeful dart of gold. She set off towards the south and found the oars' steady rhythm again.

She rowed on through the fog. Sometimes a white point of sun blushed under its mantle, a ghost sun that was almost a moon. The sea's fine weave roughened into dark pleats stitched with white. The storm swelled and the blank sky rumbled and split.

Rain started, the heavy droplets streaming down her face and between her breasts, filling the boat. The saltiness stung her raw hands until she cried out. She didn't dare drop the oars, for fear of losing her course. Hunching down lower, bracing her shoulders against the wind, she willed the boat to stay true as the trembling gold pin that could barely be seen.

79

Oona grimaced against the downpour, wanting to sink down and be at rest. Her numb hands tugged at the oars long past the point when she thought she could go no further. They worked until the gale lulled and the cries of gulls pushed through the rain.

She looked over her shoulder and saw what lay behind the fog - a grey shard of beach with black rocks rising jaggedly behind it. May's heart seemed to pause in that moment of seeing land. Oona's arms failed.

Her head fell back. She could feel the tide drag the boat through the shallows until it ran aground. Breathing hoarsely, she stared up at rough grass sprouting from the cliff. There was a blue butterfly perched on an orange flower. Another came and they circled each other like tiny moons.

The sun came out and dried the salt onto her lips and cheeks. With a groan, she tumbled from the boat. She was spent and soon fell asleep.

It was evening by the time she woke with a splutter. The sea's smallest tentacles were nudging her, nuzzling her, edging into her mouth. Coughing hard, she heaved herself onto her knees, her feet. She dragged the boat halfway up the beach before she gave up on it. The compass fitted snugly inside the bodice of her dress, a gold heart to cover May's with. She pressed her hand to it.

Along the silver strand, the new moon made jewels of sea glass. She smelled smoke and saw where it drifted from a shack tucked up on the brow of the beach where the sea would not come.

Remembering the cries of her friends and family, the pelted stones, she stopped for a moment. It might not be safe to go further, though surely it wouldn't hurt to see inside. She tiptoed up to the shack, smelling boiled cod, wood smoke, whisky, and peered through the window. Inside, an old man with white hair stirred a pot over a peat fire. She watched his hand move on the spoon, her head full of memories of Granny cooking or building a fire in the croft. She sighed. The man dropped his spoon and turned to the window, cocking his head as if he'd heard her.

She shrank down, afraid to breathe, poised to run if he flung the door open and shouted at her. When he didn't, she inched back up, pressing her nose to the mossy stones of the shack and peering cautiously at him.

He sat in the same place, his eyes looking at the window without seeming to see her. She stood straighter. Still he stared, eyes wide and pale. He had a clay pipe in his mouth and was absently mumbling the stem. The fire leapt up in the grate and she saw the same milky sheen on his eyes that old dogs got. He turned his ear towards the window.

"Hello?"

Her words came stumblingly. "The storm washed me onto the beach. I've no place to shelter."

He smiled. "Islander?"

"Aye."

"Come in, lass. There's room by the fire and it's warm."

She walked into the shack, glancing at the battered chairs ranged round the fire, the string of dried mackerel hung from the rafters and the nook bed tucked into the wall.

He gestured to an empty chair, seeming to know where it stood by habit.

She sat, breathing in the smoke of his pipe, the kippered taste of the air. The man dipped a finger into the pot and put it in his mouth, smacking his lips.

"Stew?"

He spooned it onto plates and they sat and ate in silence. Afterwards, he picked up his pipe again and lit it from the fire. Sucking at the clay, he murmured through puffs of smoke almost as if he was speaking to himself. "When I was a sailor I travelled all over the world."

"What's it like?"

"The world?" he laughed softly. "Full of all sorts. Some good. Some bad."

She tried to imagine it, but he hadn't given her much of a picture.

He drew a roll of cloth from his pocket, rooting inside for shreds of tobacco. "You web-footed islanders are ready drudges, aren't you, though it's a job in itself to find labour these days." He stuffed a pinch into the smouldering bowl. "Always work stuffing herring in barrels, though."

"I have always dreamt of seeing a big town, one with a shop in it."

He laughed hard and almost dropped his pipe. Her cheeks burned.

Then she began to laugh too. She knew how foolish she must sound. He lit his pipe from the fire. "I tell you, lass, there's cities where you can be lost for days if you choose. There's a family heading to Inverness from here in a few days. If you fancy, I'm sure they would give you space on their cart. You can help them care for their bairns."

Oona smiled. "That would be of great help to me."

"Tuck up in my bed, will you? I'll rest by the fire tonight."

He turned to the fire, puffing hard on his pipe. Oona wanted to share it with him but thought it might be pert to ask. Maybe she'd get her own pipe in Inverness and a jug of cider too.

Flames glimmered in the milky mirrors of his eyes. For a long time Oona lay awake on the narrow bed, her skin prickling with wakefulness, though her head ached for sleep. There was no curtain, so she traced the shape of the plough star over and over, thinking of how it hung above this small beach and above distant cities she could not imagine.

80

In Inverness there was a big house on the hill that was five times as big as the big house at home. Turrets and round towers stood on top of it. The kirk wasn't quite so big as that castle, but it was still bigger than the big house. You could have filled it up with the kirk from home a hundred times. All around the place were trees and fields and a huge wide burn rattling along, bigger than the fattest burn on Hoy.

The cart bumped over the muddy street and the city unfolded, vast and feverish on either side. Oona stared at the grand, grim, sandstone castles that rose up above the heads of the thronging townsfolk.

"What are those big houses?"

Mr Mackie drew on the reins and Brutus, his bad-tempered shire horse, whinnied and slowed. "They're crofts, lass, what you Orkney folk'd call crofts." His eyes were puffy from driving the cart through the night.

"Is this the New Jerusalem?"

Mrs Mackie, whose arms were wrapped snugly round two of her bairns, gave a sleepy laugh. "Shut your mouth, lass, before you catch flies." The other children asleep in her lap stretched and rubbed their eyes before burrowing back in her skirts.

The Mackies had been kind to Oona, save for the odd look now and then. At first she thought it was the sliver of scar just visible over the neck of her dress, or the golden tinge to the whites of her eyes. Or perhaps they could hear the strange heart beating. The night before, when all the bairns were fast asleep and man and wife sat arm in arm in the box, Oona heard Mr Mackie's confidential tones.

"They are a strange lot, eating with their fingers and the like."

"Aye, and you'd as soon know what a seal was saying as make out their words."

"But the lass is bonny and kind, considering."

"Aye, considering." Mrs Mackie snorted a laugh.

Some might have been offended to hear it, but Oona smiled to herself when she heard that. She was from Orkney where the funny lot lived and that was all they saw. She slept well that night, bumping over the pot-holed road.

The cart rumbled to a stop. Mr Mackie jumped down with a groan, stretched his back and tied the nag to a post. Mrs Mackie unloaded her sleepy children, placing the smaller bairns, thumbs firmly in mouths, in the arms of their older brothers and sisters. They all stood unsteadily, as if the brown ribbon of road was still unspooling under them. Mrs Mackie rummaged under the sealskin that shielded her belongings and pulled out a twist of paper. She handed it to Oona, who breathed in the yeasty scent of bread that was only a little bit stale. Her eyes stung with tears.

"Thank you."

Mrs Mackie straightened Oona's shawl. "You need a new one of these. This one I gave you's hardly more than an old horse blanket. I daresay you'll find work round here if you show them what a strong lass you are. When you do, you can get yourself a bonny new shawl and tie it like this." She made a neat knot and rested it on Oona's collarbone. "Don't frown so. I'd take you with us, but they've not space enough to swing a Cat in at my sib's house, and her so god-fearing to boot. Look out for the masts of the tall ships. They'll guide you to the harbour and there you'll find the Inn. If you give them my name and offer your help in the kitchen, Jenny will make a bed free."

Oona nodded. Her throat was too tight to say anything. She looked down at her dirty feet pressed into the cold city mud.

Mrs Mackie thrust her arms about Oona's neck, her voice thick with tears. "Heavens, I'm greeting like a bairn. I cannae stand to leave you, poor lass. You're like one of my own. Here, don't let him know I gave it you." Oona felt a cool disc slip between her fingers, felt Mrs Mackie's tears wetting her neck. She didn't want the hug to end.

They tramped off across the bridge and Mrs Mackie turned back to wave her handkerchief and dab her eyes before the crowd swallowed her. The grand buildings blurred in front of Oona, New Jerusalem warped by veils of light, its angels murmuring and crying out. She blinked. The vision grew sharp edges and drab colours. The marketplace was filled with more people than she'd seen in her life. Women walked by carrying trays of steaming bridies, bannocks and bread. They shouted loud words she didn't know. Men stopped them and winked and laughed and grabbed the pies off the trays and dropped coins in ruddy hands.

Cattle stood in stalls, huffing steam into the air, the whites of their eyes rolling round in fright at a dog that sat on his haunches and yapped. On the steps of the kirk was a gang of kids who were passing a paper full of tobacco between them, each one pinching up a dab of it and pushing it into his nose, snorting and spitting like an old fisherman in the smokehouse, though the oldest was no more than ten. Seeing them reminded her of Jamie and Roy smoking their clay pipe at the beach and throwing stones.

She struck out towards the harbour, May's heart knuckling her ribs. Two women with trays blocked her way. She pushed past them and a man herding sheep with a pipe clamped between his brown teeth. Their angry cries followed her as she jostled forward, but she didn't care as long as she wasn't stopped, pointed at, laughed at. She kept her eyes down and her arms pressed to her sides avoiding the eyes of strangers coming from the other direction. Stalls and the striped thatches of shops spilled by in a patchwork blur. She knew she should be looking for something – the Inn, a job. But she'd already forgotten Mrs Mackie's words. She broke into a half-run, treading deep in horse and cow and sheep dung, broken pies and running sewage, sweat breaking out on her forehead.

A man's chest slammed into her. She stumbled back. The man towering above her had a heavy face with a red scar running across it. One eye was covered with a patch. He smiled down with one corner of his mouth, making her look down shyly. One of his legs stopped at the knee and he rested heavily on a crutch. What if he was another creature like her, sewed out of dead flesh? She looked up at the man's face, saw Victor killing and digging, cutting and stitching.

"Aye, lass. Not bonny, I know. But take a good look if you fancy."

"Sorry."

The big man winked. "Everyone stares since I came back from France, as if they never saw a soldier before."

Oona's eyes raked the wreckage of his face.

"From the war, girl, where've you been? There's thousands of us, come back cut up and stitched up, less an arm or leg." He leaned in close. "Or head." He grinned, peering down at the neck of her dress. "You've got a few scars too, by the look of it. Been scrapping have you?"

She shook her head, face burning. "I must get to the Inn."

"That way." He pointed over his shoulder at the burn. "You daft?" His laughter rang after her.

She went along, thinking about the men from the war, who were scarred and broken like her. Like Adam. She looked at the people hustling by. Many were broken, bandaged, limping. By the time she reached the riverbank, it seemed that the place was full of people like her - the walking dead. Her heart trilled loud notes like someone singing. These days, the more she listened to it, the more it sounded like May humming a tune or gossiping or praying or scolding Oona.

The Inn was closed. A woman leaning against a pile of potatoes saw Oona gazing wistfully at the door and beckoned her over.

"Looking for someone?"

"Jenny."

"Oh aye, well Jenny's left to get her dinner. She'll be back to open up soon."

Oona thanked her and slunk back to the doorway, biting her nails, flicking the occasional hungry glance at the fat potatoes piled next to the woman's stall. She had other things Oona didn't recognise – shrivelled brown things that looked sticky - she could smell their sweet scent from the doorway - and gleaming round globes that seemed to be carved from wood and varnished.

The woman saw her staring and smiled. "Those are the sweetest fruit you'll ever taste. Apples, we call 'em, six for a farthing." She chuckled.

Oona smiled back, shyly.

"You look half starved, hen."

"I've bread for later." She couldn't take her eyes off the apples though.

"My apples are only a farthing." The woman put out a hand to her produce as if she was stroking a baby's head. "Come look."

Oona ambled over, rubbing her thumb over the coin Mrs Mackie had given her. She looked at the brown, shrivelled things - *figs*, said the woman - and the apples piled high, like something from a picture book. As she stooped, rapt, a breeze caught her shawl and it flapped up. She scrabbled to catch the edges and tied it back, but she saw the woman staring at her bare throat, the neck of her dress.

"My son's come back from the war with a scar on his face. Worse to see it on a lass." The stallholder smiled sadly. She took an apple from the top of the pile.

"Here."

"Thank you." Oona smiled at the woman and carried on down the road towards the sea. The throngs of the town dwindled on that stretch of dry road that ran along the side of the great river. Crow's nests thrust from tall ships. They drew her to them, big boats she'd only ever glimpsed sailing by in the distance before. Their sails puffed out with far-away winds. The men that clambered up and down the rigging looked like ants. She took a bite of the apple. A sharp taste filled her mouth.

Each day the ships sailed until they reached the world. Maybe she'd climb on one and buy passage to a country she heard of but couldn't imagine - France or Germany, India or China. There, in some great city she'd find a place that felt like home. Or maybe she'd just keep travelling. She gnawed the apple down to its core and threw it into the dark torrent below.

The current swept it off between the sharp prows of boats and out to sea. She pressed her hand into the half-healed space between her breasts. May's heart beat calm and steady against her ribs, not singing or scolding Oona this time, just asking her where they were.

In a soft voice she answered, *we're free.*

ACKNOWLEDGMENTS

I'd like to thank everyone who read an early draft of this novel and encouraged me to continue, especially Allan Guthrie, Adrienne Green and my creative writing tutors at Lancaster University, Graham Mort and George Green. Thanks to Martin Goodman, for knowing just how to hearten a flagging writer and for his excellent editorial skills: this book has found its true home within the discomfort zone of Barbican Press. Thanks to Mark and Sandra Atherton for their hospitality when I stayed at the Old Hall Cottage on Hoy to research Orcadian history. Finally, thanks to my family for their unfailing eccentricity, which provides more inspiration than they know: to my partner John Brewer for his patient support and creative stimulus; to Dan and Sarah Horsley, generous readers both; to small people Violet, Chloe and Annie - on whom I test many of my briefer gothic narratives; to Samuel Horsley (brother and enforcer); and to my mother, Lee Horsley, for making me a writer, even if she ran out of wool.

Lightning Source UK Ltd.
Milton Keynes UK
UKOW03f0118220714

235533UK00002B/29/P